1961: Protected by a bullet-proof cage, former Nazi official Adolf Eichmann stands trial in Jerusalem for crimes against humanity. The 15 charges against Eichmann included participation in the destruction of the Czech village of Lidice, as well as the wartime deaths of six million Jews in Germany and Nazi-occupied countries. *(Bettman Archive)*

1962: Mrs. Jacqueline Kennedy invites a TV audience into the White House for a guided tour of Camelot. Shown here in the state dining room, the elegant first lady lent a sense of glamour to the presidency and her personal style to the extensive renovation of the executive mansion, stating, "Everything in the White House must have a reason for being there." *(Bettman Archive)*

1963: Leaders of the March on Washington, including Rev. Martin Luther King, lock arms as they move along Constitution Avenue on their way to the civil rights demonstration at the Washington Monument. When the marchers assembled they were 200,000 strong, covering the ground all the way to the Lincoln Memorial to hear King's "I have a dream" speech. *(Bettman Archive)*

1964: In the early '60s American teens were captivated by the phenomenon of the Beatles. Pictured here during a performance on *The Ed Sullivan Show*, the influence of these four longhaired musicians from Liverpool, England, spread far beyond music, as many rushed to imitate the look of their irreverent idols. *(Bettman Archive)*

1964: Prizefighter Cassius Clay proved that he was "the greatest" by defeating Sonny Liston to become heavyweight champion. After converting to the Black Muslim faith and changing his name to Muhammad Ali, the champ would be stripped of his title three years later when he defiantly refused induction into the Army on grounds of conscience. *(Bettman Archive)*

1965: Astronaut Edward H. White floats freely in space outside his Gemini 4 spacecraft, making him the first American to "walk" in space. He was having such a good time during the historic 20-minute walk that he had to be coaxed back into the ship by fellow astronaut James McDivitt. *(Bettman Archive)*

THE AMERICAN CHRONICLES

VOLUME VIII

THE NEW FRONTIER

ROBERT VAUGHAN

BANTAM BOOKS

NEW YORK • TORONTO • LONDON • SYDNEY • AUCKLAND

THE NEW FRONTIER
A Bantam Book / November 1995

ISBN 0-553-56082-4

Published simultaneously in the United States and Canada

Bantam Books are published by Bantam Books, a division of Bantam
Doubleday Dell Publishing Group, Inc. Its trademark, consisting of the
words "Bantam Books" and the portrayal of a rooster, is Registered in
U.S. Patent and Trademark Office and in other countries. Marca Regis-
trada. Bantam Books, 1540 Broadway, New York, New York 10036.

PRINTED IN THE UNITED STATES OF AMERICA

OPM   0 9 8 7 6 5 4 3 2 1

To Kathy. Her heart is pure and her cause is just.

CHAPTER ONE

Chief Warrant Officer Bob Parker held the receiver to his ear and counted the telephone rings. When it reached twelve, he hung up. Stroking his chin, he stared for a long moment at the mute black instrument on the corner of his desk.

Why the hell didn't his wife answer? He had been on duty since yesterday morning and had called several times last night just to check in with Marilou, but with no success. This was the third time he had tried reaching her this morning. Even if she had gone somewhere, there should have been someone at home. The twins were only four, not yet old enough for school, so someone would have to be there looking after them. Unless Marilou took them with her.

And that, Bob knew, was very unlikely.

Marilou made no bones about being a reluctant mother. In her own words, she "had not planned to get pregnant and certainly had not planned to have two kids at once, like a bitch dog bearing a litter."

1

Because of her unwilling parenthood, Bob found himself doing many of the tasks mothers normally did. He bathed, changed, fed, and put to bed Teddy and Timmy. He was the one who got up in the middle of the night with them. And they never left the house unless *he* got them ready to leave. So where were they now? Why didn't someone answer the phone?

Of course, Marilou could well be home but just refusing to answer. If she was angry enough with him, she could easily let the phone ring without picking it up. Bob could never do that. To him a ringing phone had a sense of authority to it. Marilou not only could do it, she could revel in it.

The question was, if she was angry with him, what had escalated her enmity between yesterday and today? Hell, she was already being difficult because of the amount of time he spent with his work. Bob was certain she'd be even angrier after learning about the orders he had received this morning. But she didn't know about them yet.

He picked up the mimeographed sheet and read his orders for at least the tenth time:

DEPARTMENT OF THE ARMY
101ST AIRBORNE DIVISION
Fort Campbell, Kentucky

SPECIAL ORDERS   5 April 1961
NUMBER 68
EXTRACT

        18. TC 246. WOAVN 105. Fol WO AUTH TDY

        PARKER, ROBERT R, W2214390, CWO W2 671A 101 Trans Company, 1st Aviation Battalion, 101st Airborne Division, Ft. Campbell, KY

Rpt to: LT COL Jarred Hawkins, MACV, Saigon Post
Asg to: MACV, AVN SPT DET Saigon Post, Rep of Vietnam
Rpt date: 24 Apr 61
Tvl data: Commercial flight voucher to be issued
Sp instr: Immunization rec. Individual will remain on TDY for a period not to exceed 90 days. Per

Diem, Overseas Pay, and Flt Pay (crew member) authorized. POV not authorized. HHG not authorized. HOLD BAGGAGE not authorized. PERSONAL BAGGAGE limited to sixty-five (65) pounds.

FOR THE COMMANDER:

REED L. SAMUELS
Colonel, GS
Chief of Staff

OFFICIAL
J. A. SWINDELL
CWO W-2, USA
Asst Adj Gen

DISTRIBUTION
    2-MACV Saigon Post
  10-MACV AVN SPT DET
  10-101 Trans, 1st Avn Bn, 101 Abn Div
  20-Individual
    3-Pay Br
    3-Director OPD OPO
    3-TAGO ATTN: AGPR-WO AVN
    3-Ft Campbell TO

Translation: Bob would be going to Vietnam for three months, where he would be in charge of making flight-ready several helicopters that had recently been shipped to the Aviation Support Detachment at MACV, as the Military Assistance Command in Vietnam was called.

Bob was excited by the idea. He'd been reading a lot about Vietnam lately and knew the U.S. was getting increasingly involved in what was going on over there. This assignment would have to be interesting. Of course, Marilou wasn't going to care much for the idea. He'd have to present the news to her in the best possible light—provided he could present it to her at all.

Where the hell was she?

Though he knew it was irrational to call again so soon after the last attempt, he picked up the phone and did just that.

He got only repeated, unanswered rings.

"Mr. Parker?"

Bob looked over. Sergeant Branchfield, his technical inspector—the person responsible for the final inspection of aircraft after they came out of maintenance—was standing in the office doorway. Bob sighed and hung up the phone.

"Yeah, Brandy, what is it?"

"Two-two-five needs a test flight, sir. Can you take it?"

"I thought Mr. Lumsden was going to fly it."

"Yes, sir, I thought so, too, but he's nowhere around, and the Colonel wants his bird back by thirteen hundred. It's eleven-thirty now, and we need an hour's test flight before we can release it. If Mr. Lumsden doesn't get back in time, there'll be hell to pay."

"Okay, sure, I'll do it," Bob said, opening the bottom right-hand drawer of his desk to pull out his flight helmet. He put his TDY orders in the middle drawer.

"That your orders to go to Vietnam?" Branchfield asked.

"Yes."

"I heard you was goin' TDY over there. You don't need a tech inspector, do you?"

"Why? Do you want to go?"

"I'd love to go."

"Well, why don't you call Personnel and check into it this afternoon?" Bob asked, getting up from his desk.

"Yeah, maybe I'll do that soon as we get back from this flight."

The two men left Bob's office, which was located in the northeast corner of the large hangar building that made up the 101st Transportation Company. The 101st Trans provided field maintenance support for the helicopters of the 1st Aviation Battalion, which, in turn, provided aviation support for the 101st Airborne Division. As Bob walked across the hangar floor toward the helicopter to be test-flown, he briefly glanced at each of the numerous HU1As that sat in various stages of repair, groups of mechanics crawling all over them from bright yellow maintenance stands. Cowlings had been removed from the engine and transmission compartments, inspection plates had been opened, and doors and seats had been removed.

Bob really loved flying the HU1A, the newest helicopter in the Army inventory. It was powered by a jet turbine engine, which gave it more speed and power than anything he had ever flown before. Despite the Army's best efforts to get everyone to refer to it by its official name, the "Iroquois," the helicopter was universally called the "Huey."

Two-two-five had been rolled out of the hangar and now sat on the large concrete pad just outside the door.

"I don't mind telling you that I'm glad to see this son of a bitch out of here," Bob told Sergeant Branchfield as he watched the maintenance crew remove the ground-handling wheels, allowing the helicopter to squat on its skids.

"You and me both," Branchfield agreed. "By the way, I've got an engine analyzer hooked up to it. I'm goin' to make damn sure it's perfect when we release it."

Bob nodded. "Yeah, that's probably not a bad idea."

Two-two-five was the helicopter assigned specifically to the battalion commander, and it had been in maintenance for much longer than usual due to some difficulty in getting replacement parts. In fact, it had been down for so long, for the last week Bob had been required to give twice-daily briefings to Colonel Colby regarding its status.

He was just starting his walk-around inspection when three enlisted men came up to him.

"Can we go along for the ride, Mr. Parker?" one of them asked.

Bob shook his head. "It'd be better if you didn't. This is a test flight, and you know the regs are very specific that only those performing necessary duties should be on board during a test flight."

"Mr. Lumsden lets us go."

Bob reached up to twist the blades of the tail rotor back and forth, examining the pitch-change rods. "I'm not Mr. Lumsden," he said flatly.

"I know, sir. I just meant— Oh, here's Mr. Lumsden now," the young man said.

Bob looked around and saw Warrant Officer Ray Lumsden walking across the flight apron toward him, smiling broadly.

"What are you trying to do, steal my thunder?" Lumsden asked. "I plan to personally land this son of a bitch just outside the old man's window."

"I'd like to land it on his desk," Bob muttered. "The way he's been crapping about it."

"Mr. Parker, you're wanted on the telephone," one of Bob's clerks suddenly called from the hangar doorway.

"Who is it?"

"I think it's your wife, sir."

"Damn! I've been trying to get hold of her all day." Bob looked at Lumsden. "Okay, Ray, looks like you're going to get the flight after all, if you don't mind."

"No, not at all. I want this one."

"Thanks," Bob said, starting inside the hangar.

Lumsden watched Bob's retreating back for a moment, then opened the right front door. "Let's go," he told Branchfield.

"You aren't going to preflight?" the sergeant asked.

"You pulled the tech inspection, didn't you?"

"Yes, sir."

"And Parker's already pulled the walk-around. The colonel wants his bird back. Let's get it to him. I don't want to spend the rest of my life looking at this son of a bitch."

Lumsden climbed in, strapped into his seat, then began moving switches. The turbine engine whined into life.

Hearing the Huey's turbine starting up, Bob glanced out his office window as he picked up the phone. "This is Mr. Parker," he said into the mouthpiece.

"Bob? It's me, Marilou."

"Marilou, where the hell have you been? I've been trying to reach you since last night," Bob said, doing his best to rein in his irritation.

"I'm at home."

"Good. I'm going to take this afternoon off; I've got some news to tell you. You're not going to like it at first, but when you consider it, I think you'll see that it's the best thing that can happen to us, moneywise and careerwise."

"No, Bob, I mean I'm *really* at home," Marilou said. "I'm in Ozark."

Bob was silent for a moment, absorbing what she had just said. "Ozark? You mean you're in Alabama?"

"Yes."

He frowned with puzzlement. "Why? What are you doing down there? Where are the boys? Are they with you?"

"Yes, they're with me. Don't try to get them back."

"Don't try to get them back? What are you talking about?" So far the conversation wasn't making much sense.

"I've left you, Bob. I'm getting a divorce."

"A divorce?" Bob heard the helicopter take off; turning back to the window, he watched it climb out over the exit corridor across the base. "What do you mean, a divorce? I don't understand," he said into the phone. "We've never talked about a divorce. I mean, where did this come from all of a sudden?"

"Bob, don't tell me you didn't realize our marriage was in trouble."

He thought about his work schedule over the last few months. The company was short of officers and men and facing a command maintenance management inspection, the most demanding inspection in the Army. Sometimes, like last night, Bob had to spend the night on a bunk in the hangar. Marilou had complained bitterly about his long hours, but he had explained that there was nothing he could do about it. Evidently he hadn't gauged the intensity of her discontent.

"Well, I know the boys sometimes get on your nerves," he said. "And I admit there have been times when things could have gone more smoothly."

"Could have gone more smoothly?" Marilou gave a short, bitter laugh. "What a master of understatement you are. But then, of course, you are the writer—not I," she added acidly, referring to Bob's two published paperback novels, *Nude, Willing, and Ready* and *Lust Empire*. Neither was exactly a literary masterpiece, but they had been published, much to Marilou's surprise, since she had always considered herself a real writer and Bob just an amateur hack. Though he had done everything he could to play down any competition between them, she had never let it die.

"Marilou, let's not go into that again," he said as he watched the helicopter grow smaller in the distance. "I told you, I'm not competing with you. Our writing styles are totally dif— *Oh, my God!*"

"What?" Marilou asked impatiently.

"The helicopter! It exploded! Look, I can't talk now!"

"We have nothing to talk about, anyway," Marilou said coolly. "I'll have Daddy send the divorce papers. You just make sure you sign them."

"I've got to go!" Bob shouted, slamming down the phone. He ran outside and saw two or three men looking eastward.

"Mr. Parker!" one of them yelled, pointing.

"Yes, I know, I saw it." Bob looked around. Spotting the emergency-alert helicopter sitting on the hot pad, he ran toward it. The ready pilot, who apparently hadn't seen anything, was sitting in his seat, engrossed in a paperback novel. Noticing Bob, he put the book down.

"What's up?" he asked calmly.

"Let's go!" Bob shouted, climbing into the copilot's seat. "A helicopter just went down!"

"Shit!"

The ready pilot pulled the starter trigger, and the turbine began to spin. Bob, who hadn't even stopped to grab his flight helmet, strapped himself in.

"Fort Campbell Tower, alert helicopter on the pad for immediate takeoff," the pilot said.

"*Alert helicopter clear to depart. Be advised there is a helicopter down in the exit corridor, three miles east of the field,*" the tower replied.

"Roger, we're on our way."

Lifting up from the pad, its nose down for maximum speed, the alert helicopter beat its way over the post toward a towering, twisting column of black, oily smoke. The pilot nodded toward the headset. Bob slipped it on.

"Who was it?" the pilot asked. "Do you know?"

"Ray Lumsden."

"You sure?"

"Yeah, I'm sure. It's two-two-five. I just turned it out of maintenance. Lumsden was taking the test flight."

"Shit. His wife just had a baby, didn't she?"

"Yeah, she did," Bob said, feeling a knot in his gut.

They quickly reached the scene of the accident and circled once. The helicopter had gone down in an open field just in front of the post dental clinic, and already a hundred or more men had gathered around the crash site, watching as the ship burned fiercely.

"It doesn't look good," the pilot said, pushing the collective down to land.

They descended through their own rotor wash, the blades popping loudly. As soon as they set down, an infantry colonel came running toward them, ducking under the blades.

"What are you doing here?" the colonel shouted.

"We're rescue!" Bob shouted back.

"Rescue?" The colonel shook his head. "There's nothing here for you. No one got out."

Even as the pilot was shutting down, Bob unfastened his harness, then jumped out and ran toward the burning wreck. The fire was so hot that he could feel the scorching heat from several yards away, so hot that it stopped him from getting any closer.

The tail cone had separated from the rest of the aircraft and fallen some distance from the main wreckage, twisted but unburned. The number was very clearly visible: 014225. Two-two-five. If any secret hope remained that somehow this wasn't the helicopter he had just left, that hope was now irrevocably dashed.

Suddenly Bob's knees felt weak; his head was spinning. He momentarily thought he was going to pass out. *I was supposed to be on that helicopter,* he realized.

A staff car came bouncing across the field, and a major got out, one from the general's staff. Bob saluted him as he approached.

"Do you have any idea who it was?" Major Royal asked.

"Yes, sir. Ray Lumsden was flying. Sergeant Branchfield was the tech inspector, and Sergeant Beageux was the crew chief."

The infantry colonel overheard the conversation. "Who were the others?" he asked.

"The others?" Bob replied, confused. "There were no others. Just Lumsden, Branchfield, and Beageux."

The colonel shook his head. "Chief, my battalion was putting together camouflage nets when this thing came down —nearly on top of us. That's why there are so many men out here. And before the fire got too big, they could see inside. They all agree the helicopter was full of people."

"But it couldn't. It was a maintenance test flight." Then Bob remembered the three young men who had tried to get a ride. He hadn't seen them board the helicopter, but they must have. Lumsden must've taken them with him. "Oh, shit," he said under his breath.

"What is it, Mr. Parker?" Major Royal asked.

Bob voiced his theory.

The major looked back at the burning wreckage. "You're

saying there were three more, in addition to the pilot, TI, and crew chief?"

Bob nodded slowly. "Yes, sir, I'm afraid so."

"My God! You mean there were six men killed on a maintenance test flight?"

"Yes, sir."

"Oh, Jesus. The general will hit the roof. Six men on board a test flight, and the helicopter goes down. There's going to be a load of shit come down on us over this."

"Yes, sir, I guess so."

Major Royal was silent for a moment; then he looked hard at Bob. "Mr. Parker, they tell me you're a writer, that you've actually had a couple of books published. Is that right?"

"Yes, sir." Bob wondered why the major would bring that up now.

"Well, that's good, Mr. Parker. That's very good. Because you're going to have a great deal of writing to do to explain this away."

"Major Royal, I don't have any idea how I can explain it. I told you, when those three EM asked me if they could go, I said no."

"They got on it some way, didn't they?"

"Yes, sir, evidently they did."

"Then you had better find some reason to justify why they were on board, Mr. Parker. I want a written report for the general by seventeen hundred hours."

"Major, four of these men have wives who live on the base," Bob said, pointing to the fiery craft. "They will have to be notified."

"That's Captain Bailey's job. He's the CO, isn't he?"

"Yes, sir, but he's on leave this week. I'm acting CO."

"All right, then. It has just become your job. But that doesn't get you off the hook. I still want that report by seventeen hundred hours. Today."

"All right, sir, I'll get it to you."

Clearly the tragedy had already taken a backseat with Major Royal. All he was worried about was how they would draft their response to the Department of Army.

"Hey," somebody shouted, "the fire's burned down now. You can see 'em—or what's left of 'em. Holy shit, are they ever burned to a crisp!"

Bob felt his stomach churn, and he turned from the crash and walked away, purposely avoiding looking at the victims. He stood in front of the alert helicopter until the duty pilot came back.

"There's nothing for us here," the duty pilot said. "You want to go back?"

"Yeah," Bob answered quietly. He wanted to feel shock —or, at the very least, sadness for the men who had been his friends and co-workers. But he couldn't. He wanted to feel anger with Major Royal for his seeming insensitivity, but he couldn't feel that, either. In fact, he could feel nothing at all. He climbed into the left seat and just sat there as the pilot got in on the other side.

"I wonder who's going to tell their families," the pilot said as he turned on switches.

"I am," Bob replied.

"No shit?"

"I'm afraid so."

The pilot flipped on the booster pump. "That's sure not something I'd want to do."

"No"—Bob looked out the window as the turbine energized—"me neither."

He would have preferred using his own car to make the notifications, but Army policy required using a military sedan. Also—and he was very thankful for this—in addition to the driver he was given a chaplain and a doctor.

"Do you know all the wives?" the chaplain asked.

"I know Sergeant Branchfield's wife and Sergeant Beageux's wife. I've seen Specialist Harris's wife around the company a couple of times. But I know Janet Lumsden the best. In fact, Ray and Janet had dinner with my wife and me just the other night."

"Maybe it would help if you called your wife," the chaplain suggested.

"Yeah, she could—" Bob suddenly remembered that Marilou wasn't there anymore. "I almost forgot. She's down in Alabama visiting her parents."

"Too bad."

"Yeah." Bob sighed. "All right, let's go. We'll see Janet Lumsden first."

The driver started up, and all too soon the car pulled to a smooth stop in front of the Lumsden house. Bob got out and trod stiffly up a flagstone walkway lined with brightly colored flowers that struck him as inappropriately, almost painfully cheerful. Behind him he heard the chaplain and the doctor exiting the car.

He rang Janet's doorbell, which was promptly answered by a woman who identified herself as a friend.

"You're Mr. Parker, aren't you?" she asked. "From Ray's company?"

"Yes. Is Janet in?"

"She's in the bedroom. I have to tell you, Mr. Parker, she already knows about the crash."

"She does? How?"

"One of the neighbors was at the dental clinic and saw the helicopter go down. Janet knew Ray was going to be making a test flight, so she called the company. Someone there told her."

"I'm sorry she had to find out that way," Bob said, though secretly he was glad he wouldn't have to actually break the news.

Janet came into the living room then. She seemed fairly well composed, though her eyes were red-rimmed.

"Thank you for coming, Bob," she said, opening her arms to him.

Bob hugged her tightly. "I am so sorry," he murmured.

"When I spoke to Sergeant Haverkost, he told me you almost made that flight yourself."

"Uh, yes. Yes, I did. Under the circumstances, I feel guilty being the one to tell you."

"Don't be silly. Ray planned to take the flight. He was talking about it this morning. It's just a matter of fate, that's all."

"I guess so."

"Would you tell Marilou to drop by later? I know it won't be pleasant for her but . . ."

Bob glanced away. "Janet, Marilou is in Alabama."

Janet looked confused. "Really? My, that was sudden. I was visiting with her just yesterday morning, and she didn't say anything about it."

"Yes, well, you know how impulsive she is. She just got the urge to go home, so she went. I'm sorry."

"I am, too, for your sake." Janet put her hand on his arm. "Bob, these next few days won't be easy for you, either. You're going to be haunted by having almost been on that helicopter. It would be nice if Marilou was here for you. I think you should call her and ask her to come back."

"Yes, maybe I'll do that." He paused briefly, then introduced the chaplain and the doctor, who asked Janet if she wanted a sedative, but she declined. She did accept a prayer from the chaplain.

After a few more minutes of commiseration, the men left to call on the other wives. Bob didn't have to break the news to them, either. The NCO grapevine was far faster than the official notification system. At each house he was met by a group of the wife's friends, already on hand to offer support.

After the last visit, Bob returned to his office. First Sergeant Haverkost was waiting for him.

"Major Royal has called several times," Haverkost said. "He said to remind you not to forget the report."

"How can I? He wants me to justify why so many men were on the helicopter." Bob shook his head. "I have no idea why those other guys were on there. I told them no, but Lumsden, that dumb, dead shit, must have let them."

"Some of us've been talkin' about that, Chief, and we've got an idea if you want to use it."

"What is it? I'm desperate for anything."

"They had an engine analyzer hooked up for this flight, did you know that?"

"Yes, Branchfield told me."

"Well, Harris used to teach the analyzer when he was at Fort Eustis. Why don't you say Harris was monitorin' the engine analyzer, and the other two were there to learn how to use it?"

Bob mulled it over briefly, then nodded. "That's pretty thin, but it'll have to do. Thanks."

"It's been a pretty rough day for you, hasn't it, Chief? I mean, first your wife leavin' you, then this."

Bob looked up in surprise. "How did you know about my wife?"

"She called again this afternoon, all pissed off 'cause you hung up on her. I told her about the helicopter crash, and she said to tell you she was sorry, but she was still sendin' the divorce papers through."

Bob ran an anxious hand through his hair. "Yeah," he sighed. "First Sergeant, have you ever read *Gone with the Wind?*"

"No, sir. I seen the movie, though."

"You know that line where Scarlett says, 'I'll think about it tomorrow?' Well, right now that's the way I feel. I'll just have to think about things tomorrow."

"Actually, the only thing I remember about the movie is when Clark Gable carries her up the stairs to get a little. That was my favorite part," Haverkost said with a grin.

Despite himself, Bob chuckled.

Returning home that evening, Bob found the house cold, dark, and empty. He missed the sound of the boys' playing and laughter and felt an aching emptiness when they didn't come running to greet him. He walked over to turn on the TV, then sat down to pull off his boots and watch Chet Huntley and David Brinkley on the evening news. Huntley was in the middle of one report.

"*. . . scenes outside the U.S. Embassy in London, where thousands of Britons demonstrated against the U.S. bringing Polaris submarines into English ports. However, a spokesman for NATO said the demonstrations would not halt the deployment.*

"*At Fort Campbell, Kentucky, today, one of the Army's newest helicopters crashed, killing all six men aboard. The cause of the crash has not yet been determined, but eyewitnesses say it exploded in midair. The helicopter was on a routine maintenance test flight, though Army officials were at a loss to explain just why so many were aboard. A spokesman for the House Armed Services Committee indicated that there would be an investigation.*"

"Great," Bob groused. He walked over and shut the TV off, and the picture squeezed down to a tiny, glowing dot in the middle of the screen; then that, too, disappeared.

He suddenly realized he was hungry, not having eaten lunch because of the accident. He went into the kitchen, where the sink was piled full with dirty dishes. Uneaten portions of the meal from two nights ago were still on the table—the remains of the meal they had eaten when the Lumsdens were over. It was also the last meal Bob had eaten at home.

He found some peanut butter and jelly, made a couple of sandwiches, and took them and a glass of milk into the large walk-in closet that had been converted into a study. On the chair were two small teddy bears, one named Pepper, the other Ginger. His sons kept them there so "they could write books, too." Marilou either forgot them or, what was just as likely, didn't even know about them, since she managed to block out everything having to do with Bob's writing.

With a lump in his throat and a burning in his eyes, Bob put his sandwiches and milk down, moved Pepper and Ginger, then took his seat in front of the big gray IBM typewriter. To its left was a pile of blank paper, to the right a stack of manuscript, and rolled halfway through the platen was the page he had last written on. In the upper left-hand corner of the page was the title, all in caps: *DOWN AND DIRTY*. In the upper right-hand corner was his last name and the page number: *Parker - 117*.

Like his two previous books, this one was an erotic novel, in this case the story of a newspaper reporter who had discovered a call-girl ring operated by the mayor of a medium-sized city.

Marilou was right; it sure wasn't great literature. But he did believe he was getting better with each book, learning by experience more about the development of scenes and characters. He enjoyed writing. He could sit down at the typewriter and within a few moments completely lose himself in the story—even more than he could when reading because as a writer Bob could interact with the characters. He truly became a part of their world, leaving his own behind.

And if ever he had wanted to leave his own world behind, it was tonight.

Bob moved his hands over the keyboard. Within moments he was slipping quietly down a dark alley with his reporter, Mike Carson. Ahead, a wedge of light fell across the darkness from an open door. His orders for Vietnam, the fact that Marilou was divorcing him, the absence of his two sons, even the helicopter crash slipped mercifully into the background.

When he finally got up from the typewriter around midnight, it was to stumble, exhausted, into bed. Like Scarlett O'Hara, Bob would think about everything tomorrow.

CHAPTER TWO

APRIL 29, 1961, FROM "TRAILMARKERS" IN
EVENTS MAGAZINE:

LANDING IN CUBA FAILS

Dissident anti-Castro Cubans attempted to invade their homeland last week at a place called the Bay of Pigs. The failed invasion has greatly increased tensions between the U.S. and the Soviet Union, and Premier Nikita Khrushchev has accused President Kennedy of masterminding the attempt.

While the U.S. has not admitted complicity in the attack, it is well known that Kennedy would welcome the fall of Castro. American airplanes were said to have flown over the site during the operation, though they were not used to provide air cover.

President Kennedy is receiving condemnation from both sides—from Cubans and Soviets for supposedly backing the coup and from strident anti-

Castro elements for failing to provide enough support.

Castro, who made a personal appearance to rally his troops during the battle, has now emerged as a hero to many small countries in Central and South America. President Kennedy, on the other hand, has suffered a great blow to his personal prestige.

EICHMANN LAWYERS CHALLENGE LEGALITY OF TRIAL

Adolf Eichmann, the former Nazi official now on trial in Jerusalem for having sent six million Jews to extermination camps, was composed and impassive as his lawyers launched his defense.

Eichmann, who was chief of the Gestapo's Jewish section, was apprehended in Argentina by Israeli agents last May, then spirited away to Israel to stand trial. His lawyers are making the claim that Israel had no authority to arrest Eichmann in a foreign country, and, as no extradition was filed, had no right to bring him to trial.

NO ILL EFFECTS ON SOVIET MAN IN SPACE

Twenty-seven-year-old Yuri Gagarin, a major in the Soviet Air Force, became the first man in space this month when his spacecraft, named *Vostok*, orbited the earth.

Russian doctors have examined the space flier carefully and report that he shows no more effects from his epic flight than would a passenger on a commercial airliner.

DESTIN, FLORIDA

The young man finished his run on the beach and walked to the water's edge to watch the rolling breakers. Leaning forward, he put his hands on his knees to unwind from the run as the incoming surf bubbled over his feet, a last frothy gasp of energy.

The sun was barely a disk's width above the eastern

horizon, turning the distant water of the Gulf of Mexico golden. Nearer, the water was blue, and close in it turned a vivid green—the distinctive color that had given this part of the Florida panhandle the name "Emerald Coast."

Seagulls swept low over the frothing surf while sandpipers raced on toothpick-thin legs, staying just ahead of the line of bubbles. A school of porpoises frolicked just beyond the breaking waves, and a solitary pelican patrolled above. Farther out a marlin jumped, flashing blue and silver in the early morning sun. The young man watched the display, thinking how much he would miss all this when he was gone. He would miss a lot of things when he left for the Peace Corps, but he would particularly miss the beauty and serenity of the beach just after sunrise.

A movement to his right caught his eye, and he looked over to see someone walking toward him, following the line between wet sand and dry. As she drew closer he could see that she was a young woman in her early twenties, exceptionally pretty, with long blond hair. He had not seen her earlier because his run had taken him in the opposite direction.

"You're out awfully early," he said when she was close enough.

"I like walking this early," she replied, her bright-blue eyes appraising him. "It's my favorite time to be on the beach."

"I agree. It's mine, too."

She raked her golden hair off her face with her fingers, then looked back along the beach. Her footprints made a solitary scar in the snow-white sand, disappearing into the distance.

"I've been walking since before sunrise," she said. "I don't have any idea how far I came."

"Where did you start?"

"At the fishing pier. You can't even see it from here."

His brows arched. "That's four miles."

The girl laughed. "You say that with such certainty."

"I *am* certain. I know how far it is from here to just about every point on the beach. I use it to measure how far I run."

"Oh, you're one of *those* guys," the girl said archly.

"One of *what* guys?"

"One of those guys who run."

"It's a family tradition. My father and my grandfather were runners. Do you have something against runners?"

"No, not really. It just seems like so much work. Actually, I guess I admire anyone who does it. You aren't just here on vacation, are you? You must live here if you know the area that well."

"Well, I don't actually live here, but my family does have a beach home back there." He pointed to the area behind him. "So I've been coming down here most of my life."

"Your family has a house over *there*?"

"Yes."

"Wow, I'm impressed. There are some awfully beautiful homes back in there. Your family must be rich." She gasped and covered her mouth. "Oh, I'm sorry! I guess that was very rude of me."

The young man laughed. "That's all right. My family *is* rich. But I can't take any credit for it. It's merely an accident of my birth." He stuck out his hand. "I'm Morgan Canfield."

"Canfield? My God, of *the* Canfields? As in Rockefellers, Kennedys, and Canfields?"

Morgan laughed again. "Well, I've never really heard of us being put in a file that way. But I suppose you've got us pegged. So what's your name?"

"Sheri Warren." She smiled and looked away. A gull missing half a leg was hobbling along the water's edge. "Oh, my goodness," she said. "Do you see that poor creature? What do you suppose happened to his leg?"

"A crab, I expect," Morgan said.

Sheri looked at him in disbelief. "A crab did that? Why would a crab attack a bird?"

"A crab makes a good meal for a gull. But they don't give up without a fight. Their pincer claw can do a lot of damage."

"Oh, how awful."

Morgan chuckled. "For the crab or the seagull?"

"I don't know," Sheri admitted. "For both, I guess." She swept back her hair again. "Well, it's been nice talking to you, but I'd better be getting back."

Morgan was acutely aware that he didn't want this meeting to end. "Uh, listen, I was about to go out for some breakfast," he said quickly. "Would you like me to drive you back? Better yet, would you have breakfast with me?"

"I really shouldn't . . . I need to . . ." She stopped,

then laughed and shook her head. "What am I saying? If any of my friends found out I turned down an invitation to go out with a Canfield—even if it was just for breakfast—they'd never let me live it down," she said candidly. "I'd love to go."

"Good. Come on up to the house while I take a quick shower, will you? I'm sweaty from the run, and I'm afraid I would be unpleasant company."

She gave him a sideways look. "Are you trustworthy?" she asked with mock suspicion.

"Completely." He laughed. "Of course, you'll just have to trust me that I'm trustworthy."

The Canfield house sat high on a sand dune—so high that a long staircase had been constructed to make it accessible from the beach. The steps ended at a wooden deck, from which another set of stairs led up to a wide porch that stretched across the back of the house.

"I don't want to disturb anyone," Sheri said, staring with some reluctance up at the porch.

"You won't. Except for the housekeeper and her husband, I'm the only one here right now. My parents are home in St. Louis—although they'll be coming down for a few days next week—and my sister is back there as well."

Sheri didn't have to ask if Morgan was married. She had read about him often enough in the newspapers and magazines to know he was not. She had even seen his name once in an article about "America's most eligible bachelors."

Morgan led her up to the back porch and into a room with a glass wall overlooking the Gulf, a marble floor, a huge fireplace, and casual but expensive-looking furniture.

"You can wait here," he said. "I'll only be a few minutes."

"Thanks," Sheri replied, and he headed out of the room. She was about to sit down on the overstuffed, chintz-covered sofa when a row of photographs on the mantel caught her eye, and she went over to look at them more closely. They were a very impressive lot. One was of Franklin Roosevelt, posed behind his desk with his long black cigarette holder clenched at a jaunty angle between his teeth. He was looking up at a handsome, smiling young man who was leaning over the desk. The man looked so much like Morgan that Sheri knew it had to be his father when he was younger. Other photos showed Mr. Canfield with presidents Truman, Eisenhower, and even Kennedy, though Kennedy had only been in office for a few months.

The photograph with Kennedy was the only one in color. Far more casual than the others, it looked as if it had been taken on a back porch somewhere. Kennedy was wearing sunglasses, sitting in a wrought-iron chair, dressed in shorts and a red pullover. Mr. Canfield, wearing khaki trousers and a yellow pullover, was standing against a railing, behind which water was visible. Sheri wondered where the picture had been taken. Perhaps at Hyannis Port. She had read that the new president had a place there.

Over the fireplace was a very large family portrait. John Canfield—Sheri suddenly remembered Morgan's father's name—was sitting on a low stone wall. Morgan's mother—whose name Sheri could not recall, though she was certain she had read it at one time or another—was standing just to her husband's right, her left hand resting lightly on his shoulder. Morgan's sister, who Sheri believed was about her age, stood just behind the wall, while Morgan was standing sideways in front of his sister, one foot on the wall, elbow on his knee, chin resting on the curled fingers of his right hand. It was a carefully posed picture, though it gave the illusion that the photographer had caught the family in a casual moment.

"May I get something for you, miss?"

Startled, Sheri jumped as she turned. The speaker was a middle-aged, overweight woman with hair hovering between blond and gray.

"Uh, no, no, thank you," she said. "I was just admiring the photograph. They are a handsome family, aren't they?"

"Yes, very," the woman agreed. "If you need anything, just call out."

"Thank you. I'll be fine, I'm sure." Sheri had the distinct feeling that the woman was not as interested in serving her as she was in letting her know she was around, keeping an eye open, just in case. Sheri went back to studying the photograph. It spoke of the Canfields' wealth, even in the expressions on their faces. It wasn't arrogance as much as it was a supreme self-confidence and acceptance of their position, as if wealth were their right.

"You recognize me, I'm sure," Morgan said, coming into

the room. "That's my mother, Faith; my father, John; and my sister, Alicia."

Faith. Of course. I knew I knew it. "Where is Alicia now?" Sheri asked aloud.

"Studying law at Jefferson University in St. Louis."

"A woman lawyer," Sheri said. "I'm not sure I've ever met one."

Morgan chuckled. "Leave it to my sister to blaze new trails. She wants to be an advocate for people who can't afford lawyers. You know, like a public defender."

"Your father with all those presidents—does he really know all of them?"

"Oh, yes. He worked for Roosevelt and Truman. And he had a number of meetings with President Eisenhower, though he never actually worked for him."

"And President Kennedy?"

"My father helped in his election. And our families have been friends for a while."

"Have you ever met him?"

"Yes, several times."

"I'm impressed," Sheri said. "He's going to make a wonderful president, don't you think?"

"I certainly hope so," Morgan said with a laugh. "That's why we worked so hard to get him elected. Of course, I suppose it is still too early to know exactly how it's all going to come out."

"I think he's already made Americans feel good about themselves," Sheri remarked. " 'Ask not what your country can do for you . . . ask what you can do for your country.' "

"And I suppose it doesn't hurt that he's young and handsome?" Morgan suggested. He grinned. "At least, that's what my sister believes."

Sheri grinned back. "I agree with your sister."

Morgan held up a set of car keys. "Well, what do you say? Shall we have breakfast?"

"I'd love to," Sheri answered, smiling broadly.

Morgan ushered her out to the driveway and his car, a pale-yellow MG Roadster, its chrome wheels and grille slats edged with red to match the red leather seats.

"The car is seven years old," Morgan explained. "But I like it much better than the new MGs, don't you?"

Sheri made a wry face. "To be honest, I'm not sure I'd

even know what a new MG looks like. I'm afraid I've never gotten much beyond your basic Ford, Chevy, and Plymouth family."

"Actually, any of those cars would be much more practical if you had to take a trip," Morgan admitted. "This thing will beat you up driving no farther than Pensacola. But it's fun just to run around in. As you are about to discover. Hop in."

They drove west on Highway 98 with the wind in their hair and the high-pitched, sports-car sound of the exhaust echoing back from the sand dunes. Morgan was right. The ride was exhilarating. Finally they came to a little restaurant sitting on the north side of the highway, nestled in a stand of pine trees some distance from the beach.

"They serve grits here," Morgan said. "Do you like grits?"

"You mean that white stuff you get with your breakfasts down here?"

"Yes."

"No, I don't like them. Or it. Whichever."

Morgan chuckled. "I suppose you have to develop a taste for them. I know I did. But now I like them so much I sometimes have the cook fix them for me back in St. Louis."

They went inside and took a corner booth. The waitress hurried over, and Morgan ordered grits, eggs over easy, ham, and toast. Sheri ordered a bowl of corn flakes and a grilled ham sandwich.

Their orders were quickly served, and Sheri held up her small cereal box. "Canfield-Puritex Corn Toasties," she said, smiling and jiggling the box.

"I hope you didn't order that stuff just because you're having breakfast with me," Morgan said.

"No. Believe it or not I eat Corn Toasties every morning. It's my favorite cereal." When Morgan made a face, she added, "Really. Don't you like them?"

"No, not at all." Morgan broke the yellow of his eggs, then mixed it up with his grits. "This is my idea of breakfast."

Sheri laughed. "I can't believe that a Canfield doesn't like cereal. Especially his own cereal."

"Some of it's all right, I suppose," Morgan said with a shrug. "I like Rice Pops and Wheatos. But I've never been big on cereal." He chuckled. "Neither is my father, and neither was my grandfather—and he started the whole thing. I guess it's a good thing we didn't have to depend on people like us to make the company grow."

"Now you are making me suspicious of the whole thing," Sheri said. "What about all those athletes whose pictures are on the front of the cereal boxes? Do they really eat Corn Toasties?"

Morgan laughed. "You mean ex-athletes, don't you? Most of the endorsements we have are from people who aren't playing anymore. And I guess some of them eat Corn Toasties—but we don't give them a lie-detector test."

Sheri put her hand to her cheek in mock horror. "I'm shocked! If you can't trust your cereal boxes, who can you trust? Wait'll the folks back home find out about this."

"Speaking of home, where are you from, by the way?"

"Right now I live in Chicago, but I'm originally from Hillsboro, Illinois, which is only about fifty miles from St. Louis."

"We're practically neighbors, then. What are you doing in Florida? Are you here on vacation?"

"More like a working vacation."

"What sort of work do you do?"

"I'm a model."

"A model? How interesting. What sort of modeling do you do?"

"Lingerie."

Morgan looked up from his plate, his eyes wide.

"Careful," Sheri said, laughing. "Your eyes are popping."

Morgan grinned. "I was just thinking that I'd like to see you work sometime."

"I'm sure you would," Sheri replied dryly. "But I don't intend to be a lingerie model all my life. I have other plans."

"What are your other plans? That is, if you don't mind telling."

"I want to be a fashion designer."

"Well, that's ambitious. Have you always been interested in clothing design, or is it a result of being a model?"

"I've always been interested in it. When I was a little girl, I would cut pictures of beautiful women out of magazines, then dress them in paper dresses that I designed myself. Later I started designing and making clothes for my dolls, then for myself, my family, and my friends. Now I have hundreds of designs in dozens of portfolios."

"I'm very impressed. Have you shown them to anyone?"

"No one who counts."

"Why not? You *are* in the business, aren't you?"

Sheri chuckled. "You mean because I'm a lingerie model?"

"Yes."

"Saying that I'm in the fashion business because of what I do is like saying a theater usher is in the movie business."

"Oh. But that still leaves the question, why don't you show them to someone?"

Sheri shrugged one shoulder. "I don't know. I'm afraid, I guess."

"What's there to be afraid of? They'll either like the designs or they won't like the designs."

"You don't understand. Now I have my dreams. But if I show them around and no one likes them, I won't even have that."

"I don't understand that attitude," Morgan said. "If you think they're good, they probably are. And you should show them."

"Maybe someday," Sheri said, almost wistfully.

They chatted aimlessly for the rest of the meal, and when they were finished, Sheri took several napkins from the holder and wrapped up the ham sandwich.

"You aren't going to eat your sandwich?" Morgan asked.

"I'm taking it back to Scooter."

"Scooter? Is that your dog?"

She laughed. "My three-year-old son. His real name is Kenneth, but somehow Scooter seems to fit better."

"Oh . . . Uh, I guess it was presumptuous of me to ask you to breakfast," Morgan said, suddenly feeling very awkward. "I didn't know you were married."

"I'm not."

"Divorced?"

Sheri shook her head. "I've never been married." She looked at him, examining the effect of her words. "Are you scandalized?"

"No," Morgan replied—not very convincingly.

"But it's not the kind of thing you see in your crowd, is it?"

"Not too often," Morgan admitted. "Don't get me wrong. It isn't that such things never happen. It's just that, well, when it does, the girl in question manages to take a convenient vacation to Sweden where it can be taken care of."

"Where she can have an abortion, you mean."

"Yes."

"I didn't have that option. Unless I wanted to visit some quack in a dirty hotel room somewhere and run the risk of either bleeding to death or getting some horrid infection and *then* dying. And I certainly didn't want to turn an hour of carelessness into a lifetime of misery by marrying Scooter's father. So I had my baby alone. And now that I have him, I don't regret it for one moment. He's a wonderful kid. And great company."

"I'm sure he must be." Morgan smiled. "Well, what do you say we get this sandwich to him before he starves to death?"

Sheri smiled back. "Thanks."

She directed Morgan to the motel where she was staying —a one-story, flat-roofed, cinder-block building, painted pink, that consisted of about a dozen units.

"Wait here and I'll go get him so you can meet him," she said, climbing out of the MG when they had parked in the space alloted for her room.

Morgan got out of the car and leaned against it, listening to the surf crash and watching the morning beach walkers across the highway.

Sheri came out a moment later, leading a young boy by the hand.

"Scooter, this is Mr. Canfield. Can you say hello?"

"Hello," he said shyly.

"Hello, Scooter. Are you enjoying it down here?"

Scooter looked up at his mother. "I have to go to the bathroom," he said.

Morgan and Sheri laughed.

"Okay, run on back inside," Sheri said. "I brought you a sandwich for breakfast. It's on the bedside table."

Scooter started back inside.

"Wait a minute. Tell Mr. Canfield good-bye," his mother instructed.

Scooter smiled and waved. "Good-bye, Mr. Canfield."

Morgan laughed. "Good-bye, Scooter," he said, waving back at the boy.

Sheri watched her son, smiling proudly and lovingly, then turned back to Morgan. "Thank you very much for breakfast and the ride back."

"It was my pleasure."

"Sheri?" A man suddenly appeared in the doorway of her motel unit. About forty, overweight, and wearing just boxer undershorts and a T-shirt, he stood there lazily scratching his stomach. "Have you seen my beach shoes? I want to go for a walk."

Sheri felt her face flush with embarrassment. "They're under your bed," she said stiffly.

"Oh, okay." The man backed inside the room.

"Well, I, uh, have to go," Morgan sputtered, turning toward his car.

"Morgan, wait," Sheri said, putting her hand on his arm. "This isn't what you think. He's my boss. We're down here on a shoot. We're doing a catalog layout."

"You don't owe me any explanation, Sheri," Morgan said. "My goodness, we just met."

"You're right. I don't owe you any explanation. But I don't want you to get the wrong idea, either. Frank Corso and I aren't sleeping together, and we never have. We're here on a very tight budget, that's all. Though, of course, I don't suppose a tight budget is anything you could understand," she added somewhat waspishly.

"Listen, Sheri," Morgan said, putting his hand on hers. "Don't be so defensive. I told you, it isn't any of my business. Besides, I'll be gone in a couple of days, anyway, so you probably won't even be running into me again. If you're feeling at all embarrassed—don't."

"Going back to St. Louis?"

"No, to Ecuador. I've joined the Peace Corps."

"The Peace Corps?" Sheri laughed mirthlessly. "I might have known."

"What do you mean?"

"Your sister is going to defend the downtrodden, and you are going off to save the world. That's what people like you do. It's all a game to you, isn't it? You've had everything handed to you on a silver platter, so you do your bit for society by getting involved in 'do-good' causes. The only thing is, you never get involved in life."

"That isn't fair," Morgan snapped.

Sheri melodramatically put her hand to her forehead and turned away from the car. "Oh, do go away, Mr. Canfield. Go attend some benefit for the widows and orphans of polo players or something."

Morgan started to say something else, but he didn't. Instead he jumped into the car, shifted into first, then spun it around in the parking lot with the back wheels squealing in protest.

Sheri watched him go, feeling sad and angry.

"What the hell was that all about?" Frank Corso asked, stepping out of the room as the MG pulled onto the highway.

"Oh, Frank, you have all the grace, style, and timing of a baboon," Sheri cried.

"Yeah, well, I'm going to take a walk on the beach. You be ready. When I get back, we'll go to our first shoot."

"I have to talk to the motel attendant about finding someone to watch Scooter," Sheri said.

"Yeah, you do that. But be ready."

An hour later, as they drove away, Sheri looked through the back window at the motel. "I hate leaving Scooter like that," she said. "It has to be so scary for him, being in a strange place and all."

"Ah, don't worry about him," Frank said. "The woman who runs the motel said she baby-sits guests' kids all the time. Hell, she's got a regular playroom for 'em. It's all part of the service."

"I know he'll be all right. It's just that I'm never really comfortable leaving him with a stranger."

"She ain't no stranger. We been down here for two days now. She knows him."

She sighed. "I guess you're right."

They drove on in silence until Frank stopped in front of a warehouse. "What is this place?" Sheri asked, looking around in confusion.

"This is where we'll be doing our shoot."

"Inside a warehouse?" she asked skeptically.

"Yeah, well, they've got it fixed up inside . . . you know, like a set."

"We could have done a set shoot in Chicago. I thought we were going to find some outside location. I thought that's why we came to Florida."

"Yeah, well, we'll probably do that, too. But the real reason we came to Florida was to meet Sammy. He's the one who's putting together the catalog. He's the one with the money, and he lives down here. Besides, why are you moping? Look at it as a nice trip to Florida."

"I'm not moping," Sheri grumbled.

"Yes you are. You been moping ever since that Canfield fella left." Frank laughed. "I guess that was quite a shock to him, seeing me come out like that. He probably thought I was getting in your pants regular."

"You wanted him to think that," Sheri said, scowling.

"Yeah, well, I'm just looking out for your interests, that's all."

"Looking out for my interests?"

"Sure. If everyone thinks you belong to me, they won't hit on you. You know how this business is."

She glared at him. "Frank, do me a favor, will you? Don't do me any more favors."

Frank laughed and opened his door. "Come on. Let's go."

The warehouse took up a corner of a boat repair yard, and they had to maneuver around rotting keels and oily engines. The place smelled of fish and mildewed wood.

"Jeepers, I sure hope he's got the inside of the warehouse fixed up better than the outside," Sheri said.

"Yeah, well, look at it this way," Frank replied. "The uglier everything else is, the prettier you'll look."

Sammy—a very short man with red, blotchy skin and an imposing nose—met them just inside the door. "I've got us all set up over there," he said, pointing to the far side of the warehouse where several floodlights made a brilliant glare. "What was your name now, honey?"

"Sheri."

"Sheri. Okay, Sheri, I've got the things laid out for you over there. Why don't you get into the black outfit first? You can dress behind that screen."

Sheri studied the set. It looked like a very sparsely furnished bedroom, with a bed, a dresser, and a bearskin rug. Just off the set was a table draped with the lingerie she would be modeling. She started toward it.

"You said you want the black first?" she asked over her shoulder.

"Yeah, honey, if you don't mind," Sammy said. Then he chuckled and said to Frank, "You're right about one thing. She is one gorgeous piece. I hope she doesn't give us any trouble."

Sheri stopped short and turned around. "Trouble? What do you mean by that? Why do you think I might give you trouble?"

"Well, some girls, you know how it is," Sammy said, giving a dismissive wave. "They don't like to pose in undies."

"Sammy, don't you worry none about Sheri," Frank assured him. "She's a pro. She's been doing this for over a year now."

"Yeah, I know. I saw one of the catalogs she did. That's why I wanted to use her."

Sheri walked over to the table and picked up the black bra and panties. At first she thought they were torn. Closer inspection revealed they were supposed to be like that. The bra had cutouts for her nipples to protrude from; the panties had no crotch.

Irritated, she held up the lingerie and asked, "Frank, what is this?"

"That's what you're going to wear, honey. Now, go ahead and put it on."

"This? You're out of your mind. I'm not going to pose in this."

"I thought you said we wouldn't have any trouble," Sammy complained.

"We won't have any trouble," Frank said, holding out his hand to calm Sammy. "Don't worry about it. I'll talk to her." He walked over to the table. "What are you doing?" he hissed. "You're blowing this whole fashion shoot."

"Fashion shoot? This isn't a fashion shoot," Sheri said, holding open the crotchless panties. "This is a porno spread. My God, even if we shot this, where would you circulate the catalogs? You couldn't send this through the mail."

"You don't worry about how the catalogs are going to be

distributed. All you got to think about is looking good and spending the money we're going to make." He pointed to Sammy. "Don't you realize that he's paying three times more for this shoot than we ever got before?"

"I don't care if he's paying ten times more," Sheri snapped. "I'm not doing this."

"You'll by God do this or you're fired," Frank growled.

Scornfully dropping the panties to the floor, Sheri started walking toward the door.

"Come back here!" Frank called angrily. "Where the hell do you think you're going?"

"Home. And you don't have to fire me. I quit."

"Home? How the hell do you think you're going to get back home? I have the tickets," Frank reminded her. "And if you ain't working for me, I sure as hell won't pay the way back for you and that kid of yours. I'm cashing them in."

Sheri stopped, then turned around. "You can't do that. You're the one who brought me down here."

"Right. I brought you down here to do a job. Why'd you come if you won't do it?"

"I had no idea what you had in mind."

"The hell you didn't. You're a lingerie model, for chrissakes. You've been taking off your clothes in front of the camera all the time as it is. You think I haven't already seen everything you got? Most of the bras you pose in are so thin you can see your nipples right through the cloth anyway. And the panties you've been posing in are a joke. You might as well be naked. Half the time when we're working, I got a boner on from here to Detroit. So why is this any different?"

"You're supposed to know, Frank. I shouldn't have to tell you. If you can't tell the difference between sheer panties and panties that have no crotch, you aren't in the fashion business. You're nothing but a dirty old man."

He snickered. "Yeah? Well, I'm a dirty old man who's holding all the cards, baby, 'cause the tickets home are in my name—so you are on your own."

Morgan Canfield was sitting on the back deck, watching the sun dance on the water and thinking about the girl he had met that morning. He couldn't get her out of his mind.

He had been physically attracted to her, there was no

doubt about that. But he had been physically attracted to many women, any number of them as pretty as this woman and some even considered prettier.

He couldn't say he was attracted to her erudition. She might, in fact, be a very intellectual young woman, but he had no way of knowing since they hadn't actually had an intellectual conversation.

So what was it that made her lodge in his mind like the refrain of a song that wouldn't go away?

Maybe it was her spunkiness, her pride, her fierce determination to be taken on her own terms. She could have hidden the fact that she had a child, but she didn't. She could have lied about that child being illegitimate, but she didn't do that either. And now that he had had time to think about it, he realized that she had even brought him back to her motel knowing full well that Frank guy was there. Maybe she was telling the truth. Maybe he was just her boss and nothing more.

Morgan sighed. What difference did it make whether she was telling the truth or not?

He was about to go back into the house when he saw two figures walking along the beach. He put his hand over his eyes to shield against the glare and stared.

"Damn!" he said aloud. "Damn! That's Sheri and Scooter!"

He was absolutely certain, though he didn't know why. The figures were actually too far away for him to be able to tell anything about them except that one was obviously an adult and the other a child.

Morgan hurried down the stairs to the beach, then started toward them. A couple of minutes later his hunch was confirmed.

"Hello," Sheri said when they were close enough.

"Hello yourself."

She smiled self-consciously. "I don't suppose you thought you'd see me again. At least, not this soon."

Morgan shook his head. "No," he agreed. "I didn't think I would."

She raked back her hair, a mannerism that would forever make Morgan think of her, no matter who else might do it.

"I, uh, didn't know where else to go," she said in a small voice. She looked down at Scooter, now sitting in the sand.

"And if it weren't for him, I wouldn't have come to you at all. Poor little guy. He just walked . . . what was it? Four miles? He's worn out."

"Sheri, what is it? What's wrong?"

"I've been fired."

"Fired? Why? Because of me? Because of this morning?"

"No." She sighed. "Actually, it would be more accurate to say that I quit."

"What happened?"

"You know the shoot I said we were down here to do?"

"Yes."

"Turns out it wasn't a legitimate shoot—at least, not like anything I've ever done before. They wanted me to wear these . . . these caricatures of lingerie. Bras with no front, panties with no crotch. Believe me, this wasn't the kind of stuff that you find in a legitimate catalog. This was real porno stuff."

"And you refused to do it?"

"Yeah."

"Good for you."

"Yeah, well, the only thing is, Frank has the return tickets, and he won't give them to me. He says he's going to cash them in. He also refuses to pay me what he owes me. So, that leaves me out of money, out of a place to stay, and with no way to get back."

"I'll help you. You want some money?" Morgan asked.

"No."

"No? Then I don't understand. Why did you say I was the only one you could come to?"

"I was hoping you might know someplace where I could get some work. I intend to pay my way back."

"What sort of work will you do?"

Sheri chuckled.

"What is it?"

"The way you asked that," she said. "Not what sort of work *can* I do, but what sort of work *will* I do. That's a pretty decisive question."

"And insightful of you to notice the difference," Morgan said. "But the question remains: What kind of work will you do?"

"I won't do the kind of thing Frank wanted me to do,"

Sheri said resolutely. "Or anything remotely resembling it, if you get my meaning. But I will certainly do ordinary labor."

"Such as housework?"

"Yes."

"Would you be willing to work for Mrs. Jackson?"

"I'll work for anyone. Who is Mrs. Jackson?"

"You met her this morning. She's our housekeeper. But she's getting old and can't do as much as she once could. I've heard my parents talking about getting someone younger to help."

"Well, shouldn't I go to your parents for this job?"

Morgan laughed. "Mother and Dad are not the ones you have to please. The one you have to please is Mrs. Jackson. If she says you'll do . . . you'll do." He held his hand out to Scooter. "Come on. Let's go interview for the job."

CHAPTER THREE

MAY 6, 1961, FROM ''TRAILMARKERS'' IN *EVENTS MAGAZINE*:

ARMY EXPLAINS CHOPPER CRASH

The Army finally released the results of its investigation of the tragic helicopter crash that took the lives of six men at Ft. Campbell, Kentucky, last month. The crash was noteworthy not only because it involved one of the Army's newest jet choppers (the HU1A "Iroquois"), but also because, occurring as it did during a maintenance test flight—a routine flight that makes certain necessary repairs to the craft were properly done—usually far fewer personnel would be involved.

According to Major Royal, a spokesman for the commanding general of Ft. Campbell, "Army guidelines are very specific as to who may fly during a maintenance test flight. Only those men who have legitimate tasks to perform may be on board.

We believe those who were on board this flight met that criteria."

The six men killed were the pilot and crew chief, a technical inspector—who flies at least four hours per month on aircraft he has certified as safe —and three men operating an engine analyzer, one in charge and two learning the procedure.

It has been determined that the cause of the crash was harmonic vibrations, induced when a malfunctioning fuel control valve caused the engine to fail, thereby reducing the rotor RPM. The helicopter was literally shaken to pieces within seconds, which, according to Major Royal, "gave the appearance that the helicopter had exploded."

CHALLENGE IN VIETNAM

Even as the U.S. is being challenged in Berlin, President John F. Kennedy is careful to point out that the West is facing another, equally dangerous challenge. Five thousand miles away from Berlin, on the other side of the world, Communists are testing our mettle in Southeast Asia. "There," the President said, "the borders are less guarded, the enemy harder to find, and the dangers of Communism are less apparent to those who have so little."

Every night armed bands of Viet Cong (as the Vietnamese Communists are called), dressed in black peasant pajamas, make their way through the flooded marshes of the Mekong Delta or run silently along jungle trails, bound on their nefarious missions.

One example of their murderous activity occurred recently when two members of the National Assembly, visiting the countryside to see to the needs of their constituents, were pounced upon by a guerrilla band. After a short but bloody attack, the two assemblymen lay dead, two more innocent victims claimed by the Communists.

PEACE CORPS READY TO GO

This month the Peace Corps will be sending 27 young men and women out into the world to "light the lantern of freedom." Among them are:

HARRISON PENDLETON BRESEE JR., 30, an ex-GI with a degree in forestry from the University of the South. Bresee, whose father raises Herefords near Orange, Virginia, will serve in Africa.

VAINO ANTERO HOFFREN, 20, a political science student at San Diego who will take his experience as a poultry farmer to South America.

STEPHEN LE ROY HONORE, 23, a Negro from Urbana, Ohio, who sings calypso. A graduate student at Ohio State, he will be serving in South America.

DAN ROGER PRESTON, 23, a graduate of the Michigan College of Mining and Technology, will assist in laying water and gas lines in Africa.

MORGAN R. CANFIELD, 26, a graduate of Jefferson University in St. Louis, will serve in Ecuador. Public service is nothing new to the Canfields. Mr. Canfield's father, John, CEO of Canfield-Puritex (the nation's second largest food company), worked with FDR's economic recovery program during the Great Depression. His late grandfather, Robert, founder of Canfield-Puritex, witnessed J.P. Morgan save the nation from economic collapse by infusing millions of dollars of his own money to shore up a panicky market.

MARCELLA MILLS IS A WOMAN SCORNED

A Woman Scorned is the name of Miss Mills's latest screen embarrassment. The onetime sex kitten, who never learned to act, was able for a while to get by on her physical assets.

But that has all changed. She has added pounds along with her years, and her body has begun to sag. Despite that, the promotional photo for *A Woman Scorned* embarrassingly shows off as much of the blond-haired, green-eyed, more-than-well-rounded Miss Mills as the law will allow. *More* than the law allows in Memphis, where a court

order removed the billboard image that was slowing traffic on Crump Boulevard.

Miss Mills is now on a promotional tour, plug-
ging a film that, in all decency, should be given a
rapid burial—or at most be shown only in drama
schools as examples of how not to act.

NEW YORK

Marcella Mills sat in the lobby of the Algonquin Hotel,
poking the olive around in her martini. In New York to promote *A Woman Scorned*, she had attended the usual round of
cocktail parties, newspaper and magazine interviews, and
guest appearances on both *Toast of the Town* and *The
Demaris Hunter Show*.

The studio had provided her with a limousine and an
escort, the latter named Leonard, an aging, silver-haired man
who was charming, sophisticated, and very knowledgeable.
Leonard had been with Marcella all day, but for this evening
she had asked for, and was given, Tony, a man whose services
she had used before. He was less knowledgeable and less
sophisticated, but he was dark-haired, hard-bodied, and
much younger. And there were times when Marcella liked to
be around young, handsome men.

Marcella was forty-one, and though Hollywood was now
full of young beauties such as Raquel Welch and Jane Fonda,
the "Elder Stateswomen of Sexdom," as one wag had called
Marcella Mills and Marilyn Monroe, were still able to turn
more than a few heads.

She looked up from her martini as Tony returned.

"I called the theater," he said, sitting in the chair beside
her. "You're right. They do have our tickets at the box office."

"Have you seen *West Side Story?*" Marcella asked.

"Yeah, sure. Lots of times. In fact, I auditioned for it."

"No kidding. Are you a singer or dancer?"

"I'm whatever I need to be to get into show business,"
Tony said, smiling. "What'd you think? That I'm just a gigolo?" He pronounced "gigolo" with a hard G.

"Not at all. I thought you were an escort."

"Well, yeah, I am, but sometimes when rich women
come into New York to be escorted around, plays and restau-

rants aren't exactly what they're interested in, if you catch my drift."

Marcella sucked the olive from the end of her toothpick, holding her lips pursed for a long moment as she gazed intently at Tony. She smiled. "*I'm* a rich woman, Tony."

"Yeah, I know."

"So tell me. When a rich woman expresses an interest in things other than plays and restaurants, are you able to . . . satisfy her . . . curiosity?" She let the double entendre slide out slowly.

"Well, I, uh, haven't had any complaints," Tony said somewhat self-consciously.

"You can furnish references?"

"*What?*" He stared at her, then chuckled. "Oh, you're teasin', aren't you?"

"Yes."

"People like you, you can't always tell if they're teasin' or not."

"People like me? And just who are people like me?"

"You know. Famous people. I mean, I can remember seein' you in movies when I was a kid." He flushed, realizing he had just committed a faux pas. "I don't mean when I was *really* a kid. I just mean a couple of years ago, is all. Actually, you were just a kid yourself then."

"I did get into films very early," Marcella replied.

"Anyway, here you are . . . beautiful and famous. And I'm just me. So you see what I mean when I say I can't ever tell if you're teasin' or not." Tony looked at his watch. "Listen, if we're goin' to the show, we should get movin'."

"We don't have to go to the show."

"What do you mean?"

"Well, you said yourself that you've seen it, so you don't need to see it again, do you? And if I don't see it tonight, I'm sure I'll see it someday."

"Oh. You want to call it a night, then?"

Marcella smiled. "Not quite yet."

"What do you want to do?"

"Come on, Tony, you aren't *that* dense, are you? Surely I don't have to spell it out for you."

"Noooo," Tony replied, using his eyes seductively. "I just wasn't sure I would be so . . . lucky."

"You are a good boy, Tony. You know just what to say.

Let's see if you know what to do, as well." She stood. "Give me half an hour, and then come up to my suite."

"I'll be there," Tony said with a broad grin. "With bells on."

"With bells? Hmm, I've never tried it that way. That might be interesting," Marcella deadpanned.

Naked and satiated, Marcella sat up and reached for her diamond earrings, which lay on the table beside her bed. Smiling, she looked over at Tony, lying with his hands behind his head, the emblem of his manhood, so recently active, now lying spent and inert on his thigh.

"That's a pretty good trick you do with the earrings," Marcella said as she put them back on. "Wherever did you get the idea of removing them with your teeth?"

"Some lady asked me to do it once," Tony replied easily. "She really seemed to enjoy it, so I tried it on someone else. She liked it just as much as the first woman, so I've been doin' it ever since."

"It is a turn-on," Marcella admitted. "Maybe I'll teach that little trick to someone else."

"To Buck Campbell?"

"Buck has enough tricks of his own," she snorted. "He doesn't need any more."

"You and Buck are still married, aren't you? I mean, I read in one of those movie magazines that you're both goin' your own way but you're still married."

"Yes, we're still married."

"Why? I mean, if you're not goin' to live together, and if you're seein' other men and he's seein' other women, why are you still married?"

"I don't think that's any of your business."

"I guess not," Tony said in a chastised voice. "It's just that, jeez, you can do a lot better'n him. He's an old man."

"He's one year older than I am."

"Really? That's all? Jeez, he looks a lot older."

"He's led a hard life."

Tony snickered. "I should lead such a hard life. He's had about ten hit songs in a row."

"How the hell do you know what kind of life he's led?"

Marcella said angrily. "And it's twenty-seven hit songs in a row."

"You talk like you're still in love with him."

"Tony, I told you, my relationship with Buck is none of your business."

"Yeah, well, it's no sweat off my balls. It's just that I don't see what the big deal is with him and Elvis Presley. I mean, the way the women scream around them all the time. They don't seem all that much to me. Especially Buck Campbell. He's old, and he's not even that good lookin'."

"Some packages deliver more than they promise."

"What do you mean?"

"I mean looks aren't everything. Take Jack Kennedy, for example."

"Jack Kennedy? You mean President Kennedy?"

Marcella drew her knees up and wrapped her arms around her long, shapely legs. Though still nude, she now appeared almost chaste. "Jack Kennedy is an example of a package who promises more than he delivers."

Tony laughed. "I've never talked politics in bed before."

Marcella smiled slyly. "What makes you think I'm talking politics?"

"Well then, what the hell are you—" Tony suddenly sat up in bed. "Holy shit! Are you tellin' me you and Kennedy . . . the President of the United States . . . you and he . . . ?"

"He wasn't president then."

Tony grinned. "I'll be damned! I'll be a sonuvabitch! How about that? Me, Tony Pastola, and the President of the United States, boffin' the same woman!"

"Well, if I'd known you were going to get that big a thrill out of it, I'd've called Jack and asked him to join us," Marcella said dryly.

"What? You could do that? You mean you could just call him like that? Wow, wouldn't that be great?"

"You sound as if you might actually enjoy that. I was teasing."

"About what?"

Marcella just stared at him for a moment. "It's time for you to go, Tony," she finally said.

"Yeah, okay," he said, getting out of bed. "I guess I had better. Jeez, the President of the United States. What do you know about that?" He slid into his undershorts, then his pants. As he zipped up his fly he looked down at Marcella, who was still sitting on the bed with her arms wrapped around her legs. "You look sexy like that," he said.

"Do I?"

"Yeah. But then, I suppose you look sexy just about any way."

"Thank you."

"How'd I do, by the way?"

"You mean you want me to join your list of references?" Tony smiled. "Yeah, somethin' like that, I guess."

"Sorry. I don't do endorsements. If I did, I could make a lot of money from Lucky Strike cigarettes."

"I just mean how'd I do compared to the President?"

"As I said, some packages promise more than they deliver."

"Yeah, but who are you talkin' about when you say that? Me or Kennedy?"

"I'll let you figure that out."

"What about between me and Buck Campbell?"

"What about it?"

"How would you compare us?"

"There is no comparison."

"Wow! How about that?" Then he frowned. "Wait a minute. I'm not sure how you mean that."

"Good. A girl should keep some mystery about her, don't you think?" Marcella replied. "Do run along now, Tony. I've had a busy day."

"Okay. I'll pick you up tomorrow morning at ten."

"No. I've already arranged for Leonard to pick me up tomorrow."

"Leonard? I thought you wanted me."

"I did. Now I've had you." Marcella gave him a quick smile. "It was fun. Maybe I'll see you again sometime."

"Yeah, okay. Well, uh, good night, then."

"Good-bye."

Tony closed the door, and Marcella stayed where she was for several moments. Then she got up, put on a robe, and walked into the sitting room of the suite. She turned on the TV to watch *Route 66*. It was one of her favorite shows. She liked fantasizing about being able to lose herself in some great coast-to-coast journey, just one more invisible face.

There were probably thousands of star-struck young girls all across the country right now wishing they could be her. She wondered what they would think if they knew she was wishing just as hard that she could be one of them.

THE WILLARD HOTEL, WASHINGTON, D.C.

As Faith Canfield crossed the hotel suite to answer the knock at the door, she caught her reflection in the mirror. She was svelte and fashionably tanned from the few days she'd just spent at the Canfield compound in Destin, Florida; her blond hair had been fashioned into a new bouffant just that morning by Jacqueline Kennedy's personal stylist; and her dress, though classic in cut, came from the most chic haute couture salon in Paris. She was fifty but looked years younger, mostly because she was blessed with good bone structure but partly because of the judicious use of cosmetic surgery.

"Why should a face-lift be any more taboo than rouge or lipstick or eye shadow?" she had asked a friend of hers one day. "They are all designed to make a woman more attractive, and I see nothing wrong with it."

Faith made no attempt to defend the fact that cosmetic surgery *was* just a bit more expensive than a tube of lipstick. After all, the cost of the procedure was hardly a factor. She was married to John Canfield, CEO of the Canfield-Puritex Corporation of St. Louis, one of the largest enterprises in the country.

John Canfield's wealth and position made him one of America's leading power players, a man often called upon for counsel by leaders in both the private and public sectors. In fact, he and Faith were in Washington now because President Kennedy had asked John to pay him a visit. And, as John had learned many years before when working for Franklin Roosevelt, it was very difficult to say no to a sitting president.

Faith opened the door to find a uniformed bellboy holding a large bouquet of flowers.

"Mrs. Canfield?"

"Yes."

"These are for you, ma'am," the youth said, handing the bouquet to her. "They are from the White House," he added, obviously impressed by the fact.

"Oh, how wonderful. Just a minute." She looked around for her purse.

"Oh, no, ma'am," the bellboy said, holding up his hand. "You don't need to do that. The tip has already been taken care of."

"Oh. Well, thank you, then."

Closing the door, Faith looked around the room. On top of the television set was a large vase. Although it was in itself decorative, it would do for her purposes, and she took it over to the wet bar and filled it with water, then brought it over to the table. She was arranging the bouquet when John came into the sitting room from the bedroom.

"Was someone here?" he asked. He had just taken a shower and was buttoning his shirt.

"Flowers from the President," Faith replied. "Aren't they beautiful?"

"Indeed they are." He handed Faith his cuff links, then held out his arms as she fastened them. Like his wife, John was tan, thin, and if not younger looking than his fifty-three years, he wore his years well, with the silver in his hair giving him a look of great distinction.

"John, what do you think the President wants?" Faith asked.

"I haven't the slightest idea." He smiled. "Maybe he wants to thank us for letting Morgan join the Peace Corps."

Faith laughed. "Morgan is twenty-six years old. I hardly think we 'let' him do anything."

"I am rather proud of him for doing that, though," John said. "Aren't you? I mean, he could have stayed in St. Louis and taken a position in the company. Instead, he's down there in the jungles of Ecuador, serving his country."

"Of course I'm proud of him." Faith linked her hands behind her husband's neck. "But then, I remember being proud of another young Canfield who, instead of staying in St. Louis and taking a position with the company, went to work in Mr. Roosevelt's fight against the Depression."

"Yes, well, if I hadn't done that, I wouldn't have met Senator Dawson's beautiful daughter."

"Oh, my, you're right. Morgan might meet someone. I hadn't thought of the consequences of that," Faith said, suddenly nervous.

"What consequences?"

"Well, what sort of girl could Morgan possibly meet where he's going? Surely no one suitable."

"What makes you think that? How do you know that somewhere at this very moment the father of some dedicated young woman isn't having the same worry about his daughter? He might be concerned that she would meet someone like Morgan."

"But who wouldn't be thrilled to have their daughter married to Morgan?" Faith said. "He's a wonderful young man. Handsome, intelligent, well mannered . . ."

"Rich."

"Rich has nothing to do with it."

John chuckled. "Tell that to the girl's father. Take you, for example. Do you think for one moment Senator Champ Dawson would have let his daughter marry a sharecropper from Sikeston, Missouri?"

"Yes, well, I didn't have to marry a sharecropper from Sikeston, did I?"

"No, you didn't."

"Speaking of unsuitable young women, John, did you know that Sheri received a letter from Morgan?"

"Sheri? You mean the young woman working at the Florida house?"

"Yes."

"So she got a letter from Morgan, did she? That's nice," John said, taking his jacket from a hanger.

"Why do you suppose he would write to her?"

"I don't know. She seems like a nice girl. Anyway, it was Morgan who suggested that Mrs. Jackson hire her. Maybe he's just checking in to see how things are going."

"I hope that's all there is."

John slipped the jacket on. "Do you think there may be more?"

"I don't know. Sheri is quite pretty. I can see how a young man's head might be turned. But she does have that child. And she is . . ." Faith let the sentence hang.

"She is what?"

"A domestic."

"That's honest employment, isn't it? Besides, she is *our* domestic."

"Well, that's just the point."

"What's just the point?"

"Oh, John, don't make me out to be an old witch," Faith whined. "You know what I mean. I have nothing against the young woman . . . nothing at all. When we met her I thought she was delightful. And Mrs. Jackson is more than pleased with her. I just don't want to encourage any kind of relationship between Morgan and her, that's all."

John kissed her forehead. "Dear, I think Morgan is beyond our encouragement or discouragement. Now, tell me, how do I look?"

"Absolutely marvelous. The President will be impressed."

"To hell with the President. I'm trying to impress Jacqueline."

John F. Kennedy met John Canfield just inside the Oval Office, then ushered him over to where Robert Kennedy was standing by a couch, waiting for them. John was offered one of the leather chairs, while the President sat in his rocking chair. A lighted cigar was smoldering in the ashtray by the rocking chair, and the President picked it up and stuck it in his mouth, drawing deeply.

"I want to thank you for coming, John," he said after releasing the smoke.

"Mr. President, that is one of the perks of your office," John replied. "When you say jump, most people will ask how high."

The President laughed. "Is that a fact? There are quite a few people up on the Hill who haven't learned that yet. That's why I have Bobby."

"You've discovered the power of persuasion, have you?" John asked the President's younger brother.

"Come on; you know me better than that, John," Bobby said. "I'm not persuasive . . . I'm just mean as hell."

John laughed. "Whatever works."

The President took the cigar from his mouth. "Yes, well, evidently we haven't found what works with Khrushchev," he said. "We're going to meet in Vienna next month, but I think the son of a bitch believes he has me over a barrel with this Bay of Pigs thing." He sighed, then rocked his chair for a moment. "And he may be right," he finally said. "I don't know. Perhaps I should have sent in air power."

"Mr. President, if I may ask," John put in, "were you prepared to launch an all-out attack? I mean a full-scale invasion, using the Army, Navy, and Marines?"

"No. It never was intended to be anything like that. It was never intended to be anything more than providing some support for dissident Cubans launching a war for the liberation of their country."

"And they failed. *They* failed, Mr. President, not you—and not America."

"Yes? Well, tell that to the press, will you? And tell that to the families of the men Castro is holding prisoner."

"What is he going to do with them?" John asked.

Kennedy sighed, then clamped the cigar back in his mouth and spoke around it. "In the beginning I was afraid he was going to execute them. But it's too late for that now; he couldn't do that without being seen as a butcher. So he has put them up for sale."

"I beg your pardon?"

"He is ransoming them off to us," Bobby explained.

"And we're actually dealing with him?"

"Yes," Bobby said. "Do you disapprove?"

"I don't know. It might set some sort of precedent."

"We've dealt with foreign countries for prisoners before," Bobby reminded him. "I don't see this as anything different."

"Maybe not. What does he want?"

"Medicine, money, tractors. He's asking an outrageous price, but I think he'll come down. After all, the commodity he holds, our prisoners, has only one market. It isn't as if he can auction them off to the highest bidder."

John shook his head. "No, I guess not."

"John, what do you know about Vietnam?" the President asked abruptly.

"Not too much," John admitted, taking the shift of subject in stride. "I've seen it mentioned in news articles a few times. I can probably find it on a map."

"You won't have to find it," the President said. "The pilot will find it for you."

"The pilot?"

"John, I want you to go to Vietnam for me."

"All right," John replied, nodding slowly. "What do you want me to do there?"

"Mostly I want you to just look the place over. I have just issued orders to add four hundred Special Forces soldiers and one hundred military advisers to the six hundred or so that we already have over there."

"Are we going to get involved in Vietnam?"

"Hopefully only on a limited scale."

"Hopefully?"

"If the situation requires, I am prepared to make further increases."

"Understand, John, we need someplace to flex our muscles," Bobby said. "We can stand firm in Berlin, but all we can do is defend the status quo—we can't kick the Russians out without starting a war. And we can't go back into Cuba—not now, not after the Bay of Pigs."

"Somewhere in the world we have to draw a line and tell the Communists, 'This far and no farther,' " the President put in. "I believe Vietnam is that place."

"We couldn't do it in Laos," Bobby said, "because we couldn't find a leader we could back. But in Vietnam we think we may have someone in this fellow Ngo Dinh Diem."

"We're sending Lyndon to Vietnam, but we want you to go also, and we want you to meet Diem," Jack Kennedy added.

"Will I be part of the Vice President's party?" John asked.

"No," the President replied. "I want you to go on your own. In fact, I don't even want it known that we have had this conversation. I want you to meet Diem as a private citizen . . . say, as a businessman interested in doing business there."

"All right, Mr. President."

"Take the measure of the man. I'm not looking for a saint, but if we're going to put young men into harm's way in a place that most of them have never heard of, then I want to know that we're dealing with someone who isn't going to stab us in the back."

"We lost face when we backed out in Laos," Bobby said. "If we go into Vietnam, we have to be prepared to stay there for the long run. If not, we will lose all our credibility. Our word will never again mean anything. We must have the guts to stick it out until the end."

"And to make that kind of commitment, we must know

who we are dealing with. That's what I want you to find out,"
President Kennedy concluded.

"But won't the Vice President be doing that?"

Bobby laughed. "It was all we could do to make him go.
Here is a man who wears the Distinguished Flying Cross on
his jacket lapel, but he's afraid to go to Vietnam because he
thinks he might be assassinated."

"I take it that isn't entirely unlikely, given the volatility
of the area," John said.

The President nodded. "I agree it is a dangerous place,
and Lyndon is being subjected to some risks." He laughed.
"But I promised Lyndon that if anything happened to him,
Sam Rayburn and I would give him the biggest funeral Aus-
tin, Texas, has ever seen."

John laughed with him. "With that kind of incentive how
could he resist? So, when do you want me to go?"

"Lyndon is leaving on the eighth. I'd like you to get
there before him. Will you have any trouble with that?"

"No, Mr. President. No trouble."

Bobby stood, though it was more a signal that John could
leave than a suggestion that he should. John stood as well and
took Bobby's hand.

"Ethel sends her best to Faith," Bobby said.

"Thank you. I'll pass the word to her," John replied. He
shook Jack Kennedy's hand. "Mr. President, I'll be in touch
as soon as I return."

"I'll be looking forward to it. Perhaps we'll go out on the
boat."

"I'd like that, sir."

"Oh, John, one more question," Bobby Kennedy said as
they reached the door. "This business that's going on all over
the South now—the sit-ins and such—how do the people in
your part of the country read all that?"

"As you know, Missouri was a border state during the
Civil War," John answered. "And in many ways it still is. We
have people who think the South could work out their own
problems if the so-called Northern agitators would just stay
away. Then we have people who look at pictures of Negroes
being beaten with billy clubs, sprayed with fire hoses, and
attacked by police dogs, and they are mortified that such
things can happen in America."

"Where do you come down?" Bobby asked. He quickly

held up his hand. "Sorry. I have no right to ask you that question, especially in view of the fact that we're asking you to undertake a mission to Vietnam for us."

"That's all right. I don't mind answering," John replied. "I suppose I'm the product of my state. I am against racial discrimination and those laws that perpetuate racial discrimination. On the other hand, I think civil disobedience is a dangerous and counterproductive tactic. By forcing violent confrontations, civil rights activists are making enemies of the very moderates who could bring about the cause they're seeking. But if they *are* going to force these confrontations, I think they should be protected—by the states if the states will do so or by the federal government if that's the only recourse."

Bobby Kennedy smiled. "That was the answer of a true politician. It sounds as if you come down right in the middle."

John made a wry face. "If you don't want a middle-of-the-road answer, don't ask someone from Missouri."

When he returned to the hotel, John asked Faith if she would mind having lunch in the suite.

"I don't mind at all," she said. "What's wrong?"

"Wrong? What makes you think something is wrong?"

"John Canfield, I have known you almost thirty years—which is long enough to recognize that look when I see it. You have something to tell me, and you don't think I'm going to want to hear it."

John smiled. "Remind me never to try to lie to you."

"I'm right, aren't I? You do have something to tell me."

"The President wants me to go to Vietnam."

"When?"

"Right away."

"Right away? What do you mean, right away? Alicia graduates on the tenth. You won't be going before then, will you?"

"Darling, when the President says he wants you to do something right away, that means right away. That doesn't mean 'Wait until after your daughter has graduated from law school.'"

"But that's only four more days," Faith protested. "Surely you can wait four more days!"

"I'm sorry. I'll be leaving from Washington. You'll have to go back to St. Louis without me."

"John, that isn't fair. You aren't in Kennedy's Cabinet. You aren't even on his staff, for crying out loud."

"I wasn't in Roosevelt's Cabinet either, but I undertook a few missions for him."

"That was different."

"What was different about it?"

"Well, you were younger; the country was in trouble; times were—" Faith stopped and sighed. "We didn't have a daughter who was graduating from law school."

"Honey, Alicia will graduate whether I'm there or not," he said. "And she'll still be graduated when I come back. We'll have a big party for her then. She'll understand. She's a big girl." John chuckled. "She'll probably take it better than you are."

Faith grinned crookedly. "She'll probably take it a lot better. After all, she's one of those who have answered Kennedy's challenge to serve."

"She and Morgan."

"And you," Faith added. She smiled. "It would seem that I am surrounded by do-gooders."

The phone rang.

"So it would seem," John said, reaching for the telephone. "Hello?"

"John, this is Lyndon." There was no mistaking the Texas drawl of the speaker.

"Yes, Mr. Vice President. What can I do for you?"

"I wonder if you would have lunch with me," Johnson replied. "In my office at one?"

John looked at Faith. The Vice President's voice was loud enough that he had held the phone away from his ear so that she could hear him, too. She nodded.

"One o'clock? Yes, I'll be there."

"Good, good. I'll see you then."

John hung up. "I wonder what that's all about?" he mused.

"Maybe Kennedy gave Johnson some instructions for you."

"I doubt it. Relations between the Kennedys and Johnson aren't all that cordial." John sighed. "Darling, I'm afraid you're going to have to take lunch alone."

"Well, if you are going to be running all over the world without me, I suppose I should get used to dining alone," Faith teased. "Don't worry; I'll be fine. But I am awfully curious. You *will* tell me what Johnson wants, won't you?"

"Yes, of course," John promised. "Unless it's top secret."

He was told to go right in to the Vice President's office. When he stepped through the door, though, he found himself in an empty room.

"Mr. Vice President?"

"John, is that you?" the Vice President called. John looked toward the sound of the voice and saw an open door. Then he heard the unmistakable sound of toilet paper being taken off a roll. "I'll be out in a minute. I'm takin' a dump."

"That's all right, I'm in no hurry," John quickly assured him. What else *could* he say? He heard the toilet flush, then the water run in the sink. Johnson leaned out the door as he was drying his hands.

"Have a seat over there at the table," he said. "I'll have 'em bring in the food. Do you like barbecue?"

"Yes, I do. Though I like Missouri barbecue more than I do Texas barbecue."

"Bullshit. There's no such thing as Missouri barbecue," Johnson said matter-of-factly as he crossed the room. Opening the office door, he called outside. "Mary? Get the food in here, will you?" He walked back to a cabinet and poured himself a bourbon, then held the bottle up, offering a drink to John.

John declined.

"I suppose you're wonderin' why I asked you over here," Johnson said.

"Yes, sir, I am."

"Well, I'll tell you why. I just got word that Jack is sendin' you to Vietnam on some sort of secret mission. Is that right?"

"Mr. Vice President, I'm not sure I'm at liberty to say."

"Hell, John, I know everything that goes on over there. Don't you know that?"

"I'm sure you have your sources."

"You're goddamn right I do. I couldn't have survived in

this town for as long as I have if I didn't have a couple dozen peckers in my pocket. You know what I mean?"

"Then I guess there's no sense in denying it. Yes, I am going to Vietnam."

"You know that I'm going, too?"

"Yes, the President mentioned that."

"You know what he's doin', don't you? He's sendin' both of us over there for the same information, hopin' we'll give him two different reports."

"I'm sure he's just being thorough."

"The hell he is. He's tryin' to cover his ass so no matter what he does, he'll have somethin' to back him up. The thing is, Jack isn't smart enough to think something like this up all by himself. It's that snot-nosed little shit Bobby who's behind it. Isn't that the truth?"

"I wouldn't know, Mr. Vice President," John replied, feeling increasingly uncomfortable.

"Hell, you don't have to tell me. I know what's goin' on. But I do plan to see your report."

"Mr. Vice President, I don't want to be difficult, but my instructions are to report directly to the President."

"Hell, John, I know you can't show it to me," Johnson replied. "But don't you worry about that. I guarantee you, it'll be on my desk as quick as it will Jack's. Ah, here's the food. Eat hearty, John," Johnson said, reaching for a large piece of meat. "I never much trusted a man who couldn't put away a couple pounds of barbecue all by himself."

CHAPTER
FOUR

MAY 13, 1961, FROM "TRAILBLAZERS" IN
EVENTS MAGAZINE:

"COOP" DEAD AT 60

Sergeant York is dead. So is the sheriff who stood off the bad guys at *High Noon*. Gary Cooper, the actor who played those parts so memorably, succumbed to cancer at his home in Los Angeles.

Winner of two Oscars and known for his strong, silent roles, the rangy actor, who added "yep" to the American vocabulary, was born in Montana and got his start in the movies in 1926 with a feature role in *The Winning of Barbara Worth*. From the first Coop indelibly personified the American West.

CANFIELD CHIEF STUDIES VIETNAM
BUSINESS OPPORTUNITIES

John Canfield, President and CEO of Canfield-Puritex, left this week for South Vietnam to scope out commercial prospects there. When asked if he would really consider Vietnam a logical place for business investments, he replied:

"The U.S. is undertaking significant steps aimed at preventing Communist raids into South Vietnam. If this danger is reduced, it will take private investments to shore up Vietnam's economy. A financially sound Vietnam is the best bulwark against the further spread of Communism in the region."

SAIGON

Chief Warrant Officer Bob Parker awoke that morning to the same sounds from the street that had woken him every morning since arriving in Vietnam:

"Bun mae! Bun mae!"

The haunting cries of the bread women hawking their wares hung in the air and penetrated the walls of the small houses. The bread women, the first of the morning vendors to appear each day, carried the long, narrow loaves of golden-brown bread in straw baskets on their back. The bread was still hot from the oven and tantalizingly aromatic.

Shortly after the bread women appeared, clacking sticks announcing the arrival of the soup vendors could be heard. Old men with wispy beards and obsidian eyes who pushed about their carts heavily laden with steaming vats of noodle soup, the soup vendors employed young boys to run before them in the narrow streets and twisting alleyways, advertising the fare. The boys did this by clacking two sticks together in a distinctive rhythm. Each vendor had his own rhythmic signature, and customers who preferred a certain soup would stay in bed, listening to the clacks, until they heard the particular beat of their favored vendor.

Next on the scene were the cyclos—small, three-wheeled motorbikes with a passenger seat in front and a sputtering, popping motor in the rear. They darted in and out of the alleyways and back streets, zipping up and down Cong Ly and Tru Minh Ky, looking for riders. The cyclos trailed clouds of noxious exhaust smoke that by late afternoon lay over the city in a thick blue fog. By sunrise, Bob knew, all the streets would be veiled, not only the busy thoroughfares, but the quieter streets as well.

Only half-rested from a night spent combating heat and mosquitoes, Bob pulled the netting aside and sat up in bed. The housegirl, provided by the MACV BOQ, was already in Bob's room, sitting quietly in the corner, polishing his boots. She had her own key, and he had not heard her come in.

The first morning he was there, it had embarrassed him to get out of bed in front of her wearing only his undershorts. But she seemed not to notice him, so it no longer bothered him.

"Your President come to Vietnam today," the girl said.

"No, not the President. The Vice President," Bob corrected.

"You will see him?"

"Yes."

"*Choi, oui*. You numbah-one big shot."

Bob laughed. "I'll just be one of the crowd," he said.

"You tell him all Vietnamese like Americans. You tell him VC numbah ten."

"I'll tell him," Bob said. That was easier than trying to explain that he would probably only see Lyndon Johnson from a great distance.

Bob quickly dressed and walked over to the officer's mess for breakfast. He saw that Colonel Hawkins was already sitting at a table. Jarred Hawkins, Bob's superior while he was in Vietnam, was a big man, six foot three, with closely cropped sandy hair and clear blue eyes. He wasn't an aviator; in fact, he had nothing at all to do with aviation. He was Bob's superior only as a matter of logistical practicality. Technically, he was a military adviser to the Vietnamese Army, particularly valuable in that position because he was fluent in Vietnamese.

"Good morning, Bob," Jarred said, motioning Bob over to join him at his table. "You'll enjoy breakfast today. They've got SOS."

"Oh, good. That's my favorite," Bob said with enthusiasm.

Jarred looked at him suspiciously. "I have a theory about SOS. Only people with severely retarded taste buds really enjoy it."

"Well, for these severely retarded taste buds, SOS is a

genuine treat," Bob said, as the waiter brought a plate of the toast heaped with ground beef in a milk gravy that soldiers universally referred to as SOS: shit on a shingle.

"How are you coming along with your helicopters?" Jarred asked.

"We have two of them ready to fly, three more to go."

"Do you suppose we could make use of one of those two today?"

Bob chuckled. "Hell, they're your helicopters, Colonel. You can do anything you want to with them."

"Good. An American businessman is here in country. I don't know exactly who he is or what sort of juice he packs, but it must be substantial. I received a cable from DA that he's to get VIP treatment, meaning helicopter transportation when available."

"Where do I take him?"

"*Us,*" Jarred corrected. "I'll be going with him, and we are to go anywhere he wants to go, within reason."

"What isn't within reason?"

Jarred grinned. "If he wanted to go to Hanoi, I think I would balk. Nearly every place else is fair game."

"One problem," Bob said.

"What's that?"

"Fuel. We'll either have to stay within range of the fuel on board, or we'll have to go where fuel is available."

"Good," Jarred said, nodding. "That will give us some control over Mr. Canfield."

Bob looked up in surprise. He was just about to take another bite of his SOS but put the fork down. "Did you say Canfield? That wouldn't be John Canfield, would it?"

"Yes. John Canfield. Why? Have you heard of him?"

"Hell, yes. He's Canfield of Canfield-Puritex. You know, Corn Toasties? The 'Breakfast of Winners'?"

"Damn. I hadn't put it together. Yes, of course I've heard of Canfield-Puritex."

"I know him," Bob said.

"Really?"

"Well, sort of," Bob amended. "We're from the same area, and many years ago his uncle delivered my father."

"His uncle was a doctor?"

"No, sir, he just happened to be there when my father

was born. My grandpa was a sharecropper who farmed land that belonged to the Canfields."

"Have you met this Canfield?"

"Yes, sir, but I'm not sure he'll remember me. When I was young—very young—I went to St. Louis with my father, who was in trucking, to pick up a load of cereal from the Canfield-Puritex factory. While we were waiting, I was walking around, sort of exploring, and through a window I saw the old Mr. Canfield, John Canfield's father, grab his chest and fall. He was having a heart attack. So I ran and told my dad, who got help to Mr. Canfield in time. When he came to, he told me I had saved his life."

"He was probably right."

"Well, he's gone now," Bob said. "His son, John, happened to be there at the time. He might remember the incident, but I'm sure he won't remember me."

"Yes, of course I remember the incident," John said when he was told the story later that morning upon meeting the military personnel assigned to him. He smiled broadly and shook Bob's hand. "And I remember you. Thanks to you, Mr. Parker, my family had our father with us for several years more. It's a great pleasure to meet you again after all these years."

"The pleasure is mine, sir," Bob replied.

"Mr. Canfield, my orders are to take you anywhere you want to go," Jarred Hawkins broke in, "and I am willing to do that within reason. But Mr. Parker tells me we may have a fuel problem."

"Oh?"

Bob explained the limitations.

"Well, then, we'll just have to stay within the range of our fuel, won't we? There's a little village just north of here that I would like to visit. Phu Cuong. Could we go there?"

"Sure. I'll have you up there in about fifteen minutes," Bob promised as he and Jarred ushered their visitor onto the tarmac toward the waiting helicopter. "Let's get on board."

The helicopters that had been transferred to MACV from the Army's inventory in Korea were twin-rotor H-21's. Looking somewhat like a flying banana, the H-21 was one of the older helicopters in the Army, not nearly as powerful nor as fast as the HU1A that had replaced it in the States and in Europe. Nevertheless, it was a good performing helicopter, and Bob didn't mind flying it.

The H-21 had a reciprocating engine rather than the turbine Bob had grown used to. It didn't whine into life as a turbine did, but coughed, spit, and hacked until it broke into a deep-throated roar. When the rotor RPM was up, Bob pulled up on the collective. The nose came up first, and he corrected with the cyclic. It shifted a little, and he corrected the drift with the pedals, then began to climb out. The helicopter was built to carry ten, and he had four aboard counting himself, the crew chief, and his two passengers. Being so lightly loaded, the craft got off the ground easily, and sooner than he would have thought, he was climbing over the trees at the north end of the field.

They reached their destination and landed at the edge of town. Phu Cuong sat on a bend in the Saigon River. Its main commerce was fish, which it supplied to the markets of all nearby hamlets, whose fishmongers came to Phu Cuong every day to buy. They would walk along the bank of the river and poke through the catch, which, when laid out, stretched for almost a quarter of a mile.

The occasional visitor found the smell very strong, odious even, though Phu Cuong's residents weren't aware of it. To them the fish market was an exciting place and the center of great activity, for besides customers and vendors, it was crammed with scores of passengers from the bus line and the ferry service, both of which used the market as a terminal.

There were at least a dozen portable sidewalk cafés, marvels of logistical ingenuity, in operation in the village square. Their owners, men and women alike, would assemble the cafés every morning, then disassemble them every night, carrying them about in two large boxes suspended on their shoulders as they shuffled down the street. In one box, packed with every item carefully nested into another like Russian *matryoshka* dolls, were tables and chairs; the empty box then became part of the counter. The other box contained utensils, spices, and other paraphernalia to stock the restaurant—and, of course, the box itself completed the counter.

Within moments the portable café took on the appearance of a permanent fixture.

Leaving the crew chief to watch over the helicopter, Bob, John, and Jarred started toward the center of Phu Cuong. As they walked through the marketplace, it was all John and Bob could do to refrain from holding handkerchiefs to their noses, but Jarred, who had been in Vietnam for three years, didn't seem to notice the stench.

"Was there anything in particular you wanted to see here, Mr. Canfield?" Jarred asked.

"Not some*thing* so much as some*one*," John answered. "I want to talk to a Mr. Mot of the Cochin Business Council. According to my sources, he speaks excellent English and will be able to answer questions for me."

"I don't know Mr. Mot." Jarred pointed to a building. "But that's the Cochin Business Council over there. Suppose we try to find him."

"That seems a sensible enough place to start."

Walking across the market square, they were surrounded by chattering, laughing Vietnamese children. Though most of them hung back, the bolder ones came right up to the three Americans and pulled at the hair on their arms.

"What are they doing?" John asked.

Jarred chuckled. "Vietnamese have virtually no body hair. The children are fascinated by how hairy we are."

Just as they reached the front of the Cochin Business Council building, a smiling Vietnamese man came down the steps to greet them. He stood out from the others, not only because of the white Western-style suit he was wearing, but also because he was obviously much better fed than anyone else.

"Welcome, welcome, welcome!" he said effusively. "It is indeed an honor to have Americans visit our modest little city. I am Mr. Mot. How may I help you?"

"Mr. Mot, I am John Canfield." John pulled an envelope from his inside jacket pocket. "I have a letter of introduction from the Vietnamese minister of finance in Saigon."

Mot read the letter, then, obviously impressed by its contents, bowed deeply. "Ah, you are Mr. Canfield of the great Canfield-Puritex Corporation," he said. "I am indeed honored to meet such a rich and powerful man."

"Mr. Mot, my company is looking at certain areas in Southeast Asia for business investments. You can understand, however, that with the political climate as it is, we are somewhat concerned."

"You need not be concerned. Our government has the situation well under control," Mot insisted.

"Yes, I'm sure you do. But if you wouldn't mind, I would like to talk to some ordinary people and see how they feel about such matters."

"Of course. I will round some up for you."

"No!" John said quickly. He probably sounded rather suspicious—but, after all, he was. If left to Mr. Mot, he'd no doubt meet nothing but toadies. "Actually, I'd rather just stroll around and select a few people for myself, if you don't mind. Would you come with me?"

"Yes. That is a good idea," Mot said. He looked at the other two Americans.

"Oh, this is my guide, Colonel—"

"Jarred," Jarred interrupted, sticking out his hand.

John was surprised that Jarred introduced himself by his first name, but he said nothing. "And this is our pilot, Mr. Parker."

"It is a pleasure to meet you gentlemen," Mot said, his sincerity sounding genuine.

They wandered through crowded streets over to the teeming market area, and the first person John questioned was a woman who was buying fish.

"Ask her if she feels any danger from the Viet Cong," John requested of Mot.

Mr. Mot asked the question. When the woman answered, Mot smiled, then translated for John.

"She says there was a time when she feared the Viet Cong, but she fears them no more. She has confidence in the government to protect her."

"Ask her what she thinks about the idea of Americans helping the Vietnamese people."

Again there was an exchange in Vietnamese, following which Mot spoke in English.

"She says the Americans are very good people. If the Americans come to the aid of Vietnam, she will be very happy."

John spoke with a number of other villagers, though the

responses from all were so similar that he could almost believe they had been staged. But that would have been impossible, for he had made no previous announcement of his visit. Therefore, it seemed awfully likely that a lot was being deliberately lost in the translation.

Finally they said good-bye to Mr. Mot, got into the helicopter, and clattered off back to Saigon.

"Well," John said as they climbed down from the helicopter at Tan San Nhut airport and stood on the perforated steel planking, "that was an interesting visit."

Jarred chuckled. "Probably more interesting than you know."

"What do you mean?"

"The answers Mr. Mot gave you were not the answers the people were giving."

John shook his head. "That doesn't surprise me. They were all just a little too pat."

"But then, to be truthful, their answers didn't matter anyway since they weren't asked the questions you posed."

"Well, I'll be! You speak Vietnamese, obviously."

"Yes."

"Why didn't you say something?"

"I didn't think it the time for it. That's why when you introduced me I gave my first name instead of my last. A lot of people in Vietnam have heard of Hawkins. They know I can speak Vietnamese, and they clam up around me. I thought if he didn't know who I was, we might get a better perspective on him. And I guess we did."

"I'm curious. What questions *did* he ask?"

"None."

"None? But he said *something*."

"He told them you were a very wealthy man and you were going to give every villager one kilo of rice. But you would do this only if you were pleased by them. He told them to smile and to say their names and the names of the other members of their family. He would do the rest."

"So it was all made up? All the answers he gave me?"

"Yes, sir, I'm afraid so."

"That was pretty much a waste of time, then." John sighed. "And no doubt visiting the other people the minister of finance suggested would be an equal waste of time."

"Yes, sir, I'm sure it would," Jarred agreed. "But if you're interested, I could suggest a place for you."

"Where?"

"The village of Cao Lanh. Our engineers built a bridge there. It's being dedicated today."

"All right. Let's check it out."

Jarred turned to Bob. "We won't need you anymore, Mr. Parker. I can drive Mr. Canfield to where we are going in a jeep."

"Okay, I'll get back to work," Bob said. He shook John's hand. "It was good seeing you again, Mr. Canfield."

"After all these years and so many miles from home." John smiled. "I guess it's true what they say about this being a small world."

Bob smiled back. "Yeah, I guess so."

During the drive to Cao Lanh, Jarred told John the story behind the construction of the new bridge. The old bridge had been of wood and rope, allowing foot traffic, bicycles, and carts to cross the small river that separated the highway from the village. No motorized vehicles could use it, but there was another, larger bridge about ten miles downriver that vehicles could use and a dirt road that would bring them back to the village. Because of that, the village wasn't completely isolated, and the narrow wood-and-rope suspension bridge had served without problems until the last rainy season, when a flood destroyed it.

The Saigon government requested the U.S. Corps of Engineers to build another bridge, and Saigon drew up the plans. The villagers were pleased to get a new bridge, not realizing the replacement would be a big steel-and-concrete affair capable of carrying five-ton trucks.

"Well," John said when Jarred had finished his narration, "they certainly should be pleased with that."

"I suppose they are for the most part. But I've heard some of them say they would rather have had the bridge built back as it was."

"Why? Wouldn't this bridge be an improvement?"

"It depends on your definition of improvement. A bridge like this makes Cao Lanh an attractive military objective. Until now they've managed to avoid the fighting."

"I see. So you don't think the bridge should have been built?"

"I'm not saying that. I'm just telling you how some of the villagers feel. The truth is, it's probably a good thing. The more involved we can get the people of Vietnam with the government of Vietnam, the better chance we have of keeping the country from going Communist."

"Do you really think that's likely? Going Communist, I mean."

"If we can't make the alternative more attractive to them, I would say, yes, that's more than likely."

"Why? I mean, aren't we doing things for them?"

"You mean bridges, roads, equipment for their military?"

"Yes."

"You have to understand that a concrete road and a steel bridge are important only to people who have a need for such things. And in this country that means the ruling class and the cultural elite. To the peasants in the villages, help isn't a bridge or a road. It's a kilo of rice."

"And the Communists are giving that to them?"

Jarred nodded. "Actually, in most cases the Communists are sharing it with them. They only see Americans and their own officials from Saigon dressed in fine clothes and driving big automobiles—by the way, to the Vietnamese peasant, a Renault is a big automobile. And when the Americans and the Saigon officials take part in some staged event—the dedication of a road or bridge or public building—they literally stand apart from the citizens. The Communists, on the other hand, are at these same events wearing peasant clothes and mingling with the villagers. When the Americans and the Saigon officials go home, the Communists are still there. That night, when the villagers cook their rice by the light of a kerosene lantern, their neighbor cooking rice by the light of a kerosene lantern in the next house may well be a Communist. Given that scenario, whom would *you* trust?"

"I don't know," John answered, slowly shaking his head. "But that is an interesting observation. Have you shared it with any of our officials?"

"I'm not sure anyone wants to hear it." Jarred abruptly laughed. "Do you know what the natives in the British colonies say is the reason so many Brits wear monocles? So they'll only see half of what's going on—and thus won't see more than they can understand."

John raised his eyebrows questioningly. "And you're saying our government is like that?"

"If the shoe fits, Mr. Canfield. If the shoe fits."

When they reached Cao Lanh, Jarred parked the jeep, then took John over to meet a Vietnamese man in military dress.

"Mr. Canfield, this is Colonel Nguyen Van Tran," Jarred said. "He is chief of security of the Can Lao, which is Ngo Dinh Nhu's private police."

Colonel Nguyen removed the cigarette from his mouth with his ring and little fingers, holding it out in an almost effeminate way. He smiled at John. "Well, Mr. Canfield, welcome to our country. It is an honor to meet you. Even halfway around the world from your country we know of Canfield-Puritex. You are traveling with your Vice President?"

"No, Vice President Johnson is here on an official state visit to show our country's commitment. I am here on a private mission," John explained.

"Perhaps," Colonel Nguyen said, raising his eyebrows. "But one of your station would certainly have some influence on your new President, would you not?"

"Very little, I'm afraid."

"You are either being modest, Mr. Canfield, or your young President is a fool not to listen to you." Colonel Nguyen smiled, then looked at Jarred. "I thought you would not be able to come to the ceremony today, Jarred."

"I didn't think I would, but I convinced Mr. Canfield that it would be an interesting sight."

Nguyen nodded. "Yes. Perhaps even more interesting than you think."

"What do you mean?"

"You shall see," Nguyen said mysteriously. "Ah, it seems the band has formed. They are about to play the national anthems of our two countries. This is quite a moment, Mr. Canfield. Visible evidence through this beautiful bridge and the joining of the two national anthems that our countries are bound together in friendship and understanding."

The muscians, members of the Vietnamese Army, were dressed in starched khaki uniforms with gleaming silver helmet liners and red Sam Browne belts. At a signal from their director they raised their gleaming instruments, the bridge and the village reflected in the brass bells and tubes.

The first notes of "The Star-Spangled Banner" began. Halfway through the song—just about the point where spirited voices would have been tolling "bombs bursting in air" —an explosion rocked the area. At the first heavy, stomach-shaking *thump*, most people just looked toward the bridge in stunned surprise. The initial blast was then followed by a series of explosions, and the entire bridge went up in fire and smoke. Shaken from their reverie, the villagers screamed, and the dignitaries standing ready to cut the ribbons dived for cover, along with the soldiers and the members of the band.

John, Jarred, and Colonel Nguyen were far enough away so as not to be in any personal danger from the flying debris. They were, however, close enough to see the bridge slowly crumple, then fall into the water, a useless pile of twisted metal and broken concrete.

The smoke was still hanging in the air when a soldier reported to Nguyen, speaking rapid-fire Vietnamese.

"Colonel Nguyen," Jarred said briskly, "did this man just tell you they had the sappers trapped?"

"Yes."

"That was a lucky break, wasn't it?"

Nguyen smiled. "It wasn't luck, my friend. We had our patrols out, waiting to capture them. You see, we knew the bridge was going to be blown."

"I see."

"Would you like to be in on the capture?"

"Yes," Jarred said, speaking for himself. Then he looked at John. "That is . . ."

"By all means," John replied. "I'm game."

The two Americans followed Colonel Nguyen to a nearby jeep. Seconds later they were roaring down the road, a rooster tail of dust trailing them. Less than a mile from the edge of the village stood an armored personnel carrier and another jeep. There, three dozen Vietnamese soldiers were standing in a semicircle around four young Vietnamese men. None of the young men were armed, and none wore an armband or anything else that would suggest they were VC. One had been shot, and he was being supported by two of the others. His stomach was bright red with blood, and as John looked at him, he knew the young man would die quickly if he didn't get medical attention.

"Colonel, that man needs a doctor," he said.

"That man just blew up our bridge," Nguyen answered sharply. "He will be attended to when he answers the questions we have for him."

"But you can't deny him medical attention," John insisted.

"Jarred, would you please explain to your friend that we Vietnamese have full authority over our own domestic policy?"

"I'm sure he understands that as well as I do, Nguyen," Jarred said. "But I agree with him. Either you get that man medical attention at once, or when we return to Saigon we shall lodge a complaint at the highest possible level."

Nguyen sighed. "Very well, gentlemen. If it will make you feel any better, I will attend to his wounds." He paused. "And then I will have him executed."

He shouted orders to one of his officers, and a couple of soldiers took the wounded man over to a jeep. There he was laid down, and two Vietnamese medics bent over him to minister to his wounds.

"Thank you, Colonel," John said. "I think you will find—"

John's intended observation was interrupted by a fierce explosion. He looked toward the jeep where the wounded man had been, but now there was nothing but a puff of smoke and a pile of bloody rags. The man had managed to set off a grenade. He'd killed himself and the two Vietnamese medics.

"Oh, my God!" John breathed.

Colonel Nguyen laughed out loud, and John looked at him, shocked that anyone could laugh at such a moment.

"Oh, come now, Mr. Canfield. Don't look at me with such outrage," Nguyen said. "The blood of those men is on your hands. Yours and Jarred's. You are the ones who insisted I provide the prisoner with medical treatment. Jarred, I can understand the idealistic Mr. Canfield's misjudgment. He is a civilian. But really, my friend, you should have known better."

John turned to Jarred, fighting the urge to be sick, and said tightly, "Colonel Hawkins, if you don't mind, I would like to return to Saigon now."

CHAPTER

FIVE

MAY 20, 1961, FROM "TRAILBLAZERS" IN
EVENTS MAGAZINE:

VICE PRESIDENT LYNDON JOHNSON
REPORTS ON HIS TRIP TO VIETNAM

In a report to President Kennedy, Vice President Johnson said he assured South Vietnam's National Assembly that the United States was ready immediately to help stop the Communist incursion into their country. Among other things, Johnson said the U.S. would take steps to improve Vietnam's capacity to resist aggression and the terrorist activity of the Communist guerrillas.

"If we don't do this now," the Vice President said, "then the United States may as well pull its defensive lines to San Francisco, for if we fail here, we could wind up losing the entire Pacific."

CANFIELD-PURITEX WILL NOT EXPAND
INTO VIETNAM

John Canfield, President and CEO of Canfield-Puritex Corp., has just returned from a factfinding trip of his own to Vietnam.

Stressing it was by chance that his trip coincided with the Vice President's, Canfield insisted he was merely exploring business opportunities.

"I feel that now is not the proper time to be thinking of expansion in Vietnam," he said. When asked if he had shared his observations with the President, Canfield replied noncommittally, "As you know, I consulted with the President on a few occasions before I left and after I returned. Undoubtedly I expressed my observations on conditions in Vietnam, though we spoke of many things —including the Negro issue facing our country today."

THE ALABAMA SOLUTION

Eugene "Bull" Conner, chief of police in Birmingham, Alabama, has revealed his "solution" to the "problem" of sit-in demonstrators—those groups of Negroes, mostly students, who have been sitting in at lunch counters throughout the South, challenging segregation laws. Conner's plan is to remove them from the lunch counter by whatever means necessary—be it billy club, fire hose, or police dogs—then escort them under cover of darkness across the state line and dump them in Tennessee.

"That way," Conners explained, "the nigras [sic] will be someone else's problem."

Governor Patterson is said to have given full approval to the police chief's plan.

WASHINGTON, D.C.

Deon Booker sat in the waiting room of the Greyhound Bus station, reading the sports page of the *Washington Post*. WILL ARTEMUS BOOKER LEAVE ST. LOUIS FOR NEW YORK? the headline asked. The story went on to explain how Booker, who had spent six seasons in St. Louis, was being offered for sale by the Hawks, and the New York Knicks were expressing a great interest in the former Jefferson University basketball star.

Snorting contemptuously, Deon folded the paper over and laid it aside. He had more than a casual interest in the story; Artemus Booker was his brother. He also had mixed emotions about it. His brotherly pride in Artemus's being a basketball player of tremendous talent and great popularity was tempered by his belief that despite Artemus's talent and value, he was, as far as his brother was concerned, "dancing to the white man's tune."

"You can be bought and sold like a slave, for chrissake. Playing basketball for the white man is like being a performing monkey," Deon had told his brother in one acrimonious confrontation.

"If that's so, I'm a well-paid monkey," Artemus had countered, pointing out his $100,000-per-year salary.

"There's more to life than money," Deon had insisted.

"And there's more to life than being on the front line of every cause there is. Deon, you can't make history turn any faster, no matter how hard you try. We're all here for the ride in our appointed time and place, and the only thing we can do is make the best of what life has given us."

"I can try, big brother. I can at least try," Deon had responded, disappointed that his brother did not use his indisputable national appeal to come out more strongly for Negro rights. "That's more than I can say for you."

"You've got no right to say that. I've donated as much money to the cause as any individual in America," Artemus had said.

Deon had sneered. "You just don't understand, do you big brother? You don't understand at all. We don't want your money. We want your *soul*."

That had been their last meeting.

There was no doubt about where Deon's soul belonged. He was committed to the cause of Negro rights and had been since the Montgomery bus boycott. Artemus Booker's soul, on the other hand, apparently lay in limbo somewhere between St. Louis and New York.

Deon looked up as Joseph Perkins, a young man from

Michigan who had been on the phone, walked purposefully over to him and the others sitting near him.

"All right, listen up, people," Joseph said, getting everyone's attention. "I just got word that the Justice Department has been told of our plans, and Bobby Kennedy has offered his full support."

"That's good to know," a white member of the group said.

The little group consisted of two white women, one white man, and four Negro men—half of a total membership of fourteen who ranged in age from twenty-one to sixty. They were calling themselves Freedom Riders, and they were about to embark on bus rides—one group of seven on a Greyhound, the other seven on a Trailways—from Washington to New Orleans. Their route would cut a swath through the segregated South where they intended to violate all the segregation laws.

The trip's purpose was to raise the consciousness of America to the evils of segregated facilities for interstate travelers. To do this, they planned to begin their ride in a flurry of publicity and to that end had notified the press of their goal. It was a great disappointment to them that when their bus was called, only three reporters were there to see them off— and those were Negro reporters, writing for a limited audience that would already be sympathetic.

"Before we board, I think we ought to say a prayer," one of the group suggested.

"Good idea," another agreed, and the seven linked hands as one of them said a brief invocation.

Outside, more than a dozen buses were angled into the loading area. Small signs were mounted on stands in front of each bus, showing its destination. They walked past signs offering NEW YORK, CHICAGO, ST. LOUIS, DETROIT, CLEVELAND, and LOUISVILLE, finally coming to one reading NEW ORLEANS.

It was a muggy morning, and the smell of diesel exhaust hung heavy in the air. Nearly half the buses had their engines running, producing a loud, deep-throated rumble that made normal conversation impossible.

"Now, is everyone clear about what they're going to do?" Perkins asked, practically shouting to be heard. He had been elected group captain of the Greyhound team.

"Yeah, we know," Deon called back. "Let's get it done."

The plan was to scatter throughout the bus in various combinations, some whites in the back and Negroes in the front, with at least one seat occupied by a mixed team. One or two of the riders would also be less conspicuous by sitting in the "proper" place so that they could observe.

Deon took one of the front seats, sliding over to the window. A moment later a middle-aged white woman stepped in and stared at him.

"Young man, I believe you are in the wrong seat," she said pointedly.

Deon smiled pleasantly. "No, ma'am, I don't think so. This seat is going south, and so am I."

"You belong in the back of the bus."

"Why? Is the back of the bus going to a different place?"

"Well, I never . . . !" The woman pulled herself up indignantly, then moved on to find another seat.

The driver was the last to get on. He looked at Deon for a moment, then back two seats at another Negro sitting quietly with a white man. Since it was apparent that the white man didn't mind sitting with the Negro, the driver just shrugged and slipped into the driver's seat. Putting the gearshift into reverse, he backed the bus out of the terminal to begin the trip.

The first stop would be Fredericksburg, Virginia, fifty-two miles away. As the bus drove down the highway, Deon leaned his face against the green-tinted window and looked out at the countryside rolling by.

"I can't tell you how proud we are to have a Booker with us," one of the organizers had told him when he volunteered to make the Freedom Ride. *"Yes, sir, the name Booker will make folks sit up and take notice."*

Some Negro names everyone, black and white, recognized. Some were more recently famous, though their fame, coming as it did from the area of civil disobedience, actually bordered on the infamous. Dr. Martin Luther King, for one. Scarcely a white person in the country did not know his name, but for all who revered him, an equal number vilified him.

There were, of course, well-known and respected Negroes in the entertainment field: Sidney Poitier, Harry Belafonte, Sammy Davis Jr., Nat King Cole, and Marian Anderson were examples. There were also Negroes known and esteemed for their sports skill, such as Joe Lewis, Jackie Robinson, Jim Brown, Bill Russell, and Deon's brother, Artemus Booker.

But as skillful as Artemus was on the court, the Booker name had been known and revered long before he ever put on a basketball uniform. His grandfather, Loomis Booker, was in a league with George Washington Carver. Scarcely a schoolchild in America, black or white, didn't instantly recognize that illustrious name. And as they knew that George Washington Carver had "unlocked the secrets of the peanut," they knew also that Loomis Booker was the quintessential self-made man: starting out as a janitor at St. Louis's prestigious Jefferson University and educating himself with salvaged books to such a degree that, though the school was a segregated institution at that time, he was awarded a doctorate in humanities; working alongside Dwight D. Eisenhower during World War I, coordinating all the transportation that enabled American doughboys to serve "over there"; and, finally, a brilliant academic career as a beloved and respected university president.

Whenever people learned Deon was the grandson of this famous man, they felt awed just to be around a relative. They didn't realize, and Deon couldn't make them understand, that he didn't share their enthusiasm for his grandfather's greatness.

He viewed Loomis Booker as a man who had always stayed in his place. Even his graduation from an all-white school was through the back door—a special dispensation granted by the university's board. On top of that, Dr. Booker had served his entire academic career in an all-Negro school —just as he was supposed to. He did not one thing to change the status quo. Not one Negro was freer because of anything Loomis Booker did. Not one unjust law had been changed. In fact, in the most bitter irony of all, Loomis Booker's accomplishments were being used as an argument *for* the status quo by the very people Deon considered his archenemies.

"Niggers don't need to mingle with the white folks to make somethin' of themselves," the segregationists liked to say. "Why, you take that Loomis Booker fella. From all I've read, you'd never want to meet a nicer man. *He* wasn't always agitatin' an' breakin' laws. *He* stayed with his own kind, but he turned out to be someone that even presidents listened to. I don't hardly see how segregation kept him down."

It was a cruel twist of fate, Deon thought, that his grandfather's accomplishments, long a source of pride for Negroes, were being used as a weapon against them.

Deon heard a click, then a rush in the bus's speaker, indicating that the driver had just turned on the microphone.

"This is Fredericksburg," the driver's amplified voice said. "We'll be here for thirty minutes."

The bus stopped in Fredericksburg with a clack of gears and a squeal of brakes. Deon was one of the first ones off, and as he waited for the others, he spotted two signs directing passengers to the separate waiting rooms—one marked WHITE, the other COLORED.

We'll just see about that, he said to himself.

The other Freedom Riders disembarked, and all seven proceeded to the whites-only waiting room. They had to endure numerous icy glares, but there were no incidents. When they reboarded the bus a half hour later, it was with relief that nothing had happened.

Their next stop was Richmond, once the capital of the Confederacy. Despite their worries, Richmond, too, offered no resistance to the group as they continued to defy the segregationist signs. The stop in Petersburg, where the Freedom Riders would spend the night as guests in the homes of members of a local Negro church, was equally uneventful.

Deon was escorted to the house where he would stay, and he had just settled into a big, comfortable chair when one of the sons, a teenager, asked, "Is Artemus Booker really your brother?"

"Yes."

"He's my favorite basketball player," the youth said. He raised his hands over his head in a pantomime of someone making a jump shot. "Up, shoot, swish," he said. "I can do it just like him."

"No, you can't," his younger brother said.

"Yes, I can."

"No, you can't. If you could, you'd be playin' in the NBA."

"I'm not old enough to play in the NBA, but I'll be there one day."

"Not many people make it to the NBA," Deon cut in.

"You ought to think about something else . . . like being a lawyer or a doctor or an engineer."

The teen laughed. "You crazy? Colored folks don't do jobs like that. The only kind of job there is for colored folks is loadin' trucks or bein' a janitor or maybe a preacher. Preachin' is good. Preachers wear suits."

"That's not true," Deon said. "You can be anything you set your mind to."

"Don't be fillin' them boys' heads with false hopes, now," their mother cautioned.

"They aren't false hopes," Deon countered. "They're attainable goals—though I admit the goals are harder for our people than they are for whites."

"Why is that?" the younger boy asked.

"That's a good question," Deon replied caustically. "That's why my friends and I are making this bus trip."

The teenager laughed. "You tellin' me that ridin' a bus is goin' to make it easier for colored folks to get good jobs?"

"Yes. Among other things."

"Well, I got nothin' but respect for you for doin' it," the boys' mother said. "But I ain't gettin' my hopes up."

"But we have to have hope, don't you see? Without hope, without dreams, we have nothing. Besides, the trip seems to be working. We were in three white waiting rooms in bus stations today, and nobody did anything to stop us."

"You ain't in Alabama yet," the woman warned. "I got a sister lives in Alabama, and she says the folks down there done heard you be comin'. It ain't goin' to be pretty when you get to Alabama."

"You don't have to tell me anything about Alabama," Deon said. "I live in Montgomery, and I went through the Montgomery bus boycott. Only that was then and this is now. And now we've got the United States Justice Department on our side."

"It don't do no good to have anybody on your side 'less you got 'em standin' *by* your side, if you know what I mean. I'm prayin' for you . . . I'm prayin' for all of you. I think what you doin' is 'bout the bravest thing I ever heard of. That's why I told the reverend I'd be glad to put one of you up. But you keep your eyes open when you get down there, son, 'cause it ain't goin' to be nothin' at all like it's been up here. No, sir. Nothin' at all."

*   *   *

The Freedom Riders boarded two new buses the next day to continue their ride to New Orleans. The first stop was Farmville, where the COLORED WAITING ROOM sign had been freshly painted over. Though there were a few stares and whispers when the passengers came into the lunchroom, no one actually said or did anything to prevent them. They were served a meal without incident.

Their next stop was Lynchburg, also visited without incident, then Danville—where for the first time they were turned away from the white waiting room. They convened outside to decide if this was where they wanted to make their stand, concluding that having their trip interrupted by being thrown into jail in Danville wasn't a good idea.

"I don't think we ought to give Danville the honor of being the one to jail us," one of the young men said, and the others laughed.

"All right," said Joseph Perkins, the group's de facto leader. "Back on the bus. *We'll* pick the time and place, not them."

The first physical confrontation came the next day in Rock Hill, South Carolina. As the Freedom Riders filed into the white dining room, John Lewis walked to the front of the group. Deon sensed right away that this bus terminal was different from all the others so far. He could feel an electric tension in the air.

"John," he said softly, "be careful."

"Nothing's happened yet," Lewis replied.

"Yeah, but I don't like the looks of this."

The Rock Hill bus station featured several pinball machines. The white youths arrayed around them were similar in type to the young white men who had been the prime challengers at lunch counter sit-ins. Wearing jeans and T-shirts, the young whites strutted toward the door when they saw the Negroes entering.

The apparent leader of the white toughs, a pack of cigarettes rolled up in his left sleeve and a cigarette dangling arrogantly from his lips, stepped in front of John Lewis.

"Niggers belong on the other side," he growled. He jerked his thumb toward the colored entrance.

Lewis cleared his throat. "Negroes and whites have the right to equal access on grounds of the Supreme Court decision in the Boynton case," he said.

The young white tough took the cigarette from his mouth, looked at the end of it for a moment, then flipped it away. He smiled coldly.

"That's a crock of shit," he said, and he shoved Lewis back. When Lewis started forward again, the tough threw a punch that caught Lewis in the mouth. Lewis went down, and several other white youths rushed forward.

Albert Bigelow, one of the white Freedom Riders, was an imposing figure. He was a big man, a retired Navy captain who had seen enough death and carnage during the war to convert him into a confirmed pacifist. He was, in fact, a pacifist of such conviction that he had once sailed his private yacht, *The Golden Rule*, into an atomic bomb test site in the Pacific.

When Lewis went down, Bigelow rushed to put his body between the white youths and the fallen Freedom Rider. "Leave him alone!" he ordered.

"What's this, another nigger lover?" one of the youths sniggered.

"Naw, he's a white nigger, that's all," another jeered.

Someone threw a punch at Bigelow, and when they saw he wasn't going to return the blow, it emboldened the others to join in. Four of them rained blows to Bigelow's head and body. He stayed on his feet as long as he could, but finally he dropped to one knee.

Several Rock Hill policemen showed up then, and the police chief rushed into the fracas to rescue Lewis and Bigelow. With angry shouts and curses, he shoved the white boys away, then helped the two victims, both bruised and bleeding but conscious, back to their feet.

"You think you're tough, do you?" the police chief shouted at the white youths. "Beatin' up on a couple of men who won't fight back? Why don't you take *me* on?"

The white boys backed away sullenly.

"What's the matter? No stomach for it?" the chief challenged.

"We was just tryin' to uphold the law," one of the white

boys said. "Niggers ain't got no business in here. The law says they belong next door."

"You let me worry about upholdin' the law," the police chief said. "Which I now plan to enforce by throwin' the whole lot of you in jail for assault and battery." He looked over at the two bruised Freedom Riders. "Just as soon as these folks prefer charges."

Lewis was holding a handkerchief to his nose. Bigelow's wife, who was also one of the Freedom Riders, was tending to a cut over her husband's eye.

"No," Lewis said, shaking his head. "We won't be preferring charges. We don't want any trouble."

"Trouble? It's no trouble for you; it's trouble for these guys," the police chief said.

Lewis shook his head again. "No."

"Goddammit!" The cop pointed at each of the other protesters in the terminal. "I'm goin' out on a limb for you people, do you realize that? The least you can do is back me up."

"We appreciate it, Chief, really we do," Bigelow said. "But we think it would be best if we just let it alone."

He sighed. "All right. I'll keep my men here until the bus leaves." He glared at the white boys and told them sternly, "If these folks want to go in there, they are goin' to, and you won't do a thing to stop them. Do you understand that?"

"It ain't right."

"It's none of your business whether it's right or not," the chief said. "You boys just stay the hell out of their way!"

No further physical confrontations marred the Freedom Riders' passage, and they continued on unmolested to Atlanta, Georgia. There a celebration dinner was given in their honor, and there, too, they learned that Dr. Martin Luther King had made a special trip to Atlanta just to pay homage to them.

Excitement ran high through the little group as they arrived for the dinner that evening. Though of course everyone knew of Dr. King, not everyone had met him. Deon was one of the few in the group who had not only met Martin Luther King but actually knew him quite well. They had met during the Montgomery bus boycott, the incident that had propelled King into the national spotlight.

King was escorted over to the group and introduced to each of the Freedom Riders. Seeing Deon, he smiled. "It's good to see you again, Deon. I might have known you would be in the thick of things." He looked over at Wyatt Walker, also present. "This young man," he said, indicating Deon, "was one of the most loyal, dedicated, and effective fighters of the entire bus boycott. He gave his all to the cause. Of course, that's no more than you would expect from the grandson of Loomis Booker."

"You are Loomis Booker's grandson?" someone asked.

"Yes, sir."

"What a great, great man he was. You have quite a name to live up to."

"Yes, I know."

"And," King went on, "I am happy to say that his brother, Artemus, has also been very helpful to our cause, to the tune of several thousand dollars of personal donations. I am told he is a basketball player of some note."

One of the others laughed. "You were told he's a basketball player 'of some note'?"

"Yes," King replied. "Why? I haven't been misinformed, have I?"

"No, Dr. King, you haven't been misinformed. But to say he's a basketball player of some note is like saying Willie Mays is a baseball player of some note. They're both far more outstanding than that."

"Well, I would say it all depends upon how much . . . *authority* you give to the word 'note.' In this case I would say it has great enough authority to encompass men of the caliber of both Mr. Mays and Mr. Booker."

The lesson in semantics was terminated when someone abruptly called, "Gentlemen, the ladies have dinner ready. And judging by the look and smell of the food they have prepared, I would say we have quite a treat in store for us."

At the conclusion of the meal, Dr. King spoke to those assembled, the Freedom Riders and the people who had turned out in support of them. Everyone waited expectantly, anticipating one of his vintage speeches. He didn't disappoint them.

"We are met here tonight to sup at the table of brotherhood," King began.

"Amen," someone said.

"We are in communion with the finest that our country has to offer, young and old, man and woman, Negro and white . . . all of God's children, drawn together for the common purpose of shining the bright light of truth into those dark areas of injustice."

"The light of truth, Lord, the light of truth," a woman said in counterpoint.

"We are in the midst of a mighty crusade," King said. "There are those who tried to stop us, but the crusade will go on."

"Yes, Lord, amen."

"We started the crusade in Montgomery, when one tired Negro lady refused to give up her seat to a white man. The crusade went on, Lord, on those terrible, dark, bleak winter mornings when we watched those empty buses rattle by. Our people shivered with the cold, ached with fatigue, and yearned for the sweet, lighted warmth of those buses, but they did not falter. The crusade went on."

"The crusade went on, Lord," the crowd responded, picking up on King's theme.

"The crusade went on, Lord, at those sandwich counters in Montgomery and Birmingham and Jackson and Atlanta and all over the South when our people endured the evil stares and hateful curses of an intolerant society. The crusade went on."

"The crusade went on, Lord."

"The crusade went on, Lord, in those prisons and jails where men and women, boys and girls, were incarcerated for seeking justice where no justice is to be found. The crusade went on."

"The crusade went on, Lord," the crowd chanted as more people picked up the mantra.

"The crusade went on, Lord," King said, becoming more intense with the crowd's feedback, "when men and women of character, conscience, and courage—the very ones we are honoring here tonight—climbed into those Greyhound and Trailways buses and put themselves in harm's way in order to right the wrongs of an intolerant nation. The crusade went on."

"The crusade went on, Lord."

"But now, Lord, for the crusade to go on these fine men and women and boys and girls must draw on every ounce of their strength and from their last reserve of courage to continue. After we have fed them and housed them and given them our love, brothers and sisters, they must gird themselves with the armor of the Lord to enable the crusade to go on. For tomorrow, and the day after that, they will pass through areas of the fiercest segregation in our nation. The crusade will go on when they face bigotry and intolerance, hatred and violence on a heretofore unprecedented scale.

"But these men and women will do this for us, brothers and sisters. The crusade will go on because these brave souls are facing persecution, prosecution, incarceration, and even death. They will do this because this crusade is bigger than the ignorance of bigotry, bigger than the evil of violence, bigger than the fear of death. This crusade is about the principle of racial freedom. It is a testament to the strength of their will and the righteousness of their cause. *The crusade will go on!*"

King's final words were met with tumultuous cheers and applause.

Getting up from their seats, the Freedom Riders mingled with the crowd, shaking hands and accepting everyone's best wishes. Catching Deon's eye, King signaled that he would like to speak to him alone.

Deon made his way through the crush to Dr. King's side. "I have nothing but the greatest admiration and respect for you and the others for what you are doing," King told him. "But I must warn you that there is terrible trouble brewing in Alabama. In fact, I'm not at all certain any of you will make it through Alabama alive."

"But we're riding on a public bus, Dr. King. And by now news of what we're doing has preceded us. Surely the glare of publicity will provide us a shield."

King shook his head. "If you were dealing with people of reason I would agree with you. But these aren't people of reason. These are bigots of the worst kind. These are men who would kill a Negro and then wear his scalp as a badge of honor."

"That may be so, sir, but fear cannot be allowed to stop us."

"I was certain you would feel that way, Deon," King said, pride in his voice. "And I'm sure the others share that determination. But I could not, in all good conscience, allow you to continue without making sure you understood what lies before you."

Deon smiled and took Dr. King's hand. "Thank you for your concern, sir. But as you yourself said, the crusade will go on."

The following day, when the passengers reboarded the bus after a brief stop at the Tallapoosa terminal, Deon saw the driver call Joseph Perkins over to speak to him. Perkins listened and nodded but said nothing, then climbed into the bus. After the bus had pulled out of the station, Deon got up from his seat and went back to sit down alongside Perkins.

"What was that all about?" he asked.

Perkins, who seemed distracted, looked at Deon. "What?" he asked.

"I saw the driver call you over as we were getting on the bus. What did he want?"

Perkins sighed. "He says he's been hearing from the drivers of the buses coming this way. There's a big mob waiting for us in Anniston."

Deon nodded. "I expected as much. Fact is, I thought it would come before now. We've been pretty lucky up to this point."

"You know this area, Deon. What will the mob do?"

"Anything they can get away with. Hopefully the publicity we've gotten will put some check on what they do."

"Are you afraid?" Perkins asked.

Deon smiled tightly. "Yeah," he admitted. "I don't mind being a hero, but I wouldn't care to be a martyr."

When the bus pulled into its parking slip at Anniston, an enormous crowd of men was waiting. They were holding clubs, bricks, iron pipes, and knives.

"Hey, you! Freedom Niggers!" one of the mob shouted, and the others laughed at his corruption of their name. "Come on out, Freedom Niggers! Come on out and integrate our waitin' room!"

This was much more than a handful of arrogant white youths like those at Rock Hill. This was a huge mob of enraged adults, all armed with weapons. The Freedom Riders, and even the passengers who weren't affiliated with them but just happened to be on the bus by chance, were too terrified to get off. They sat stiffly in their seats, immobilized by the size and anger of the crowd.

"Come on out here, niggers! Come on out or, by God, we'll come in after you!"

A couple of the men in the mob tried to force open the door. At that point two of the passengers suddenly ran to the front of the bus, brandishing pistols.

"We're with the Alabama State Police!" one of them shouted through the door's window. "Back away! Back away from the door!"

The two undercover policemen braced themselves against the pull lever to keep the door shut. Outside, the mob began slamming the side of the bus with bricks and pipes. A few of them slashed at the tires with their knives.

"Go! Get out of here!" one of the state troopers bellowed at the driver.

The driver didn't protest. He started the engine, shifted into reverse, and backed away as the crowd rushed forward.

"That way!" one of the undercover cops shouted, pointing at several Anniston city policemen who had just arrived and were directing the bus safely out of the station.

"Mother of God!" one of the passengers whispered hoarsely as the bus pulled away. It was a white woman, and she was sitting in a seat just behind Deon. "Did you see the looks on their faces? That was the most terrifying thing I have ever seen!"

"Yes, ma'am, I saw the looks," Deon replied. "Only it wasn't the most terrifying thing *I've* ever seen. I've been seeing those looks all my life."

"I never knew," the woman said, eyes wide and brimming with tears. "God in heaven, I never knew what you people have to go through. I am so sorry. I am so terribly, terribly sorry."

"Holy shit!" someone shouted from the back of the bus. "They're coming after us! Faster! Go faster!"

Deon twisted around to look through the rear window and saw dozens of cars chasing after them.

"Oh, my God!" the woman passenger moaned. "What will we do? What will we do?"

Deon looked into her eyes. "Just pray the guy handling this bus is a good driver."

He was a good driver, and for a few moments Deon thought they were going to get away. Then he felt the bus listing to one side. At first, he hoped it was only his imagination, but the listing got worse. Even the woman behind him noticed.

"What is it?" she asked fearfully. "What's happening?"

"I don't know," Deon replied. "But I don't like it."

The bus began slowing down.

"What is it, man?" someone screamed. "Go faster!"

"I can't!" the driver yelled. "They got the rear tires. In another minute we're goin' to be ridin' on the rims."

The driver pulled the bus over and stopped, then shut the engine down. He got out of his seat and looked back at his passengers. "I'm gettin' out of here," he said. "And if you've got any sense, you'll do the same!"

He opened the doors, jumped out of the bus, then ran into a thicket of trees bordering a field.

For a moment there was absolute silence, so quiet that Deon could hear birds singing and the wind rustling the leaves in the trees. It was peaceful and calm, and he almost felt as if they should all get out and have a nice picnic lunch while they waited for help.

Then he heard the cars stopping behind them, one by one. Doors opened and slammed shut, and the men in the mob were shouting to each other.

"*Whoooeee!* Boys, we got us some niggers now!"

"Come outta there, niggers! This here's your bus stop!"

A brick was thrown against a window, shattering it and sending shards of glass over the passengers. A woman passenger screamed, and a man shouted fearfully.

"Get down!" another passenger called. "Everyone get down!"

Several people fell to the floor in the aisle while others got down between the seats. Another window was shattered, then another, and another still until every window in the bus was smashed out. After that the mob began battering in the sides of the bus with pipes.

"Hey!" one of the pack shouted from outside. "Hey, I got the luggage compartment open! Let's see what kind of clothes them niggers is bringin' with 'em!"

Moments later somebody laughed. "Well, I got me some purple pants here. My, my. Anybody found an orange shirt to go with 'em?"

Deon rose and looked toward the front of the bus. He saw that the mob had jammed a pipe behind the door handles to keep them shut, imprisoning the passengers. Now, why was that? They had been trying to get in; why the sudden change in tactics?

The answer quickly became clear when a bottle of gasoline with a flaming wick was thrown inside the bus through the smashed-out rear window.

"Jesus Christ, it's a firebomb!" someone screamed.

The warning wasn't necessary, for the flaming gas rapidly spread down the aisle and into some of the seats. The bus was filled with a thick, black, acrid smoke.

"My God! They mean to kill us all!" someone shouted. The passengers began choking and coughing. Besides the burning smoke, Deon felt the bile of fear rising in his throat. He knew beyond a shadow of a doubt that he was going to die right here, right now, on a lonely stretch of highway, at the hands of this mob.

One of the two state policemen, coughing and hacking, desperate for air, pulled his pistol again and worked his way to the front door. When he saw two men just outside the door, holding it shut, he aimed point-blank at one of them and pulled the hammer back. The man outside the door saw him, then turned and ran. When the other ran as well, the trooper shattered the window in the door with the butt of his revolver, removed the pipe, and pulled the door open.

Albert Bigelow, his head still bandaged from his encounter with the young thugs in Rock Hill, grabbed the passengers, urging them, shoving when necessary, to the open door.

The trooper who had opened the door now stood guard outside, his aimed pistol keeping the mob away as, one by one, coughing and hacking, the passengers spilled off the bus. Some immediately collapsed, but others, fearing the bus would explode in a great fireball, pulled the fallen ones to their feet and prodded them on.

The mob, held somewhat in check by the two troopers, nevertheless managed to crowd around, hurling taunts and occasionally swings at those escaping. One of the Freedom Riders was knocked down by a blow to the head, and Deon moved in quickly to help him to his feet.

Suddenly several gunshots sounded, and Deon felt his stomach rise to his throat. "The bastards have guns!"

"No, look!" the white woman who had been riding behind him shouted. "It's the highway patrol! We're saved!"

For a moment Deon wasn't sure whether they had been saved or not. Then he saw that the troopers were, indeed, herding the mob back to their cars. Finally, one by one, the cars were started, turned around onto the highway, then driven off. The occupants of the cars shouted taunts and curses into the wind.

"Get in the patrol cars!" the troopers ordered the passengers. "All of you who were on the bus, get in the cars!"

"Where are you taking us?" Deon demanded.

One of the troopers stared at Deon with ill-concealed hatred. "We ought to take every goddamn one of you to jail," he growled. He pointed to the flaming bus. "Look what you caused!"

"I'd like to remind you, Officer, that we were on that bus," Deon said angrily. "Doesn't it seem unlikely that we would set fire to it?"

"It doesn't make any difference who actually set fire to it. You bunch of out-of-state agitators are the cause. Now, get in the fuckin' car. We're takin' you all to the hospital in Anniston."

During the drive into Anniston, the troopers chatted with each other over their radios; thus the fact that the hospital was their destination was no secret. Not surprisingly, when they arrived, a large mob was waiting for them.

"Here, what is this?" the hospital administrator asked belligerently as the Freedom Riders and the other passengers, some of them bleeding from blows and shards of glass, many of them weak from smoke inhalation, came in. "Why are you bringing those people here?"

"There was no other place we could take them," one of the troopers said. "They're your responsibility now. There's another bunch of 'em bein' beaten up at the Trailways station back in Birmingham. We have to go."

When the police left, the hospital administrator looked at the pitiful group of travelers. He nodded at a thin, middle-aged white man and asked, "Are you one of them?"

The man had a badly cut lip. "I was on the bus, yes," he said.

"That's not what I asked. Are you one of the so-called Freedom Riders?"

"No. I'm just a passenger who got caught up in this."

"Who else is just a passenger?"

Nearly a dozen men and women raised their hands.

"Okay, we'll take you," the administrator said. "Come over here."

"What about these others?" the white woman who had been sitting behind Deon asked. "You aren't just going to ignore them, are you? Some of them are badly hurt. They need care!"

"Lady, I've got over a hundred patients in here. Do you want to see that mob out there burn this hospital like they burned the bus?"

"No. No, of course not."

"I'd like to help, but there's nothing I can do about it."

"You . . . you aren't going to turn them over to that mob, are you?" the woman asked, pleading their case.

The administrator stroked his chin for a moment, then sighed. "Who's in charge here?" he asked.

"I guess I am," Joseph Perkins said. He introduced himself.

"Perkins, take your people down to the laundry room," the administrator said. "You can wait there."

"Wait for what?"

"For the mob to leave. Then all of you will have to go, too."

"Is there a telephone we can use?" Deon asked.

"What do you want a phone for?"

"I want to call some friends in Montgomery."

"That's a long-distance call."

"I'll pay for it." Deon smiled. "Besides, look at it this way. If I call them, they'll send several cars up to get us. We'll be out of your hair quicker."

"Yeah, I guess that's best all around," the administrator

said. He snickered. "I guess you folks won't be getting on another bus anytime soon, huh, boy?"

"I can't speak for the others," Deon said, looking around. "But as for me . . . I'll be on another bus tomorrow afternoon."

CHAPTER SIX

JULY 1, 1961, FROM "TRAILBLAZERS" IN *EVENTS MAGAZINE*:

BRITISH TROOPS LAND IN KUWAIT

Citing the possibility of an Iraqi takeover, Great Britain began landing its troops in Kuwait this week. "Kuwait has been granted the status of an independent country," a British spokesman said. "To stand by and watch a larger county take it over would be a dereliction of our duty."

The Iraqi have let it be known that they do not recognize Kuwait as an independent nation because it was carved out of their country by an arbitrary settlement forced upon them by a foreign power. Iraq considers Kuwait its nineteenth province.

Critics of Britain's action accuse them of being more concerned over Kuwait's oil supply than Kuwait's independence.

RUDOLF NUREYEV MAKES FIRST
WESTERN APPEARANCE

The great Russian ballet star Rudolf Nureyev has wasted no time in performing for Western ballet fans. Nureyev, who has perhaps more power and grace than anyone else performing ballet today, bolted from his Soviet keepers only last month at Orly Airport in Paris.

Though he has asked for political asylum, the Soviet government announced that it wasn't politics that caused the defection of their ballet star but love. "He was attracted by a beautiful young red-haired Parisian girl," the Soviet statement said. "How can politics—or even art—compete with that?"

IN THE AIR ABOVE IDAHO

The droning noise of the twin-engined Beechcraft Super G-18 changed in intensity as the pilot throttled back in preparation for his descent. He eyed the young man in the copilot's seat. "Want to go tell them we're here?"

The copilot looked over his shoulder through the bulkhead opening into the passenger compartment. The Super G-18 was large enough to carry ten passengers, but this particular craft had been configured in an executive design—two fully reclining seats, a leather couch, a galley, and a lavatory—and was engaged by only two passengers, a man and a woman. The man, Eric Twainbough, was sitting upright, his bearlike body folded artfully into the commodious seat. His white hair and beard gleamed in the sun streaming in through the window by his right shoulder; his glasses had slipped down on his nose as he concentrated on the book he was reading. Across the aisle was his wife, Tanner. Her seat was tilted back, and she was sleeping, her mouth open slightly. Though her once-blond hair was now quite gray, the years had been kind, granting her a body that was still quite slender and features that belied her advancing years.

The copilot got up and, stooping to pass through the doorway, walked back into the passenger section. He was wearing dark-blue trousers and a white short-sleeved shirt with dark-blue epaulets. His left sleeve sported a shoulder patch that read: TANNENHOWER EXECUTIVE AIR. This airplane was one of a fleet of such planes, all belonging to the Tannenhower Brewing Company. Tanner Twainbough, granddaughter of Adolphus Tannenhower, one of the founders of the company, was the majority stockholder, though she was no longer active in the day-to-day operation of the company. Her son, Hamilton, was now in charge as the chief executive officer.

Eric Twainbough, on the other hand, had never had anything to do with the operation of the brewery. He was a Nobel-laureate writer who, over the past thirty years, had consistently landed on the best-seller lists with his efforts. Several of his books had also been made into movies, so he enjoyed a substantial income independent of his wife's enormous inheritance.

The copilot stood over his seat. "Excuse me, Mr. Twainbough . . ."

Eric looked up from his book.

"I thought you might like to know that we're coming into Sun Valley, sir. We'll be landing in about five minutes."

"Thanks," Eric said, closing his book and putting it aside.

"Hey, I read that, too," the copilot said, pointing to the book, which was Harold Robbins's *The Carpetbaggers*. He had, in fact, greatly enjoyed it. On the other hand, he had never read any of Twainbough's books, having always considered him to be a "highbrow" writer like Hemingway or Faulkner.

"Did you? Did you like it?"

"Yeah, especially the juicy parts," the copilot said with a broad smile. He leaned over to awaken Tanner.

"That's all right. I'll wake her," Eric said.

"Very good, sir," the copilot replied and returned to the cockpit.

Eric glanced out at the rugged terrain of northern Idaho. Then he reached across the aisle to gently shake his wife's arm.

"Tanner," he called softly. "Tanner, wake up. We're about to land."

She opened her eyes and looked around momentarily,

getting her bearings, then returned her seat to the upright position. "We're here already?"

"Yes."

She took a small mirror from her purse and looked at herself. "Oh, Eric," she groaned. "Why did you let me fall asleep like that?" She brushed at her clothes and ran her hand through her hair. "I look a mess."

"You look fine. Anyway, Mary and Hem won't be meeting us at the airport. You'll have plenty of time to freshen up on the drive to Ketchum."

"Since we have to find a motel for tonight anyway, could we do that first and stop in the room for a few minutes?"

"If you want to."

"I do. Thanks." Tanner glanced out the window, then looked back at her husband. "I wonder what he'll be like now," she mused.

"What do you mean?"

"I've heard all sorts of stories. I mean, what if he has really gotten strange?"

Eric laughed. "How would we ever know? Ernest Hemingway has always been strange."

"You know what I mean. With his, uh, problems. I just don't want it to be uncomfortable, that's all. For Hem or for us."

"Don't worry about it. It'll be all right. Besides, Mary said she thought it would be good for him to see us. You know he's been working on a book about the early days in Paris. She thought he might enjoy talking to a couple of us who were there with him then."

Tanner reached across the aisle to take Eric's hand. "Those *were* good days," she said, smiling.

Eric snorted. "If you call living in a cold-water garret with only one bucket of coal a day to keep you warm in the winter good, then I guess they were."

"Well, I seem to recall that the cold didn't bother us all that much," Tanner said slyly. "We had ways of keeping warm . . . if you remember."

"Don't talk sexy, wench, or I'll throw you down in the aisle and take you as we land," Eric deadpanned.

Tanner laughed. "Oh, my, and wouldn't the pilots enjoy that? A couple of old geezers like us getting it on like dogs in heat."

"Speak for yourself," Eric said. "You're an old hag of nearly sixty, but I'm just a lad of seventy-two and as randy as I was the day we met."

"Good Lord! If I had known reading *The Carpetbaggers* was going to affect you like that, I would've—"

"Taken it away from me?"

She laughed again. "My word, no! I would've suggested you read it a long time ago. How is it, by the way?"

Eric picked up the book. "The copilot likes it. My guess is, Mr. Harold Robbins is going to sell a lot of books."

"Yes, but how *is* it?"

"He's going to sell a lot of books."

At that moment the airplane touched down on the macadam runway, its wheels making a chirping noise. Eric put the book back down and looked out the window. "Lafayette, we are here," he murmured.

KETCHUM, IDAHO

"There's the road," Tanner pointed out, just after the Oldsmobile convertible they had rented at the Sun Valley airport crossed a little bridge.

"Are you sure? That looks more like a driveway than a road."

"Well, technically I suppose it is a driveway. Hemingway's house is the only one up there."

Eric turned onto the narrow gravel road, driving alongside a swiftly moving stream until the road ended at the house, a big two-story building made from unpainted lumber. Its rustic aspect was further enhanced by the fact that it had no neatly trimmed lawn, just wild sage grass growing in profusion on both sides of the stream. Towering spruce trees stood like sentinels next to the house.

When they pulled to a stop, Mary came out to meet them, smiling broadly.

"It's so good to see you again!" she gushed. "I'm so happy you could make this stopover on the way to your ranch. Come. Papa will be so glad to see you."

"How is he doing?" Eric asked, putting his arm around Mary as they walked up to the house.

"Oh, somewhat better, I think. He has his good days and his bad. Come on in. You must be tired from the trip."

"Oh, Mary, it is so lovely here," Tanner said, looking around admiringly.

"Yes, I've always liked it—though I must say I did like our place in Cuba better. But things are in such chaos down there. And now with this Bay of Pigs mess—" She shook her head. "I'm afraid we'll never get back."

"Where's Hem?" Eric asked as they entered the house.

"He's in the den. It's down that hall. Go on in. He's waiting for you."

Leaving Mary to show Tanner around the house, Eric made his way to the den. He didn't see Hemingway at first; then a movement in the corner of the room caught his eye, and he saw Hemingway standing in the shadows behind a large leather chair, almost as if he were hiding. This was the first time Eric had seen him in quite a while, and he was shocked at the change in his appearance.

Hemingway had always been a big man, with longshoreman's shoulders and arms. Now the shoulders were sagging, the arms loose and flabby. But beyond the loss of bulk and muscle tone, the expression in Hemingway's eyes was also shocking. More than his size and his leonine head, what had always been most vivid about him to Eric was his eyes: dynamic, intense, arresting. But the eyes now looking at him out of this gaunt face were vacant, lost, and frightened.

"Were you followed?" Hemingway asked suspiciously.

"I beg your pardon?"

"The feds. Did they follow you?"

"What feds?"

"Goddammit, don't be coy with me, Twainbough. You know what feds. The IRS boys. They're after me, you know."

Eric stared at him for a moment. It didn't escape his notice that Hemingway had called him Twainbough instead of one of his patented made-up monikers, such as Twainberry or Twainstein.

"Uh, no, I wasn't followed," Eric said.

"Are you sure?"

"I'm positive. I checked, several times," he added, thinking that was what Hemingway wanted to hear.

"Good." Hemingway came out from behind the chair, apparently willing to be seen now, and walked over to the window to peer around the edge of the shade. "It looks clear," he agreed. When he turned back, he was grinning broadly, and there was a hint of his old self. "Twainberry, how the hell have you been?" he asked effusively. "Damn, it's good to see you!"

"I'm doing well. How about you?" Eric replied, relieved at the sudden change.

"I'm doing a little better." He gestured to Eric. "Come on into the kitchen. I've got some wine breathing."

Eric followed him into the kitchen, where a bottle of beaujolais sat uncorked on the counter. This was more like the old Ernest, and Eric felt himself relaxing.

Hemingway poured a glass for Eric, then, very pointedly, turned the other glass upside down.

"I don't know what Mary is trying to do," he growled. "She knows I can't drink."

"Oh, I'm sure one glass of wine wouldn't hurt," Eric said easily. "In fact, it would probably be good for you."

Hemingway glared at Eric. "Are you in cahoots with them?" he snapped.

"With whom?" Eric replied, puzzled.

"Never mind." The frown left Hemingway's face nearly as quickly as it had come, replaced with gruff bonhomie. "So, you were at Kennedy's great coronation, were you?"

"Yes. Unlike Frost, I had no role in the inauguration. But I was there. And you were supposed to be. You were missed, my friend."

"I caught it on television. He gave a good speech." Hemingway cleared his throat, then gave a passable imitation of Kennedy's broad Boston accent. " 'Let the word go forth from this time and place, to our friends and foes alike, that the torch has been passed to a new generation of Americans. We will explore the stars, conquer the deserts, eradicate disease, tap the ocean depths, and engage in the arts. So, ask not what your country can do for you. Ask what you can do for your country.' Or something like that," he concluded.

Eric laughed. "Damn, no need to watch a newsreel. You've got it down pat."

"What do you think of him?"

"I don't know. The jury isn't in yet. He has style, I'll give him that. But he sure screwed up on Cuba by withholding air support."

Hemingway shook his head. "He did exactly the right thing," he countered. "If he had committed air, we would have gotten that much deeper into it, lost that many more men, and accomplished nothing."

"You don't think a little air power could have made the difference?"

"Eric, do you know how big Cuba is? More than eight hundred miles long. During World War II, we lost thousands of men trying to take islands that were no more than one one-hundredth the size of Cuba. What makes people think a little air power would have made a difference?"

"I don't know," Eric admitted. "I guess it's assumed that if we had shown a bit more resolve, the Cuban people would have joined in the uprising."

Hemingway grunted. "It would have been just the opposite. A *yanqui* invasion is all it would take to put the average Cuban behind Castro."

"I guess you're right. After all, you know the Cubans a damn sight better than I."

"What the hell is *that* supposed to mean?" Hemingway barked.

Hemingway's mood shifts were so abrupt that Eric felt as if he were riding a roller coaster: everything going along smoothly one second and the bottom dropping out the next. "It's not supposed to mean anything," he said soothingly. "Just that you used to live there, that's all."

"I might have lived there, but I never swallowed Castro's line. If I had, do you think I would have left everything there? I've got papers, manuscripts, mementos—hell, half a lifetime back there."

"Hem, I didn't mean anything by what I said."

"People talking when they don't know what they're talking about is why I'm in trouble with the feds now."

"I didn't know you were in trouble with the feds."

"They're tapping my phones, opening my mail, following me every time I go out." Hemingway got up from the table and checked through the doorway. Then he walked back and said secretively, "Even Mary is reporting to them. She doesn't think I know, but I do."

"Oh, come on, Hem. Surely you're mistaken," Eric protested. "Mary loves you deeply. She would never do anything to hurt you."

"She wouldn't, huh? Who do you think put me into that loony bin for shock treatments? Mary, that's who."

"I'm sure she was just trying to help."

"Help? There is no help," Hemingway groused. "I can't eat, I can't drink, I can't make love, I can't write. Don't you understand? Those are the only things that make life worth living." Suddenly, inexplicably, his face broke into a large smile. "But what the hell, I've had my share of drinking, loving, and writing. And when I release my big book, the one about the land, sea, and air, it's going to knock a lot of critics right on their collective asses. So whaddya say. You and Tanner are only going to be here a couple of hours. Let's not waste any time arguing."

Caught off guard by yet another of Hemingway's mood swings, Eric could only stare at his old rival and nod.

THE FLYING E RANCH, WYOMING

Eric and Tanner Twainbough rode their horses out of the stand of trees into the clearing at the top of Table Rock and looked down on their ranch. It was actually Tanner's first visit to the place, for Eric had purchased it in the period between their long-ago divorce and their not-too-long-ago remarriage.

It was early morning, and the blood-red sun tinted Devil's Tower several miles to the east with a crimson blush. Between Devil's Tower and the ranch compound lay sixty-five thousand acres of rangeland, fed by the serpentine Belle Fourche River. The compound consisted of a bunkhouse, cookhouse, smokehouse, barn, corral, granary, machine shed, garage, private airstrip, and the main house—a large two-story, white-frame gothic with screened-in porch, turrets, dormers, and a big bay window. A ribbon of smoke rose from its kitchen chimney, for the cook, currently preparing breakfast, still insisted on using a wood-burning stove. From Eric and Tanner's position they not only had an excellent view of the entire compound, they could also smell woodsmoke and bacon and the hot, sweet smell of heated syrup.

"Smells good," Eric said, sniffing appreciatively.

"It sure does." Tanner laughed. "I don't know what's gotten into me, but I've been eating like a horse ever since we came out here."

"It's the western air. It gives you a good appetite."

"I'll say it does. It's a wonder all the cowboys here don't weigh three hundred pounds apiece."

"They work hard enough to burn it off."

"So, this is where you started," Tanner mused, her gaze sweeping the ranch. "You were a cowboy on this place. A real cowboy."

"Yeah. I came here soon after my parents died. It's funny, but when I think of growing up, I don't think of my parents or my home, I think of this place . . . and I think of Mr. Ebersole."

"He's one of the people buried down in the little cemetery?"

Eric nodded. "Rodney Ebersole. He lived in America for sixty years, but on the day he died his English accent was as strong as it had been on the day he got off the boat."

"And the other two graves?"

"Jake Quinn and Marcus Parmeter."

"They were your friends?"

"My best friends. Until they got themselves killed in some damn-fool attempt to hold up a train."

"You're kidding! They tried to hold up a train? You mean like Jesse James?"

"No, not like Jesse James. Jesse James got the job done. We didn't."

"*We?*" Tanner gasped. "Eric, you mean . . . *you* were involved? *You* tried to hold up a train?"

Eric was silent for a long moment. "Yeah," he finally said. "I was involved."

"My God! I've known you for nearly forty years. I had no idea you had anything like that in your background. Why have you never told me about this?"

"It's not something I'm very proud of," Eric confessed.

"What happened? Will you tell me now?"

Eric leaned on the saddle horn and gazed out over the ranch, a distant look in his eyes as if he were seeing not only across the ranch but across the years. "I haven't even been honest with you about my name," he said softly. "My real name is McKenzie. Eric McKenzie."

"Oh, my God," Tanner breathed, staring at her husband. "Eric, if it's so bad that you had to change your name, I don't know if I want to hear this or not."

Eric looked at her. "That's all right with me. I'm not that anxious to tell it."

"Oh, no, I didn't mean that. No, please tell me, Eric. You must," Tanner insisted.

"All right. But it isn't a pretty story. Part of it you already know—but only part. . . ."

He was from Montana originally and was only twelve when both his mother and father contracted pneumonia and died during a blizzard, and he had been snowed in and incapable of going for help. Unable to bury them in the frozen ground, he had wrapped them in tarpaulins and carried the bodies out to the barn where they would remain frozen until, come the spring thaw, he could inter them. For the rest of the winter Eric spent all his time just trying to survive.

When the neighbors came to call that spring, they were shocked to find the boy living alone. He had cut his own firewood, hunted and cooked his own food, and even fought off an attack by a starving, frenzied pack of wolves. Well-meaning authorities immediately put him in an orphanage, but within a year he ran away, eventually making his way to Wyoming and Rodney Ebersole's ranch, where he convinced the foreman that he was old enough to work. There he met and befriended Jake and Marcus, who didn't care about his age—only about the fact that he pulled his own weight, minded his own business, and made his word good.

Mr. Ebersole had been a scholar with a vast library; taking a liking to the boy, he instilled in him an early love of books. When Eric read in a newspaper about the 1904 Louisiana Purchase Exposition—the St. Louis World's Fair—he, Jake, and Marcus, with Mr. Ebersole's blessing, started out to "see the wonders."

"But within days, like a bunch of greenhorns we had our money stolen," Eric explained to Tanner. "We couldn't face going back to the ranch with our tails tucked between our legs, so Jake and Marcus came up with the idea of robbing a train. They figured if we could catch one late at night when it stopped for water, we could get some money from the mail car, and then we'd disappear into the darkness. We didn't want much. Maybe a hundred dollars or so—just enough for train fare to St. Louis, a couple of nights in a rooming house there, a bit of spending money, and the fare back for the three of us." He gave her a crooked smile. "A hundred dollars went a long ways back then." He fell quiet for a moment, then continued, "What we didn't realize was that the train we chose happened to be carrying a large payroll shipment and extra Pinkerton guards. When we banged on the side of the mail car for them to open the door, the guards came out firing shotguns. They didn't say a word, just blasted away. Neither Jake nor Marcus had a chance."

Tanner studied her husband's somber face. "Thank God you got away," she said softly.

"I was back some distance from the car. I was the lookout. What a joke, huh? The guards missed me with the first volley, and I managed to get away before the second. I started running and didn't stop running until I reached St. Louis. Along the way I changed my name to Twainbough." He smiled. "I coined it on the spur of the moment one day when someone asked me what my name was—all I could think of was 'Twain,' like 'Mark Twain'; then, thinking that wouldn't sound convincing, I quickly added the 'bough' . . . and so it's been ever since."

Tanner reached out and put her hand on her husband's shoulder. "Now I understand."

"Understand what?"

"Why you had to buy this ranch. I thought you were just living out some boyhood dream. Now I know you were fulfilling an obligation. And it really is a lovely place, Eric. I could understand it if you wanted to come live here."

"You mean hide out like Hemingway is doing?" Eric chuckled. "No, thanks."

"Will he get better, do you think?"

"I don't know. He's gotten so damned paranoid. Though sometimes when we were talking he seemed perfectly lucid. For example, we were discussing President Kennedy's Cabinet choices, and he was making very cogent observations on each one of them. He also has a very good grasp of what's going on in the world. Then, just when you start wondering what all the fuss is about over his condition, he comes up with something from left field . . . such as accusing Mary of working with the feds—whoever the feds are in his mind—to get the goods on him."

"I know. Mary shared that with me." Tanner sighed. "It must be awful for her. Did you know she found him standing at the gun rack the day before we got there, holding the shotgun in one hand and a couple of shells in the other?"

Eric started. "No. I didn't know."

"She said he had the breech broken open, and he was just staring at it."

"What did she do?"

"She acted as if she didn't even notice the gun and started talking to him about going to Mexico. She told him that Gregorio could bring their boat over to the Yucatán peninsula, and they could get in some marvelous fishing. Finally, Dr. Moritz came over, and they managed to talk him through it."

"They're going to have to keep a really close eye on him, I'm afraid."

"Why is he like that, Eric?"

"He's depressed because he says he can't write. But the irony is, he's writing better now than he ever has. He let me read some of his book about Paris. *A Movable Feast*, he's calling it. It's good, Tanner. It's very good."

"Mary also told me he isn't really doing too poorly, physically," Tanner added. "True, he's eating very little, and he gets no exercise to speak of, so he doesn't look as robust as he once did. But despite that, he's in pretty good shape. Oh, Eric, when I remember what he was like in Paris, in the old days . . ." She sighed again. "It is so sad. What makes him like that?"

"I don't know. We may never know."

"Mr. and Mrs. Twainbough?" They turned at the sound of the young voice. It was fourteen-year-old Donnie Clark, whose father, George, was Eric's ranch manager.

"Hello, Donnie," Eric said, smiling at the young rider. "What can we do for you?"

"Cookie asked me to come up here and tell you that breakfast is ready."

"We'd better get down there, then. If he's anything like the cook we had when I worked here as a boy, he'll throw it out if we aren't there fast enough to please him."

"You mean the cook would actually throw the food out?" Tanner asked, appalled.

Eric grinned. "Well, to tell the truth, I don't know. He always threatened to—but I never knew any working cowboy who was ever late for a meal."

*   *   *

Eric had just piled his plate with a second stack of pancakes when the phone rang. George Clark got up and walked into the hall to answer it; a moment later he returned to the dining room.

"It's for you, Mr. Twainbough," he said.

"Thanks," Eric said, spearing a sausage link to take with him.

"He's looking really good," George said to Tanner when Eric had left the room.

"Yes, he is, isn't he? And coming out here is a great tonic for him. He really loves this ranch."

"Coming here recaptures his youth. There aren't a lot of people in the world who are lucky enough to be able to do that."

"Mrs. Twainbough, did you know his name is carved in the wall of the bunkhouse?" Donnie asked.

"Really?"

"Well, the name 'Eric' is right above the back door. That has to be him, don't you think?"

"I wouldn't be surprised," Tanner agreed.

Eric suddenly reappeared. He stopped just inside the dining room doorway and stood there, a look of disbelief on his face.

"Who was it, Eric?" Tanner asked, trying to read her husband's expression.

"It was Mary. Mary Hemingway."

"Oh, how sweet of her to call. What did she have to say?"

"Ernest is dead."

"What? My God! How? When?"

"This morning at about five-thirty. He took a shotgun into the entry foyer, then blew off the top of his head. She's going to say it was an accident . . . that it happened while he was cleaning his gun."

"He did it in the foyer?" Tanner asked, aghast.

"Yes."

"Oh, that *bastard*! What a cruel, cruel thing to do to Mary."

CHAPTER

SEVEN

AUGUST 19, 1961, FROM "TRAILMARKERS"
IN *EVENTS MAGAZINE*:

COMMUNISTS BUILD WALL IN BERLIN

Fourteen years ago, in a speech given to students and guests at Westminster College in Missouri, Winston Churchill applied the phrase "Iron Curtain" to Communist apportionment and domination. It had been only metaphorical. But now the Soviets and the East Germans have made the Iron Curtain a reality by erecting a wall dividing East Berlin from West Berlin.

The wall was built with amazing speed, using prefabricated concrete blocks. Reinforcing the physical barricade are East German border guards, armed with machine guns and orders to shoot to kill.

The wall's purpose is to prevent East Berliners from "voting with their feet" by leaving the Eastern sector to seek refuge in the West. The mass exodus, some 2,000 per day, was proving highly embarrassing for the Communists, who continually preach that their political system is far better than democracy.

RUSSIAN COSMONAUT IN SPACE
OVER 25 HOURS

The Soviet Union continues to make impressive gains in space flight. Cosmonaut Gherman S. Titov, the second Soviet in space, orbited the earth some 17 times before making a safe landing. He returned to earth close to where Yuri Gagarin, the first man in space, landed on April 12.

The U.S. has also sent two men into space but has not yet achieved manned, orbital flight.

MIXED TEAMS OF NEGROES AND WHITES
WILL GO SOUTH IN '62 TO HELP
REGISTER NEGROES TO VOTE

Stating that Negroes will never realize the American dream unless they are allowed to participate in it, the Congress of Racial Equality (CORE) announced that biracial teams of Negro-rights activists will be going to Alabama, Georgia, and Mississippi next summer to register Negroes to vote.

"1962 is an election year," a spokesman for the group said. "These deep southern states are prime targets for our efforts because they have the greatest disparity between Negroes, who are left out of mainstream society, and whites, who enjoy all that freedom has to offer. Not until the Negro has the ballot will that condition change."

However, a spokesman for the White Citizens Council warned, "Outside agitators would only succeed in making the summer of '62 a seething cauldron of hate. If that turns into violence," the spokesman added, "the niggers [sic] will have only themselves to blame."

OCTOBER 1961, ST. LOUIS

The Braniff Airlines Convair from Nashville pulled into Gate 7. Inside the terminal, clustered around the gate, was a joint welcoming committee composed of people from the Southern Christian Leadership Council and Jefferson University. Besides the official welcoming committee, an unofficial one composed of newspaper, radio, and TV reporters was on hand, anxious to get a few words from the newsworthy passenger on board the Convair, Dr. Martin Luther King.

After deplaning and giving the reporters a few minutes of his valuable time, Dr. King was whisked away to his destination, Jefferson University, where he was to give an eagerly awaited speech.

He walked onto the auditorium stage and was greeted by a thunderous ovation. Standing at the podium, Dr. King had to wait for several minutes before the applause finally subsided and he could begin his speech.

And what a speech it was. Alicia Canfield, in her last year at Jefferson University Law School, sat in a third-row seat listening raptly. King's voice filled the auditorium with its resonance, the melodic cadence characteristic of the southern Negro preacher carried to the highest state-of-the-art form. From King's lips the words took wing, and every heart in the auditorium responded to his clarion call.

". . . and I say to our white brothers and our white sisters in Mississippi that though you may be filled to the brim with hate for us, we are just as full of love for you.

"If you curse us, we will love you.

"If you lash out with your fists, we will love you.

"If you hurl slings and arrows at us, we will love you.

"Do to us what you will, we will overwhelm your oppression by our willingness to suffer and our capacity to love."

At the conclusion of the speech, Alicia made her way to the student center, where a reception was to be held. She showed her pass to the policeman on duty in front of the building, then entered the lobby and started down the hall for the meeting room. The hall was crowded, but she had expected that. She wasn't going to be put off by a crowd. She was going to see Dr. King if she had to get down on her hands and knees and crawl under everyone's legs.

It took Alicia several minutes of skillful maneuvering, but finally she found herself in the meeting room. Standing on tiptoe, she saw King on the other side of the room. Someone was talking to him, and he was looking intently at that person with his deep, dark eyes that carried so much of his power.

"Hey, girl!" someone said angrily, as Alicia pushed closer to King. "What do you think you're doin'? Ain't no white girl got any business in here."

The speaker was a young Negro woman, and her eyes reflected years of anger and resentment.

"I . . . I'm sorry," Alicia stammered. "I just wanted to get closer to Dr. King."

"You ain't got no right to be in here. Why don't you go to the country club or the white man's swimmin' pool or somethin'?"

"I'm sorry," Alicia said. Hurt and embarrassed, she turned to leave.

"Please," a voice called. "Let the girl through."

Alicia felt her heart stop for a moment; the voice was Dr. King's.

"Deon, bring that girl to me, would you?" King asked.

Deon Booker, who was traveling with King, pushed his way through the crowd, then reached out and took Alicia's hand in his own. He pulled her back through the crowd until she was standing in front of King.

Alicia felt a fluttering in her stomach and nervous perspiration under her breasts. King reached out to shake her hand.

"Bring the other young lady to me as well," he instructed.

A moment later the young black woman who had spoken so harshly to Alicia was standing with them. She looked sheepishly at the floor.

"What is your name, my dear?" King asked Alicia.

"Alicia Canfield."

"And yours?" he asked the black girl.

"Violet Simmons."

He took Violet's hand and Alicia's hand and put them together, holding them in place with his own hand.

"Violet, behold your sister, Alicia," he said. "Alicia, behold your sister, Violet. You are sisters now, in the sight of

God, and what God has joined together, let no work of man put asunder."

Alicia looked at Violet. She smiled, and both women embraced. The others in the room cheered, and Alicia had never felt a warmer, more loving feeling in her life than she did at that very moment. It was a feeling she didn't want to end.

"You're going to do *what*?" Faith asked her daughter that night when Alicia laid out her plans for the immediate future.

"As soon as I graduate next May, I'm going south to help register Negroes to vote," Alicia repeated.

"You are going to do no such thing! I've never heard of anything so ridiculous," Faith insisted.

"Mother, I'm over twenty-one," Alicia reminded her. "And come spring I will have graduated law school. I would think I have the right to decide what I want to do with my own life."

"We'll see what your father has to say about this."

Alicia folded her arms. "It won't make any difference what he says," she said stubbornly. "I'm going to do what I'm going to do."

"We'll discuss this later tonight," Faith said. "After your grandmother leaves." She effectively ended the conversation by going into the kitchen to check on the cook's preparations for dinner.

Watching her mother's retreating back, Alicia silently fumed. Boldly, she decided she would broach the subject during the meal that evening—while her grandmother was there to take her side . . . and she was sure that an old suffragette like Connie Canfield *would* be on her side.

"Dad, I have something I want to talk to you about," Alicia said soon after they had all sat down around the dining table.

Knowing what her daughter had in mind, Faith tried to head it off. "Let's not talk about it now, dear. Wait until after dinner."

"It needs to be talked about now, Mother," Alicia insisted.

"There is no need to bring it up in front of your grandmother. She certainly doesn't have to be involved in any of our family disputes."

"Why not? She's family, isn't she?" Alicia asked.

Connie laughed. "She has you there, dear. I am family."

Faith looked pointedly at her daughter. "It's just that this would best be served, I believe, by postponing the discussion."

"Postpone it? For how long? Until it's too late to do it?"

"Too late to do what?" John asked, picking up his wine glass.

Alicia smiled. "See? Dad wants to know."

Faith put down her fork. "All right. It's already too late to have a peaceful meal. I suppose we may as well discuss it now."

Suddenly John looked at his daughter sharply. "Alicia, you aren't . . . uh . . . you aren't about to get married, are you?"

Alicia laughed loudly. "Heavens no. And I'm not pregnant, either."

"Alicia!" Faith gasped.

"Well, look at him, Mother. He turned absolutely white when he thought I might be pregnant."

Connie laughed. "She's right, dear," she told her son. "It did give you a start."

"Well, it was a passing thought," he admitted.

"Now that the worst is out of the way, you can handle anything else, right, Dad?"

John dabbed at his lips with his napkin, then smiled. "Pretty good move. No wonder you went into law. But you aren't going to trap me with that tactic. Now, what is this thing that is so important it can't wait until after dinner?"

"After I graduate, I want to get involved in the Negro rights movement," Alicia said.

"Involved?"

"I want to help the Negroes."

John looked at Faith. "I don't see anything wrong with that. In fact, it's commendable."

"Wait until you hear how she wants to be involved," Faith warned.

John looked back at Alicia. "What do you mean? You want to represent them in court or something?"

"No, Dad, I want to get much more involved than that. As you know, there's going to be a concerted effort to register Negroes to vote in next year's elections—and I want to help."

"I see." John leaned back in his chair and crossed his arms. "And just what role will you be playing?"

"I'll be going down to Mississippi with Deon Booker."

"Deon Booker? Loomis's grandson?" Connie asked.

"Yes, Grandmother." She turned to her father. "You knew Loomis Booker, right? He was a good friend of Grandfather's."

"Yes, I knew him well."

"Well, then you know that with Deon, I'll be safe."

"Safe? Correct me if I'm wrong, missy, but wasn't Deon one of those who got beaten up during a freedom ride?"

"And hasn't he been thrown in jail a half-dozen times?" Faith added.

"So has Martin Luther King been beaten and jailed," Alicia countered. "But they were thrown into jail for exercising their rights, not for any criminal violation."

"Jail is jail, no matter what the reason," John said. "What if you get thrown into jail for exercising *your* rights? For the rest of your life you'll be stigmatized. That's something you can never overcome, no matter how unjust your incarceration."

"Oh, that's not necessarily true, John. After all, *I* was thrown into jail," Connie said.

"You were put in jail, Grandmother?"

Connie smiled at her granddaughter's astonishment. "I surely was."

John cleared his throat. "That wasn't the same thing, Mother, and you know it."

Connie laughed. "Oh, but it *was* the same thing. The exact same thing, as a matter of fact. You see, dear," she explained to Alicia, "like Dr. King I was thrown into jail for advocating the right to vote. Only in my case it was the right for women to vote."

Alicia's eyes flashed. She had been right. Her grandmother was her ace in the hole. "There, Dad, do you see? I have to do this. It's in my genes."

"In your genes," John snorted.

"Alicia, dear, there is a tremendous difference between

what Grandmother Canfield did and what you are propos-
ing," Faith said.

"What's the difference?" Alicia replied.

"Well, if you can't see it, I'm not sure I can tell you."

"Mother, look at this family," Alicia said patiently.
"Grandmother demonstrated for the right of women to vote.
Great-uncle Billy ran off to Europe to join the Lafayette Es-
cadrille even before the U.S. got into World War One. Dad
joined President Roosevelt's crusade to help America recover
from the Great Depression, and my own brother is down in
South America with the Peace Corps, helping impoverished
people improve their lives. We are a family of activists for
what is right. So my question is, why is it all right for everyone else in the family to make some sort of grand gesture for
what they believe in, but it isn't all right if *I* do it?"

"Is that what this is to you?" John asked. "A grand gesture?"

"I don't know; maybe it is," Alicia admitted. "And maybe
I'm more than just a little drawn to the cause by the excitement of it. But I also have a deep, abiding sense that it is the
moral thing to do."

John looked at Faith. "We can't really stop her, you
know."

"I know."

He looked back at Alicia. "If you feel you really must do
this thing . . ."

"Yes, Dad, I do feel it," Alicia insisted.

John sighed. "All right. Go—and go with our blessings.
But please, be careful."

"Oh, Alicia, if anything were to happen to you—" Faith
couldn't complete the sentence.

"Don't worry, Mother. Nothing's going to happen to me.
I told you, I'll be with Deon. He knows how to handle these
things."

ZAMORA, ECUADOR

Morgan Canfield lay on his cot in the tiny one-room hut
and stared through the open window at the sky. He shivered
and pulled the blanket over him more tightly to keep out the

cold, wishing he had the strength to get out of bed and light a fire.

Ecuador. It was supposed to be hot in Ecuador. It was located right on the equator—hence the name—and it was hot at the equator, right? So why was he freezing to death?

He was freezing, he answered himself, because he was ten thousand feet up in the Andes mountains. And at this elevation it was damn cold.

The sky grew somewhat grayer outside his window. It would be light soon, and by midmorning it would start warming up a little. But only a little.

Morgan felt an all too familiar urge building up again, so he forced himself to get out of bed and cross the room to squat over the foul-smelling bucket. He had been suffering from diarrhea for four days now. Four days without letup. At what point, he wondered, did diarrhea turn into dysentery? He didn't think people could die from diarrhea, though he knew they did from dysentery.

Well, he would just continue to call it diarrhea.

The green apple quick-step.

Montezuma's revenge.

Make jokes about it, he told himself, and it would go away.

He strained against the cramps, added only a tiny bit more to the offal in the bucket, then returned to his bed.

Outside it grew grayer, and he could smell the early-morning breakfast fires and hear the goats milling about restlessly, their hard little hooves rattling on the rocky ground. The goatherds would be coming soon to take them down the side of the mountain to find a place to graze.

Morgan was in a tiny village that had no name of its own but was close enough to Zamora that that was how the Department of Census located it. He had come here armed with ideas from the Peace Corps training center and imbued with enthusiasm for helping the poor unfortunates of the world.

He was the one who had learned.

Nothing was as he thought it would be. In the first place, he was totally unprepared for how primitive the living conditions were. He had had some sort of romantic idea about huts with thatched roofs, but he hadn't really given much thought to such basic necessities as food and water. He was here to help others, yet it took so much effort just to sustain himself that he had very little time to be the great American benefactor he had envisioned. It didn't make any difference how much money he had; there was no convenient grocery store to supply his needs. For the first month he struggled from dawn to dusk just to survive.

Finally, after it became apparent that he *would* survive, he looked around to see how he might be of help to the villagers. None of the officially recommended help projects were applicable here. The villagers already had chicken pens and a good, effective catchment system for water. They were better able to grow gardens than he was, and they knew where and when vegetation could be found for their goats. And teaching them English would be virtually worthless.

What he did discover, almost by accident, was that the villagers had very little idea about the outside world and a consuming curiosity about it. None of them had ever seen a television set, and few had heard a radio. They knew airplanes only as mysterious white trails high in the sky, and most were truly amazed to discover there were actually men up there.

Morgan became not so much a teacher of science or history as he was a window on the world beyond. Every evening the villagers would gather around his hut to listen to his stories. He told them of the continents of North and South America, of Europe, Asia, and Africa, and of the great seas that surrounded them.

"Are the great seas bigger than the Zamora River?" he was asked.

"Yes, many times bigger."

They talked among themselves, trying to fathom how large the ocean must be by stretching the river in their imaginations. One elderly villager asked if the sea was greater than the distance from the mountaintop to the great lowlands. He was one of the few who had once undertaken that journey, walking for five days to span the distance.

"It is bigger than the distance you could walk in one hundred days," Morgan told them, and they gasped and oohed and aahed at the greatness of such a body of water.

He told them about great cities and fields of grain and huge herds of cattle. He told them about highways and automobiles and airplanes and ships—and even rocket ships. He told them of wars and of democracy and communism. He spoke of art and music and literature, and, because he had a book of Shakespeare's plays, he read to them from *Hamlet*, *MacBeth*, and *Romeo and Juliet*. Many of the villagers, men and women alike, cried over the sad ending of *Romeo and Juliet*.

He wasn't sure he was doing what Peace Corps volunteers were supposed to be doing, but he had no one to tell him he should be handling things differently. And if the primary purpose was to create goodwill, then he was doing that.

Morgan decided he had drifted off to sleep because when he awoke again, the grayness of predawn was gone and sunlight was streaming in the window opening. He heard a scraping sound, and he turned on his cot to see one of the village women putting his night-soil bucket back in the corner, while another was sweeping the dirt floor with a straw broom.

"You don't have to do that," Morgan said, speaking in the mixture of Spanish and Quechuan by which they communicated. He sat up.

"No," one of the women said. "You stay."

"I'll be all right," Morgan assured them. "As soon as I get over this."

"You will not get well without medicine."

"Yes, well, there's nothing I can do about that. I haven't seen a Walgreen's drugstore lately."

The woman with the broom put it down, then walked over to the table to pick up a cup. She brought the cup to him.

"What is that?" Morgan asked.

"You drink."

"Thank you, no. I don't believe I could hold anything down."

"Medicine. You drink," the woman ordered. She held the cup under his nose. It had a strong turpentiney smell. "It will make you better."

Morgan looked at the cup for a moment. "Oh, what the hell," he mumbled. "If it kills me I won't be much worse off than I am now." He closed his eyes and drank it down. It tasted godawful. "Now I know how Socrates felt," he said, scrunching up his face.

"Qúe?"

He smiled and lay back down. "Never mind. I guess we'll just have to wait and see what happens."

"Letter come for you," the other woman said.

Morgan sat up again. "I have a letter?" The woman handed it to him. "Thank you," he told her.

It was from Sheri Warren.

Dear Morgan,

I am so excited that I can scarcely write. I wish you had a telephone in that village so I could call you. Better yet, I wish there was an airport there so I could fly to you to tell you the news in person. But that isn't possible because from all I can determine, you are somewhere on the dark side of the moon.

Do you remember those fashion ideas I told you I had? You tried to talk me into showing them, but I was too frightened. But about six months ago I showed Mrs. Jackson my portfolio of designs, and she also encouraged me to show them. Well, I don't know if she's more persuasive than you or if she just had more time to work on me. At any rate, I finally gave in and sent them to E. J. Buckner and Company. They're a big women's sportswear manufacturer in New York, like Evan-Picone. I chose E. J. Buckner because I once did some modeling for them, and when I sent them the portfolio, I reminded Mr. Buckner of it.

Well, guess what? I got a letter back from him, offering to buy every one of the designs, for A LOT of money! Well, maybe it isn't a lot of money to you, but for me and for the average person, believe me, it is. And he wants me to come to New York to work for him. So the next letter you get from me will be from New York, with my New York address.

It'll be sad leaving Destin. I have loved living here and working here, and I'm going to miss the ocean. I'm also going to miss Mrs. Jackson. Did you know that the first time she saw me, she was afraid I might be thinking about stealing something from the house? She confessed that at one point—but I already knew she had thought that. Anyway, we have gotten along beautifully, and Scooter just loves her. She is a WONDERFUL person. Your family is so lucky to have her, and I have been very lucky to know her.

I've got to run now. I have a million things to do to get ready. I hope you are well, and I hope no pretty señorita catches your eye. It's funny how much I miss you, even though we met for such a brief time. I'll be glad when you have fulfilled your obligation to the widows and orphans of polo players and come back to the good old U.S. of A.

Love,
Sheri

Morgan got up and retrieved the box that held all his letters, those from his mother and father and his sister, Alicia, plus at least a dozen others from Sheri. Sometimes when he felt himself growing melancholy, he would pull all the letters out and reread them.

As he stood there refolding Sheri's latest letter, he suddenly realized it had been a while since he had had an attack of diarrhea. Maybe that witch-doctor concoction was working after all. Grinning, he asked aloud, "Walgreen's, who needs you?"

OZARK, ALABAMA

When Bob Parker passed the Chisum Truck Stop and the Ozark Motel, he felt himself tensing. He was getting very close. In fact, it was only about three miles until he crossed the Fort Rucker highway. Once there, he would turn left into town, go past the square, then turn onto Broad Street. Marilou and the boys were now living in a garage apartment behind one of the old antebellum homes on the first block of Broad Street.

As he came into town, Bob felt conflicting emotions sweeping through him. For one thing, he felt an unusual degree of nostalgia at seeing Ozark again, since in some ways it was as much his hometown as was Sikeston, Missouri, where he had been born and where he graduated from high school. In a real sense he had grown up in Ozark. He had been an immature kid when he arrived at Fort Rucker, fresh out of basic training and ready for helicopter crew-chief school. It was here that he met and married the mother of his children. And it was here that he graduated from flight school and received his appointment to warrant officer.

Aside from the nostalgia, he was incredibly excited about seeing the boys again. Yet despite the excitement, he was apprehensive. This would be the first time he had seen Marilou or the children since she left him. A lot had happened since then. First the helicopter crash that had taken the lives of six men from Bob's company, then his brief tour in Vietnam. . . . He believed he had in many ways changed more in the last few months than he had in the previous six years.

Bob pulled onto Broad Street, found the right house, and, his heart thumping, drove back to the garage. He had no sooner braked to a stop than Marilou came out to meet him. She was wearing a one-piece orange jumpsuit, and she looked better now than she had at any time since they were first married.

"Shit, Marilou," Bob said under his breath, "why'd you have to look so damned good?"

"Hello, Bob," she said, smiling broadly at him. "You're looking good. Tan and trim. Vietnam must have agreed with you."

"I wouldn't go so far as to say that. On the other hand, something is definitely agreeing with you. You're looking fantastic."

"Well, thank you. I've been on a diet, and I've changed my hair. I had to do something. After all, when I start school this fall I'm going to be the old mother on campus."

"Yeah, you said in your letter you'd be going to school. Auburn?"

"War Eagles," Marilou replied. "Where else would I go?"

"Uh, are the boys here?"

"They're both inside, watching television."

"Didn't they know I was coming?" Bob was a little disappointed that they hadn't rushed out to meet him, and Marilou sensed it. She smiled.

"Are your feelings hurt?"

"What?"

"They didn't come running out here. I think your feelings are hurt."

"No, not really."

Marilou laughed. "Yes they are. Your feelings are hurt. Well, they shouldn't be. It's Saturday-morning cartoon time. You don't really think you can compete with Mighty Manfred the Wonder Dog, do you?"

Bob smiled wryly. "I guess not."

Marilou looked at her watch. "Listen, I have to run down to Dothan to take care of a few things. As long as you're here, you don't mind staying with the boys, do you?"

"No, no, of course not. I mean, that's why I'm here in the first place. To see them."

"I'll be back by three," Marilou tossed over her shoulder as she walked over to a little red Corvair hardtop convertible.

"Whoa, hold it!" Bob said, pointing to the car. "Where did you get that? What happened to the Lark?"

"Well, now, you don't really expect me to drive a Lark to college, do you? Daddy bought this for me. Isn't it cute?"

"Yeah," Bob said, envious. "It's nice."

"You and the boys have a good time." Marilou started the car, then drove away with a roar from the dual exhausts.

Turning, Bob climbed the side stairs up to the apartment and let himself in. He found Teddy and Timmy on the floor. Teddy was lying on his stomach, Timmy was sitting up, and both were eating dry sugar-coated cereal from a bowl that sat on the floor between them. Their eyes were glued to the flickering cartoon images on the TV.

"Hi, boys. Remember me?"

Timmy looked around. "Daddy!" he shouted.

"Daddy!" Teddy echoed.

Both boys ran to him, and he picked them up and embraced them, wishing with all his heart that things had not turned out as they had.

They had a full, busy day. At noon they went to Hambone's for burgers and fries. After that they went to the schoolyard, where Bob let them play on the swings and sliding board. Then they washed Bob's car, getting as much water on themselves as they did on the car. Then they went to Novak's Drugstore for ice cream. Before taking the boys home, Bob stopped by Walker's Grocery to renew old acquaintances and to buy franks and buns and a couple of steaks. He didn't know if Marilou had a grill, but if she did, he would cook hot dogs for the boys and a steak for the grown-ups.

Marilou's car was there when they returned.

"Well," she said when they went inside, "did you have a good time?"

The boys began telling her in great detail about their day.

"And now Daddy's going to fix hot dogs," Timmy added.

"Oh, my, that sounds good," Marilou said.

"I, uh, got a couple of steaks for us," Bob said, holding out the sack. "If you don't mind."

"No, I don't mind at all. I think that would be wonderful. There's a grill out back."

Bob went out behind the garage, found the grill, and, with practiced ease, had a pile of charcoal briquettes burning in no time. When he went back up to the apartment, Marilou was washing vegetables at the sink.

"I'll make us a salad," she offered.

"Sounds good," Bob said. He held up his grimy hands. "I need to wash."

"Oh, use the bathroom off my bedroom, will you?" Marilou asked. "The boys are taking a bath in the other one."

"Okay."

When Bob went into Marilou's bedroom, he stopped short. The bedroom furniture was the same set they had used all during their marriage, and a barrage of familiar sights, smells, and impressions came flooding back to him. For a moment he felt an overwhelming sadness for things lost; closing his eyes, he willed the thoughts away.

As Bob passed by the dresser, he noticed a pair of army aviator sunglasses. They were in a leather case, embossed with a pair of wings and gold lettering: CAPTAIN ROGER MORRIS, UNITED STATES ARMY.

What were these glasses doing here? Was Marilou sleeping with this Roger Morris, whoever he was?

Bob hated himself for doing it, but when he went into the bathroom, he opened the medicine cabinet and the vanity doors, peering among the bottles of makeup and toiletries until he saw what he was looking for: Marilou's diaphragm case.

He opened the case and ran his finger over the latex. There was a little sheen of spermicide jelly down in the cup that had somehow missed being washed out. It had been over five months since their divorce; it couldn't still be there from the last time they had had sex.

Feeling guilty for looking—and hurt for discovering what he hadn't wanted to discover—Bob closed the case and put it back in place.

After supper Bob helped get the boys ready for bed. They kept trying to find excuses to stay up longer, but they finally grew too tired to fight about it and reluctantly went to sleep.

The apartment was quiet as Bob and Marilou sat on the sofa in the living room, drinking gin and tonic. The sofa, like the bedroom furniture, had come from their quarters in Fort Campbell. Bob lifted one of the cushions to look beneath it, and Marilou chuckled.

"If you're looking for the wine Paul Gareth spilled that night after we did *Bus Stop*, you will no doubt see that the stain is still there," she said.

"Good. I'd be disappointed if it had changed any." Then, because that was an awkward statement bordering on the maudlin, he changed the subject quickly. "Is Dale County still dry?"

"Oh, honey, as long as the preachers and the bootleggers have their say, it's going to *stay* dry. You know that."

"What does your dad think about it?" Marilou's father was the county sheriff.

Marilou laughed. "You remember Daddy. It all depends on whose vote he's after. By the way, I got a letter from Janet Lumsden."

"Did you? How's she doing?"

"She's doing well. She's gone back to New Mexico." Marilou studied his face, then said gently, "That crash must have been awful for you, losing so many of your friends like that."

"It was. It's been over a year and lots of things have

happened in between—we were divorced, I was in Vietnam —and yet it still affects me every time I think about it."

"Janet said you were on that helicopter, but you got off just before it took off."

"I wasn't actually on board yet, but I was about to take the flight when you called me. Ray was there, so I asked him to take it so I could talk to you."

Marilou gasped. "My God! You mean my telephone call kept you from flying that helicopter?"

"Yes."

Marilou shivered. "I had no idea. That's really heavy, isn't it? What made it crash, anyway?"

"The fuel valve shut down, stopping the flow of fuel. That caused the engine to quit, and Ray didn't realize it until his RPM had already deteriorated too far. When the RPM got too low, it set up a harmonic vibration that literally shook the helicopter to pieces."

"Couldn't he hear it when the engine quit?"

"No. The transmission sits between the pilot and the engine. The noise you hear inside the aircraft is actually transmission and rotor noise. The only way he would have known he'd lost his engine was if he'd been monitoring his gauges more closely."

"You're a good pilot. Maybe you would have noticed the gauges," Marilou suggested.

"I don't know if I would've or not. I can tell you I certainly monitor them more closely now," Bob admitted. "Plus now they're putting on a low-RPM warning light and audio signal."

They fell quiet again. After a minute or two Marilou asked, "What's it like in Vietnam?"

"Hot, muggy, lots of mosquitoes. Actually, it's rather pretty, in a tropical-jungle sort of way."

"Do you think we'll ever get into a war over there?"

"We may send a few more advisers over, but I don't think we'll ever get into an actual shooting war. The VC are a nuisance, but I don't see them as a real threat to the Vietnamese government."

"I hope you're right. I met someone who thinks it's going to turn into a real war."

"Would that be Roger Morris?"

Marilou looked up sharply. "Who?"

"Roger Morris. I saw his sunglasses in the bedroom. You're sleeping with him, aren't you?"

Marilou blinked a few times, and tears began to form. "Bob, you have no right," she said angrily. "You have no right to question my life. We aren't married anymore."

"I'm just concerned about the children, that's all." But from the moment he made the statement, he wished he could call it back.

"That was a cheap shot," Marilou said quietly.

"You're right," Bob agreed. "It was a cheap shot, and I apologize." He reached out to take her hand in his, and she made no effort to resist. "Listen, I'm sorry. I really am sorry."

Marilou smiled at him through her tears. "All right. You're forgiven."

Bob looked at his watch. "Wow, I didn't realize it was this late. I don't know if I'm going to be able to find a room or not."

Marilou laughed. "Are you hinting that I should ask you to stay here?"

"I don't know. Maybe I am." He patted the sofa. "It wouldn't be the first time I've slept here."

"I'll go get a pillow and blanket," Marilou said, getting up.

"I'm not ready to go to bed yet."

Marilou smiled. "You sound like the kids. You don't have to go to bed yet. I'm just getting things ready, that's all."

"Oh."

"You want to watch TV?"

He shrugged. "No. Not particularly. I'd rather just talk for a while, if you don't mind."

"Well, there's a switch. It used to be you were either writing or watching TV. We never talked." Marilou walked back into her bedroom. "How is your writing coming, by the way?" she called. "Anything new?"

"I sold *Down and Dirty*," Bob called back. "To Tower Books."

"Tower? That isn't who you were with before, is it?"

"I was with Saber before. They're a California company. Tower is in New York."

"Well, that's quite a step up, isn't it?"

"I hope so. They gave me a thousand dollars. That's a lot more money than I ever got from Saber."

When Marilou returned with the blanket and pillow, she was also dressed differently. The orange jumpsuit was gone, replaced by a yellow silk gown that showed off her body very well, even to the two nipples standing out in bold relief.

"I hope you don't mind that I changed," she said.

"Are you kidding?"

Marilou sat down beside him, and when Bob put his arm around her, his hand fell easily and comfortably to her breast.

"Titty rump, titty rump, titty rump, rump, rump," he said softly. It was the last line of an old and very inside joke between them. He hadn't said it, or even thought it, since their good days together, and he surprised himself by saying it now.

Marilou looked up at him, and there were tears in her eyes. "Oh, Bob. If only things could have been different between us."

He kissed her. The kiss, like his arm around her, felt familiar and comfortable, and he felt an aching sweetness.

"I've missed some things," she said.

"So have I."

"Maybe we can make up for some of what we've missed," Marilou suggested. "That is, if you'd like to."

"I would like to, very much," Bob said, his voice husky with desire. He kissed her again. "Marilou, I want to go to bed with you. I want to make love to you the way we did when we were young and I was a private and we didn't have anything but each other."

Marilou stood up, tugging on his hand. "Let's go into the bedroom."

Bob followed her, and as soon as they stepped through the bedroom door, she turned around and kissed him again, this time more demandingly. Their mouths opened, and tongue pressed against tongue as they hungrily tasted each other.

"Bob, wait," Marilou said, breaking away from him. She went into the bathroom, and he knew that she was inserting the diaphragm. When was the last time she used it? he wondered. He closed his eyes tightly and banished the thought. She was right, it wasn't any of his business now. He couldn't very well expect her to live like a monk—or a nun, as the case might be.

When Marilou came back into the bedroom a few moments later, she turned off the light.

"Why did you do that?" Bob asked. "I want to see you."

"It'll be nicer. You'll see."

Marilou lit a candle on the bedside table. The flame flickered a bit at first, then straightened into a smooth point of light perched above the slender white taper. She turned to look at him. "Now," she said softly, "isn't this better?"

This was a new wrinkle. She had never bothered to light a candle when they had had sex before. Bob saw that it was burned down halfway. Was that a measurement of some sort?

"You didn't answer," Marilou said.

"How's this for an answer?" he asked.

He kissed her again, and the kiss grew deep and urgent. They separated, but only to take off their clothes. Because she had fewer clothes to remove, Marilou was nude before Bob, and she stood in front of him, waiting anxiously. The tip of her tongue flicked out to wet her lips, and her eyes looked at him hungrily. Her body glistened like gold in the candlelight, and the triangle of her pubic hair stood out boldly against her incredibly smooth skin.

"It will be good to wake with the smell of you in my bed again," Marilou whispered.

By now he was as naked as she, and she put one hand behind his neck and used the other to trace patterns of pleasure across his chest, then down to his most sensitive part.

"I'd like to shake hands with an old friend," she joked in a smoky voice as she grabbed him. "I haven't had the pleasure in quite a while." She lay back on her bed and pulled Bob down with her.

Afterward, they walked back into the living room, still nude, and Marilou sat on the sofa while Bob ate a piece of cheese he had found in the refrigerator. He looked back at her. There were a couple of damp spots on her thigh, evidence of their lovemaking. They glistened in the soft light, and Bob found it very exciting.

"You look cute standing there, eating your curds and whey," Marilou said.

"You want some?"

"No." She was silent for a moment, then she said, "Bob, I wish it hadn't happened."

"The divorce?"

"No. The divorce was inevitable. In fact, it should have happened years ago. What I wish is that we hadn't made love just now."

"You didn't enjoy it?"

"You know damn well I did. I enjoy having sex, and if I like my partner, I enjoy it even more."

Bob felt a hollowness in the pit of his stomach, and he looked at Marilou. "*If* you like your partner?" he said in a quiet, choked voice.

"Yes."

Bob had not had sex with anyone since he and Marilou were divorced, and he had not been unfaithful to her during their marriage. "Let me get this straight. Are you telling me that you have such frequent sex that you even have it with partners you don't like?"

"After the fact, they have sometimes proven to be disagreeable, yes," Marilou said easily.

"But you like me?"

"Yes. I like you."

"And Roger Morris? Do you like Roger Morris?"

"Yes, Bob, I like Roger Morris," Marilou said pointedly. It was clear where Bob was going.

"Well, if you like me, and you enjoyed the sex, why do you wish it hadn't happened?"

"Because I can't trust you to keep it in its proper perspective."

"And just what is its proper perspective?"

"I know you, Bob. You are such a straight arrow that you're probably already thinking we should remarry. You probably think it would be wonderful for the boys."

"I must confess to having given it some thought, yes."

"I figured as much. Oh, Bob, don't you understand? I don't want to be married to you—or to anyone. I didn't like myself very much when I was married to you. I didn't like living a lie."

"What lie were you living?"

"The lie of being a dutiful wife. Didn't you know? Are you trying to tell me that you had no idea about all the affairs I had?"

"No," Bob answered dully. The hollowness turned to nausea. He wished with all his heart he hadn't started this conversation. It was taking him places he didn't want to go. "I didn't know. I thought all those people hanging around all the time were queer."

"Actually, most of them were bisexual," Marilou said. "But because you thought they were homosexual, it made a great cover. You never suspected a thing. One night—this is scandalous, I know—but one night while you were writing, there were four of us in the bedroom screwing like minks, trading partners, boy-boy, boy-girl." She shivered. "I still get excited thinking about it."

He couldn't look at her. "You mean you did that while I was home?"

"Yes."

"Couldn't you have at least had the decency to wait until I was asleep?"

"Don't you understand, Bob? The very fact that you could have come in at any moment and discovered us added to the excitement we all felt."

"Please," Bob begged in a choked voice. "Don't tell me any more." He was suddenly acutely aware of his nakedness, so he grabbed his clothes and began to get dressed.

"Are you getting dressed to go to bed? That doesn't make any sense, does it?"

"Listen," Bob said, pulling on his trousers, "make my apologies to the boys, will you? I think I'll start back to Fort Campbell tonight."

"You're upset."

"Gee, don't be foolish. Why should I be upset?"

"Don't be upset, Bob. I just wanted everything to be up front with us, that's all. I owe you that much."

Bob stared at her for a moment, then bent over to tie a shoe. "Yeah, well, consider the debt paid."

CHAPTER EIGHT

JUNE 23, 1962, FROM "TRAILMARKERS" IN
EVENTS MAGAZINE:

TWO AMERICAN SOLDIERS SLAIN
IN VIETNAM

Two U.S. Army officers, advisers to the Army
of the Republic of Vietnam (ARVN), were killed by
Viet Cong when the convoy in which they were
traveling was ambushed. The ambush occurred on
Highway 1, about 35 miles north of Saigon.

The entire convoy of 7 vehicles was destroyed
in the well-planned and well-executed ambush,
which involved at least 200 VC guerrillas. In addition to the American casualties, 15 South Vietnamese soldiers were killed.

In the same week, the U.S. Army announced
that it used its fleet of H-21 helicopters to transport
South Vietnamese soldiers to Landing Zone D for
an offensive operation against the VC.

COMMUNICATIONS SATELLITE SET TO
TRANSMIT TV OVERSEAS

Within a matter of weeks, officials say, Americans will be able to see live telecasts transmitted via satellite from Europe. The satellite, known as Telstar, will pick up the signals from a ground station in Europe, then transmit them to a ground station in Andover, Maine.

"I don't think the average person fully understands the impact and significance of this event," a spokesman for the TV industry said. "But when a television viewer in Paris, Tennessee, can watch an event as it is happening in Paris, France, we are truly living in a global village. This rivals in significance the first telegraphed transmission by Samuel F.B. Morse, more than a century ago."

BASE CAMP ALPHA, REPUBLIC OF VIETNAM

Sitting on the canvas field cot in his tent, Lieutenant Colonel Jarred Hawkins covered his face, neck, ears, and hands with mosquito repellent, then tried to decide whether or not he should take off his boots before retiring. Normally he would be sleeping in his private apartment on rue Le Loi in Saigon; tonight he was out in the field, paying an inspection to one of the many base camps the South Vietnamese Army had established. A base camp was a fortified enclave, the idea being that soldiers from the Army of the Republic of Viet Nam, accompanied by their American advisers, would patrol the area by day, then retreat into their base camps at night.

Jarred did not believe in the concept. He felt retreating into an enclave each night was merely telling the enemy that after the sun went down, the jungle belonged to them—and to the damn mosquitoes, he added to himself as he slapped at one. He felt the ARVN should make a show of being in command of the countryside, night *and* day. But despite his urging, the base camp concept remained in effect, partly because Jarred's point of view, even among the American military, was the minority one.

Often the VC launched attacks against the heavily fortified base camps. The camps were so well defended it was quite rare that the VC could actually overrun the position, but they didn't have to win to score a psychological victory. It was enough that they would even attack.

"Do you see?" the VC told the Vietnamese peasants who lived in the villages near the base camps. "The corrupt Saigon government says they are here to protect you, but where do the government soldiers and the American bandits go at night? They go into their enclaves and hide under their beds like children. Don't put your trust in them. Put your trust in the National Liberation Front, for we are the true representatives of the people."

This particular base camp was commanded by a South Vietnamese captain named Sanh, though an American adviser, Captain Jeff Cathcoat, and two American sergeants, Cox and Delaney, were also part of the forces on site. Only the three American advisers were actually under Jarred's command, but in their advisory capacity they exercised a lot of leverage over their Vietnamese counterparts.

"It's like this," Jarred had told an American reporter recently. "We aren't connected to the Vietnamese commanders by steel rods; we are connected to them by rubber bands. We can't force them to do anything, but we can influence them."

Captain Cathcoat abruptly pushed through the two canvas flaps that prevented light from escaping and into the little sandbag bunker. He stood looking down at Jarred in the circle of golden light given off by a stubby candle as Jarred sat on the edge of the cot looking down at his feet.

"Trying to decide whether to take off your boots?" Cathcoat chuckled.

"Yes," Jarred replied. "If we're hit during the night, I don't want to have to go running out across the compound in my socks. On the other hand, it's a hell of a lot more comfortable trying to sleep with my boots off than it is with them on —espcially given how damn hard it'll be to get any sleep anyway." He slapped at another mosquito.

"Tell you what, sir. Go ahead and take your boots off. Either Sergeant Cox, Sergeant Delaney, or I will be awake all night long. If it looks like anything is about to happen, we'll get word to you in plenty of time to get your footwear on."

"Okay, Captain, I'm going to count on that," Jarred said,

loosening the laces in his boots. He pulled them off, then wiggled his toes. "Damn, those things get hot over here," he moaned.

Cathcoat's cot was across from Jarred's, and he began rummaging through a canvas bag sitting on top. Finally he found what he was looking for: a small olive-drab can of C-rations.

"Peaches," he said, smiling broadly. He pulled out his dog tag chain and located the little finger-operated can opener. "Far as I'm concerned you can shit-can everything in those damn C-ration kits except the fruit." He sat on his cot and worked open the top.

"You mean you don't like the beans and franks?" Jarred asked, lying back on his cot with his hands folded behind his head.

"They're okay, I guess. Not as bad as *some* of the crap they try to pass off as food. Like the ham and eggs. Whoever came up with that should be forced to eat it for thirty days. Want some?" He held the open can toward Jarred.

"Thank you, no."

Cathcoat ate the contents by tipping up the can and pouring them directly into his mouth.

"How long you been out in the bush?" Jarred asked.

"Six months," Cathcoat replied. A piece of peach was hanging from his lip, and he sucked it in. "How long you been over here?"

"A little over four years, this time."

"This time? You mean you were here before?"

"I was an American observer during the French occupation. And I stayed on for another year after they left, to help the Vietnamese military make the transition."

"Damn, Colonel, you've put in *enough* time over here. You ought to be able to go home by now."

"Saigon *is* home," Jarred replied.

"Really?"

"Well, it's as much home as anyplace, I guess. I don't have a family, or anywhere to go back to."

"If I were you, I'd *get* me some sort of family—a dog or something—before I spent any more time over here." Cathcoat finished the fruit, then stood up and grabbed his carbine. "Well, I better get going. If nothing happens, I'll see you in the morning."

"Be careful," Jarred said.

Cathcoat grinned. "You don't have to tell me that, sir. Hell, over here 'careful' is my middle name."

After Cathcoat left, Jarred reached over and pinched out the candle, then lay in the darkness, listening to the sounds drifting in from outside. Some Vietnamese soldiers were playing cards nearby, and a spirited discussion was going on about the value of their hands. Someone else was listening to music on a small battery-operated radio. The song, sung by a young woman, was a sad lament about her lover killed by the forces of evil. Jarred couldn't help but muse about the feelings that had gone into writing the song, for those loyal to the Saigon government could think of the evil forces as VC, whereas those who supported the VC could think of the evil forces as the Saigon government.

Jarred thought of his third-floor apartment on Le Loi Street in Saigon, how he would often sit out on the veranda just before dawn to watch the colorful sunrise. He liked to observe the morning people: the bread women, the soup vendors, the sidewalk merchants. He thought of the streets of Saigon: Cong Ly and Duong Troung Tan Buu, Tru Minh Ky, Tru Minh Gaing, and Le Loi. Oddly, those streets with their strange-sounding names were much more familiar to him than the streets in his hometown of Jackson, Mississippi: Bailey Avenue, Fortification, Poindexter, Capitol. These were only names to him now; try as he might, he could no longer conjure up clear images to go with them.

The only image Jarred could still recall was that of the Baptist orphanage where he had been raised. He never knew his parents and didn't even know if his name, Hawkins, was their name. He had no idea how he came to be raised in an orphanage, though he suspected his mother had been a woman scorned who abandoned him rather than face the shame of being an unwed mother. He had no real reason for believing that, other than the vague hope that somewhere— even if he never saw her, even if he never found out who she was—she might still be alive.

With such thoughts swirling around in his head, he finally drifted off to sleep.

*   *   *

"Colonel! Colonel!" Cathcoat hissed. He was shaking Jarred's shoulder.

"Um? What is it?" Jarred asked sleepily.

"Better put your boots on, sir. We've been hearing people move around out there. I've got a feeling we're about to be hit."

Immediately awake, Jarred sat up and pulled on his boots.

"Colonel, did you bring any weapon other than your pistol?" Cathcoat asked.

"No, that's all I have."

"That's what I thought. Here's an extra carbine. You better take it."

"Thanks."

Jarred followed Cathcoat out of the little bunker to a sandbag circle near the north wall of the compound. This mortar bunker was ostensibly manned by a Vietnamese gun crew, but Jarred saw that Sergeant Delaney was with them.

"How close in you want us to come, *dai ui*?" Sergeant Delaney asked Cathcoat. Vietnamese for 'captain,' the words were pronounced *dye wee*, though Delaney, who was from Georgia, managed to make it sound distinctly southern.

"If they're still coming, you can follow them inside the wall as far as I'm concerned," Cathcoat replied, adding, "By the way, Colonel, I should warn you to keep an eye on our own troops. Never can tell when one of them might be VC. Also, let out a yell if you hear anything heavy fall in here so we can bail the hell out. It could be a grenade."

"You got it," Jarred said.

Four or five hollow popping sounds sounded out in the jungle, followed by a line of sparks climbing up into the night sky.

"*Mortars! Incoming!*" Sergeant Delaney yelled.

A few seconds later there were four deafening explosions from inside the compound. One of the mortar rounds started a fire in the long barracks, and as it blazed it cast a wavering orange light over the compound, illuminating every foxhole and mortar bunker.

"Great, that's all we need," Cathcoat muttered. "Now we're backlit by the friggin' fire."

Delaney dropped a round down in the tube, and it popped out with a ringing *thunk*. Three other mortars returned fire as well, and high explosive rounds burst outside the walls. But almost immediately there were four more blasts from incoming rounds. Two of them were phosphorous, and they sent up huge fountains of white-hot fire. Several defenders were showered by the flaming phosphorus, and they burned like torches, screaming in their agony. Again the compound was well lighted, whereas beyond the fence there was total darkness.

"Where the hell is our illumination?" Cathcoat shouted into the radio. "Get us some light here! Fast! They're chewing us to pieces!"

Jarred couldn't hear the answer, but he knew it wasn't to Cathcoat's liking by the way the blood vessel in his temple was throbbing.

"What do you mean, half an hour?" the captain shouted. "You're supposed to have someone on station! You want us to wait half an hour? We by God may not even be here in half an hour!" He signed off. "Shit!" he spat. "We're blind as friggin' bats in here."

"What about artillery support?" Jarred asked. "Maybe they can send up some flares."

"There's an ARVN artillery unit a couple miles down the road," Cathcoat said. "Only thing is, they don't have any American advisers with them. I don't know if we could get a fire mission from them or not. And even if we could, I wouldn't know how to give them coordinates. Captain Sanh isn't much good at translation. Hell, it's all I can do to make him understand *me*."

"Let me handle that," Jarred said, reaching for the radio. "You know their call sign?"

Cathcoat picked up the signal operating instructions book. "Here's the SOI," he said, handing the book to Jarred. They were racked by another round of explosions, which forced them down.

Jarred found the call sign, then reached for the radio. He spoke in quick, authoritative Vietnamese, surprising everyone in the bunker, the Vietnamese as well as the Americans. When he was finished he handed the phone and the book back.

"I think we'll have some illumination soon," he said.

"I didn't know you could speak that shit," Cathcoat said. "I'm impressed as hell."

Ignoring the plaudit, Jarred moved close to the sandbags and raised his carbine. "We'd better get ready for them."

"Yes, sir. Pass the word!" Cathcoat shouted to the next bunker. "We've got illumination on the way! Get ready!"

High overhead came a sound like the rushing of empty cars down a railroad track. Then came a half-dozen pops, followed by a wavering yellow light that lit up the entire open space between the compound walls and the jungle—including the nearly one thousand black-clad VC moving slowly across the field toward them.

"Holy shit! Look at them! I've never seen so many in one place before!" Cathcoat said.

"They're in range," Jarred said. "We'd better open up before we lose the light."

"Yes, sir, you're right. Fire!" Cathcoat shouted, even though it was rightfully Captain Sanh's place to issue the order. Whether Cathcoat had that authority or not, the order was carried out, for immediately every weapon inside the compound began firing. Machine guns hosed out solid streams of tracer fire, while the Vietnamese soldiers opened fire with M-1 rifles. Jarred and Cathcoat joined in the melee with their carbines, while Sergeant Delaney and his Vietnamese gun crew kept up a smooth, steady mortar barrage.

"Walk it in toward us, Delaney, walk it in!" Cathcoat yelled. "The sonsabitches are almost to the wire!"

"Charge two!" Delaney ordered the mortar crew, decreasing the amount of propellant for the mortar rounds and thereby shortening the range.

Even before the first illumination rounds had burned out, a second barrage of artillery-launched flares was in the air, bathing the earth in its eerie light. Tracer rounds zipped back and forth between the defenders in the compound, and the faceless black shadows, who, though their numbers were gradually decreasing, continued forward. The night was rent by the bang and chatter of rifles and machine guns and the boom and *whoosh* of mortars and the .57- and .75-mm recoilless rifles the VC were employing against the defenders.

"Cap'n Cathcoat, they're in the concertina!" Delaney shouted as the attackers reached the wire fencing strung up around the compound.

"Drop your rounds right on the fence!" Cathcoat ordered.

"Yes, sir. Charge one!" Delaney shouted to his gunners.

"Captain Cathcoat, you'd better pull the perimeter in," Jarred suggested. "Otherwise our guys are going to get chewed up by our own mortars."

Cathcoat picked up the field phone and twisted the crank. "Dai ui Sanh! Dai ui Sanh!" he shouted to the Vietnamese commander.

Sanh apparently answered, though Jarred couldn't hear his response above the storm of battle.

"Pull your men back to the final defensive position!" Cathcoat barked into the phone. "Now! On the double!"

He hung up, then pulled a metal box from a niche in the sandbag wall of the mortar bunker. He opened the lid, revealing a bank of tiny twist switches.

"Claymores?" Jarred asked.

Cathcoat smiled broadly. "You bet your ass we've got Claymores out there. Three rows of nine. Enough to level the whole friggin' force if they get in the way."

Though Jarred had not spoken his fears out loud, he had been considering the possibility of their being overrun. Now he relaxed. Each Claymore could send out a cone of death and destruction fifty yards deep and fifty yards wide.

Jarred saw the Vietnamese defenders beginning to pull back across the open spot between the outer defensive perimeter and the line of holes and sandbags that made up the final defensive line. Sergeant Cox was at the outer wires, directing movements, when suddenly he went down.

"Cox has been hit!" Jarred shouted.

Cathcoat looked up from the box of Claymore switches. "Damn! I'd better go get him." He started over the edge of the sandbags, but before he could climb out of the bunker, another soldier was running toward the fallen American, zigzagging back and forth as bullets hit the ground at his feet and zipped all around him.

"Wait!" Jarred said. "Captain Sanh has gone after him."

"Will you look at that little shit?" Cathcoat breathed in an awed vioce.

Sanh reached Sergeant Cox, then—even though the American was bigger than he—managed to get him up across his shoulders in a fireman's carry.

"He'll never make it back," Jarred said. "Cox is too heavy."

"Don't sell him short just because he's little," Cathcoat said. "He's strong as an ox."

True to Cathcoat's word, Sanh carried Cox back, running the same zigzag pattern he had used going out to the wire.

"Is everyone back?" Cathcoat asked.

"Looks like it," Jarred answered.

"Good. Get your head down!" Cathcoat warned.

He began twisting the switches in the box. With each twist there was a searing blast out at the fence until all nine Claymores were detonated. Cathcoat then pulled the old wires out of the firing generator and started inserting wires for a second barrage. While he was doing so, Jarred raised up to take a look at the attacking hordes. In the wavering light from the flares he saw that the first blast had taken out everyone who had reached the concertina wire plus nearly half of the remaining attacking force. The surviving VC, stunned by the sudden devastation of the Claymore mines, stopped dead in their tracks. The defenders continued pouring fire out toward them.

Finally, hesitantly, the VC regrouped and continued their attack.

"Okay, assholes, here comes another one!" Cathcoat shouted. Again he twisted the firing switches, and again a series of fiery explosions rippled down the line. This charge was farther back than the first, and now Jarred could see the necessity for making sure that all the friendlies were back. Had Cox still been where he fell, he would have been cut to pieces by shrapnel from a mine that ripped right through where he had been.

The second blast took out half of the VC who had survived the first charge. This time there was no stunned silence or hesitation. This time the survivors turned and ran back toward the jungle, leaving their dead and wounded on the field behind them.

The South Vietnamese defenders shouted taunting challenges to the attackers and, leaving their holes and bunkers, rushed out to the wire to throw several parting shots at them. Cathcoat, grinning victoriously, sat down in the bottom of the bunker and leaned back against the sandbags. He reached for his shirt pocket with shaking hands and pulled out a crumpled pack of cigarettes, offering one to Jarred, who declined.

Raising the pack to his mouth, Cathcoat extracted one of the filterless white cylinders with his lips.

"When I've finished a hard day at the office, I like to relax with a Lucky," he said blithely.

Sergeant Delaney, who had also pulled out a cigarette, offered Cathcoat a light. Both men inhaled deeply, then let out a long stream of smoke. The field phone rang, and Delaney picked it up.

"Sergeant Delaney," he said. "What? Oh, shit." He paused. "Yes, yes, I'll tell him. Thanks, Dai ui Sanh." He replaced the phone.

"What is it?" Cathcoat asked.

Delaney shook his head. "Sergeant Cox is dead."

ONE WEEK LATER

The Continental Hotel sat on a busy corner in the heart of Saigon. An open patio afforded customers the opportunity to sit quietly over a drink or a meal while watching people pass by. Overhead fans turned briskly, and white-jacketed waiters darted about, balancing cooling drinks on serving trays.

Jarred pulled his jeep into the no-parking zone in front of the hotel, then passed a chain through the steering wheel and locked it. Among Jarred's many duties, he was military adviser to Colonel Nguyen Van Tran of the Can Lao, Ngo Dinh Nhu's private police force, so the jeep Jarred was driving was marked with the colors and imprint of the Can Lao—which meant he didn't have to worry about the no-parking area, even though a white-clad member of the National Police was standing nearby. The "white mouse," as the Americans called the white-uniformed men of the National Police, was not a part of the Can Lao, so even he shared the Vietnamese people's fear and distrust of them—and of anyone connected with them. As he looked toward Jarred, his face reflected that fear.

Jarred had tried to convince Nguyen, and even Nhu, that the image of the Can Lao was going to have to change if they were ever to win the people's trust and support. But Nhu had replied that he didn't need the people's trust and support. "That is for my brother to worry about," he had said, speaking of Ngo Dinh Diem. "He is the politician. I am an administrator. I need only the people's obedience, and I have learned that fear is the best tool for accomplishing that."

Today Jarred was scheduled to escort Colonel Nguyen's wife, Ly, to an orphanage in a nearby village. Visiting orphanages was something Ly enjoyed doing, and, as she was Nguyen's wife, her presence represented the Can Lao. Her visits were the one ray of goodwill exhibited by the Can Lao, so, as a concession to the Americans, Nhu allowed them to continue.

Jarred was about to enter the hotel's patio when an old man shuffled up to him. Long wisps of white hair protruding from his chin formed a beard that waved in the gentle breeze. The man clasped his palms together and dipped his hands several times in groveling respect. He stared at Jarred with the eyes of a man who had lived beyond his time and had been turned out by his family to beg or to die.

"Venerable one, it is I who should honor you and the wisdom of your years," Jarred said gently, returning the gesture and then pressing a hundred piasters into the man's hands.

The old man was clearly so shocked at hearing Jarred speak Vietnamese that it was several seconds before he realized the enormity of his prize. He grasped it tightly to prevent it from getting away and scuttled quickly over to a sidewalk vendor to buy a bowl of *my ton* soup and the special treat of a bottle of beer.

Jarred stepped into the patio. He would have preferred a table right at the entrance, but it was occupied by an enormous man whom Jarred recognized as the minister of imports. He was reading a newspaper, and the fat, sausagelike fingers of both hands were adorned with diamond rings. Rolls of flesh from his thick neck lay in layers across the silk collar of his expensive suit.

The conversations being conducted on the Continental's patio were in French, Vietnamese, and Chinese. Jarred couldn't follow the Chinese, but the French and Vietnamese exchanges dealt with things as diverse as the price of rubber on the international market and a ballet being performed in Cholon. No one was talking about the war going on out in the countryside, and Jarred saw this as a perfect example of something he frequently tried to point out to other Americans but was unable to make them grasp: The stratum of society represented by the people with whom Americans normally had contact was totally isolated from the mainstream Vietnamese people. It curled and seeped through the general population like an oil slick on water, moving with the current, seemingly a part of the whole but never actually emulsifying.

A taxi pulled to a stop at the curb, and Jarred watched as a woman sitting in the shadows of the backseat passed money across to the driver. When she stepped out of the car, Jarred recognized her, having met her once before: Madam Nguyen Ly.

She approached the patio entrance. Jarred guessed her age as just over thirty. She had high cheekbones, not prominent but well accented, and even at this distance he could see that her eyes sparkled like jewels and were framed by eyelashes like the most delicate black lace. Her skin was smooth and golden, her movements as graceful as palm fronds stirred by a breeze. She was wearing the Vietnamese national dress, an *ao dai*, of blue-green shimmering silk that clung to her upper body, then fell in two flowerlike petals, front and back, from her waist over white silk pants. It was both amazingly seductive yet prim and proper. Jarred believed that he had never seen a more breathtakingly beautiful woman.

He met her at the entrance, and when she smiled and offered her hand he took it. "Madam Nguyen, it is a pleasure to see you again. I am sorry that I must be a poor substitute for your husband. He has been unavoidably detained by pressing business."

Ly laughed, the delicate sound falling from her lips like the tinkling of wind chimes. "That is his excuse. The truth is, he didn't want to meet me. I must go to Di Hoa, a small village not far from here, and visit the orphanage my father started. My husband does not like this."

"Madam Nguyen, it is my pleasure to be your escort," Jarred said.

"You may do so only if you call me Ly and not Madam Nguyen. In your country, friends, even men and women, address each other by their given names. Is this not so?"

He smiled. "Yes. I am called Jarred."

"Then *I* shall call you Jarred," Ly said. Because of her accent, she pronounced it "Zharred." It was almost a caress to

the ears, and Jarred derived a great deal of pleasure hearing
her say it.

"Would you like a drink before we go?" he asked.

"I think not. The children will be looking for me."

He smiled and gestured toward the entrance. "Then let
us not keep them waiting."

The drive to Di Hoa was very pleasant once they crossed
the river and the congestion of Saigon was behind them.
Highway 13 wound through lush green fields and quiet little
villages, with brilliant splashes of color lining the road from
the profusion of flowers.

The location of the orphanage provided a graphic symbol of the dual religious identities of Vietnam, sitting as it did
halfway between a large Catholic church and a centuries-old
Buddhist pagoda. However, the sign in front left little doubt
as to which camp the orphanage belonged in: ST. MARY'S
BLESSED FOR THE CHILDREN.

Jarred kept himself off at a distance while Ly visited
with the children and spoke with the staff. He had seen other
official visits, where members of the government mingled
with ordinary people like gods coming down from Mount
Olympus, but this was nothing like that. It was obvious that
Ly enjoyed this role, and it was equally obvious that the
children and the staff truly enjoyed her presence.

Finally the long afternoon came to a close, and Ly, carrying a very small girl and with several children flocking around
her, walked across the grounds to the jeep. Jarred was leaning against the front of the vehicle, his arms folded across his
chest, waiting patiently.

"Have you grown tired of waiting for me, Jarred?" Ly
asked, smiling.

"No," he replied. "Watching a beautiful woman enjoy
herself is a pleasant way to spend an afternoon. And you are
an exceptionally beautiful woman."

Ly blushed.

"I'm sorry," he said quickly. "I meant no offense or
disrespect."

"That is all right. I know no offense was meant. It is just
that I am embarrassed to have you compliment me so."

"Ahh. Then in the future I will be very careful to say you are ugly."

Ly looked up sharply, clearly surprised by the remark. Realizing he was teasing, she laughed out loud, covering her mouth with her hand as she did so.

"Why do you laugh, fairy princess?" one of the children asked in Vietnamese.

"Because the American said something funny," Ly answered.

"Is the American your hero?"

Ly looked at Jarred, then smiled. "Of course he is my hero. Don't you think he is handsome? He is going to carry me away to his castle."

"And you will live happily forever after?" one of the children asked.

"Yes. We will live happily forever after." As Ly spoke the words, the easy laughter left her voice, and she sounded almost plaintive. As if clearing her mind of the thought, she shook her head and smiled. "I must go now, children. Good-bye to you. Good-bye to all of you." She climbed into the jeep.

Jarred started it up, waving good-naturedly to the larger children who continued to chase after them for several hundred feet.

"Why do they call you fairy princess?" he asked when they were on the road again.

"Because sometimes I read stories to them. And they think I am the fairy princess in the stories, so they—" Ly gasped and stopped in midsentence. She stared at Jarred, eyes wide. "You understood what they said? You speak Vietnamese?"

"Yes." Jarred smiled. "You wouldn't want a hero who couldn't speak your language, would you?"

"I . . . I am very embarrassed by that," Ly said, looking down at her lap. "I hope you do not take offense."

"Ly, I don't think I could take offense at anything you said or did."

The remainder of the drive was spent in relative silence. A few times Jarred sensed Ly looking at him, but when he glanced at her, she quickly dipped her gaze, only the smallest trace of an embarrassed smile playing across her lips.

When they reached Saigon, Jarred felt at once that something was going on. He could feel an air of tension about the city, unlike anything he had experienced before. All up and down both sides of the street people were milling about and jabbering excitedly. It was especially noticeable because despite the crowds, the markets were not doing business. Many of the vendors were sitting on their haunches, chewing on the end of a stick treated with betel nut as they looked dispassionately out over the crowd. Other vendors had abandoned their wares entirely and stood clustered along the edge of the street, waiting expectantly.

Particularly unusual was the scarcity of traffic. Even the cyclos, both the motorized and the pedal powered, were parked along the sides of the streets. The cyclo operators sat in their own passenger seats, passing cigarettes back and forth, waiting along with everyone else.

As the jeep approached Phu By Street, they saw several armed members of the Can Lao.

"What is it?" Ly asked. "What is wrong?"

"I don't know." Jarred pulled over to the side of the road and stopped. "I'm going to try to find out what's going on here, but I think it would better if you didn't come with me."

"Why not?"

"I don't know that there's no danger—and I would rather not take a chance with you. Please, take a cyclo home."

"Very well," Ly said, stepping lightly, gracefully, from the jeep. She started toward one of the cyclos, then turned and looked back at him with an almost coquettish smile. "See? You *are* my hero, the way you are concerned for my safety."

Jarred waited until he was certain Ly was safely on her way, then continued on. At the end of the block was a large crowd of civilians, and when Jarred reached them, he saw they were so congregated because they were prevented from going any farther by a roadblock, manned by the Can Lao. When one of the policemen saw the markings on the jeep Jarred was driving, he shouted to the crowd to open up a path. Then, pulling one of the barricades aside, he waved the American on.

Jarred drove through. No civilians were on this side of

the barricade, just several soldiers and men from the Can Lao. He parked the jeep between a three-quarter-ton truck and a half-track, then got out and walked forward to see what was going on. Spotting Colonel Nguyen standing with a knot of officers, he walked over to him.

"Ah," Nguyen said, smiling broadly. "Back from the orphanage, I see. And did my wife make a big impression on the urchins?"

"Her visit was most appreciated, by the children and the staff," Jarred replied. "Colonel Nguyen, what is going on here?"

"You are just in time for a little entertainment, Colonel Hawkins." Nguyen smiled. "Though I do not think it is the kind of entertainment you would particularly relish."

"What is it?"

"An execution, Colonel. We are about to execute a traitor."

"You're right," Jarred said. "I don't think I would enjoy watching an execution."

"I do not understand how you can be so squeamish about such a thing. Especially as you are a veteran of battle. Ah, here comes the traitor now."

Two soldiers hauled someone down from the back of a two-and-one-half-ton truck. Since they were walking away from Jarred toward a post that had been erected in an open space, they were presenting their backs, so he couldn't see the condemned man's face. He was just as glad. He did not want to see the fear that would be in the man's eyes.

"I don't want to watch this," Jarred muttered.

"Then go, Colonel Hawkins, by all means," Nguyen said. "This is, after all, a concern for my government, not yours."

Just as Jarred started to turn away, the soldiers escorting the prisoner reached the post. They turned the prisoner around to secure him to the post for the firing squad, and Jarred saw his face. And recognized him.

"Captain Sanh!" he shouted.

Sanh wildly scanned the crowd. "Colonel Hawkins!" he called, spotting the American. "Tell them I am no traitor!"

Jarred put his hand on Nguyen's shoulder. "Colonel Nguyen, what are you doing?" he demanded. "You are making a great mistake! That man's no traitor! I saw him fight bravely last week. If anything, you should give him a medal!"

"There is no mistake," Nguyen said.

"But there *has* to be. He's no VC! My God, I saw him kill ten or twelve of them myself!"

"I did not say he was VC."

"You said he was a traitor."

"Yes, but not VC. He is a traitor because he belongs to a group of men who would overthrow President Diem."

"*What?*"

Nguyen smiled coldly. "There is more than one way to betray your country, Colonel." He turned to the major standing beside him. "Order the firing squad to do their duty," he commanded.

The major saluted, then walked over to a group of seven soldiers. A moment later the soldiers lined up, raised their rifles, and pointed them toward Captain Sanh. Jarred looked at Sanh for a moment, remembering how he had braved enemy fire to carry a fallen Sergeant Cox back from the concertina wire. Sergeant Cox was dead and was probably already dead when Sanh went out to rescue him, but that didn't diminish the bravery of Sanh's deed.

Now Sanh was about to be executed for treason, and there was nothing Jarred could do to stop it. He didn't even know if the charge was true. He knew that Sanh wasn't VC, but he could very well be a member of one of the dissident groups springing up against Diem. If so, Jarred wasn't entirely unsympathetic to his cause. To that degree, Diem was his own worst enemy.

The commander of the firing squad barked out the firing sequence, then gave the order to fire. A volley of shots rang out, and Sanh was slammed back against the post. His body sagged but did not fall, held up by the ropes as he was. The firing squad commander gave the command to order arms as the echoes of the gunshots were fading away; then he walked up to check the body.

"Colonel Nguyen," he called. "The traitor is not yet dead. Shall I order another volley?"

"No," Nguyen said, taking out his pistol. He strutted out to Sanh's sagging form. "No need for that."

He put his pistol to Sanh's temple and, without a second's hesitation, pulled the trigger. A little mist of blood, brain matter, and bits of bone sprayed out the opposite side of Sanh's head.

"Now he is dead," Nguyen said, putting his pistol away. When he saw that he had blood on his hand, he pulled out a handkerchief and wiped it off.

Jarred walked back to his jeep and stood there for a long moment. It took all the willpower he could muster just to keep from throwing up.

ATLANTA

Over a thousand delegates from forty-two states had gathered for the annual convention of the NAACP. Atlanta had been chosen because it, among all southern cities, was beginning to make some moves of accommodation. The "white" and "colored" signs had come down from drinking fountains, integrated baseball games were being played in the parks and playgrounds, and some—though not all—lunch counters had taken down their "whites only" signs.

A few pockets of resistance to integration remained. One such place was the Rebel Restaurant, and Deon Booker was with a group of picketers outside. Initially, the plan had been to enter the restaurant in a large group, thereby forcing a police confrontation. But it was decided that if they did that, they might well wind up in jail and miss the proceedings at the convention.

Three policemen were on duty in front of the eatery, keeping a wary eye on the protesters. The little group had been told they could picket as long as they stayed far enough away to allow unrestricted entry to the restaurant's customers.

A middle-aged white couple arrived, and one of the women protesters stepped out of the picket line to hand them a circular.

"Get away from me, nigger!" the white man spat, giving her a shove.

"Watch who you're pushin' aroun' there, ofay!" one of the men shouted, throwing down his sign and starting toward the white man. The white woman let out a gasp of fear, and the three policemen moved quickly, but Deon was quicker. He grabbed the bellicose black youth and pushed him back into the line.

"George, you stay there!" Deon ordered. "You want to undo everything Dr. King has accomplished?"

"Did you see what he done to Iris? I ain't goin' to let him shove her around like that," George sputtered angrily.

Deon looked over at the young black woman who had been shoved. "Iris, you hurt?"

"No."

"Then there's no harm done," Deon said soothingly. "Remember, this is a nonviolent movement."

"Yeah? Well, how long we got to be nonviolent, anyway? How many times we got to be knocked aroun' before we figure out this nonviolent shit ain't goin' to work?"

"It *is* going to work," Deon insisted.

"Suppose it don't? What then?"

"There is no 'then.'"

"The hell there ain't. We could fight for what's ours. It's been done before."

"George, there are twenty million Negroes in America, and a hundred and sixty million white people. You like those odds?"

"Listen to the man, George," Iris said, returning to the picket line. "He's right."

"They got no business pushin' you aroun' like that," George insisted.

"You don't worry about that. I'm not goin' to let you use me as an excuse to get your own head bashed in."

Muttering, George picked up his fallen sign, and the tension was defused.

Deon stepped aside. His hand was throbbing, and he held it up and looked at it. When he had rushed to stop George, his hand had hit the stake of the sign George was carrying, and a splinter had lodged under the skin. Deon started picking at it.

"Get a splinter, did you?" one of the white policemen asked.

"Yeah."

"Come over here to the car. I've got a first-aid kit. I'll get it out."

"It'll be all right."

"It could get infected," the policeman warned.

"Yeah, okay," Deon said. He walked over to the police

car and held out his hand while the officer removed the splinter, then coated the wound with an antiseptic. Deon suddenly chuckled.

"What is it?"

"I was just thinking. Last week I was in Birmingham, and a policeman turned a fire hose on me. Here, a policeman removes a splinter. Maybe we *are* making some progress."

"Yeah, well, it's a good thing that splinter wasn't in your ass," the policeman joked. "I don't think we've made that much progress."

Deon laughed with him. "I don't think I ever *want* to make that much progress."

He returned to the picket line and walked for another hour before being relieved by a second shift. From the restaurant Deon went straight to the convention headquarters. Nearly as many people were gathered outside the building as would be inside, for this was a convention of national importance. Police were here, too, but their job was mainly to keep traffic flowing since there was no trouble except for a knot of white men dressed in KKK robes and carrying a Confederate flag. One of the robed men was giving a speech, shouting through a bullhorn.

"If the Kennedys in Washin'ton have their way, that little Bobbysox Kennedy and his big brother, the President—"

He was interrupted by the laughter of those immediately around him.

"—the nigra children and the little white children will all be mixed together in one schoolhouse. You know what will come out at the other end? A mongrelized race that will destroy both the nigras and the whites. It ain't just the white race we're fightin' for. We're fightin' for *all* races, and I'm tellin' you, there ain' goin' to be no integration of the schools, of the buses, of the restaurants, there ain't goin' to be no integration *anywhere* as long as free white men are willin' to stand up and be counted!"

The large crowd of black men, women, and children gathered outside the convention headquarters began to sing to drown out the heckler's speech. The song was one that Deon, and indeed the entire country, had come to recognize as the anthem of the civil right's movement: "We Shall Overcome."

Feeling a swelling of pride, Deon made his way inside.

"Deon! Deon, over here! I saved a seat for you!" a female voice called.

Deon looked toward the voice. His benefactor, Violet Simmons, a young student he had met at Jefferson University in St. Louis, was waving to him. He pressed through the crowd and finally reached her. "Thanks," he said, sitting beside her.

The comedian Dick Gregory had just been introduced and was himself in the process of introducing Dr. Martin Luther King, Jr. to the audience.

"How did it go at the restaurant?" Violet asked.

"They wouldn't let us in," Deon said dryly.

"Ha, ha. Very funny. You should be up there with Dick Gregory."

"Shhh. Let's listen."

". . . I've been thinking about all the times Dr. King has been arrested," Gregory was saying. "And I have come to the conclusion that because of this, Dr. King may be the only celebrity in America who gives out more fingerprints than autographs."

The audience exploded with laughter.

"Isn't this excitin'?" Violet asked.

Deon smiled at her youthful enthusiasm. "Sometimes it's more excitement than I want."

"What do you mean?"

"We have a long, rough road ahead of us. And the worse may be yet to come."

Violet studied his face. "You're not leavin' the movement, are you?"

"No."

"Good. You had me scared there for a minute."

"I want you to be scared. I want you to know what you're getting into," Deon cautioned.

"I think I have an idea."

"Girl, you have no idea at all. I've been sprayed with fire hoses; beaten with clubs; bombarded with rocks, bricks, and bottles; and gassed with tear gas."

"I know what to expect," Violet insisted. "But I *will* be a part of this."

"No, you don't have any idea what to expect," Deon warned. "I'm telling you that I've been through all that, and

I'm still not prepared. I'm afraid it's going to get worse, much worse, before it gets better."

"Well, now, how much worse can it be?"

"I'm afraid we're going to do a lot of dying," Deon replied somberly.

Before Violet could respond, Dick Gregory was announcing Dr. King's name, and the crowd erupted into wild applause. King stepped to the podium and held up his hands; the crowd quieted, and he spoke.

"We have met here today to bridge the divisions which separate us, not only Negro from white but Negro from Negro. You represent the NAACP and I the Southern Christian Leadership Council. However, I would suggest to you that we are two different organizations with but one soul. And though I am not an officer of the NAACP, many of my SCLC officials are also officers of the NAACP. By now I have addressed NAACP chapters in more than twenty states, and it is obvious that we are a people bound for the same destination. Unfortunately we are sometimes separated and confused by what paths we should take. I hope, by my few words here today, to draw these paths closer together.

"Some say that we are not ready for freedom if it prolongs the confrontations between the Negro and the law. They say that what we really want is peace. They say that we are ready to put aside the festering hate and the angry standoffs so that we can have a period of lessened tensions and blessed peace.

"But I say to you, my friends, that peace is not merely the absence of tension; it is the presence of justice. And if we as Negroes are denied justice, then we as Negroes are denied peace."

"Amen!" someone shouted.

"They ain't no peace!"

King leaned forward and grabbed each side of the pulpit as he stared out over an audience electrified by his words.

"My friends, I want to share with you something that I have learned about freedom. I have learned that no person can be truly free until he is free of the fear of dying. I am free because I am not afraid to die.

"Now, don't get me wrong. I love life as well as the next man, as we all should. I love the sweetness of it, and I hope for a long and fruitful life so that in the golden years I can enjoy the company of my grandchildren. But I do not let that love of life shackle me with the fear of death, for only when death hath no dominion over us are we really free.

"When we have reached that stage, we can stand up to any man, to any government, to any unjust law and say, 'I may have no money, I have no position of authority, I am not a person of fame or power, I have no awards or honors, I have not been educated in the finest schools, I cannot read or write, but I possess the capacity of dying!'"

There was a smattering of applause, though some, listening to the words, felt a sense of foreboding.

"And with the sting of death removed, we can begin to bring about change through the most powerful of all ways: the way of nonviolent civil disobedience.

"Now, there are newspapers and timid Negroes and well-meaning white people who are against civil disobedience. They say they are for rights for the Negro, but they are against any violation of existing laws. 'If you don't like the law,' they say, 'go to the courts or the ballot boxes to change the law.' But legislation and court orders can only declare rights; they can never thoroughly deliver them. Only when the people themselves begin to act are rights on paper given lifeblood, and I submit to you that any individual who decides to break a law that conscience tells him is unjust, and willingly accepts the penalty for it, is, at that moment, expressing the very highest respect for law.

"Listen to what Peter said. 'We must obey God rather than man.' And, to this end, the earliest Christians practiced civil disobedience to the point that they were willing to be thrown to the lions to stand up for what they believed."

"You got that right!" someone called.

"Amen!"

"In our own lifetime, we must never forget that everything Hitler did in Germany was legal. It was illegal to aid and comfort a Jew in the day of Hitler's Germany. And I believe that if I had lived there with my present attitude, I would have disobeyed that law, and I would have encouraged people to aid and comfort our Jewish brothers.

"Some of our timid brothers and sisters may say that we have made some gains, that it would be better for us if we would just take the gains we have and move forward more slowly. But I say to you that I want *all* of our rights, not just some of them. I want them *here*, and I want them *now*. All! Here! And now! We want all of our rights!"

"Amen! All our rights!" the crowd responded, shouting and clapping rhythmically.

"We want our freedom here, in America; here, in the black belt of Mississippi; here, behind the cotton curtain of Alabama; here, on the red clay of Georgia!"

Again the audience responded with shouting and applause.

"We are not willing to wait any longer! We want freedom *now*!"

The entire crowd leaped to their feet, exploding in thunderous cheers and applause that hit the walls, floors, and ceilings with the shock wave of an explosion.

"He's done it again!" Deon said, grinning and shaking his head.

"He's done what?" Violet asked.

"He's come into the enemy's camp and stolen their people."

"The enemy's camp?" she asked, confusion in her eyes. "You call these people his enemies?"

"Not anymore I don't." Deon pointed to the NAACP officials who were sharing the dais with King. Like the audience, they were applauding—but their expressions showed that they were not altogether happy with what had just happened.

SAIGON

In Jarred's third-floor apartment, the balcony was more like an outside room, or, more properly, an extension of the living room because there was no wall between the living room/kitchen and the balcony. The floor of the living room/kitchen, which was covered with a light green tile, extended out onto the balcony, which had a mosquito net that could be let down at night and a canvas awning that could be lowered if the rains grew too heavy. Beyond that there was no divider, making it one great room, half of which was open to the sky and half of which was roofed. The glass-topped wrought-iron dining table was out in the open part of the room. Every time it rained, the tables and chairs, being entirely exposed to the elements, were soaked. Bridging the space between the open and enclosed areas was a lacquered bar, which sat back just far enough under the overhang to avoid all but the spray that bounced up from the tile floor, and during the monsoon season—like now—it often doubled as the dining table.

Jarred was sitting behind the bar, drinking a beer and watching the monsoon sweep across the skyline of the city. From this vantage point he had an excellent view of two of Saigon's more famous hotels: the older, more sedate Continental and the newer, brassier Caravelle. Though visiting dignitaries and media people from the States invariably chose the Americanized Caravelle, Jarred much preferred the Continental, with its Old World charm still intact.

A voice, soft and melodious, called to him. "Zharred?"

Jarred turned toward the voice and saw Madam Nguyen standing just inside the door. She was wearing a raincoat and carrying a dripping umbrella, which she now folded shut.

"Hello," Jarred said.

"I . . . I didn't see you at first," Ly said. "I wasn't sure you were here."

"Do you really think I would break a date with you?"

"I didn't know," Ly replied softly. "It is just that now I have found happiness, and I am frightened that it will be taken away."

Jarred walked toward her. "Let me take your raincoat," he said solicitously. "It's all wet, and you'll catch a cold."

Ly took off her raincoat and handed it to him. He hung it on a hook, then turned back to her. He was certain that never in his life had he seen anyone more beautiful, or desirable, than she was at that very moment. He took her in his arms and they kissed.

Jarred and Ly were now fully involved in an adulterous relationship. The first time Jarred had made love to Ly, he had felt more than adulterous; he had felt treasonous. She was, after all, the wife of his colleague. Ly had also felt a terrible sense of guilt—so much so that they had agreed never to do it again.

That agreement had lasted for one day. Now they were seeing each other as often as they could, and on more than one occasion they had come dangerously close to getting caught.

The kiss deepened, and Jarred felt Ly leaning her body into his, clinging to him with an irrefutable intensity. When at last they separated, she exhaled a long, deep sigh, her minted breath caressing his cheek as gently as the strokes of a butterfly's wing.

"Ly," Jarred murmured, kissing her eyes and ears tenderly, "something amazing has happened to me. All my life I believed there was really no such thing as love. I thought it was just something poets wrote about—or a device the movies used to sell popcorn. But I was wrong. I was terribly, terribly wrong. Now I know what the word 'love' means."

"And what does it mean?" Ly asked, shivering under his continuing kisses.

"It means us. You and I together. I am in love with you, Ly. Truly in love. If I died tomorrow, I would die happily, knowing that finally in my life I had found love."

"No, please," Ly said, putting her arms around his neck and pulling his face down to hers. "Don't speak of dying. You must never speak of dying."

Jarred could feel the soft resilience of her lips as he kissed her and the perfumed cage of her mouth as it opened hungrily on his, as if she could consume him.

After that, events unfolded in a dizzying sequence. At some point they must have removed their clothes because Jarred became aware of his naked body against hers, though he wasn't sure how or when it had happened. He could hear the heavy raindrops slapping against the tile floor of the balcony, and he felt the light mist of a cool spray against his heated skin, inflamed by his growing need for her. Jarred guided Ly to his bedroom and his bed.

The rain continued to move across the city, pushed now by the increasing winds of a full-blown storm. As the storm worsened, the rain was falling too hard to be evacuated by the several drains at the base of the balcony walls. Water pooled on the patio floor and backed up into the great room. Heavy sheets of rain blew in, worsening the situation, but the canvas awning stayed unfurled. Jarred and Ly were oblivious to everything except the storm of their own passion.

CHAPTER
NINE

JULY 14, 1962, FROM "TRAILMARKERS" IN
EVENTS MAGAZINE:

"SHERIWEAR," A NEW LINE OF WOMEN'S CLOTHES, IS HOT, HOT, HOT!

The hottest designer in New York is Sheri Warren. Bursting on the scene less than a year ago, her sexy styles are now the rage of the industry. "We can't produce them quickly enough to satisfy the demand," a spokesman for E. J. Buckner and Company said.

While it is too early to suggest that Sheri Warren is on a par with such recognized giants as Geinrich, Halston, or Blass, she has nevertheless made an impact. Eleanor Lambert, head of the New York Couture Group, has called her "not just a designer, but a creative force within the fashion world."

Radically departing from the traditional, Sheri-Wear shows more leg, more back, more of everything. With a built-in bosom support, the dresses, cut as low on top as they are high below, are designed to be worn without bras.

"If you ask me, the styles should be outlawed," a New York police officer said. "They're a bloomin' traffic hazard is what they are."

TWO CIVIL RIGHTS WORKERS MISSING IN MISSISSIPPI

Mississippi law enforcement officials and the FBI have stepped up their search for Vivian Goodman and George Tatum, two civil rights workers who have been missing for over a week. Miss Goodman, who is white, and Mr. Tatum, a Negro, were working as a team.

"I don't condone violence," a spokesman for the Mississippi State Police said. "But they should've had better sense than to team up a white girl with a colored boy. All this outside agitation is unsettling enough, but that's just waving a red flag in the bull's face."

A member of Robert Kennedy's staff said that the attorney general is very concerned about the situation and has asked for daily reports on the progress of the search.

NORTHERN MISSISSIPPI

Deon Booker pulled the '58 Ford station wagon off to the side of the road and stopped. He and two of his three companions coughed and fanned at the dust that roiled up through the open windows. Riding beside Deon on the front seat was Violet Simmons; in the backseat were Alicia Canfield and Jerry Wiggins, a young white graduate student from Ohio State who was asleep at the moment and had been for the last several minutes.

True to her vow, Alicia had come to Mississippi to work on registering Negroes for the vote, but her time down here had not been easy. She and the other volunteers had been subjected to high-pressure fire hoses, dogs, and truncheons. They had been cursed at, spat upon, and pelted with rocks, bottles, rotten fruit, and even excrement. However, they were still alive, which was more than could be said for Vivian Goodman and George Tatum. Officially, the young black man and white woman were listed as missing, but there was little doubt in the minds of the civil rights workers as to what had happened to them.

Deon turned off the Ford's engine. When he did, Jerry woke up and looked around. There was nothing to see but a swampy-looking forest.

"Where the hell are we?" he asked, yawning and stretching.

"State Highway Three-fifteen, about halfway between Sardis and Delta," Deon answered.

"Right. Like that means something to me. I'll bet you're just as lost as I am."

"No way. I was born here, man."

"Here?"

"About ten miles from here. In the noble town of Delta, Mississippi. If you squint at a map, you might be able to find it. My father was a doctor there."

"No shit? You were raised here?"

"I didn't say I was raised here. I said I was *born* here," Deon said. "Both my folks were killed when I was a kid, so my brother and I moved to Missouri, where we were raised by my grandparents."

"Loomis Booker, yeah, I knew he was from Missouri. I sure wish I could have met him," Jerry said.

"Why?"

"I've always admired him."

"Along with George Washington Carver and Booker T. Washington."

"Well, yes, but you make it sound so patronizing."

"Ask white folks about Negroes they admire, and those are the only names you hear. They aren't the only Negroes who have ever accomplished anything, you know."

"I know that," Jerry said defensively. "I know about people like Crispus Attucks, Sojourner Truth, and Absalom Jones."

"Absalom Jones?" Deon asked with a chuckle. "You got me there. Who is Absalom Jones?"

"He was the first Negro priest in the Episcopal church."

"Are you Episcopalian?" Alicia asked.

"No."

"Then how did you know that? I'm Episcopalian, and I didn't know that."

"I don't know. It's just something I read once, and it stuck with me."

"What do you know about Andrew Booker?" Alicia asked.

"Andrew Booker? Not much, I'm afraid. I have to admit, I'm not much of a basketball fan," Jerry replied.

Alica laughed. "I guess not. *Artemus* is the basketball player. Andrew Booker was Deon's father."

"The doctor?"

"He was more than just a doctor," Alicia said. "He was a medical researcher. He helped develop blood plasma."

"No shit! That's quite an accomplishment, isn't it? I mean, think how many lives that's saved over the years. You must be very proud of your father, Deon."

"I am. Unfortunately, developing blood plasma didn't do him any good."

"What do you mean? He got cheated out of the patent or something?"

"Something like that," Deon said wryly.

"Deon's mother and father were in a terrible automobile accident," Alicia explained. "His mother was killed instantly, but his father survived the crash and would have lived if he had been given blood plasma."

"Oh, wow! The very thing he developed could have saved his life and they didn't have any at the hospital. What a horrible shame!"

"You don't know how much of a shame," Alicia said. "They *did* have plasma at the hospital—but it was reserved for white use only. By the time they got some plasma from a source set aside for Negroes, it was too late. Dr. Booker had died."

Jerry sat silently for a moment. "My God, Deon," he finally said softly. "How can you stand to even look at a white person?"

"It hasn't always been easy," Deon admitted. Suddenly he laughed, breaking the somber mood. "Especially if it's an ugly white boy with red hair and freckles."

"Hey, Deon, speak for yourself," Violet said. She

reached back and rubbed her hand through Jerry's bright-red hair. "I think Jerry is a *pretty* white boy."

"Hey, cut that out," Jerry said, pushing Violet's hand away as the others laughed at his discomfort. "So, why have we stopped, anyway?"

"I'm hungry," Deon replied. "I thought maybe we could get something to eat from that place back there."

Jerry turned in his seat and looked back at a ramshackle little store Deon was pointing toward. "You want to go in *there*?" he asked. "Man, are you crazy? If we're going to integrate something, I don't want to get my skull crushed in over some redneck dump like that."

"I'm not thinking integration, I'm thinking eating. I'm so hungry my stomach thinks my mouth went on strike."

"Baby, in all the time I've known you, your mouth has never gone on strike," Violet teased.

"I'm hungry, too," Alicia said.

"Come on, are you folks serious? You really want to go into that place?" Jerry asked.

"We don't all have to go," Deon said. "You and Alicia could go and get some stuff for all of us. You know, cheese, bologna, bread, mayonnaise, stuff like that."

"Yeah, that's a good idea. We could have a picnic," Alicia suggested.

"Get a pickle, will you?" Violet asked. "I love big dill pickles. They're really good on hot days like this."

"Come on, Jerry, let's go," Alicia said.

"All right," Jerry said, climbing out of the car. "I guess I wouldn't mind having something to eat myself."

As they walked away toward the store, the breeze stirred the leaves of the trees that lined the road. Frogs croaked from the cypress trees, and, from somewhere deep in the forest, a woodpecker drummed loudly on a hollow tree, its efforts amplified by the resonance of the swamp.

"Listen to that," Alicia said. "Doesn't it sound peaceful?"

"Sure, if you like rattlesnakes, cottonmouths, alligators, and pythons," Jerry muttered.

Alicia laughed. "I don't seriously think there are any alligators out there, and I know there aren't any pythons."

"Yeah, well, whatever. I just know I wouldn't want to go walking through there."

It was midsummer hot, but the trees, though somewhat back from the road, were tall enough to provide shade for Alicia and Jerry to walk in. The weeds and grass growing alongside the road were full of dust, and as they walked through them, little puffs rose from their feet. Grasshoppers and other insects fluttered before them, and occasionally cockleburrs stuck to their pant legs, and they stopped to pick them off.

Alicia thought about these last few weeks in Mississippi. The highlight had been the registering of several new voters. Negroes in their sixties and seventies who had never in their lifetime had the privilege of casting a vote would be able to in this year's election. Alicia felt very good about that.

There had been some bad times, too. Several times hecklers had gathered, and the mood had grown ugly. The police were present during those times, and the civil rights workers were told they were there to protect them from the angry citizens of the state. Alicia wondered, however, why the police stood in somber, helmeted lines facing them instead of the crowd of hecklers. She also wondered why, when the citizens shot BB guns at them, the police made no attempt to stop the assault. And when the police did go into action, the person on the receiving end of a billy club always seemed to be a civil rights worker.

They were almost to the little general store. The wood was unpainted, and a sagging, rotting porch hung on the front. Many of the wallboards were no doubt as rotten as the porch floor, but they were covered with large sheet-tin signs that hid the decay.

IF YOUR SNUFF'S TOO STRONG, IT'S WRONG. USE TUBE ROSE.

R.C. COLA. BEST, BY TASTE TEST.

PURE SALT. JEFFERSON ISLAND SALT.

In front of the store were two old, round gas pumps with glass cylinders at the top and hand pumps on the side. Alicia hadn't seen one of them in years. She remembered her father once explaining that the gas was dispensed by pumping the handle back and forth until the glass was filled, then letting gravity feed the gas through the hose. The glass container was graduated to mark up to ten gallons, and the amount of gas sold was determined by the graduation marks in the glass cylinder.

An old pickup truck was parked to one side of the store. It might have been red at one time, but it was so badly rusted that it was difficult to tell what color it was supposed to be. One of the doors was wired shut. Fresh tire marks behind it showed that it was a working truck, however, and not merely an abandoned vehicle like the '37 Ford coupe on the opposite side of the store. The wheels, hood, and engine were all gone from the Ford, and weeds grew up through the space where the engine should have been. A rusting license plate on the front bumper of the car said "Mississippi" at the top of the plate, and "Panola" at the bottom, indicating the car had last been registered in Panola County. The plate was dated 1954.

Two men were sitting on the edge of the porch, listening to a portable radio broadcasting a baseball game.

"Two outs, two men on, and the next batter is Stan 'the Man' Musial. Sandy Koufax watches Musial come to the plate as he takes off his hat and wipes the sweat from his brow."

"That Jew bastard better wipe the sweat off *his* face," one of the two men cackled loudly to be heard over the radio. "Musial's goin' to knock the cover off the ball."

"Yeah, I don't know. Koufax is good when his stuff is workin'," the other said, his brow knitted with worry.

"Here's the windup, and the pitch. Strike one, just cutting the inside corner of the plate. The count is one and oh. The crowd is nervous. They want a hit here. The Cardinals are down by one here in the last half of the ninth. And here's the second pitch. Strike two!"

"Shit! What'd I tell ya? That Jew bastard is going to strike him out."

"Musial ain't out yet."

The door to the store opened, and a man came out sipping an orange drink. He was dressed in coveralls, and his face was wrinkled, either from age or hard life.

"Hey, John, whaddya think?" the first man yelled. "Is Musial goin' to get a hit or not?"

"Don't think much about it one way or the other," John replied. He glanced over at Alicia and Jerry entering the dusty yard—though she wasn't sure he even saw them—then got into the old pickup, started it with a whining grind of starter and engine, and drove away with the rattling nearly drowning out the crunching sound of the tires on the gravel.

"Swung on and fouled back out of play. The count stays at two and oh."

Alicia and Jerry nodded at the two men on the porch and entered the store. It was hot inside, despite a tall floor fan roaring near the counter. The fan was pointed toward the grocery clerk, a heavyset woman in a bright print dress. She was sitting on a stool behind the counter, listening to the same ball game as were the men out front. Her radio, a small brown plastic model with a round dial, sat on a shelf behind her, between a roll of twine and a hot plate. The radio, hot plate, fan, and at least one other electrical device were all plugged into the same outlet through a collection of extension cords and adapters.

"Here's a ball, low and outside. The count goes to two and one."

The store smelled of animal feed and soap. The bare, unpainted plank floor looked just like the porch. Alicia and Jerry walked back to the meat counter and peered through the glass. The clerk hauled herself off the stool and wandered back to them.

"Heavens to Betsy, I didn't even hear y'all drive up. 'Course, I been listenin' to the baseball game and wasn't payin' no attention. That Harry Carey can make 'em sound so excitin', can't he? Can I help y'all with somethin'?"

"We'd like two pounds of sliced bologna," Alicia said.

The woman began cutting the meat from a large roll.

"Ball two. Musial is really working Koufax now."

"Did y'all hear about them two Freedom Riders they just found over to the dam?" the clerk asked as she carved thick slices with a butcher knife.

"Freedom Riders?"

"Well, whatever you call 'em. Them folks that come down from N'Yawk agitatin' our coloreds. I'm talkin' 'bout that white girl and colored boy that was travelin' together. They found 'em dead."

The blood drained from Alicia's face. "Vivian Goodman and George Tatum?" she managed to ask.

"Ball three! It's a full count now."

"Yeah, I think that's who it was. I 'member the name Goodman, anyway. That's a Joosh name, ain't it?"

"I . . . I don't know," Alicia said. She felt sick and put her hand on the edge of the counter to steady herself. Until this moment she had held on to the irrational hope that they would be found alive and well.

"Well, I tell you the truth, it's a shame," the woman said. She tore a length off the roll of brown butcher's paper and wrapped the meat carefully, then taped it down. "I mean, I don't want no Yankees comin' down here agitatin' our colored folk any more'n anyone else. But I sure don't want to see any of 'em get kilt. The press up north got enough bad to say 'bout Mississippi as it is, without addin' on to it by some damn-fool killin's. 'Course, I don't know what them two young folks was thinkin' of, comin' down here like that, a colored boy with a white girl. They was just askin' for trouble. It just breaks my heart to think about what their poor mamas and daddies must be goin' through now. Okay, what else can I get for you?"

"Swung on and hit hard down the right field line, curving, curving . . . foul ball! Koufax is only one pitch away from winning this ball game now, but Musial is hanging tough."

When Alicia didn't answer, Jerry spoke up. "We'll have a loaf of bread, a pound of that cheese, and a jar each of mustard and mayonnaise. Oh, and do you have any dill pickles?"

"Sure do, hon. We got 'em in a jar and in a barrel," the woman answered.

"Swung on and there it goes . . . deep, deep into right field! It's way, way back there! It might be . . . it could be . . . IT IS! A home run for Musial, and the Cardinals win the ball game!" Harry Carey shouted. Adding to the cheers of the thousands at the stadium were the whoops and shouts from the two men who were listening out front.

"I'll take one from the barrel," Jerry said. "You have any pop?"

"Beg your pardon?"

"Soft drinks?"

The woman still looked confused.

"Holy cow! What an end to this game! Listen to that crowd!"

"Pepsi? Coke?"

The woman smiled. "Oh, you mean sodies? Course we do, hon. Over there in that box. Watch yourself when you dip them out, though. That water's ice cold."

Jerry went over to the drink box, rummaged around in the frigid water, and pulled out four drinks.

"Well, now, will that be—" The woman suddenly noticed that Alicia was crying. "What is it, hon?" she asked, her brow furrowed. "Why you cryin' like that, girl? Is it about them two Freedom Riders? You cryin' about them, ain't you? Did you know them?"

Alicia nodded. "Yes. I knew them."

"Oh, my!" The woman looked through the dirty front window of the little store. "Oh, my, you're one of 'em, ain't you? You're one of them Freedom Riders. Are y'all here with coloreds?"

"Yes," Jerry admitted.

The woman's eyes grew wide with fear. "Look here, I ain't never caused nobody no trouble, an' I swear I didn't know nothin' 'bout them two Freedom Riders gettin' themselves kilt till I heard about them findin' the bodies this mornin'. Please, don't let the coloreds hurt me!"

The woman's reaction so surprised Alicia that she quit crying and stared at her. "Why are you so frightened?" she asked. "Just what do you expect to happen?"

"Please!" the woman implored. "Y'all don't have to pay nothin' for the stuff. Take it! Just don't let 'em hurt me."

"Don't worry, they aren't even with us. They're parked down the road. And we have every intention of paying for our purchases."

Alicia gave the clerk the money; then she and Jerry left the store, puzzled and even a bit angered by the woman's irrational response.

When they got back to the car, they found that Violet had already spread a blanket on the grass on the other side of a drainage ditch, and she and Deon were waiting patiently.

"Did y'all get my pickle?" Violet asked.

"Pickle? Nobody said anything about a pickle," Jerry replied.

"Jerry," Violet whined.

"He got it," Alicia said softly. "We got everything."

"Good, good. Let's eat," Deon said. He studied Alicia's face. "You've been crying," he challenged. "What happened?"

"They found them, Deon," Jerry said.

"Found who?" Violet asked. Then, reading their expressions, she knew who. "You're talkin' 'bout Vivian and George, aren't you?"

"Yes."

"Dead?" Deon asked.

Jerry nodded.

"Shit!" Deon shook his head. "Where'd they find them?"

"Over at some dam," Jerry answered.

They were pensive as they spread out the food on the blanket and made their sandwiches.

"I don't know," Deon finally said. He sighed. "Maybe we're crazy thinking we can do anything to get through to these redneck bastards. Maybe we're just wasting time here."

Suddenly a pickup truck stopped just in front of their car, sending up a cloud of dust. Two men rode in the cab, two more in the bed.

"Uh-oh. I wonder what they want?" Jerry muttered.

"I don't know. But I have a feeling they didn't stop to offer us dessert," Deon answered. "Check out the flag."

A ragged and faded Confederate flag fluttered from the radio antenna.

The four men got out of the truck and started toward them. All were either carrying pistols or had pistols stuck in their belts. Two of them, Alicia noticed, were the men who had been listening to the ball game on the porch of the store.

"What'd I tell you, Harley Mack?" one of the two from the store said. "Didn't I tell you they was some of them agitators?"

"That you did, Charley, that you did," Harley Mack replied. Something about his attitude suggested that he was the leader of the group.

Deon, Violet, Jerry, and Alicia stood up apprehensively, nervously watching their visitors.

"What y'all want?" Violet asked.

"What y'all want? What y'all want?" Harley Mack mimicked. "It's 'what *do* y'all want.' Come on, girl. If you're goin' to live with white folks, you're goin' to at least have to learn how to speak English good. Now, let me hear you. What *do* y'all want?"

Violet was silent.

"Goddammit, girl, I said say it!" Harley Mack demanded menacingly.

"What . . . do . . . y'all . . . want?" Violet said in a small, frightened voice.

"I'll tell you what I want," one of the other men said. He squirted a stream of chewing tobacco, then wiped the back of his hand across his mouth. He didn't get it all, and brown juice dribbled down his chin. He grinned broadly, showing crooked, yellow teeth. He rubbed the front of his pants. "I want a little poontang."

One of the other men laughed. "Hey, Pete, would that be *coon*-poontang?"

All of the men laughed at that one.

"Why don't you just go away and leave us alone?" Alicia said. "We aren't bothering anyone."

"Well, now, we can't just let you go," Harley Mack said. "We the law, now. We got to take you in."

"You're the law?" Alicia said.

"You deaf, girl? Didn't I just tell you we was? I was made a deputy to look for them two civil rights workers, and I deputized these here boys to help me. That makes us the law."

"We haven't violated any law," Deon said.

"Yeah, you have. You're trespassin' on private property."

"We just stopped for a few minutes to eat," Jerry said.

"Yeah, but you done crossed over the ditch. The ditch is the boundary of the road easement. On the other side of the ditch where you folks are is private property."

"Whose property is it?" Alicia said.

"Whose property? Fuck, what difference does it make?"

"The property isn't posted," Alicia said. "We've caused no physical damage to it. Unless the property owner files a complaint for trespassing, we have violated no law."

"Is that a fact? Well, me and my deputies say you have."

"That's another thing. Even if you are a deputy, you don't have the authority to deputize others."

"Where you gettin' all that? You a lawyer or somethin'?" Harley Mack asked with a sneer.

"Yes."

Harley Mack snickered. "Now, ain't that the shits! Well, let me tell you, Miss White-nigger Lawyer. This here property belongs to a white man, and if any nigger gets on any white man's private property in these parts, it's a violation of the law. And if I want to deputize some of my friends to help me keep the law, then I'll goddammit deputize 'em!"

"Cool it, Alicia," Jerry said under his breath.

"Excuse me," Deon said. "Would any of you happen to be from Delta?"

"I'm from Delta," one of the men replied.

"Marvin, you dumb shit, shut the fuck up!" Harley Mack said.

"If you're from Delta, ask Stump Pollard about me. My name is Deon Booker, and these are my friends."

"Ask Stump Pollard?" Harley Mack said. "You think any of us care what that Communist sonuvabitch says?"

"Stump Pollard a Communist? What are you talking about? He was the chief of police."

"He was, but he ain't no more. Now he's just a nigger-lovin' Commie."

"I think we had enough of this lip flappin'. What are we goin' to do with 'em, Harley Mack?" Charley asked.

Harley Mack looked over his shoulder. "There's an abandoned machine shed just beyond the trees there. Let's take 'em there."

"What about the car?" Pete asked. "There's still lots of feds pokin' aroun'. They'll see it here, and they'll start askin' questions."

"I could torch it," Charley suggested. "I done a pretty good job on the one that nigger boy and white girl was in."

"You?" Alicia gasped, horrified. "You burned their car?"

"Charley, you got a big mouth, you know that?" Harley Mack said angrily. "Don't listen to him, girl. He didn't do nothin' of the kind."

"Shit, why don't we just kill 'em an' dump 'em somewhere in the slough?" one of the others asked.

"No," Harley Mack answered. "Let's take 'em to the shed and leave 'em there while I figure out what to do with 'em."

"What about the car?"

"Leave it. There's so many sightseers an' all now, it'll be a couple of days 'fore anyone gets suspicious over it."

"Let's go, niggers," Charley ordered. "An' I'm referrin' to all of you as niggers, 'cause as far as I'm concerned that's what you all are."

"Hey!" Harley Mack chortled. "Why ain't y'all singin'?

What's that song you always singin'? Oh, yeah, 'We shall overcome.' Sing it for me."

The little group was silent.

"I said, sing it for me!" Harley Mack raised his gun.

Violet started to sing, but Deon shut her up.

"Hey, what you doin', nigger? Don't you tell that little girl to shut up."

"We aren't going to do tricks for you," Deon said.

"The hell you ain't. 'Case you didn' notice, we all got guns. We got 'em, an' you don't. That means you goin' to do any fuckin' damn thing we tell you to do."

"We aren't going to sing," Deon said.

"You'll sing or I'll kill your black ass."

Deon remembered what Dr. King had said in Atlanta—how no one was really free until they were free of the fear of death. As Deon stared at the hate-filled eyes of his adversaries, he suddenly felt a calmness descend over him, and he knew what Dr. King was talking about.

"Go ahead," he said quietly. "Kill me."

"Goddammit! Goddammit, I'm serious!" Harley Mack sputtered.

"I am, too," Deon said. "I'm not going to sing for you. If you're going to kill me, do it."

"You heard 'im, Harley Mack. He wants us to kill 'im," Charley said. He raised his pistol. "Shit, I say let's do it!"

"Charley, you're crazy!" Marvin said. "We're just havin' some fun here! We ain't out to kill nobody."

"You heard the nigger; he wants us to kill 'im," Charley said. "I'm willin' to oblige."

"Put your gun down, Charley," Harley Mack growled.

"Come on, Harley Mack."

"I said put your gun down! Let's get 'em over to the shed. Move, niggers," he ordered gruffly.

Nothing else was said about singing.

They headed into the slough, slogging through water and mud and fighting branches slapping against them. Violet was walking just in front of Alicia, and Alicia saw that she was shaking with fear.

"It'll be all right, Violet," Alicia said with more conviction than she felt.

"I'm so scared!" Violet whispered.

"Don't let them know," Alicia cautioned. "Whatever you do, don't let them know."

"Hey, you, white-nigger bitch. I didn't say you could talk. Did I tell you you could talk?" Harley Mack snarled. "Y'all just keep movin' there, and keep your fuckin' mouths shut."

Mercifully, they reached the machine shed several minutes later. Harley Mack opened the door and motioned with his pistol that they should all go inside.

Violet started through the door, but Pete stopped her with the barrel of his gun.

"Not you." He smiled wickedly. "I'm gonna change my luck with you."

"Whooee! Listen to ol' Pete," one of the others said. "I do believe he's goin' to get in a little sport-fuckin' with this girl."

Pete reached for the front of Violet's shirt and jerked it so hard that the buttons popped off. It hung open, her white bra contrasting sharply with her dark skin.

"No!" Alicia screamed, starting toward Pete. "Leave my sister alone!"

Alicia had just reached Pete when she caught a quick, angry movement from the corner of her eye. She felt a sharp pain on the back of her head; then everything went black.

Like a weighted cork resurfacing from deep within a pool, Alicia floated back to consciousness. She opened her eyes and realized she was lying with her head on Violet's lap. Violet was rubbing her forehead gently with long, cool fingers.

Alicia focused on Violet's face and was horrified to see that it was puffy and bruised. One eye was nearly swollen shut.

"Violet, oh, no! They . . ." Alicia tried to sit up, but a wave of dizziness and nausea overtook her, and she slipped back down.

"Shush," Violet said, holding her finger over her lips. "Everything's goin' to be all right."

"Okay, now, pull," Alicia heard Deon say, and she turned her head to see Deon and Jerry yanking on one end of a plank. The other end was jammed against a crack in the wall. The two young men pulled and strained, but nothing happened.

"Hold it, hold it," Jerry said. "If we pull any more, we're going to break this board, and we won't make a dint in the wall."

"Those rednecks wrapped a chain around the door handles," Violet explained to Alicia.

Thunder sounded in the distance; a few moments later rain splattered noisily on the tin roof.

"Well, if it rains hard enough, at least we won't have to worry about them coming back and setting fire to the place," Deon said.

"Fire? You mean they're going to burn us up in here?" Alicia asked, feeling the blood drain from her face.

"They were talkin' about it," Violet said.

"But don't worry," Jerry assured her. "We'll find some way out of here, long before that happens."

It grew dark, and the rain continued falling. It hammered against the roof and walls and puddled on the ground. It blew in sheets across the swamp and drummed into the trees. The steady rhythm of the rain was punctuated now and then by jagged streaks of lightning—barely visible through cracks in the plank walls—and loud reports of thunder, cracking sharply at first, then rolling through the valleys, cascading out of the hills like pounding surf.

Alicia shivered. "I can't see a foot in front of my face. And I'm cold."

"You want to snuggle for warmth?" Jerry invited.

"You don't mind?"

Jerry chuckled. "Well, it's not exactly my idea of a romantic evening. But it might keep us from freezing to death."

The four young civil rights workers huddled together and soon drifted off to sleep from exhaustion.

"Wake up!" Deon hissed. "Wake up! Someone's trying to get in here!"

Alicia opened her eyes, then sat up. It was morning. The rain had stopped, and the inside of the shed was dimly lit by slits of sunlight that slipped through the cracks between the planks.

Violet, a frightened look on her face, listened intently.

Jerry sat up and rubbed his face. "What's going on?" he asked.

"There's someone outside," Alicia whispered.

"What are we going to do?" Jerry asked, alarmed.

Deon looked around. A low partition jutted out from the back of the room. "Violet, you and Alicia get back there behind the wall. Here, Jerry"—he bent down and handed Jerry a short length of planking that was lying near one wall—"take this." Then he found a piece of a two-by-four for himself.

"These aren't much against guns."

"Maybe not, but I'm not going down without a fight."

"Me, neither," Jerry agreed.

Hefting their makeshift clubs, the two young men crept toward the door. With their weapons at the ready, they waited.

From outside came the sound of the chain being pulled loose. The door creaked open, and a brilliant bar of light splashed inside. A gray-haired white man stuck his head in.

"Deon? Deon, are you in here?"

"*Chief Pollard?*" Deon gasped, relief flooding into his voice. "Chief Pollard, is that really you?"

The man chuckled. "I haven't been chief in over fifteen years, but, yeah, it's me. How you doin', son?"

Deon laughed. "I'm doing a lot better now that you're here."

"Come on. Let's get out of here before those crazy bastards come back," Stump said. He saw Jerry, smiled, and stuck out his hand. "Stump Pollard."

"I'm Jerry Wiggins. This is Alicia Canfield and Violet Simmons."

"You kids all right?" He studied Violet's bruised face. "No, I can see that you're not. Let's get the hell out of here and get you to a doctor, young lady."

They piled out of the machine shed and stood blinking in the bright light for a moment, then started walking back across the slough.

Deon asked, "How did you know where to find us?"

"Marvin told me where you were."

"Who's Marvin?"

"Marvin Posey. He's my nephew."

"How'd *he* know we were in there?"

Stump grimaced. "Hell, boy, he was one of the fellas who put y'all in there."

"Some nephew," Jerry grumbled.

"At least he had a change of heart," Alicia said.

Suddenly a shot sounded; with a grunt, Deon fell on his face.

"*Deon!*" Violet screamed.

"Get down!" Stump shouted, pulling out his revolver, and they all dived for the ground. Alicia heard him fire a shot, and she lifted her head slightly and looked around, seeing for the first time three men near a clump of trees. One of the three men slumped to the ground.

"Throw your guns down!" Stump shouted at them.

"You killed Harley Mack, you crazy old bastard!" one of the two remaining men called back.

"Throw your guns down or by God I'll kill you, too!" Stump yelled.

One of the two men started to raise his gun, and Stump cocked the hammer on his. The one who had made the threatening move threw his pistol down; the other man followed suit.

"Now, get your hands up and get over here," Stump shouted.

As the two men complied, Stump walked back to Deon, lying facedown in the dirt. "Deon," he said anxiously, "are you hurt?"

"I think so," Deon answered calmly.

"Where were you hit?"

"I don't know. I can't feel anything."

"We'll get you out of here," Jerry said, reaching for him.

"No!" Stump warned. He knelt beside Deon, then pinched his leg. Hard.

"Can you feel that?"

"Can I feel what?"

"This." Stump pinched him again.

"I don't feel anything. Help me up. Let's get out of here."

Stump shook his head. "I think we'd better keep you right here until we get an ambulance." He stood up and glared at the two men by the trees. "You boys, get over here! Now!"

The two men reached them, and Alicia recognized them as the ones called Charley and Pete from the night before.

"Take the shoestring out of your left shoe, both of you," Stump ordered.

"Say what?" Charley asked.

"Do it!" Stump snapped, making a threatening move with his pistol.

Quickly the two men dropped to one knee and began removing their left shoelaces.

"Now put your hands behind your back. Alicia, you and Violet tie their thumbs together. That'll hold 'em better'n anything. Jerry, just keep walking straight and you'll find yourself back out on the highway. Hurry on over to the general store and call the sheriff in Sardis. They got an ambulance service there. Tell him to send it on the double."

"Yes, sir," Jerry said.

"You think the sheriff is goin' to take your word over ours, nigger lover?" Charley asked Stump scornfully. "You just kilt one of his deputies. He's goin' to put *you* in jail, not us."

Stump glowered at the man. "We'll just have to see about that, won't we?"

NEW YORK

Sheri Warren had taken an apartment in a grand old residential hotel on Central Park South. It was large, comfortable, and tastefully if not expensively decorated. The living room had two brocade-covered sofas facing each other across a teakwood coffee table. A very good imitation Persian rug covered most of the parquet floor. Original oil paintings hung on the walls, and though they appealed to Sheri and she thought them impressive, she was certain none were too costly.

Besides the large living room, the apartment featured a small wood-paneled den, an unusually large dining room, an excellently equipped kitchen, and two bedrooms. Both bedrooms had wonderful views of Central Park and the regimented tall buildings flanking it.

Sheri sat at the dining-room table, nursing a second cup of coffee and looking over a portfolio of new designs she had been working on. They were done in colored inks to show not only the lines but the bold, almost outlandish hues. More than an evolution, these would be a revolution against traditional design. The collection was, in fact, such a radical departure that it would either propel her to the top of the fashion world or drop her into obscurity overnight. It was a risk she wanted to take, and she wanted to take it on her own. She was going to submit her resignation to E. J. Buckner and Company today.

The apartment door opened, and Mrs. Edith Spranger stepped inside. The stout, middle-aged housekeeper tucked her keys back into her oversized black purse, then walked over to the closet to put it away.

"Good morning, Mrs. Warren," she said.

Sheri had told her housekeeper many times that it was "Miss" and not "Mrs." Warren, but the housekeeper either couldn't or wouldn't remember that her employer was an unwed mother.

"Good morning, Mrs. Spranger. Does it look like rain?"

"It's a little cloudy, but I don't think it's going to rain. Is Scooter better today?"

"Much better, thank you. He coughed very little during the night."

Mrs. Spranger smiled broadly. "It was the spice tea," she insisted. "That's what cleared him up."

"I'm sure it was." Sheri finished her coffee, then stood up. "Well, I must be going. I have a ten o'clock meeting."

"But you've had no breakfast, Mrs. Warren. Let me fix you a bite of something."

"Thank you, but there's no time."

"It is only just after eight."

"Yes, I know, but there are some things I must take care of."

"You should have three balanced meals," Mrs. Spranger told her in a motherly fashion. "You can't work if you don't eat enough to keep up your energy." Mrs. Spranger's stout build was ready evidence of her belief in the need of keeping up her energy.

"I'll eat a good lunch," Sheri promised. "Scooter!

Scooter, I'm going now!" she called. "Come kiss me good-bye and say hello to Mrs. Spranger."

Scooter came dashing into the living room, holding his arms aloft. Sheri hoisted him up.

"Ooof," she grunted. "You're getting so big I'm not going to be able to pick you up much longer. Pretty soon you're going to have to pick *me* up."

Scooter laughed. "That's funny. Little kids can't pick up their mommies."

"Well, one day you'll be able to. Now, you be a good boy for Mrs. Spranger."

"Oh, Scooter is always a good boy. Aren't you, Scooter?"

"Yes," Scooter agreed, nodding emphatically. "I'm always a good boy."

Sheri kissed him, grabbed her purse and portfolio, and waved at Mrs. Spranger as she stepped out the door. Five minutes later she was in a taxi headed for E. J. Buckner and Company.

Sheri had mixed feelings about leaving the company. On the one hand, Mr. Buckner had been the first person to take her seriously. As a designer, she had been a complete outsider who dropped in out of the clear blue sky. Her attaining recognition for her designs was as unlikely as an amateur performer wandering in off the street into a Broadway theater and being made star of the production. And yet Buckner had seen something in her work that made him take the risk with her.

Although Sheri hadn't known it at the time, it hadn't been a totally magnanimous move on Buckner's part. He had been desperately in need of a design hit. He had broken into the fashion scene in the forties—and some wags insisted he hadn't had a good idea since shoulder pads. He had seemed totally incapable of coping with the dazzling, dizzying sixties. It had been a long time since the company had produced anything fresh and new, and by the time Sheri came along, it was try something different or go under. With nothing to lose, he took the gamble with her, and it paid off. Right now, E. J. Buckner was *the* stellar fashion manufacturer in the industry.

But it wasn't all rosy. Sheri had discovered that even though her line of clothes was the hottest in the field, she was the least compensated of all the designers she knew. Despite that, she would have been content to wait for her reward had

Buckner not started marketing some of his other lines under the SheriWear name.

Sheri recalled the conversation she had had with him about it, "It's merely a marketing ploy," he had explained. "It's business, that's all. When you have a hot brand name, you go with it for as long as you can. Let's face it, my dear. Your name is hot, hot, hot."

"It won't be hot for long if you flood it with inferior designs," she had argued.

"Inferior designs? May I remind you, my dear, that two of those designs are my own?"

"Yes, yours, not mine. If it bears *my* name, it should be my design."

Buckner had smiled patronizingly. "Oh, but I thought you understood. It isn't your name, my dear. It's my name . . . bought and paid for."

Sheri felt her resentment rising as the taxi worked its way through garment district streets clogged with trucks and clothing racks, and by the time the driver stopped in front of the Buckner Building on Seventh Avenue, she was itching for a confrontation. After paying the driver, she tucked her black leather portfolio under her arm and marched inside.

Like the street outside, the interior of the building was a beehive of activity. The lower floors housed the shipping department, where the clothes were wrapped and packed to be sent out to customers across the country. Upstairs were the manufacturing areas, cutting rooms and sewing rooms where scores of sewing machines hummed; fitting rooms, where models changed dresses dozens of times per day to parade in front of buyers from stores on both coasts and a dozen places in between; and, in the front of the building—off the operations areas—the designers' studios and the executive offices. It was very hot upstairs year round, since the heat was kept high for the models, who were often nude or nearly so.

A tall, bony young woman wearing only skimpy bikini panties was leaning against the door of one of the fitting rooms as Sheri walked by. The model was smoking, and she reached over to grind the cigarette butt out in a fruit-jar lid that sat on the windowsill. Brown paint was peeling off the sill. A dingy gray pigeon sat just outside the window. It didn't move when the model's hand came toward it, as if it were aware of the pane between them.

"Hello, Mindy," Sheri said. "Have you seen Mr. Buckner this morning?"

"He's in there," Mindy answered, tossing her head toward the fitting room.

"Thanks."

Buckner, in his midfifties, was short and chubby. He had wavy blond hair, watery blue eyes, and sensual lips. His fingers were stubby, but his fingernails were long and impeccably manicured. He was leaning against the wall, arms folded across his chest, watching a model slip into one of the company's new bra dresses. This model was also naked except for panties. Dorothy Hoffman, Buckner's executive assistant, was helping the young woman get dressed. It was a well-known secret among all the models that Dorothy was more of a sexual threat to them than Buckner. However, he seemed to enjoy watching Dorothy lust after the girls.

"No, no, no," Buckner complained. "I want to see more tit, not less. Pull the top down a little."

"If you pull it down any farther, her nipples are going to show," Dorothy insisted.

"And is that a problem?"

"Only if you want to sell the dress, E.J.," Dorothy replied. "While they are lovely nipples, I agree, I'm afraid we would find a somewhat limited market for a dress that exposed everything."

"The whole idea of the bra dress is to titillate, isn't it? Find some way to be more titillating without showing more nipple," Buckner said. "I'm sure you can do it. Oh, good morning, Miss Warren. I thought you weren't going to be in today."

"Scooter is much better," Sheri said.

"Good, good. Listen, I've got some more designs I want to put into SheriWear. Why don't you take a look at them . . . maybe make a suggestion or two? That way they will be like yours."

"Not quite. Mr. Buckner, we need to talk."

Buckner sighed. "Not again. I thought we had all this settled. Oh, very well. Come on into my office."

He led Sheri into his large, lavishly decorated suite at the front of the top floor.

"Tea?" he offered, walking over to a silver samovar.

"No, thank you."

"I hope you don't mind if I indulge." He drew a cup of tea in a gold-rimmed china cup, then settled down in a baronial leather chair. "And now, my dear, you wanted to discuss something with me?"

"Yes." Sheri drew a deep breath. "Mr. Buckner, I don't want you to think I am unappreciative of what you have done for me. You took a chance on me and my designs."

"I don't think you have any idea how big a chance that was," Buckner said. "To introduce an unknown quantity into a major company . . . It could have been disastrous. We might well have gone under."

Sheri checked the desire to say that the company would have gone under if she *hadn't* come along. Instead, she continued in a conciliatory vein. "Yes, well, as I say, I am very appreciative of all you've done for me. But I think the time has come for me to move on. I am herewith submitting my resignation."

Buckner took a swallow of his tea before he replied. "The SheriWear line is well established now. You've done some good things, and you've made some money. Why rock the boat? Why don't you leave things just the way they are?"

"I don't want to leave things just the way they are," Sheri replied. "For one thing, I know that your most successful line of clothes is the SheriWear line. And I also know that I am the lowest paid of all your designers."

"Oh, come, now. You haven't fared that badly, have you?" Buckner insisted. "You have a nice apartment, lovely new clothes. . . . You're doing quite well, actually."

"But I'm not doing as well as I could be doing."

Buckner finished his tea, then set the cup and saucer very carefully on a pedestal table with lions' heads carved on the legs. "Perhaps if I increased your compensation somewhat?" he suggested.

Sheri shook her head. "No. I do thank you for making the offer, though. But I really feel it's time for me to go out on my own."

"If you feel that's what you must do, then by all means, do so." Buckner stood. "Is that all?"

Sheri, surprised by the ease with which he acquiesced,

stood as well. "Uh, yes. That's all. I will, of course, stay on for two more weeks."

"That won't be necessary. I can see no real purpose in your continuing here." He smiled wanly. "I doubt that we would get the full measure of your creative talents."

"Well, I must say, this is very gracious of you. And I am very pleased that you aren't making it difficult."

"I wish you all the best," Buckner said. "I do feel it is only fair to tell you, however, that even though you might leave, your name must stay here."

"You mean SheriWear."

"No, I mean Sheri Warren."

"What?"

"The name 'Sheri Warren' is the sole property of E.J. Buckner and Company. We hold the copyright."

Sheri felt a pulse in her temple begin to throb. "What do you mean, you hold the copyright? It's *my* name. You can't take my name away from me."

Buckner chuckled. "Oh, my dear, I haven't taken your name away from you. Sheri Warren is still your name. You just can't use it to market a line of clothes, that's all."

An hour later Sheri sat in one of the leather chairs that surrounded the huge, highly polished oval, mahogany table in the conference room of the law firm of Evert, Evert, McConnel, and Daigh. John Daigh sat across from her, one hand resting on his bald forehead as he studied Sheri's contract. After several moments he sighed, then took off his glasses and laid them on the table beside the document.

"I'm afraid it's all quite legal," he said.

"You mean Buckner owns my name?"

"Yes."

Sheri leaned back in her chair and scowled at the lawyer. "I don't see how that's possible."

Daigh tapped the contract with his index finger. "It's possible because you gave it to him. It isn't all that unusual. This sort of thing is standard practice. If an established business undertakes to develop and promote a particular brand or name, then they have a right to expect some return on their investment. I will say that what is, perhaps, a little unusual about this particular contract is that there is no provision for you to draw royalties from their use of your name."

"Well, can we fight it on that?" Sheri asked.

Daigh shook his head. "I'm afraid not. This is a work-for-hire contract. It was an unwise business move on your part to sign it; it is perfectly legitimate and would stand the test of a court challenge. Just out of curiosity, Miss Warren, whatever possessed you to sign such a contract?"

Sheri raked back her hair from her face. "I don't know," she said, sighing unhappily. "It was the first time anyone had ever shown any real interest in my designs. I was so excited, so eager to get them produced, that I never took the time to really study the contract. Frankly, even if I had studied it, I don't know that I would have noticed this. The only thing I looked at was the money—and at the time it seemed like a fortune."

"But you don't think it's a fortune now."

"I guess it's relative. My previous job was as a housekeeper, and to a housekeeper, eighteen thousand dollars a year is an enormous sum. But when I can go into any department store in America and see a line of clothes that I designed, it seems there should be more due me. Is that greedy of me?"

"Not at all," Daigh said. "You have every right to earn as much as your talent and skills will generate. Unfortunately, as a result of the contract you so unwisely signed, you have no legal right to produce a line of clothes using all or any part of the name 'Sheri Warren.' "

" 'What's in a name?' " Sheri quoted. " 'A rose by any other name would smell as sweet,' I suppose. I still have the —what did you call it? Talent and skill? That's the marketable commodity here, after all, not my name."

Daigh closed the contract folder, then slid it back toward her. "Would that that were true," he said, shaking his head dubiously. "I do wish you luck, Miss Warren."

Sitting in the loan office of the North American Commercial Bank, Sheri looked across the conference table and studied the faces of the chief loan officer, August Raymond, and the president of the bank, Carter Holbrook, who were examining the figures she had prepared for them.

"These are very impressive numbers, Miss Warren," Holbrook said, looking up from a ledger. "Can you verify that SheriWear is selling this well?"

"The figures *are* verified, Mr. Holbrook," Raymond put in. "When Miss Warren first came to me to discuss arrangements for a loan, I investigated the matter myself."

"Very, very impressive," Holbrook murmured. "I am tempted to make the loan, even though you are a woman. As you may or may not know, my dear, it is against bank policy to make business loans to women unless there is a male co-signer."

That took Sheri aback. "Why?" she asked.

Holbrook chuckled. "Well, it's obvious, isn't it? Women are notoriously bad business risks. I can think of no quicker way to get into difficulty with bank examiners than to have a lot of ill-advised loans out."

"But I am only asking for a hundred and fifty thousand dollars," Sheri insisted. "And, as you can see, SheriWear has netted well over that each month for nearly a year now."

"That's true," Holbrook said, stroking his chin. "As I say, this is an intriguing situation. What do you think, Mr. Raymond?"

"My initial inclination was to grant her the loan, Mr. Holbrook," Raymond replied. "But as there is a problem here, I wanted to come to you for your approval."

"You mean because she is a woman?"

"Yes, that, and . . ." Raymond let the sentence hang.

"And what? Is there something else?"

Raymond looked at Sheri. "Do you want to tell him, Miss Warren?"

"I can't use my name," Sheri said.

Holbrook looked puzzled. "I beg your pardon?"

Sheri cleared her throat. "My name, Sheri Warren, belongs to E. J. Buckner. He holds the copyright on it, and he is going to continue marketing SheriWear."

"Oh, my."

"But it doesn't matter," Sheri said quickly. "He doesn't have the rights to my talent." She reached for her portfolio. "Let me show you my ideas for a new line I am creating. It is far, far better than anything I've ever done for Buckner. And I don't even need my name. I'm going to call the line Contempowear." She opened the folder to show the bold lines and colors of her designs.

"Miss Warren, you may as well close that folder," Holbrook said, waving his hand toward it. "I wouldn't know a middy blouse from a pair of pajamas. I know absolutely nothing about fashion."

"Well, I *do* know about fashion, Mr. Holbrook. And these are good," Sheri said. "If you would just—"

Holbrook waved his hand impatiently. "What I *do* know," he interrupted, "is business. The sales numbers you showed me for SheriWear are impressive. I might have been persuaded to give you a loan against such a market position. But now you tell me that the name SheriWear—indeed, the very name 'Sheri Warren'—cannot be used by you. If you cannot use that name, then you do not have a market position, and if you have no market position, you have no collateral. I'm sorry, Miss Warren, there is nothing I can do. My hands are tied."

Once, when Sheri was a little girl, she fell from a tree. The fall knocked the breath from her body, and she lay there unable to breathe, terrified that perhaps she would never breathe again. That event came back to her with startling clarity, for she was feeling that very sensation at this very moment. She leaned back in the chair and looked across the table at the two men who, for now at least, had such control over her life. It had not occurred to her that she would not be able to get the money she needed to start her business. She hadn't thought beyond this point.

"What . . ." She stopped. She couldn't seem to get her brain to work.

"I beg your pardon?" Holbrook asked.

"What do I do now?" she asked in a very small voice.

Holbrook folded his hands in front of him. "Oh, come now, Miss Warren, it isn't as bad as all that. If E. J. Buckner has your name, I'm certain he would want to keep *you* as well. Why don't you go back and work for him? You were making a very good salary with him. There aren't many young women your age who could command that kind of money."

"No, I . . . I can't go back," Sheri said.

"Well, have it your own way," Holbrook said, standing. "I've explained why we can't loan you any money. I'm sorry, but I'm sure you understand. I must answer to my stockholders. If you were my own sister, Miss Warren, I would have to tell you no. Good day to you now."

He started out of the room; August Raymond stood as well and went with him. Still stunned by the fact that she was not going to get the loan, Sheri remained seated at the table.

She overheard Holbrook hissing angrily on the other side of the door.

"That's it!" Holbrook snapped. "No more women, period. I don't even want you to come to me with the suggestion that we'll make a business loan to a woman. Did you see how she took that? With a man, it's 'no,' a gentleman's handshake, and good-bye. With a woman, there's no telling what she's going to do. I thought she was going to faint on me, for God's sake. Now, get her the hell out of here!"

"I'll take care of it, Mr. Holbrook," Raymond said quietly.

Sheri pulled herself together, then stood and closed up her portfolio. She was just zipping it when the loan officer came back into the room.

"I'm sorry," he said. "I shouldn't have even brought you in to see him in the first place. I was afraid he would act that way, once he learned you had given your name away. Still . . ." The word dangled into silence.

"Still what, Mr. Raymond?" Sheri asked in a flat, emotionless voice.

"I think you do have something here," he said, tapping the portfolio. "I'm certainly not a fashion expert or anything, but there is something about these that is upbeat, modern, jazzy. I think they will sell."

"They'll never get the chance."

"Perhaps they will," Raymond countered. He stepped over to the door and looked up and down the hall, then came back to the table. "If you don't mind, I'm going to have someone give you a call."

"Who?"

"I'd rather not say, in case it doesn't work out."

"Then how will I know who it is if the person calls?"

"He'll identify himself and say I asked him to phone you," Raymond said mysteriously.

"Then what?"

"If he's interested, you will get the money you need."

"I don't know. This all sounds a little strange to me."

"Miss Warren, *you* aren't taking the risk here," Raymond said. "*I'm* taking a risk for arranging a loan for you through a source other than the bank I work for. I could be fired. And if the loan goes through, then the person who is lending you the money will be taking a risk. Now, if you would rather I not do this—"

"No, no," Sheri said quickly. "I . . . I'm willing to try anything."

Raymond smiled. "Then go home and wait by your telephone. I have a feeling you'll be getting a call today."

The call came shortly before three that afternoon.

"Miss Warren?"

"Yes."

"A mutual friend, August Raymond, asked me to give you a ring. He suggested I might be interested in investing in a business proposition of yours."

"Who is this?"

"The name is O'Braugh, Miss Warren. Kerry O'Braugh. Perhaps we can discuss the matter over dinner this evening?"

"Where?"

"I'll send a car for you."

"Mr. O'Braugh, forgive me if I seem overly cautious, but I'm going to have to arrange for a baby sitter, and I don't like to be somewhere where the sitter can't reach me."

"Mama Tantini's," O'Braugh said. "It's an Italian restaurant on West Fifty-sixth."

"Yes, I know it. All right, Mr. O'Braugh. Send your car."

The car was a Lincoln—a limousine, in fact. That in itself wasn't too unusual. If someone was wealthy enough to make such investments, then he would certainly be wealthy enough to afford such an automobile. What was unusual was the presence of the man other than the driver. The driver was sitting behind the steering wheel; the other man was standing by the rear door, holding it open for her when she came down to the street.

"Are you Mr. O'Braugh?" she asked, not really expecting him to be. O'Braugh had, after all, said he'd be sending a car, not picking her up.

"No. We'll take you to him," the man answered. He, like the driver, was swarthy, short, and stocky.

Something about him made Sheri uneasy, and for a moment she almost changed her mind. She hesitated.

"Get in, please," he said.

Throwing caution to the wind, Sheri shrugged, then got in. She did want the loan, and if this person was making her a little uneasy, it was just because her imagination was working overtime. The man closed the door, then climbed in the front seat beside the driver. The car pulled away from the curb so smoothly that Sheri almost didn't realize they were in motion. She turned and looked out the window, keeping her face averted from the front seat for the length of the mercifully short ride.

Mama Tantini's Restaurant on West Fifty-sixth, just off Eighth Avenue, was packed with tables and diners. There were six big rooms, filled with statues of the Madonna, angels, splashing fountains, figures of birds, potted plants, oversized paintings, and hanging tapestries. The restaurant was also festooned with Christmas decorations, even though it was not the Christmas season.

Mama Tantini's was the preferred eating spot for New York's large population of Italian-Americans because of the quality and quantity of the food served. As soon as a diner was seated he would be brought a huge hunk of cheese and a large loaf of Italian bread, plus an enormous plate of antipasto. That would be followed by steaming bowls of pasta, then by the entree of veal parmigiana, chicken cacciatore, roast chicken, or filet of sole. After that, if one was still hungry, there was a huge assortment of cannoli, pies, cakes, and ice cream.

Mama Tantini's was also a very popular tourist attraction, so on any given night its clientele was equally divided between its regular trade and visitors from middle America. It was one of the first places Sheri had visited after arriving in New York, though this would be the first time she had been back since.

The man who had helped her into the car now helped her out of it and escorted her into the restaurant. He spoke in Italian to the maître d'. The maître d' smiled at Sheri.

"Would you come with me, please, Miss Warren? Mr. O'Braugh is in the private dining room."

Sheri followed him through various dining rooms, then down a gilt-papered hall and through a set of double doors into a private dining room considerably smaller than the public rooms—and much more tastefully and expensively decorated.

The man sitting at the table stood when Sheri came into the room. He was about five eight, with broad shoulders and narrow waist and hips. His gray hair was cut in a brush-cut. His blue eyes flashed brightly, and he smiled as he came toward her, walking with a distinct limp.

"Miss Warren, I'm Kerry O'Braugh. It's good of you to come," he said. He then spoke to the maître d' in quick, confident Italian. "I've ordered champagne. I hope you'll forgive the liberty."

"Champagne is fine," Sheri said. "I'm confused."

"About what?" Kerry held a chair out for Sheri.

"Your name is O'Braugh. But all this"—she waved her hand around—"and you spoke in such flawless Italian." She smiled. "Or I assume it was flawless Italian; I don't know the language."

"My father was Irish, my mother was Sicilian," Kerry explained.

"Oh, so you *are* Italian, then. On your mother's side."

"Sicilian," Kerry corrected. "There is a distinct difference. And, in fact, I was born there."

"I've always thought I would like to visit the Mediterranean," Sheri mused. "Places like Sicily, the Greek isles."

"Yes, it's beautiful over there," Kerry agreed. "But I've lived in both places, so give me the good ol' U.S. of A."

Waiters suddenly appeared, carrying steaming trays of food.

"Good heavens, Mr. O'Braugh. Just how many people are coming to this dinner?"

He looked confused. "No one else. Just the two of us."

Sheri made a wry face. "Then you must be trying to fatten me up for the slaughter."

Kerry looked at all the food, then smiled. "I'm sorry. I'm just trying to be a gracious host."

"It does all look good," Sheri said, hoping she hadn't offended the man. "I'll do what I can to hold up my end."

Kerry O'Braugh was a fascinating man, full of such entertaining anecdotes that by the time the meal was over Sheri had nearly forgotten the purpose of their eating together. It was only when he reminded her that it came back to her.

"And now, Miss Warren, tell me about this business proposition of yours," he said as he poured her after-dinner wine.

"Have you heard of a product called SheriWear?" she asked, reaching for her wine glass.

"Yes."

Sheri was surprised. "You *have*?"

"It is currently the fastest-selling line of designer sportswear in the country," Kerry said. "It is 'interesting, attractively dangerous, and delightfully sexy.' "

Sheri laughed. "You've been reading John Fairchild's articles in *Women's Wear Daily*."

"Yes, I have," Kerry admitted. He took out a gold cigarette case, offered her one, and when she declined, took one for himself. "I also know that you can't use the name SheriWear for your own line of clothes, nor can you even use your own name in the marketing. I am right, aren't I?"

"Yes, you are. I must say, Mr. O'Braugh, I am surprised by how much you know about this."

"Yes, well, if I'm going to invest a great deal of money in someone, then I want to know something about that person. I took the time to research you today." He lit the cigarette, then exhaled a long stream of smoke. "And I do consider a half-million dollars a sizable investment."

"A half million? Oh, but I'm not asking for that much."

"If we go into business together, that's the amount of money you will be getting from me. I don't want you to fail because you are undercapitalized. And I am willing to invest five hundred thousand dollars in your business, providing you are willing to take my money."

"Yes, of course I am!" Sheri said happily.

"Not so fast," Kerry said, raising his hand. "I want you to wait a couple of weeks. If after that you are still willing to take my money, then we have a deal."

"I don't understand. Of course I'm willing to take your money. Why wouldn't I be?"

"Why, indeed," Kerry retorted. He chuckled. "That's for you to find out. Do your homework." He pulled a card from his pocket and handed it to her. "Call this number by the first of August. If it's yes, I'll deposit the money into your account.

If it's no, well, then, we've had an enjoyable evening, and I think you would agree we haven't gone hungry."

He pushed a button under the table, and almost instantly someone came into the room. "Have my car brought around," Kerry said. "Miss Warren is ready to go home."

"Sì, Padrone."

CHAPTER TEN

JULY 28, 1962, FROM "TRAILMARKERS" IN *EVENTS MAGAZINE*:

AIRPLANE SOARS 59 MILES HIGH

Although rockets have propelled man into space, they are inherently expensive, cumbersome, and limited. "Rocketry *looks* exciting," a spokesman for the National Aeronautics and Space Agency (NASA) said, "but for all the excitement, we're still in the Stone Age as far as space flight is concerned. Going aloft in a rocket is like tying someone to a cannon shell; it is nothing but a glorified projectile. The entire mission is ballistic from takeoff to landing.

"With the X-15, however, we just may have crossed into the Bronze Age," the spokesman continued. "The X-15 is an airplane—albeit unlike any airplane ever flown before—totally under the control of the pilot. When Robert White flew the X-15 to an altitude of 59 miles, he went to the very threshold of space, then returned to a controlled landing on a runway at a predetermined point. That is something even the Russians, with all their achievements in space, have been unable to accomplish."

KING AND ABERNATHY JAILED IN GEORGIA

When Georgia's Judge Durden sentenced reverends Martin Luther King and Ralph Abernathy to a fine of $178 each or a period of 45 days in jail for leading a civil rights protest, he expected them to pay their fines. To his surprise, both men accepted the prison sentence instead. After being searched and issued green prison togs, they were escorted off to begin serving their sentences.

VIOLENCE ERUPTS IN MISSISSIPPI AS FORMER CHIEF OF POLICE IS CHARGED WITH MURDER

Last week in Mississippi the civil rights movement suffered a lamentable setback when violence broke out near the site where the bodies of Vivian Goodman and George Tatum were found.

According to Panola County Sheriff Clyde Quade, civil rights workers Alicia Canfield (daughter of St. Louis tycoon John Canfield), Jerry Wiggins, Violet Simmons, and Deon Booker (grandson of Loomis Booker and brother of basketball great Artemus Booker) were being detained by a group of young white men led by Deputy Sheriff Harley Mack Teasdale for allegedly trespassing. Two witnesses stated that the deputy found the civil rights workers on private property, and when they refused the lawful order to leave, Teasdale arrested them, confining them to a vacant machine shed while he returned to the sheriff's office for further instructions.

"I ordered him to go back and release them on their own recognizance, pending their agreement to show up in court for a hearing on the trespassing charge," Sheriff Quade said.

But when Teasdale returned, according to the two men who were with him, the civil rights workers had already been freed by the former police chief of Delta, Mississippi, Emil R. "Stump" Pollard, an old friend of the Booker family. From there, accounts of the story differ. According to Pollard, an unprovoked Deputy Teasdale fired at the four young people, at which point Pollard, defending them, shot back. Results of the gun battle: Deputy Teasdale dead, with a bullet in the heart; Deon Booker paralyzed, with a severed spinal cord.

However, according to the two men with Teasdale that morning, the former police chief fired first. Indeed, they say that it was Pollard who shot Deon Booker since neither they nor Teasdale even fired. Charges of second-degree murder have been brought against Pollard.

MARCELLA MILLS EMBARRASSES PRESIDENT KENNEDY AT CANCER BALL

Perhaps no First Family has been as big a boon to the arts as the Kennedys. Opera divas, prima ballerinas, violin virtuosos, and entire casts of Broadway musicals have entertained the Kennedys and their guests at the White House. But none raised the temperature to a more sizzling degree than did Marcella Mills when she showed up last week with some fellow movie stars to kick off the national Hollywood Campaign for Cancer Research, a project designed to honor such Hollywood greats as Gary Cooper, Humphrey Bogart, and others who have succumbed to the disease.

There were the usual song-and-dance numbers, skits, and stand-up comedy routines, but Miss Mills, wearing a skintight white-sequined dress, sang a personal song to President Kennedy that delighted the crowd but, some said, actually caused the President to blush. The song, "I Want to Be Loved by You," was performed with wiggles, jiggles, shimmies, writhes, pouts, winks, and blown kisses.

"For all that Marcella didn't remove a single

item of clothing, Gypsy Rose Lee couldn't have been any more seductive," one White House official said—though whether with irritation or admiration was unclear.

ITALY'S EXPORTS ARE AMERICA'S CRIMINALS

Crime bosses Vito Genovese and Kerry O'Braugh have much in common. Both started their criminal careers just in time for the lawless era of Prohibition to launch them to the top—Genovese hooked up with Joe "the Boss" Masseria while O'Braugh threw in with Al Capone. Both then formed their own organizations, O'Braugh leaving Chicago to go to St. Louis while Genovese killed his mentor to further his advancement in New York.

Shortly before World War II, however, both men returned to their native Italy. Genovese did so of his own accord to escape a possible murder rap. O'Braugh—whose Irish father had fled his homeland for Italy, where he subsequently married a Sicilian woman—was deported by the U.S. State Department for his involvement in several violent labor disputes, one resulting in the death of a union striker (allegedly by O'Braugh, though it was never proven) and in a serious injury to O'Braugh that left him with a permanent limp.

During the war, however, both Genovese and O'Braugh provided valuable assistance to the U.S. Army in Italy, thus winning powerful allies in their bid to return to the States. Reentry was granted to each, whereupon they immediately picked up their criminal ties where they had left them years earlier.

Their rise to prominence conferred inclusion at the infamous Appalachian crime syndicate meeting in 1957 of the top one hundred Mafia bosses (where it is said that Kerry O'Braugh led the campaign to name Vito Genovese boss of bosses).

There the similarity ends between the two mafiosi, for the government finally collected enough evidence on Don Vito Genovese to send him to prison, where he remains. Kerry O'Braugh, on the other hand, has not had any direct encounters with the law since the congressional hearings in 1937 and has managed to stay out of legal trouble since his return to the States. Living in New York, O'Braugh somehow manages a lavish lifestyle with no known source of income. He can often be seen dining in Mama Tantini's restaurant, where, according to the waiters, he is "a fine gentleman who tips well."

LAS VEGAS, NEVADA

It was the perfect hideaway, just on the edge of town, more in the desert than in the city. A high cinder-block wall insured seclusion. Inside the wall was an open area patrolled by guard dogs, then several strands of concertina wire and an electric fence. The grounds were further guarded by TV cameras and dozens of electric sensors.

When Marcella Mills was in residence at her Las Vegas home, she felt as secure as if she had been at a presidential retreat—which made sense, since the same people had installed both systems. But in the case of the Las Vegas hideaway, the purpose of the system wasn't so much protection against harm as protection against invasion of privacy. There was, after all, a public image to maintain.

Public images aside, Marcella had learned early in their affair that his marriage was being maintained for political reasons, although she could detect no rancor or animosity in the relationship. Marcella had spent time with the couple on several occasions, and she had never heard a cross word pass between them, nor had she ever heard him say anything bad about her. His wife seemed to accept his philandering as the cross she had to bear, and she bore it with such grace and dignity that she managed to project to the whole world a marriage made in Camelot.

Marcella's knowledge of the situation had made it easier for her to enter into the affair. She never fooled herself into thinking she was in love with him, and she knew that he wasn't in love with her. But he represented excitement and power to her, and she represented glamour and forbidden pleasure to him, and that was all that was needed to draw them together.

The security men knew, of course, but they had become such a part of the landscape that they were all but invisible. When Marcella and her powerful lover had sneaked into a hotel room for their first tryst, she never gave a second thought to the two men who stood guard just outside the door.

Over the next two years they had found several opportunities to get together. She would receive a cryptic call from someone, asking if she would accept a visitor to her Las Vegas home at such and such a time and on such and such a date. That would be her signal.

Often Marcella would wait for him in vain. Sometimes she would get a call telling her the plans had changed; sometimes she wouldn't. She had absolutely no control over the situation. Today was one of those days. She had been told to expect a visitor before three o'clock that afternoon. Whether he would come or not she had no way of knowing, but she would be there for him if he did.

Marcella finished her novel, then looked at her watch. It was just after two, and she hadn't had any word if he was coming. With a sigh, she laid the book down, then walked over to turn on the TV. She chuckled. In place of the soap opera that should have been on was a live telecast from Nellis Air Force Base.

"The arrival of Air Force One created a lot of excitement on this base today," the announcer's voice was saying over the picture of the big Boeing 707. *"Just why the President dropped in on Nellis is unclear. In fact, there was no advance notice given of his arrival. However, considering the security that must always surround a presidential visit, officials are quick to stress that it is not all that unusual that his visit was unannounced."*

Smiling and humming a happy tune, Marcella turned the TV off, then went into the bathroom to take a bubble bath. It was going to be an interesting day after all.

ST. LOUIS, MISSOURI

Deon Booker rolled his wheelchair out into the solarium of the Jefferson University Medical Center. In the winter the solarium was warmed by the sun, but now, at the height of summer, the overhead glass was kept shaded, and air conditioners had to work overtime to keep the room cool. The solarium was located on the fifteenth floor, overlooking Forrest Park. From there Deon could see the Jewelbox, the only structure still remaining from the 1904 World's Fair.

"Oh, what a grand and glorious event that fair was, Deon," his grandfather had once told him. "They gathered the largest number of automobiles ever to be assembled in one place for the great motorcar parade. And the pikeway and all the buildings ablaze with electricity, the grand canal . . . I tell you, it was something to behold."

When others thought of Loomis Booker, they thought of his contributions to society, of his preeminence as a Negro leader during an era when blacks were, for the most part, background shadows. Loomis Booker was a bigger-than-life figure to most Americans, a name in history books to school-children, an unapproachable demigod to others. But to Deon Booker, Loomis had been Grandfather, a man who could—even at the end of his life, with all the accolades and awards heaped on him by government, business, and academia—still be excited by his memories of the great St. Louis Exposition of 1904.

There were a few others in the solarium this morning, patients and nurses, but Deon didn't know any of them. Some, like him, were in wheelchairs. Others had walked out slowly, unsteadily, to sit on one of the chairs or couches. A couple of men were playing checkers, but most, like Deon, were just gazing out the windows, keeping their distance from each other, quietly lost in their own thoughts.

A nurse's voice broke into Deon's reverie. "Mr. Booker, there's a writer here to see you," she announced.

"I don't want to talk to any more reporters," Deon said. Since the shooting, a constant barrage of journalists, both print and television, had tried to get his side of the story. All the more so recently, now that Stump Pollard was being tried for second-degree murder.

"He's not a reporter," the nurse said. "He's that famous

author, Eric Twainbough. He says he's a friend of yours. Is that true? Do you really know him?"

Deon turned his wheelchair around to face the nurse. "Yes, I know him."

"Goodness, I'm impressed."

"Tell him to come in."

He watched the nurse leave, then return a moment later, leading a big, bearded man. Deon more than knew him. Eric Twainbough was virtually a part of his family. When Eric had been little more than a boy—and determined to see the same St. Louis World's Fair that had so entranced Deon's grandfather—he had been beaten and thrown off a freight train by an overzealous brakeman. Loomis Booker had found him alongside a St. Louis track, more dead than alive, and nursed him back to health, then became his mentor, adviser, and friend. It was a friendship that would last until the day Loomis Booker died.

Eric strolled across the floor with his hand extended, smiling broadly. "Hello, Deon. How the hell are you?"

"How do I look?" Deon replied.

"You look like the only Negro in the world I could beat in a footrace," Eric cracked.

At first Deon's eyes flashed in quick anger; then the anger disappeared, replaced by his usual good humor. He was convulsed with laughter.

"You got that right," he said, wiping his eyes when the spell of laughing had passed. "Listen, it's good to see you. It's good to see *anyone* who isn't shoving a microphone in my face."

"Yeah, well, that's the way it is when you're famous."

"Listen to who's talking about being famous. You're the famous one around here. Nobel Prize. Petzold Prize. Every other kind of prize. Plus all the movies they've made from your books. I really made a hit with the nurse just now when I told her I know you."

"Yeah, we're both famous, and we're both wonderful. Listen, are you going to the trial?"

"I don't have any choice. I've been subpoenaed as a witness."

"You're talking as if you wouldn't go if you didn't have to."

Deon turned his chair around and rolled back over to

the windows to look down at the park. "I don't think I would," he said after a long moment.

"Why not? Don't you think you owe it to Stump?"

"What if I do? You think a crippled nigger is going to do him any good?"

"You can tell what happened."

"Hell, I don't *know* what happened. One minute we were walking across a damned slough, and the next minute my face was in the muck. I didn't hear anything and I didn't see anything."

"What do you mean, you didn't hear anything?"

"Just what I said. I read once that you don't hear the bullet that hits you. Well, in my case it's true. I didn't hear it."

"They're trying to say that Stump shot you by accident while he was shooting at Teasdale and the others."

"That's a crock of shit."

"How do you know, if you didn't hear anything or see anything?"

Deon turned his wheelchair around to look into Eric's face. "I know that Alicia and Violet and Jerry believe the deputy shot me first, then Chief Pollard returned fire. But I didn't see anything at all, so I'm afraid I'm not going to make much of a witness unless I lie."

"No, don't do that. There's nothing they would like better than to have you commit perjury. If they could nail you with that, you'd wind up in jail with a longer sentence than they'd give Stump, even if they found him guilty."

"Yeah, I know." Deon sighed. "My only consolation is that while my testimony can't strengthen the defense, I don't see how it can help the prosecution."

"What are you going to do when all this is over?"

"Haven't you heard? Artemus is getting me a tryout for the NBA," Deon said bitterly.

"Don't give me that shit, Deon," Eric retorted. "Like you could have played for the NBA before you wound up with wheels for legs."

Despite himself, Deon chuckled again. "You do cut to the heart of it, don't you, old man? All right, I'll be truthful with you. I don't have an idea in hell what I'll do now. I've been so involved in the civil rights movement for the last few years that I've never given a thought to anything else."

"Then why think about anything else? Why would anything have to change, just because you're in a wheelchair? You can still work for civil rights."

"Like this?"

"Deon, once, when you were a little boy, I came to visit Loomis. You and Artemus were out in the backyard playing basketball, and you were doing a pretty good job of holding your own with him. When I commented about it, Loomis said that you had as much athletic skill as Artemus. The only difference, he said, was a matter of a few degrees . . . from sixty-five to seventy-five degrees. Any colder and you wouldn't play, any hotter and you wouldn't play—whereas Artemus would be outside shooting baskets no matter if it were zero or a hundred. Did he ever say anything to you like that?"

"A few times," Deon admitted.

"He said you were so lazy, you were always looking for something you could do while sitting down."

"Are you supposed to be inspiring me or something? 'Cause if you are, you read the wrong book."

Eric raised a finger. "No, wait a minute. Hear me out. It'll get better, I promise. Because, you see, Loomis also said that you could do more in one hour of sitting on your ass than most people could do in a full day of running around. Okay, Deon, here's your chance to prove that." Eric pointed to the wheelchair. "You're sitting on your ass, and you're going to be sitting on your ass for the rest of your life. Seems to me it's time for you to prove that your grandfather knew what he was talking about."

Deon grinned. "You aren't going to break out the flag, are you? I mean, I don't think I could take it if you break out the flag."

"Would it do any good?"

Deon shook his head. "Don't need it. I figure you've given me enough to think about. Actually, I think I'd make a dramatic figure, crusading for civil rights from a wheelchair. Don't you? Dramatic, hell. You might even say heroic."

"You aren't feeling sorry for yourself anymore?"

"No."

Eric grinned. "Good. Then what do you say we go have some dinner, then catch the Cardinals tonight?"

"Okay, but I warn you, it's a pain in the ass moving me around in this thing," Deon replied, shaking his head slowly.

"Sportsman's Park isn't built to accommodate wheelchairs the way this hospital is. You think you're up to it?"

Eric laughed. "I don't have to be up to it. That's the beauty of being rich. I've got a chauffeur who'll go with us. I'll just have *him* haul your ass around."

"Who's pitching tonight?"

"Bob Gibson."

"Ah, good. One of my kind."

"No shit! Wonder how he does it."

"Does what?"

"You said he's one of your kind. I wonder how he pitches from a wheelchair."

SARDIS, MISSISSIPPI

The domed and columned courthouse was the grandest building in Sardis. Though not set in a town square, it was situated far enough off the street to accommodate a big lawn with several large shade trees, which almost gave it the illusion of being on a green.

The overflow from the packed spectators' gallery had spilled onto the lawn, and many people had sought relief from the hot Mississippi sun by huddling under the trees. Besides the locals, the area was packed with reporters—with their attendant cars and trucks and ancillary personnel—from all the television networks and wire services, for the trial of Stump Pollard had drawn national attention.

Alicia Canfield, newly admitted to the bar in Missouri, had been recognized by the Mississippi bar to assist in Stump's defense. It was a unique beginning to her law career. For one thing, here it was, her very first case, and it was being tried in a state other than the one she had passed the bar in. For another, she was not just cocounsel; she was personally entangled in the case and would be called by the defense as a witness. And finally, this case was being tried in the glare of national publicity.

The principal counsel for defense was Eddie Bender, the doyen of lawyers in and around Sardis, Mississippi. Eddie Bender and Stump Pollard had known each other for many years, but they weren't exactly friends—quite the opposite, in fact. They had been political opponents in a part of the country where politics, church, and motherhood were so closely entwined, it was almost blasphemous to befriend someone of the opposite political stripe. Eddie had once lost a race for the state senate, and he had blamed Stump for his defeat. According to the story, when the ballot count was posted on the big tote board in front of the courthouse, showing Eddie Bender going down to defeat, the two men finally came to blows. Stump, who was nearly twice as large as Eddie, managed to hold his temper in check, even after Eddie got in the first two or three punches. Friends of Eddie's, realizing that, unrestrained, Stump could break every bone in his body, quickly intervened before Stump got too riled.

"Not only that," Stump told Alicia, "but the ornery son of a bitch had a habit of getting people off with no more than a slap on the wrist when they should've been sent to prison. It was frustrating for me to arrest someone only to watch Eddie Bender get 'em off. I said a long time ago that as much as I disliked the bastard, if I ever got my ass in a crack, he'd be the one I'd want to represent me."

Eddie was in his early sixties, a smallish man—smaller even than Alicia—with thinning white hair; bushy white eyebrows hovering over hard, appraising blue eyes; and a nose like the beak of a hawk. He was somewhat of a dandy who always wore a suit and a vest and perspired very little—even now, in the sweltering un-air-conditioned courtroom.

Stump, on the other hand, was perspiring mightily and suffering from the heat, despite his constant working of a hand-held fan that promised JESUS SAVES.

Alicia, who was suffering from the heat almost as much as Stump, was seated at one end of the defense table, Eddie was in the middle, and Stump was at the other end. Alicia focused her attention on the front of the courtroom, studying the Mississippi state flag that hung on the wall behind the judge's bench. The field of the flag was the stars and bars of the Confederacy. It made her recall the Confederate flag fluttering from the antenna of the pickup truck their assailants had been driving on that day and night of terror. She shivered involuntarily.

"You cold, girl?" Eddie asked, looking at her.

"No," Alicia replied. She didn't want to mention the flag. "I just shivered."

Eddie chuckled. "That means someone's just stepped on your grave."

"Comforting thought," Alicia mumbled.

"All rise!" the clerk suddenly intoned.

Amid much noisy shuffling, the packed gallery stood.

"The court of Panola County is now in session, the Honorable G. B. Dowling presiding."

Judge Dowling entered the room. His three-hundred-pound body seemed even more massive under the flowing black robe. He had globular cheeks, multiple chins, and a high forehead. Gathering his robe, he stepped up to his seat, then sat down.

"Be seated," he instructed.

As the courtroom settled itself, the judge studied the papers before him for a few minutes, then looked up.

"Is the defense ready?"

"The defense is ready, Your Honor," Eddie replied.

The judge looked at Alicia, sliding his glasses up his nose the better to see her. "Who is that?" he asked in a gruff voice. "Who is that little girl sitting there with you?"

"I'm Alicia Canfield, Your Honor."

"I asked Mr. Bender, girl, I didn't ask you."

"Sorry, Your Honor," Alicia said.

"Your Honor, this is Alicia Canfield. She is actin' as my co-counsel in this case."

"Your co-counsel? That little girl?"

"She is qualified before the bar in Missouri, Your Honor, and has been recognized for this case by the Mississippi bar. I filed the motion with the court for permission to use her, and it has been approved."

"I approved it?"

"Yes, Your Honor."

Judge Dowling rubbed his primary chin. "You don't say." He glanced at the prosecutor. "What do you say about this, Mr. Conway? Does prosecution have any objections to the use of this girl as co-counsel?"

"We have no objections, Your Honor," the prosecutor replied. "If Eddie thinks he needs help from this little Yankee gal, then he can have her with my blessin's."

The spectators laughed.

The prosecutor was James Conway, a candidate for attorney general of Mississippi. A high-profile case like this was wonderful for publicity . . . provided he won.

"Is prosecution ready?"

"Prosecution is ready, Your Honor."

"Very well. With the defendant represented by counsel and with both counselors ready, Mr. Prosecutor, you may make your opening statement."

Conway got up from the table and walked over to look at the jury, which consisted of eight men and four women—all white. He took an oversized red handkerchief from his jacket pocket and wiped his face.

"Ooo-weee, it's hot!" he declared. "It's so hot I saw a hound-dog chasin' a rabbit . . . and they were both walkin'."

It was an old joke, but there was a respectful tittering of laughter from the jurors.

"Course," Conway went on, "we're Mississippians. An' Mississippians are used to the heat. The problem is, we been gettin' more'n our share of heat here lately. It started last year when those busloads of coloreds and whites come down here from the North, all fired up to change a way of life we been livin' peacefully for all these years. Well, we all know the kind of problems that started. Then this year we got all the coloreds and whites comin' down here to register our colored folk to vote. Well, now, I don't mind a colored person votin' . . . long as he votes for me," he added, provoking genuine laughter. "But the problem is when someone else comes to register our coloreds, then our coloreds get to thinkin' they got to vote the way the folks who got them registered want them to vote. You know what that means? That means folks from *outside* the state are goin' to start controllin' what goes on *inside* our state. They're goin' to do that by influencin' our simple-minded coloreds. That's wrong. That's mighty wrong."

Alicia leaned over and whispered to Eddie, "Aren't you going to object or something?"

"Object to what?"

"Object to what he's saying."

Eddie shook his head. "Why, hell, honey, so far I haven't heard him say anythin' I disagree with."

"But what he's talking about now is irrelevant. It has nothing to do with the case at hand," Alicia protested.

"Then it can't be hurtin' us none."

"But we shouldn't just sit here and do nothing," Alicia insisted. "He's getting away with it."

"Girl, he wants us to object, can't you see that? Right now he's preachin' to the choir. I guarantee you, there's not a person on that jury that doesn't agree with everythin' he's sayin'. And if we object to it, then all we'll be doin' is puttin' ourselves on one side of the fence while ol' Conway is on the other side—along with all twelve members of the jury. Let him ramble on."

"Right here in this courtroom," Conway was saying, "there are reporters from newspapers and magazines all over the country. Outside, on the lawn, you can see the cars and panel trucks belongin' to all the TV networks. I'm told that there are even reporters here from England and France and places like that. They are watchin' us, ladies and gentlemen. They are watchin' us from all over the world to see if we have the courage of our convictions. Can we maintain law and order in our society while being in the fishbowl for the world? Or will the presence of all this outside interest sway our judgment?

"I think we can send them an answer, don't you? I think we can show the world that no outside intimidation is goin' to keep us from doin' what is right.

"The questions we are to decide here are quite simple. The first question we need an answer to is: Did Harley Mack Teasdale die as a result of a bullet fired from Stump Pollard's gun? The second question we want an answer to is: Did Stump Pollard violate the law in dischargin' that gun? If the answers to those two questions are yes, then Stump Pollard is guilty as charged of murder in the second degree.

"And I will tell you what the answers are. The answer to the first question is yes. How do we know it's yes?" Conway turned toward the defense table, dramatically jabbing his finger toward Stump to prove a challenged point. "We have eyewitnesses who saw Stump Pollard fire his pistol at Harley Mack Teasdale."

He jabbed his finger toward Stump a second time. "We have a ballistics match proving the bullet that killed Harley Mack Teasdale was fired from Stump Pollard's pistol." He jabbed his finger a third time. "And last, but certainly not least, we have Stump Pollard's own confession that he fired the gun."

At first Alicia wondered why he was making such a dramatic show over what was uncontested information. Whether or not Stump fired the gun was not the question, nor had it ever been. Then she realized that by doing this, James Conway made it appear as if the prosecution had won a round. It was nothing more than psychological theater, performed for the jury. For a moment Alicia was able to detach herself from the proceedings, to observe with objectivity the considerable skill of this country lawyer.

"Now, havin' proved the answer to the first question is yes, we come to the second question: Did Stump Pollard violate the law in dischargin' that gun? Ladies and gentlemen, the answer to that question is also yes. The state of Mississippi will introduce evidence showin' that Stump Pollard and the deceased had an adversarial relationship goin' back several years. We will also show that Stump Pollard has no current association with the police force of Delta, and thus the discharge of his firearm could not in any way be said to be official duty. Now, Mr. Pollard is going to claim he fired in self-defense, but we will introduce witnesses who will swear that neither they nor Harley Mack Teasdale fired their weapons. That leaves us with only one inescapable conclusion: There was no justifiable reason for Stump Pollard to shoot at Harley Mack Teasdale. When we are finished with this case, I feel very strongly that you will be able to put aside all the media attention and the interference from the North, and just concentrate on doin' what is right. And what is right is to find the defendant, Stump Pollard, guilty as charged of murder in the second degree."

With one final wipe of his face, James Conway sat down.

"Opening remarks, Mr. Bender?" Judge Dowling asked.

Eddie Bender stood up, but he did not leave the table.

"Ladies and gentlemen of the jury, let's please not lose sight of one fact," he said in a soft, southern drawl. "We are tryin' Mr. Pollard here. Mr. Pollard and that's all. We aren't sallyin' forth to send any messages to the Yankee media. We aren't fightin' for state's rights. We aren't strikin' a blow for southern freedom. And we aren't campaignin' for the office of attorney general. What we are doin' here is lookin' for the truth, pure an' simple. And, finally, I'd like to remind you that the man on trial is one of our own."

Bender sat down.

NEW YORK

Once again Sheri Warren found herself in the conference room of the law firm of Evert, Evert, McConnel, and Daigh. A secretary, a woman around thirty, came in, carrying a cup of coffee.

"Thank you," Sheri said.

"You're welcome. Oh, and Miss Warren, I want to tell you how much I love your designs. I think your clothes are just beautiful."

Sheri smiled. "Thank you very much."

"Mr. Daigh said he would be with you in just a few moments," the secretary said as she withdrew.

Sheri nursed her coffee and looked at the objets d'art that decorated the conference room. A full suit of armor stood in one corner, a shield and crossed swords were hanging from the wall, and the far wall was painted with a large mural depicting a jousting tournament. Sheri wondered whether the law partners saw themselves as knights errant, rushing forth to courtrooms to do battle against the enemy. Or maybe it was just that the firm's decorator was a Middle Ages nut.

The door opened and John Daigh came in, carrying a brown envelope. "I'm sorry," he said. "The messenger carrying this report just arrived."

"Report? What report?"

Daigh sighed. "Miss Warren, when you told me you had located a source of backing for your venture, I was excited for you. But when you told me who your backer was, I became frightened."

"Frightened? You didn't say anything to me about being frightened," Sheri said, frowning. "You just told me you wanted to take the time to check out my backer's credentials. I assumed you meant his financial credentials. Why would you be frightened?"

"Because Kerry O'Braugh is a Mafia figure."

Sheri laughed.

"I'm very serious."

"Mafia? I thought everyone in the Mafia had names like Carmine or Luigi. And their last names *end* with an *O*, they don't *start* with an *O*."

"He has an Irish name, but he is very Sicilian." Daigh looked at her through narrowed eyes. "Good heavens, Miss Warren, don't you read the newspapers or news magazines? He was splashed all over *Events* two weeks ago."

"I've been too busy to do anything but work on my designs," she admitted sheepishly. "I confess that he did tell me he was Italian on his mother's side. And I know that he speaks Italian fluently. But Mafia? He seemed like a respectable businessman to me. He was very much the gentleman the whole evening."

"The Mafia is a business," Daigh said. "The only thing is, its business is crime."

"Well, designing dresses is certainly no crime. And he offered to back me to the tune of a half-million dollars. No one else has offered to help. Are you telling me now that I should turn him down?"

"That would be my recommendation."

She thought it over briefly. "Well, I'm sorry, but I have no intention of turning him down. This is my one chance, Mr. Daigh. If I don't take it now—"

"Miss Warren, didn't you tell me that you are friends with the Canfield family?"

"I *worked* for the Canfield family," Sheri corrected. "I was the assistant housekeeper in their Destin, Florida, home."

"Still, the Canfields are one of the wealthiest families in America. Perhaps you could ask them for the money."

"No. I won't trade on that relationship."

"It would be an investment, Miss Warren," Daigh explained. "You wouldn't be going to them hat-in-hand. I would be glad to prepare a letter of intent for you."

"No," Sheri said firmly. "You don't understand." She thought of her relationship with Morgan. He would think she had only been using him. "I can't ask them."

Daigh sighed. "All right, Miss Warren. But before you make a final decision on whether you are going to accept backing from Mr. O'Braugh, I want you to read this." He pulled a sheaf of papers from the brown envelope and handed them to her. "Sit there and take a few minutes. It may be the most important few minutes of your life."

"What is it?"

"I hired a detective agency to put it together for you. Please, just read it. I think you'll find it explains itself."

Sheri leaned over the papers, brushing her hair back from her face, and began reading.

JACOBY & ANDERSON INTELLIGENCE SERVICES
315 WEST 56TH STREET
NEW YORK 19, N.Y.

AGENT: Michael Carmack
Confidential Report (for client's eyes only)
Subject of report: Kerry O'Braugh

Kerry O'Braugh, 61, was born in Palermo, Sicily. It is alleged, though this agent was unable to confirm, that Kerry's father, Ian O'Braugh, was a member of the Irish Republican Brotherhood. According to an unconfirmable account, the senior O'Braugh killed a British soldier in a pub and was forced to flee Ireland, whereupon he settled in Sicily.

There he married the daughter of a *capo consigliere*. Although his Irish birth prevented him from becoming a member of the Mafia, he nevertheless became a trusted aide-de-camp to his father-in-law and was ultimately killed with him in a vendetta.

In 1914, at the age of thirteen, Kerry O'Braugh and his mother left Sicily and came to the U.S., settling in Chicago. After several brushes with the law, including incarceration in a reform school, O'Braugh joined the gang of Big Jim Colossimo, the leading underworld character in Chicago at that time.

When Colossimo refused to engage in bootlegging during Prohibition, he was murdered by his lieutenant (and nephew) Johnny Torrio. By then, O'Braugh had become Torrio's protégé.

When Torrio and Al Capone became partners

in the Chicago mob, O'Braugh's loyalty was to Torrio, who, fearing correctly that Capone would one day take over the rackets in Chicago, persuaded O'Braugh to set up shop in St. Louis, where he would be able to operate away from Capone's influence and without incurring his enmity.

Before O'Braugh left Chicago, he is reputed to have become a made member of the Mafia—an extremely rare event for someone not a full Sicilian. Although O'Braugh's membership has never been challenged by others nor repudiated by him, it is known that there are some who resent it.

During the 1920s, after wresting control of all bootlegging and other criminal activity in St. Louis from a rival gang leader—by joining forces with the leader of a Negro gang operating out of East St. Louis, Illinois—O'Braugh was the undisputed king of organized crime in St. Louis. It was alleged, but never proved, that he murdered a man in retaliation for the death of his girlfriend.

During the 1930s Kerry O'Braugh was engaged in so-called labor negotiations—violent confrontations with picketers to break up their lawful strikes. As a result of this activity, O'Braugh was deported back to Italy in 1936.

During the war, O'Braugh commanded a brigade of anti-German partisans. In addition to disrupting German communications and transportation lines, he rescued several downed Allied airmen. When the Allies invaded, O'Braugh provided, to quote an official report from the U.S. Fifth Army, "invaluable assistance." This enabled him to successfully petition the State Department to rescind his deportation order.

Since his return to the U.S. in July 1954, O'Braugh has been engaged in several seemingly lawful business ventures. Although he is suspected of being a front man for Mafia investment in legitimate enterprises, three separate investigations have failed to bring about an indictment. With no outstanding warrants or pending prosecution against him, he continues to operate unhampered and has become a very wealthy man.

When Sheri finished reading the report, she returned the pages to the envelope and looked up at John Daigh.

"I'd never heard of him before this," she said.

Daigh threw open his hands. "Consider yourself educated."

"According to this, the law isn't after him."

Daigh chuckled. "That's not quite true, my dear. The law would like nothing better than to get something on him. They have just been unsuccessful so far, that's all."

Sheri drummed her fingers on the table for a moment. "Would I be committing a criminal act by accepting money from him?" she finally asked.

"You would be committing a questionable act."

"Would it be criminal?"

Daigh sighed. "Technically, no. If you don't know that the money he gives you has been obtained by illegal means, then you are not in violation of any law."

"Can this man be trusted?"

"It depends on what you mean by trusted."

"Will he do what he says he is going to do? Will he advance me all the money he says, and will he not change any of the terms of the agreement after the fact?"

"I don't think you'd have to worry about that," Daigh said. "In their own peculiar way, mafiosi are very trustworthy. They set quite a store by their peculiar concept of honor. O'Braugh will keep his word to you."

"Good. That's all I care about."

Daigh held up a finger. "But," he added quickly, "be advised that this 'honor' cuts both ways. He will fulfill, to the letter, everything he promises. He will expect—no, make that *enforce*—the same agreement on your part."

Sheri laughed. "You mean if I don't make a payment on time he'll come break my knees?"

John Daigh looked at her with an expressionless face. "You will notice, Miss Warren, that *I* am not laughing."

CHAPTER ELEVEN

"Do you swear to tell the truth, the whole truth, and nothing but the truth, so help you God?"

"I do."

"Would you state your name, please?"

"My name is Charles W. Good."

"Thank you. You may be seated."

Charles Good, who was wearing a white shirt, a narrow maroon tie, a dark-gray wool jacket—way too heavy for the heat but apparently his only "proper" attire—khaki trousers, and work boots, took his seat in the witness chair. Prosecutor James Conway approached him.

"Are you employed, Mr. Good?"

"Yes, sir, I am."

"Where do you work?"

"Right now I'm doin' part-time work over at the sawmill. Come fall, I'll be workin' full-time in the cotton gin for Mr. Copeland."

"Did the decedent work there as well?"

"Who?"

"Harley Mack Teasdale. Did he also work at the cotton gin?"

"Yes, sir. Me an' Harley Mack an' Pete, we all work there."

"That would be Peter Field?"

"Yes, sir, Peter Field, that's him."

"Peter Field was with you and Harley Mack Teasdale on the mornin' Mr. Teasdale was killed?"

"Yes, sir. We was all three together."

"Would you please tell the jury, in your own words, exactly what happened that mornin'?"

"Yes, sir. Well, Harley Mack, he'd been made a depitty for Sheriff Quade on account of ever'one had been lookin' for that nigger boy and white girl—"

"Objection," Eddie Bender said laconically. "The use of the term 'nigger' is prejudicial to colored folks."

"Well, now, why would you be objectin' to that, Eddie?" Conway asked. "You're not defendin' colored folks, you're defendin' a white man."

"Conway, you know the racial overtones of this case. Now, I'm tellin' you, I object to the use of the word 'nigger.' And I'd like a rulin' on that, if you please, Your Honor."

"That's all right, Judge," Conway said. "I agree with the learned counselor. There's no need for us to add any more fire to this case. Mr. Good, I'm goin' to have to ask that you not use the word 'nigger.'"

"Yes, sir."

"Now, please, continue with your story."

"Yes, sir. Well, sir, like I said, Harley Mack was depittyin' for Sheriff Quade 'cause ever'one had been lookin' for that"—he said the next word slowly and distinctly—"*nigra* boy and white girl that was lost. But then they was found, so Harley Mack, he started lookin' for some other depittyin' to do. So he asked me 'n Pete an' some others to come along with him. That's when we seen them four agitators trespassin' on private property. Harley Mack decided we ought to"— Good paused for a moment as if looking for a word, then continued—"detain 'em. So we done that while he come back to check with the sheriff to see what should we do next."

"And what did the sheriff say?"

"He said we ought not to have done that, an' he told us to go back an' let 'em out."

"So did you go right back to let them out?"

"No, sir, by then it was too dark to be walkin' through the swamp, you know, what with the quicksand an' snakes an' ever'thin' else out there. So Harley Mack, he decided it would be best to wait until mornin' to let 'em out." Good stopped and scratched his head. "Don't s'pose it was the right and legal thing to do, but that's what he done. Well, anyway, so the next mornin', Harley Mack, he come got me an' Pete an' asked did we want to go with 'im to let the agitators out, so we said, 'Yeah, we might as well, seein' as how we helped lock 'em up.' And that's when we seen Stump Pollard."

"Where did you see him?"

"He was comin' across the slough with them agitators."

"What happened next?"

"Well, sir, Harley Mack, he raised up his hand like this, pointin' at Stump. 'What you reckon he's a-doin' with them folks?' he asked me an' Pete. And when he done that, why Stump, he started in a-shootin'."

"Stump started shootin'?"

"Yes, sir."

"Wait a minute now, Mr. Good. We want to get this straight. You are sayin' that Stump Pollard opened fire without provocation?"

"Without what?"

"None of you shot at Stump before he started shootin' at you?"

"No, sir. None of us shot a'tall."

"Why do you suppose Stump opened fire like that?"

"Well, sir, I been studyin' on that," Good replied, nodding sagely. "And near as I can figure, Stump must've thought Harley Mack had a gun. I mean, the way Harley Mack was pointin' at him an' all. That's the only reason I can come up with that would make Stump just start shootin' like that."

"Now, Mr. Good, I direct your attention to the colored man present in this courtroom who's sittin' in the wheelchair there. Do you see him?"

"Yes, sir. Well, he ain't hard to pick out. He's the only nigger in a wheelchair in here."

The assembly laughed.

"Objection."

"Sustained," Judge Dowling said. He frowned at the witness. "Mr. Good, you have been warned about the use of that term."

"Yes, sir. I'm sorry, Your Honor, I forgot. It won't happen no more."

"Was that colored man present that mornin'?" Conway asked.

Charley Good pointedly studied Deon Booker. "Yes, sir," he finally said. "He was there."

"Mr. Good, as you can see, the colored man you have identified as being there is in a wheelchair. Do you know why he is in a wheelchair?"

"Yes, sir. He's in a wheelchair 'cause he got shot that mornin'. Messed up his spine, from what I heard."

"Who shot him, Mr. Good?"

"Stump Pollard shot him."

"Mr. Good, why do you say that Stump Pollard shot Mr. Booker?"

" 'Cause it's like I said. Harley Mack didn't have no gun in his hand. All he done was point his finger at Stump. And when he done that, Stump started shootin'. Well, the next thing you know, the . . . *nigra* goes down, an' then, right after that, Harley Mack goes down."

"What happened next?"

"I knelt to look at Harley Mack, and I seen that he was dead."

"How do you know he was dead?"

"Hell, Stump hit 'im right betwixt the eyes. He was prob'ly dead 'fore he ever hit the ground. Then I yelled at Stump and told him he had kilt Harley Mack."

"And what did Mr. Pollard do then?"

"He told us he was by God goin' to kill me an' Pete, too, if we didn't put our guns on the ground."

"Hold it, hold it. I thought you said you didn't have any guns."

"No, sir. What I said was, Harley Mack didn't have no gun in his hand. None of us did. We was all carryin' our guns, but they was stuck down in our belts."

"Did any of you discharge a weapon that mornin'?"

"No, sir. Only Stump Pollard. He was the only one that done any dischargin'."

"How many times did he shoot?"

"I don't know for sure. He discharged two, maybe three or four times. All I know is, right after he commenced dischargin', the nigra went down, an' then, right after that, Harley Mack, why, he went down, too."

"Thank you, Mr. Good," Conway said. He turned to Eddie Bender. "Your witness, Counselor."

With great deliberation, Eddie got up and walked over to stand in front of the witness chair. He stared at Charley Good for a long time without speaking. Good began shifting nervously in his chair.

"Your Honor, I object!" Conway shouted.

"Object to what, Counselor?" Judge Dowling replied. "For God's sake, Mr. Bender hasn't even said anything yet."

"Yes, sir, that's just what I'm objectin' to. He's makin' my witness nervous."

Judge Dowling sighed. "Mr. Bender, either start your questioning or get off the pot."

"Yes, sir, Your Honor. I was just formulatin' my questions, that's all," Eddie replied. He looked at the witness. "Charley, what does the word 'detain' mean?"

"Beg pardon?"

" 'Detain.' You said Harley Mack made the decision to 'detain' them. Did Harley Mack talk like that? Was that his word?"

"I don't know what you're talkin' about."

"If you don't know what I'm talkin' about, why did you use the word? Mr. Conway told you what to say, didn't he?"

"Objection, Your Honor. He's leadin' the witness."

"Sustained."

"Charley, did you shoot at Stump Pollard that mornin'?"

"No, sir."

"Did Harley Mack shoot at him?"

"No, sir."

"Now, are you sayin' that you know for a fact that Harley Mack didn't shoot? Or are you sayin' that you don't know whether he shot or not?"

"I'm sayin' he didn't shoot."

"Did Peter Field shoot at them?"

"Nobody shot at 'em. I told you that."

"Do you know what perjury means?"

"Objection, Your Honor. He's badgering the witness."

"I'm hardly badgering the witness, Your Honor," Bender protested. "I'm truly concerned that this witness understands neither the meanin' nor the seriousness of perjury."

"Overruled. You may ask the question."

"Charley, do you understand the word 'perjury'?"

"Don't it mean somethin' like you don't like nig—uh, nigras?"

The courtroom laughed.

"No, Charley, it means lyin' on the witness stand. If you lie on the witness stand, it is a crime. You can go to prison for that, Charley. Did you know that?"

He seemed to freeze. "No."

"Now that you understand that, do you still insist that Stump Pollard is the only one who discharged his weapon that mornin'?"

Good ran his hand across the top of his brush-cut blond hair, then blinked once or twice before he answered, "That's what I said, and I'm stickin' by it."

"No further questions, Your Honor."

"Your Honor, the state calls Peter Field to the stand."

Peter Field was considerably larger than Charley Good, with dark hair that framed his wide-set brown eyes and a flattened nose. Field's account of the events of the morning was virtually word-for-word identical to the testimony given by Good, even to the use of the term "detain."

"Your witness, Counselor," Conway said when he was finished.

Eddie nodded and started his cross-examination. "Mr. Field, why did Mr. Teasdale find it necessary to detain the four civil rights workers?"

"Well, 'cause, like Charley said, they was trespassin' on private property."

"And so when you detained them, you took them onto that same private property, and you even entered and used without permission a private buildin'?"

"Well, there wasn't no place else to keep 'em."

"Why didn't you take them into town to jail?"

"I don't know," Field answered with a shrug. "Harley Mack, he was the one in charge."

"Did you rape Miss Simmons?"

"Objection, Your Honor! This question is immaterial!" Conway shouted.

"Your Honor, Miss Simmons's contention that she was raped goes to the heart of this entire incident," Eddie countered. "It changes it from the so-called arrest that prosecution is claimin' to criminal kidnappin', assault, and rape. People who are capable of criminal kidnappin', assault, and rape are also capable of murder. As a longtime police officer, my client understood the mentality of people like Teasdale, Good, and Field and was thus extra cautious. It is easy to see why he thought his life, and the lives of those in his charge, were in danger."

"Objection overruled."

"Thank you, Your Honor." Eddie turned back to Peter Field. "Now, did you rape Miss Simmons?"

Confused, Field looked toward the prosecutor. "You told me I wouldn't have to answer that question."

"Mr. Field, you may decline to answer on the grounds that it may incriminate you," Conway said.

"Yeah, that," Field said, looking back at Eddie. "I decline to answer your question."

"No further questions," Eddie muttered.

"Redirect?"

"Yes, Your Honor," Conway said. "Mr. Field, disregarding all that happened on the night before, did you tell the truth about what happened on the morning Harley Mack Teasdale was shot?"

"Yeah. Ever' word of it is gospel. I didn't shoot nobody, Charley didn't shoot nobody, an' Harley Mack didn't shoot nobody. The only one that done any shootin' was Stump Pollard."

"Thank you. You may stand down. And now, Your Honor, the state calls Dr. Nathan Peterson to the stand."

Dr. Peterson was sworn in, and Conway began his questioning.

"Dr. Peterson, on the morning of the shootin', you treated both Harley Mack Teasdale and Deon Booker, did you not?"

"Well, I treated Deon Booker," Dr. Peterson answered. "There was no treatment that could be done for Mr. Teasdale. He was DOA."

"I'm sorry, Doctor, I misspoke. I meant you looked at them both. You saw both wounds."

"Yes, sir."

"Would you describe the wounds for us, please?"

"Yes, sir. In the case of Harley Mack Teasdale the wound was an intrusive defect just above and to the left of the right eye socket. It was caused by the introduction of—"

"Excuse me, Doctor," Conway interrupted, holding up his hand. "Couldn't you just tell us in plain words what the wound was?"

"Yes, sir. A bullet entered here and exited here," Peterson said, putting the tip of his finger first at a point on the bridge of his nose, then on the top of his head.

Conway walked over to the evidence table and picked up a spent bullet. "Would you describe the wound as being consistent with a wound that would be caused by this missile?"

"Yes, I would say so."

"Your Honor, this is a bullet picked up at the scene by Deputy Marion Wilson. Harold Cargill, the ballistics expert for the Memphis Police Department, has verified that this bullet came from the thirty-eight-caliber Police Special belonging to Stump Pollard. I ask that it be entered as state's evidence, item two."

"It is so entered."

"And now, Dr. Peterson, how would you describe the wound suffered by Mr. Booker?"

"It, too, was caused by the penetration of what was probably a bullet—though in the case of Mr. Booker no bullet has been found."

"Do you see Mr. Booker in the wheelchair there?"

The doctor removed his glasses, polished them, then put them back on and stared at Deon for a moment. "Yes."

"Is he the one you treated?"

"Yes."

"As you can see, Doctor, he can't walk. Why is that?"

"The bullet, or some invasive object, severely damaged the spinal cord, rendering him paralyzed from the waist down."

"That's a very tragic thing to happen to a young man in the prime of life, isn't it?"

"Yes, of course. But at that he was lucky. A fraction of an inch more, and the entire cord would have been cut, leaving him totally paralyzed from the neck down. And a fraction of an inch beyond that and he could have been killed. As it is, he is still alive, and he still has use of his upper body."

"Doctor, what was the path of this 'invasive object'?"

"The wound followed a line between the side and the lower middle part of the back."

"Which was the entry wound, Doctor? The hole in Mr. Booker's back, or the hole in his side?"

Doctor Peterson shook his head. "I'm afraid that is impossible to determine."

"Why?"

"The invasive object penetrated the body with very little deformation, which means that the exit wound was as small and compact as the entry wound."

"Was the wound in Deon Booker larger or smaller than the wound that killed Harley Mack Teasdale?"

"They were about the same, I'd say."

"Both wounds could have been made by the same gun?"

"Perhaps."

"We have already identified and tagged the bullet that killed Harley Mack Teasdale as a thirty-eight-caliber bullet. Would you say that the wounds you saw in Deon Booker were consistent in shape and dimension with wounds caused by a thirty-eight-caliber pistol?"

"They could be."

"Objection, Your Honor," Eddie Bender called. "This is pure speculation."

"Sustained."

"Dr. Peterson, you have testified in court on gunshot wounds before, have you not?" Conway asked.

"Yes, sir, lots of times."

Conway turned his back on Dr. Peterson and began walking slowly toward the jury box. "Then I'm sure you realize that Mr. Bender is quite correct in lodgin' his objection, for without the bullet that wounded Deon Booker, you cannot be sure both wounds were caused by the same gun, can you?"

"No, sir."

Conway suddenly spun around and held up his finger. "Let me ask you this, Doctor. Was one wound much larger than the other? Misshapen? That sort of thing?"

"No, sir."

"Then you did not see anything in your examination that

would disprove the theory of both wounds being caused by the same weapon, did you?"

"No, sir, I did not."

"Thank you, Doctor. No further questions."

Eddie stood up, mopping his brow with a handkerchief, and crossed to the witness chair. He assessed the witness for a moment, then asked, "Dr. Peterson, you aren't tryin' to tell the court that both wounds were caused by the same bullet, are you? In other words, you don't think the bullet went through Mr. Booker's back, out his side, then flew a hundred and fifty feet to strike, with deadly accuracy, Mr. Teasdale between the eyes, do you?"

"No, sir, I'm not trying to tell the court that."

"Then you are willin' to concede at least two bullets were fired that day?"

"Objection, calls for a conclusion."

"Your Honor, this is prosecution's own expert witness," Eddie replied. "If we can't get a reasonable assumption from him, then what is he doin' here?"

"Overruled. Witness may answer the question."

"Yes," Dr. Peterson said, "I do believe there were two bullets fired that day."

Eddie Bender walked over to the table and picked up Stump Pollard's pistol.

"Dr. Peterson, this is Stump Pollard's weapon. As you can see, it is a revolver. Which means that, unlike an automatic, when the bullet is fired, the shell casin' stays in the gun. In this case, it stays in one of the chambers of the cylinder. You do understand how that works, don't you?"

"Of course. I have shot both automatics and revolvers."

"Yes, sir, I know you have. I just wanted to explain it so that the jury would understand. Now, Dr. Peterson, you do know that when the police came, Stump surrendered his weapon to them."

"Yes, sir."

"Do you also know that when the police examined his revolver, there was only one spent cartridge in the cylinder?"

"No, I wasn't aware of that."

"Well, now, do you have any explanation for that?"

"What do you mean?"

"Doctor, you have conceded that you believe the wounds in Mr. Booker and Mr. Teasdale were made by two bullets. If Stump Pollard's gun was only fired one time, where did the other bullet come from?"

"I . . . I don't know."

"Dr. Peterson, what treatment did you give Deon Booker?"

"I gave him trauma treatment only. He was moved to a hospital in St. Louis as soon as it was determined that he could be moved."

"I see. And since Harley Mack was already dead, you didn't do any more than look at him and pronounce him dead?"

"That's all."

"What about the others? Did you treat any of them? My associate in this trial, for example. She suffered a blow to the head, didn't she? Did you look at her?"

"Yes."

"And what did you determine?"

"That she fell, or was struck, on her head. The nature of the wound was such that I couldn't be sure. I cleaned it and applied antiseptic. I told her I didn't think she would have any long-term effects from the wound."

"Did you treat anyone else?"

"Not really."

Eddie had been walking away; now he turned back toward Dr. Peterson. "Oh? What about Violet Simmons?"

"You mean the colored girl? Well, she complained of—"

"Objection, Your Honor! Whatever the colored girl complained of has no bearing on the case!" Conway yelled.

"Your Honor, why did the prosecutor sit there quietly while the doctor described his treatment of Miss Canfield's wound, but when the doctor started to talk about Miss Simmons being raped, he suddenly objects?"

"In the first place, Your Honor, what we are talkin' about here is an allegation of rape, not a charge. And it was filed, I might add, by an hysterical young woman. And in the second place, it has nothin' at all to do with the case we are tryin'."

"Your Honor, Miss Simmons was present while all this was goin' on. She was a witness, and I will be usin' her testimony. I would think that her condition on the mornin' in question might be a valid point of consideration here."

The judge looked from man to man. "Counselors, please, approach the bench."

Eddie started toward the bench; then he turned and looked back at Alicia. "Come on," he said. "That means you, too."

Quickly, Alicia stood and joined them.

"All right, Mr. Bender, you tried to open this bag before. Now, what is your purpose in bringing this up again?"

"Your Honor, on the night before the shootin', Miss Simmons was raped by Peter Field. Rape is a crime of violence, and anyone who would do somethin' like that would have no compunctions against killin'. That is enough to give any reasonable person a legitimate right to be frightened for his life. The fact that a rape took place is critical to establishin' the frame of mind of my client when he saw three armed men comin' toward them."

"There is only an allegation of rape, Your Honor. It is not a fact," Conway argued.

"Have charges been filed?" the judge asked.

"Your Honor, she's a colored girl from out of state. How seriously do you think her complaint would be taken?"

"It would be taken seriously in my court, Mr. Bender," Judge Dowling said. "Rape is rape, and it doesn't matter whether the victim is a white woman or a colored woman. Now, have charges been filed?"

"I can answer that, Your Honor. No charges have been filed," Conway said.

"I'll file them today, if necessary," Eddie offered.

"So what if he does file them, Your Honor? What does that have to do with the case at hand? We are tryin' second-degree murder here, not rape."

"Your Honor, when Violet Simmons takes the witness stand, she is going to testify that she was raped by Peter Field. I want it on record now that she made the same complaint to Dr. Peterson on the morning after, if for no other reason than to let the jury know that this isn't somethin' that just came up."

Judge Dowling tugged on his earlobe for a moment, then nodded. "Very well, Mr. Bender, I will let you walk down this path for a short distance—but I intend to keep you on a tight leash. Now, let's continue."

As Alicia walked back to the defense table to sit down, her gaze found Violet, and she nodded slightly toward her.

"Dr. Peterson, did Miss Simmons complain of any problems?" Eddie Bender asked, walking over to the witness chair.

Peterson looked over at the prosecution table at Conway, who pointedly averted his eyes.

"Answer the question, Doctor," Judge Dowling instructed.

"She, uh, complained that she had been, uh, assaulted the night before."

"Assaulted?"

"Yes, sir."

"Is that what she said? Did she say she was assaulted?"

"She said she was raped."

"Had she been raped?"

"It is impossible to tell if a mature, sexually active woman has been raped."

Eddie started to ask another question when Judge Dowling interrupted him.

"Mr. Bender, I do believe the little gal you've got sittin' at the table with you is tryin' to get your attention," he said.

"Thank you, Your Honor." He walked back to the table and leaned over while Alicia whispered something in his ear.

"You ask him that," Eddie said.

"Me?"

"Sure. You're one of the lawyers of record." He turned toward the judge. "You Honor, my cocounsel is going to continue the cross-examination." He sat down, and Alicia nervously stood up for what was about to be the first cross-examination question of her legal career.

She cleared her throat. "Dr. Peterson, did you believe Miss Simmons when she told you she had been raped?"

"No, ma'am, I didn't."

"Why didn't you believe her?"

"It just seemed farfetched to me, that's all. I mean considerin' who it was and all."

"You mean because she is Negro and the assailant was white?"

"Objection. Alleged assailant," Conway said.

"Sustained."

"Because her alleged"—Alicia said the word softly, paused briefly, then emphasized the next word—"*assailant* was white?"

"You might say that."

"Doctor, you say now that you don't believe she was brutally raped by Peter Field. But on that morning you treated her as if you did believe her, did you not?"

"What do you mean?"

"You administered a sedative . . . and a blood test. What was the blood test for?"

"It was just routine, that's all."

"You didn't give any of the rest of us blood tests. Nor did you prescribe a sedative."

"You were sufferin' a concussion. A sedative would have been the last thing I would prescribe for you."

"What was the blood test for, Doctor?"

"To test for VD."

"Isn't that prescribed by law when you are treating a rape victim?"

"Yes."

"So then you did believe her?"

"I thought it was better to be safe than sorry, that's all," Peterson replied waspishly. "But that doesn't mean—"

"Thank you, Doctor," Alicia said, cutting him off. "No further questions."

"Redirect, Mr. Conway?"

"Yes, Your Honor," Conway said. "Dr. Peterson, regardless of this alleged rape smoke screen thrown up by the defense, the question we are here to decide is not whether or not the girl was raped, but whether or not Stump Pollard was justified in shootin' Harley Mack Teasdale. Now, the defense pointed out to you there was only one empty shell casin' in the cylinder of Stump Pollard's revolver, correct?"

"Yes, sir."

"What Mr. Bender failed to point out to you was the fact that though there was only one empty shell casin', there were two empty chambers. Were you aware of that, Doctor?"

"No, sir, I was not aware of that."

"Dr. Peterson, how difficult is it to poke one of the empty cartridges out?"

"It isn't hard at all. In fact, there's a cartridge ejector on the gun. You could poke one out in less than a second."

"So if Stump Pollard wanted to poke one of the empty cartridges out and leave one in so that it would look as if he only fired once, he could do so easily?"

"Yes, very easily."

"Thank you, Doctor. No further questions. Your Honor, the state calls its next witness."

Conway called the ambulance driver and the police officer who had worked the case. They testified that Harley Mack Teasdale was dead by the time they had arrived, that Deon Booker was lying facedown unable to move because of his wound, and that Charles Good and Peter Field were being held prisoner by Stump Pollard.

"Held prisoner how?" Conway asked Deputy Marion Wilson.

"He had made them put their arms behind their back, then tied their thumbs together with their shoestrings," Wilson said. "It may not sound like it, but it's a very effective way of keepin' someone prisoner."

"Deputy Wilson, you found the bullet that killed Harley Mack Teasdale, you did not?"

"Yes, sir, I found it."

"Where was it?"

"It was about fifteen feet beyond Teasdale's body."

"Was it hard to find?"

"No, sir. There was a blood pattern that sprayed out from the wound. I just followed that pattern, and there was the bullet."

"Did you find the bullet that wounded Deon Booker?"

"No, sir."

"Were any of the civil rights workers armed?"

"No, sir."

"Besides Stump Pollard, who else was armed?"

"Harley Mack, Charley, and Pete were all armed."

"What were they carryin'?"

"Charley was carryin' a forty-four revolver. Pete was carryin' a twenty-two target pistol. And Harley Mack was carrying a German P-Thirty-eight automatic."

"An automatic? The kind that kicks out the empty cartridge when it fires?"

"Yes, sir."

"Did you find any empty cartridges?"

"No, sir."

"Thank you. I have no further questions."

Eddie stood up. "Deputy Wilson, did you check Harley Mack's gun to see if it had recently been fired?"

"Yes, sir."

"And had it been?"

"Yes, sir."

"Didn't you find that significant?"

"No, sir, not particularly. The boys told me they'd been doin' some target shootin' the night before."

"Did you do a paraffin test on Harley Mack?"

"No, sir. Didn't see any need. They said they'd been doin' target shootin'."

"And you let it go at that?"

"Yes, sir."

"I see. Well, now, you have testified that you found no empty cartridge to indicate that Harley Mack fired his weapon, is that true?"

"That's true."

"What about where Stump was? Prosecution has made a suggestion that perhaps Stump fired two rounds and poked one of the empty cartridges out of his revolver. Did you find an empty thirty-eight caliber shell casin'?"

"No, sir, I did not."

"Thank you. No further questions, Your Honor."

The ambulance driver was the next witness for the prosecution, but his testimony was unremarkable, and Eddie Bender chose not to cross-examine him.

After the ambulance driver, the state called Mildred Foreman. She, along with her husband, was the owner of the general store where Alicia and Jerry had bought groceries for the picnic. She testified that she had been terrified when Alicia and Jerry came into the store, and she had not been at all surprised when trouble broke out a while later.

Alicia cross-examined her.

"Mrs. Foreman, did either my friend or I say anything to you that you considered threatening?" Alicia asked quietly.

"Not directly."

"Indirectly, then?"

"Indirectly? Yes, ma'am, I guess that's the way it was. It was indirect."

"In what way?"

"Well, when I told you about them findin' the bodies of that colored boy and the white girl, you got real upset. Then you told me you knew them and that you was one of them. I got afraid that you and your friend and the coloreds you said you had with you might want to hurt me in some way. I was afraid you might be blamin' me for what happened to them."

"Did we give you any cause to feel that way?"

"No, not really," Mrs. Foreman admitted.

Alicia smiled at the woman. "What about now, Mrs. Foreman? If I came into your store now, would you be frightened?"

"No, knowin' what I know now, I don't reckon I would."

Alicia started back to the defense table, then stopped and looked back toward Mrs. Foreman. "Knowing what you know now, Mrs. Foreman, would you be frightened *for* us?"

"Objection, Your Honor!"

"Withdraw the question," Alicia said quickly. The big smiles on Eddie's and Stump's faces as she sat down told her that she had scored with the question, withdrawn or not.

"Your Honor, the state calls Mrs. Emma Teasdale to the stand."

Alicia turned in her seat to watch Emma Teasdale, the mother of Harley Mack Teasdale, approach the stand. She was a frail woman, with a pinched face and dingy-gray hair pulled back in a severe bun. Her eyes were sad and tired, and her lips were so thin as to be little more than a line drawn across the lower third of her face. Her sunken jaws were the result of missing teeth, lost no doubt through neglect and poor diet. She wore a blue-print dress that was a shade too big for her, and as she walked up to the front of the courtroom she clutched the collar together with her right hand. She might have been forty or seventy; Alicia had no way of determining. Despite the fact that this was the mother of a monster like Harley Mack, Alicia couldn't help but feel an immediate sympathy for her.

Emma was sworn in, then took the witness stand. Conway approached her.

"Mrs. Teasdale, first I would like to thank you for agreein' to testify. I realize it's goin' to be hard on you, but I know you understand we must do this to see justice served. Now, I would begin by askin' if you know Stump Pollard."

Emma looked over at the defense table, then raised her right hand and pointed a long, bony finger toward Stump. "That be him a-sittin' there at the table, next to Lawyer Bender."

"How long have you known him?"

"I don't know him for him to speak to me, but I've know'd who he was, ever' since he kilt my first husband."

There was a surprised gasp from everyone in the court-room.

"That would be Harley Mack's daddy?"

"Yes, sir."

"Damn!" Eddie said under his breath. He turned to Stump. "Did you kill Harley Mack's daddy?"

"I don't know," Stump whispered back.

"You don't know?" Eddie whispered fiercely. "Well, just how goddamn many men have you killed? Have you killed so many you don't even know them all?"

"Counting Harley Mack, I've killed three," Stump said. "And one of them was a black man."

"Who was the other?"

"A guy named Deekus Farley."

"What was Harley Mack's daddy's name?" Conway was asking the witness at that point.

"It was Deekus Farley," Emma Teasdale said. "That was Harley Mack's name, too, till I married Maynard—Mr. Teasdale. Maynard, he adopted Harley Mack."

"What were the conditions that led up to Stump Pollard killin' your first husband?"

Emma sighed. "Poor ol' Deekus, he never was none too bright. He was always gettin' hisself into first one fix, then another. Only one day he got hisself into a fix he couldn't get out of. He robbed a grocery store over in Delta, and he shot an' killed a nigra woman what was workin' there. Then when he tried to leave by the front door, he seen lots of folks comin' to see what was the shootin' about. So he run out the back door and down the alley. By then folks had called the police. Stump Pollard—he was the chief then—got wind of where Deekus was an' chased him down and shot him dead in the graveyard out at the edge of town."

"And what about Harley Mack? Did he ever have any run-ins with Mr. Pollard?"

"Yes, sir. First it was just tomfoolery kinds of things. You know, things like boys do. That was when Mr. Pollard was still with the police. But even after he left, seems like he was always findin' somethin' to do to get my boy into trouble. Two, maybe three times he done somethin' he called a citi-zen's arrest. Never heard of that till Mr. Pollard started usin' it on Harley Mack. Maynard—Mr. Teasdale—he didn't like it much, an' he complained to the police over in Delta that Mr. Pollard was harassin' my boy, but they didn' do nothin' about it."

"Where is Mr. Teasdale now?"

"He's dead. He got likkered up and was kilt in a car wreck two years ago. It's been a hard life for me, but long as I had my boy, my Harley Mack, I was able to get along." She took out a handkerchief and dabbed at tears. "Now I got no one," she sniffed.

"Again, Mrs. Teasdale, let me thank you for testifying today. I know it was very difficult for you." He looked over at Eddie. "Counselor, I leave this poor woman in your hands."

Eddie half stood. "I have no questions," he said.

"Eddie!" Stump hissed. "Ask her about Deekus! He not only shot and killed the Negro woman in the store, he also shot and wounded three more people as he was running down the alley. And one of them has a game leg till this day. When I cornered him in the graveyard, he refused to give up. He started shooting at me, and I had no choice. It was a good shoot."

Eddie shook his head. "The longer Emma Teasdale stays up there, the sadder a figure she becomes. Let's get her the hell out of there before she does any more damage."

"He's right, Mr. Pollard," Alicia said.

Eddie smiled. "See. Even the little girl agrees with me."

"Your Honor, Mrs. Teasdale was my last witness," Conway said. "Prosecution now rests its case."

The judge nodded. "Okay, Mr. Bender, it's up to you now. Is defense ready to present its case?"

Eddie stood. "Your Honor, we have a case developed that will prove the homicide was justifiable homicide by reason of self-defense. But I see no need to waste the state's time or money by going any further. It should be obvious to anyone that prosecution has clearly been unable to make a case for second-degree murder. I move that the case be dismissed."

"Thank you, Mr. Bender, for what I am sure is your heartfelt concern over a waste of the people's time and money in this case," the judge said dryly. "But let's go on with it, shall we?"

"Very well, Your Honor. I'm prepared to call my first witness."

"Will it be lengthy?"

"I don't know, Your Honor. I intend to take it as far as necessary."

"Yes, well, due to the lateness of the hour and the fact that I mean to give you as much time as you need to fully develop your case, I am going to adjourn until tomorrow. Members of the jury, you are cautioned not to discuss this case with each other or with anyone else."

Judge Dowling slapped his gavel on the block. "Court is adjourned until nine o'clock tomorrow morning."

"Our case is suckin' muddy water," Eddie Bender said as he mixed himself a bourbon and Coke at the bar in his office. He offered the liquor bottle to Stump, Alicia, Deon, Jerry, and Violet. When they declined, he nodded toward a refrigerator that stood against the back wall. "I've got beer and soda pop in there if anyone wants somethin'."

Jerry got drinks for all of them.

"What do you mean, our case is sucking muddy water?" Stump said, popping the cap off a beer bottle. "Goddammit, Eddie, I've seen you weave magic when the sonsabitches you were defending were as guilty as sin. Now you've got an open-and-shut case of self-defense and you can't make it?"

Eddie took a swallow of his bourbon before he answered. "Open and shut, is it? What makes you say that?"

"Because in the first place, Harley Mack and those other bastards kidnapped these four kids. Then Pete Field raped Violet. And when they caught me letting them out, Harley Mack opened fire on me."

"That's not the way Field and Good are tellin' it. They say you shot first."

"They're full of shit. Harley Mack fired first."

Eddie looked at Alicia. "Is that true, Alicia? Did Harley Mack fire first?"

"Yes, of course he did."

"What makes you so certain?"

"Because I heard more than one gunshot."

"Yes, I did, too," Jerry said.

"So did I," Violet insisted.

"Uh-huh. And how far away from you was Teasdale when the shootin' started?"

"About fifty yards."

"That would be one hundred fifty feet."

"Yes."

"Uh-huh. That's about halfway down the line to the right-field fence," Eddie said.

"What the hell are you talking about?" Stump asked.

"You played football in college, Stump, so I don't expect you to understand. But I played baseball," Eddie explained. "Right field. One of the earliest adjustments I had to make was to play the ball off the batter's bat by sight—not by sound. Because even at a hundred fifty feet, there's enough delay between sight and sound to cause you to lose track of the ball."

"What are you getting at?" Jerry asked.

"If you all were one hundred fifty feet away from Harley Mack and his two cohorts, the sound of their shootin' and the sound of Stump's shootin' might be on top of each other."

"What if it was?"

"If that's the case, how could you be sure who shot first? In fact, how can you be sure Harley Mack shot at all? Maybe the two gunshots you heard were both from Stump's gun."

"I only shot one time," Stump said.

"What about you, Deon? Do you think you were shot by Harley Mack Teasdale?"

"I know I was."

"How do you know?"

"Because it's the kind of thing that rednecked bastard would do."

"And, of course, Stump would never shoot you in the back."

"Of course not."

"Unless it was an accident."

"Come on, Eddie," Stump snapped. "I nailed Harley Mack right between the eyes from one hundred fifty feet. You think I could accidentally shoot Deon?"

"I don't think so. But Deon did tell the doctor that he had been shot in the back."

"I didn't know any better then."

"Why did you say it?"

"Because I thought I had."

"Why did you think that?"

"Because that's . . . that's what it felt like to me," Deon hedged.

"Uh-huh. The only thing is, your back was to Stump, not to Harley Mack."

Alicia shook her head angrily. "Mr. Bender, that doesn't mean anything and you know it. You heard the doctor say that Deon wouldn't be able to tell whether he was shot in the back or the side."

"I know," Eddie answered. "Which means that as a witness, Deon is useless to us." He looked at Deon. "I know I called you down here to testify, but I think I'm not even goin' to put you on the stand. If Conway has a whack at you, you could do some serious damage to our case just by tellin' the truth."

"Shit, I thought he was our star witness," Stump said.

"He was."

"And you're not going to use him?"

"No." Eddie sighed. "Now do you see what I mean when I say our case is suckin' muddy water?"

"What are we going to do?" Alicia asked.

"Here's where you learn one of the most important tactics in a lawyer's book of tricks."

"And what's that?"

Eddie looked at each of them in turn. "You learn how to pray."

NEW YORK

When Sheri Warren stepped into the expansive office, Kerry O'Braugh came around his desk smiling, his hand extended.

"Miss Warren, it is good to see you again. How have you been getting along?"

"Fine, thank you," she replied. She looked around the office, taking note of the walnut desk and table, the leather sofa and chairs, the antique Oriental carpet, and the works of art on the walls and on the shelves. "You have a lovely office. Very elegant."

Kerry chuckled. "You mean it's more like a businessman's office than a gangster's, right?"

"Well, no . . . not exactly. That is . . ."

She paused, and Kerry laughed again.

"Don't worry about it," he said, dismissing her embarrassment with a wave of his hand. "Look, I know you had me checked out. Hell, that's why I told you to take a few weeks to think it over. So, now you know. My background hasn't been all that clean."

"No, it hasn't," Sheri agreed.

"On the other hand, did you find anything on me since I returned to the States?"

"No."

"Well, all right then. There you go. You didn't find anything, and you won't find anything because I've been straight ever since I came back." He opened a silver cigarette box and held it out toward her. "You want a smoke?"

"No, thank you."

"Do you mind if I do?"

"No, go right ahead."

Kerry lit a cigarette, then exhaled a blue plume of smoke. "I suppose I ought to give these things up," he said. "I've been reading articles saying cigarettes cause cancer. Do you believe that?"

"I don't know. It probably can't be good for you, putting all that stuff in your lungs."

"Yeah, that's what I think. I'd really like to quit, but it's hard, you know?"

"I'm sure it is."

"Listen, have a seat over here so we can talk," Kerry said, ushering her over to the sofa. She sat down and was surprised when he sat on the sofa beside her rather than in one of the facing chairs. "I want to explain a little about my past to you."

"You don't have to."

"I want to. I mean, young people like you, you don't know what it was like in the old days. Life was hard, and if you were an immigrant kid with nothing going for you, you had to use all your wits just to survive."

"I'm sure you did what you thought you had to do," Sheri said. "Really, Mr. O'Braugh, you don't owe me any explanations."

He smiled. "I know I don't. But if we're going to do business together . . . We *are* going to do business together, aren't we? That *is* why you're here?"

"Yes. If you're still serious about investing."

"I'm very serious about it, Miss Warren. Which is why I want you to understand a little of where I'm coming from, as the kids like to say today."

Sheri nodded. "All right."

"For someone like me in the old days, the only way up was to make the right friends."

"You mean like the Mafia?"

"Miss Warren, what do you know about the Mafia?"

"Not much, really," Sheri admitted. "I've read about it, of course. The Cosa Nostra, that sort of thing."

Kerry smiled. "I find it interesting how many people know of the Mafia, but know nothing about it." He stood up. "Let me show you something."

He led her over to a wall displaying an old shield bearing a coat of arms. Next to the shield was a sword and a mace. There was also an old parchment, framed and carefully preserved. Sheri tried to read it, but it was in Italian.

"What is this?" she asked.

"It is a proclamation, given to my grandfather."

"What does it say?"

"It says, 'The citizens of Taormina gratefully acknowledge the help given them by Luigi Sangremano, and, from this day forward, accord upon him and all his descendants the title of Don. The citizens also recognize the claim of the Mafia to be the arbitrators of justice, and swear by the code of *omertà* to hold the secrets of Luigi Sangremano in sacred trust.' It's dated 1871," Kerry concluded.

"Is this real?"

"Of course it's real. It's the recognition of a grateful community of services rendered to them by my grandfather."

Sheri shook her head. "I can't believe you actually keep a charter on your wall that connects your family with the Mafia." She laughed nervously. "That's a little like keeping your parole from prison framed, isn't it?"

"That is the popular concept of the Mafia, yes. And, to be honest, the history of the Mafia in America deserves that reputation. But that doesn't change the legitimate contribution the Mafia has made to Sicilian society, nor the historic significance of this charter. You see, when it started—back in the 1600s—it was a patriotic organization."

"Like the VFW, no doubt," Sheri deadpanned.

Kerry chuckled. "No, nothing like that. More like the French Underground during World War Two or the partisans in Italy during the same era. In fact, many of the partisans were members of the Mafia."

Sheri remembered reading in the report that Kerry had been a partisan.

"For such people during the war, it was considered patriotic to go around blowing up police stations, military barracks, bridges, trains, even banks," he explained. "But times have changed, and anyone who would do such a thing today would be considered a criminal."

"So you're saying that when the Mafia first started, it was a clandestine political organization?"

"Absolutely. In the early days of the Mafia, it was the only justice the Sicilian people had against Bourbon rule. The Mafia fought against terror and oppression and helped gain freedom for the Sicilians. But, as frequently happens to many good things, its noble purposes were soon perverted, and corruptible men found that the power they had taken up was just too enticing to put down. The good name they had established, along with the code of omertà, enabled them to keep the Mafia intact, even though its goals were no longer so noble."

"What is omertà?"

"Code of silence. It means that no one will tell the police of any criminal activity. That code of honor has been *the* one thing that allowed the Mafia to survive and flourish."

"Code of *honor*?"

"Yes. Honor is very important to me—and to people like me."

Sheri recalled her lawyer's warning about Kerry O'Braugh's code of honor. "You are what they call a 'made man,' aren't you?"

"Yes," Kerry said.

"Are you proud of that?"

Kerry stood looking at the document on the wall for a moment; then he walked back over to the sofa and sat down. Sheri went with him.

"I really don't know how to answer that question," he admitted. "At the time I perceived it as the proudest moment in my life. For one thing, I'm half Irish—I even bear an Irish name. To be accepted by the others under such conditions . . . well, it was—and is—unheard of. For that recognition I still feel a sense of pride. But over the years I have had to do a lot of things that I'm not so proud of now. Maybe that's why I'm trying so hard to be legitimate. I will tell you of my past, Miss Warren, but I make no apologies for it. That was then, and this is now."

"I thank you, Mr. O'Braugh, for being so forthright with me," Sheri said, feeling a strange kind of admiration for the man.

"It's all out on the table," Kerry said. "Now, are you still willing to do business with an old reprobate like me?"

"I would be happy to do business with you," Sheri replied solemnly.

Kerry smiled broadly. "Great! Now, how about another dinner to seal the deal?"

"All right, but please, not Mama Tantini's again," Sheri said, laughing and holding up her hand. "Too many dinners like that and I won't be able to wear the clothes I'm designing."

"Okay, you pick a place."

"I know a place where they serve only salads. It's wonderful."

Kerry laughed. "Yeah, I guess I can put up with leaves and twigs for one meal. I'll have my *consigliore* draw up the contract and advance you the money and we're in business."

"I beg your pardon? Have who draw up the contract?"

"Consigliore." Kerry smiled. "That's lawyer, to you."

CHAPTER
TWELVE

AUGUST 6, 1962, FROM "TRAILMARKERS" IN
EVENTS MAGAZINE:"

MARILYN MONROE ENDS HER OWN LIFE
AT THE AGE OF 36

A bottle of sleeping pills beside her, Marilyn
Monroe was found dead in the bedroom of her Los
Angeles home yesterday. According to her psycho-
analyst, Marilyn had tried twice before to kill herself, though each time she made a telephone call in
time to save her life. When her body was found, her
arm was reaching toward the phone, as if she had
intended once more to undo what she had done.

SHERI WARREN ANNOUNCES NEW
COMPANY: CONTEMPO CLOTHES

Sheri Warren, the hot, hot fashion designer
who created the SheriWear line of women's clothing for E. J. Buckner, has left to form her own
company. Although she is prohibited by contractual

agreement to use the name SheriWear or even any part of her own name in the marketing of her new line of clothes, that apparently won't stop her success. The enormous talent is still there.

"I have seen her new line of clothes," fashion critic Eleanor Lambert said. "They are sensuous, sassy, and scintillating. They will make quite a bold statement about the sexy sixties."

MARTIN LUTHER KING FREED FROM GEORGIA PRISON

City officials in Albany, Georgia, freed Dr. Martin Luther King and Dr. Ralph Abernathy this week, just days into their 45-day sentence, thus avoiding threatened mass demonstrations.

The two civil rights leaders had been jailed when they led a group of antisegregationists to the steps of the Albany city hall to attempt to force a meeting with the mayor of Albany. When the mayor refused to appear, the group knelt in prayer, after which the chief of police arrested King and Abernathy as the leaders of the disturbance.

This was the third time this year that King and Abernathy have been arrested in Albany.

SARDIS, MISSISSIPPI

On the second day of Stump Pollard's trial, Eddie Bender called Alicia Canfield to the stand.

"Tell the court in your own words what happened to you and your friends on the night before and the morning of the incident in question," Eddie instructed.

A well-composed Alicia told how only she and Jerry had gone into the general store to buy food for a picnic, wanting to avoid any kind of confrontation that the presence of Deon and Violet might cause. She told how frightened they had been when the pickup truck carrying the four men had stopped—a fear quickly justified when they were ostensibly arrested and led through the swamp to the abandoned toolshed. She told how Peter Field had made sexually explicit threats toward Violet and how, when she had stood up for her friend, she was hit from behind. And she told of the long, fearful night they spent in the toolshed before being rescued the next morning by Stump Pollard.

"Then, as we were walking through the swamp back to the road that morning," Alicia continued, "Mr. Pollard abruptly shouted for us to get down. At about the same time I heard a shot and saw Deon fall. Then I heard another shot. That's when I looked over toward the trees and saw the three men, one of whom was lying motionless."

"Were these men armed?"

"They were. But at Mr. Pollard's orders they put their weapons on the ground."

"Thank you, Miss Canfield," Eddie said. "Your witness, Mr. Conway."

The prosecutor stood. "Thank you, Counselor. Miss Canfield, did you see the three men comin' out of the trees before Stump's warnin'?"

"No."

"Did you see them shoot Mr. Booker?"

"I heard them shoot him."

"You *heard* them?"

"Yes."

"How do you mean that?"

"I heard the sound of a gunshot. Deon went down. The gunshot came from where the three men were standing."

"By that you mean it sounded like it came from one of the three men?"

"Yes."

"Have you been in many gun battles, Miss Canfield?"

"Objection, Your Honor," Eddie said, his tone disdainful. "The prosecutor is bein' facetious and inflammatory."

"Sustained."

"All right, I'll reword my question. Have you done much huntin', Miss Canfield?"

"No."

"Have you ever hunted?"

"No."

"Have you ever had occasion to be in an area when guns are being fired? Before this incident, I mean."

"No."

"That's too bad. Because if you had, Miss Canfield, you would know what every man in this courtroom who has ever been in battle or has ever been huntin' would know: It is nearly impossible to judge, exclusively by sound, where a gunshot comes from . . . or even how far away it is. And for someone who admittedly has no experience at all, I daresay it is impossible. Now, given all that, Miss Canfield, are you still tellin' the jury that you know the gunshot came from the three men? Or are you just tellin' us that you believe it did?"

"I'm sure it did."

"You saw the muzzle flash? The puff of gun smoke?"

"No."

"You heard it?"

"Yes."

"Then what you are tellin' us is you believe it came from one of the three men. You believe it, but can you swear to it, Miss Canfield?"

Alicia was silent for a long moment. Finally, with a re-signed sigh, she said, "No. I cannot swear to it."

"Thank you, Miss Canfield. No further questions."

"You may step down, Miss Canfield," the judge in-structed.

The examination and cross-examination of Jerry Wiggins produced basically the same responses.

Defense then called Marvin Posey, one of the men who had accosted the four young civil rights workers. Taking the stand, he admitted to being in the pickup truck and to harass-ing them while they were having their picnic. He then testi-fied how he started having second thoughts about it when Harley Mack decided to lock them in the toolshed and when Pete Field said he was going to rape Violet. Not wanting to be a party to such a thing, he left.

"Mr. Posey," James Conway asked on his cross-examina-tion, "did you try and talk those fellas out of anything?"

"No, sir."

"Why not? If you felt that what they were doin' was wrong, why didn't you try to stop them?"

"It wouldn't've done any good for me to try," Marvin said. "They had their minds made up what they were goin' to do."

"Uh-huh. Well, Mr. Posey, did you actually see Peter Field rape the colored girl?"

"No, sir," Marvin admitted. "I told you, I left."

"So then you don't actually know that he did do it, do you?"

"He said he was goin' to."

" 'He said he was goin' to.' Is it not possible that he was just talkin' big but really had no intention of actually carryin' through on his threat?"

"I don't know. I sure thought he was going to do it."

"You thought he was, but you don't know for a fact that he did do it, do you, Mr. Posey? I mean, you didn't see him do it, did you?"

"No, sir, I told you I didn't."

"Then what you are testifyin' to is what Mr. Field *said* he was goin' to do . . . not what he did. Is that right?"

"Yes, sir, I guess it is."

"Tell me, Mr. Posey. What is your relationship to the defendant?"

"He's my uncle."

"Thank you, Mr. Posey. No further questions."

Violet Simmons was the next witness for the defense. She testified in a soft voice how, after being forced by gun-point through the swamp to the toolshed, one of the men, Peter Field, took her off a ways from the shed and raped her.

"Did you try to fight him off?" Eddie Bender asked.

"Yes, sir. But he hit me in the face. Several times. Finally I just couldn't fight anymore."

"What about the others? Did they also rape you?"

"No, sir."

"Well, did they help Field? Did they hold you down or anything?"

"No, sir. They just stood nearby and watched," Violet said in a flat, emotionless voice.

"Now, Miss Simmons, tell us what you know about what happened the next mornin'."

Violet's account was substantially the same as Jerry's and Alicia's. Finally it was Conway's turn to cross-examine.

"Miss Simmons, I know it was difficult for you to testify about the events that took place the day before the shootin' incident. In fact, I don't intend to challenge you on your account of what happened. You have been through enough on that score," Conway said in a surprisingly conciliatory tone. "So I will confine my questions to the events of the followin' mornin' since that is what we are here to determine. Did you see—and I mean actually *see*—anyone firin' at you?"

"No, but I know they—"

"Yes or no, please," Conway said, holding up his hand. "Did you see Harley Mack Teasdale shoot Deon Booker?"

"No, sir."

"No further questions."

Stump Pollard was the last witness called, and he took the stand to testify on his own behalf. He told how his nephew, Marvin, had come to him, telling how the day before he and a group of his friends had kidnapped four civil rights workers and locked them in a toolshed on the old Trotter place. Stump then went out to the Trotter place to release them, and while they were walking across the slough to his car, Harley Mack Teasdale, Charles Good, and Peter Field came upon them.

"We saw each other at about the same time," Stump said. "I was about to talk to them when Harley Mack raised his weapon and shot. The bullet hit Deon, and he went down. I shouted at the others to get down, and I returned fire. Harley Mack went down, and I aimed at the others."

"Did you shoot again?" Eddie asked.

"No."

"Why not?"

"I didn't have to. They knew I meant business, and they put their guns on the ground."

"How many times did you shoot that mornin'?"

"Only once."

"Now, Mr. Pollard, the prosecutor has made a big deal out of your pistol havin' two empty cylinders. Could you explain that?"

"Yes. It's a habit I got into while still on the force. I always kept an empty chamber under the hammer. That way there was less chance of the gun going off accidentally."

"Thank you, Mr. Pollard. Your witness."

"How many men have you killed, Mr. Pollard?"

"Objection!"

"Your Honor, it seems like a perfectly legitimate question to me. Here is a man who carried a gun in his line of work for many years. I think it would be helpful to know how often he used it."

"Objection is overruled. Answer the question."

"I have killed three men," Stump said.

"Harley Mack, his daddy, and one more?"

"Yes."

"How do you feel when you kill someone?"

"Objection!"

"Sustained."

"Other than this particular incident, Mr. Pollard, has anyone ever shot at you?"

"Yes."

"Have you ever been wounded in the line of duty?"

"Yes, I have."

"So it would be fair to assume that you are very careful of anyone who has a weapon and who is also a potential adversary?"

"Yes, of course."

"Might it not also then be reasonable to assume that you would be so careful as to be overly cautious? For example, might it be possible for you to react to danger before the danger exists?"

"I'm not sure I know what you mean."

"Is it not possible, Mr. Pollard, that you might have shot at Mr. Teasdale because you *thought* he was goin' to shoot at you?"

"He *did* shoot at us. He hit Deon."

"Don't you find it strange, Mr. Pollard, that of all the witnesses on the scene that mornin', you are the only one who can make that statement? Even your own friends admit they can't be certain. If Harley Mack shot at you, where is the empty shell casin'? And where is the spent bullet?"

"I don't know."

"You don't know," Conway mocked. "Then how do you expect us to believe you?"

"Mr. Conway, I had a career of honorable service as a law enforcement officer, and I have a lifetime of honesty and integrity. I would assume those things will have some weight with the jury."

Conway sighed and turned away from Stump to face the jury. "Mr. Pollard, with no witnesses to back you up and no physical evidence to substantiate your claim, you are askin' this jury to make quite a stretch to believe you just because you are a nice person. No further questions."

"Your Honor," Eddie said, rising from his seat, "Mr.

Pollard was my last scheduled witness, but, with your indulgence, I would ask that we adjourn until tomorrow to give me a chance to prepare for the summation."

"Does prosecution have any objections?"

"Your Honor, if Mr. Bender wants to prolong the misery I have no objections," Conway said airily.

"Very well. Court is adjourned until nine o'clock tomorrow morning."

"Stump, I don't mind tellin' you, there's been many a time when I wanted to see you in the fix you're in right now," Eddie Bender said when they had all gathered in his office after court was adjourned. "But, goddammit, not when I'm defendin' you. Your ass is in a crack, and I'm right in there with you."

"You do believe me, don't you, Eddie?" Stump asked.

"Yeah, I believe you. If I didn't believe you, I wouldn't have taken your case in the first place. I would've been sittin' out there in the gallery, rootin' for you to get yours." He poured himself a bourbon and Coke. "The question is, will the jury believe you?"

"Well, excuse me, please, but I just don't understand the problem here," Jerry Wiggins put in. "Stump says Harley Mack shot first. All of us, except for Deon, have testified that we also believe he shot first. Only Good and Field say otherwise. Now, by my count, that makes it four to two. Isn't that good enough to convince the jury?"

"No," Eddie said. "You are testifyin' to what you believe, not to what you know. Pardon my language, ladies, but in the final analysis, your testimony isn't worth a pitcher of piss."

"All right, but the burden of proof is with the prosecution, isn't it?" Jerry persisted.

"Yes."

"So even if it is Stump's word against Good's and Fields, he's a law enforcement officer with a spotless reputation, while it was pretty damn clear they both perjured themselves on the witness stand. That should discredit them, shouldn't it? And when you get right down to it, we don't have to prove anything, prosecution does. Right?"

"Wrong," Eddie answered.

Jerry frowned. "What do you mean, wrong? The burden of proof is with the prosecution, isn't it?"

Eddie stared at Jerry for a moment, then turned to Alicia. "Explain it to him, honey," he said.

"Jerry, we are pleading not guilty by reason of self-defense," she said. "And although you're right, the burden of proof technically does lie with the prosecution, the practical matter is that we also have something to prove. We must convince the jury that Stump believed his life was in such mortal danger that shooting Harley Mack was the only option open to him. For all intents and purposes, that effectively switches the burden of proof to our side. And it's going to be extremely difficult to prove if we don't find something that will shift the balance in our direction."

"Oh."

"Okay, look, you didn't put *me* on the stand," Deon said. "Put me on. I'll swear Teasdale shot first. That'll be two of us against two of them."

"But you cannot testify to that with absolute certainty, can you?" Eddie challenged. "As a matter of fact, you saw and heard less than the other three."

"What difference does that make? At least I'll be testifying to something I believe is true. Good and Field lied, and everyone knows they lied."

Eddie shook his head. "It's no good, Deon. You would be discredited immediately."

"Why? Because I'm a Negro?"

"Partly so," Eddie admitted. "But also because you didn't swear a statement to that effect, and you haven't testified before now."

Deon slammed his hand on the arm of his wheelchair. "Man, I can't believe this! I mean, there is no doubt in my mind but that those three men were coming out there to burn down the shed and kill us. Stump Pollard saved our lives, and for that he's on trial for murder!"

The phone rang, and Alicia answered it.

"What can I tell you?" Eddie said to Deon, as Alicia spoke quietly behind them. "No one said that life is fair."

"*What?*" Alicia suddenly exclaimed, catching everyone's attention. "Are you sure?"

"What is it? What's goin' on? Who're you talkin' to?" Eddie asked.

Alicia covered the mouthpiece. "This is a man who works as an ambulance attendant for the hospital. I think maybe you ought to speak to him."

"What does he want?"

"He says he has the bullet that hit Deon."

Brad Mitchell was a small man with thinning blond hair and light-blue eyes magnified by thick glasses. He sat in a chair in Eddie's office and looked around nervously.

"I know you," Alicia said, appraising him. "You were one of the men who came to pick up Deon."

"Yes, ma'am," Mitchell affirmed, "I was there."

"Why didn't the prosecution call you to testify?" Eddie asked.

"I don't know. Mr. Conway, he know'd I was there, but he just didn't want to use me, I guess."

"Well, never mind that now. You told my associate that you have the bullet that hit Mr. Booker. Is that true?"

"Yes, sir, I got it. I truly do."

"Where is it?"

"Right here." Mitchell pulled an envelope from his pants pocket and handed it to Eddie, who opened it and shook out the spent bullet.

"Damn!" Stump said excitedly. "That's it! That's from Harley Mack's gun!"

"How do you know?"

"Well, look at it! It's a nine millimeter. You know how many guns around here use nine-millimeter ammunition? Not very damned many. But the gun Harley Mack was carrying that day was one of those German P-Thirty-eights that Maynard Teasdale brought back from the war. The P-Thirty-eight uses nine-millimeter ammunition."

"Tell me, Mr. Mitchell, where has this bullet been until now?" Eddie asked.

"Hidden in a locked drawer in the controlled-drugs room of the hospital," he said.

"How did you know it was there?"

"Because that's where I put it."

"I see. And what makes you so certain that this is the bullet that hit Mr. Booker?"

"Because this here bullet is the same one I picked up off the ground that very mornin'," Mitchell said.

Eddie squinted at the man. "Wait a minute, let me get this straight. You mean to tell me that all this time, with all the publicity and all the talk about not being able to find a bullet, you have not only known that a bullet existed, you have known where it was?"

Mitchell averted his eyes. "Yes, sir."

"How many other people know about this bullet?"

"Near as I can figure, there don't nobody else know about it."

"Then would you mind tellin' me why in hell you haven't come forth before now?" Eddie growled.

Mitchell pouted. "I don't know why you're so mad at me. Seems to me like you'd be more'n happy that I've come to you now."

"Yes, well, I'm not askin' you any more than the prosecutor is going to ask. You say you're the only one who knew about this bullet. Why are you just now makin' it known?"

"Well, sir, the truth is, I thought maybe I'd wait and see if"—Mitchell took a deep breath—"see if I could somehow make some money out of it," he concluded.

"And just how did you plan to make money from it? What were you goin' to do? Blackmail Good and Field?"

"Shit, Mr. Bender, you know them boys don't have no money," Mitchell chortled. "No, sir, I was goin' to sell it to some of them newspaper folks. Only, when I called a couple of them, they said that without I had some proof that this here bullet was the actual one, it wasn't worth nothin'."

"I see. So the only reason you've come forth now is to get the proof you need. Is that it?"

"Somethin' like that," Mitchell admitted.

"What about obstruction of justice, Mr. Mitchell?" Eddie asked heatedly. "Have you ever heard of that?"

Mitchell shook his head. "Nope. Don't know what you're talkin' about."

"I'm talkin' about you, Mr. Mitchell. By withholdin' evidence, you have obstructed justice. That is a felony. You can go to prison for that."

"Hold on here!" Mitchell said, his hands up as if warding off misfortune. "I come here to help you out. I didn't come to hear no talk 'bout you puttin' me in prison."

"Bullshit. You didn't come here to help us out. You came here to get this bullet validated so you could make some money from the news media," Eddie said angrily.

"Well, what if I did? Won't that be helpin' you? You got no call to be talkin' 'bout puttin' me in prison."

"It won't be me doin' it, Mr. Mitchell. It'll be the prosecutor. And you can rest assured he will do it."

"What . . . what if I don't say nothin'? I mean, what if this here ain't the bullet? What if I just made all this up?"

Eddie shook his head. "Uh-uh. It's too late now. You've squeezed the toothpaste out of the tube, and you can't put it back. The only hope you have now is to follow through with it, or you'll just get yourself in deeper."

"Shit," Mitchell muttered. "All I wanted to do was make a few bucks, is all. I didn't know nothin' 'bout no obstruction of justice."

"I'll tell you what I'll do," Eddie said. "You cooperate with us now, you testify on the witness stand to what you just told us—how you found this bullet on the ground under Deon and how you've kept it hidden all this time—and I'll see what I can do for you. If it comes down to a trial, I'll defend you."

Mitchell looked from Eddie's face to Stump's, then back. "Yeah, all right. I'll do whatever you want. I swear I didn't know I was goin' to get myself into trouble. I just thought I could—"

"Make a little money," Eddie interrupted. "Yeah, we know."

AUGUST 7

"Your Honor, defense has another witness to call," Eddie Bender said the following morning as soon as court reconvened. "I realize I told the court that I would only be makin' my summation this mornin', but this witness came forward only late yesterday afternoon, and I assure you he is crucial to our defense."

Judge Dowling nodded, jiggling his chins. "Very well. You may call your witness."

"Thank you, Your Honor. Defense calls Brad Mitchell to the stand."

Nervously, Brad Mitchell stepped through the swinging wooden gate and approached the witness stand, then held his hand up while he was sworn in. Taking out a handkerchief, he wiped his face as he took his seat.

"Mr. Mitchell, what is your occupation?"

"I'm an ambulance attendant for the Panola County Ambulance Service."

"On the morning of July twenty-third, did you accompany the ambulance driver and Deputy Wilson to a spot off State Highway Three-fifteen, about halfway between Sardis and Delta?"

"Yes, sir, I did."

"Now, Mr. Mitchell, you have heard both the ambulance driver and the police officer testify, have you not?"

"Yes, sir, I heard 'em."

"Did either of them give any testimony inconsistent with your own recollection?"

"What?"

"Did what they said pretty much match up with the way you remember things?" There was only the slightest hint of impatience in Eddie's voice.

"Oh, yeah. Uh, yes, sir. What they said was pretty much the way things was."

"In the sworn affidavit you gave Mr. Conway, you did nothin' more than verify their stories, is that correct?"

"Yes, sir."

"So it is understandable why the prosecution did not call upon you to testify, since your statement was on record and you would only be secondin' what was already said."

"Yes, sir, I reckon so."

"But there was somethin' you left out of your statement, wasn't there, Mr. Mitchell? Somethin' you called my office about last night?"

"Yes, sir."

"And last night, on your own initiative, you called my office to advise me of this missin' piece of information, did you not?"

"Yes, sir."

"And what was the nature of this missin' information?"

"I called to tell you I had the bullet that hit the colored man."

A gasp rose from the spectators' gallery.

"Is this the bullet?" Eddie asked, walking over to the evidence table and picking up a clear plastic bag containing the spent slug.

Mitchell squared his glasses. "Yes, sir, that's the one," he said.

"Your Honor, I enter this spent bullet, marked as defense exhibit *D*. I also enter into evidence another spent bullet, marked as defense exhibit *E*. Bullet *D* was picked up from the field where Deon Booker was shot. Bullet *E* is a bullet fired from the pistol belongin' to Harley Mack Teasdale. And, finally, I enter into evidence the findin's of Mr. Harry Cargill, ballistics expert for the Memphis Police Department, statin' both bullets were fired from the same pistol. Mr. Cargill, as the court may recall, is the same ballistics expert who verified that the bullet that killed Harley Mack Teasdale was fired from Stump Pollard's gun."

"Mr. Conway, has the prosecution had a chance to examine the bullets and the ballistics report?" Judge Dowling asked the prosecutor.

"We have, Your Honor."

"Very well; the exhibits may be entered as marked."

"Now, Mr. Mitchell," Eddie continued, "would you please tell the court how you came by this bullet, where it has been until now, and why you are just now makin' it public?"

Mitchell admitted to finding the bullet and pocketing it when no one was looking, then joining the others in searching for it, even though he already had it in his possession.

Eddie then asked if Mitchell had also retrieved the spent shell casing.

"No, sir, I don't know nothin' about that."

"You are familiar with how the pistol Harley Mack was carrying works, aren't you?" Eddie asked. "You know that every time it shoots, it kicks out an empty shell casin'."

"Yes, sir, I know."

"Where is the empty shell casin', Mr. Mitchell?"

"I don't know."

"You do see my dilemma, don't you? If there is no empty shell casin', then prosecution might well claim the gun wasn't fired there. And by your own admission you had planned to make money out of this bullet. What would you tell Mr. Conway if he wants to suggest that you got this bullet from somewhere else and are just sayin' it came from the scene of the shootin'?"

"The only thing I can tell him is the truth," Mitchell said. "That there bullet came from the scene of the shootin', just like I said it did."

"Mr. Mitchell, there is another facet of your testimony that we must dispose of. Are you aware that by withholdin' evidence as you did, you committed a crime for which you could be prosecuted?"

"Yes, sir. You told me that last night."

"Then you understand fully, do you not, that the testimony you have just given could very well be all that is required to send you to jail for the crime of obstruction of justice?"

"Yes, sir."

"Knowing that, do you still stick by your story?"

Mitchell nodded glumly. "Yes, sir."

"Thank you, Mr. Mitchell. I have no further questions."

"Redirect?"

Conway got up and started toward the witness. He stopped about halfway, stroked his chin for a moment, then sighed.

"I have no redirect, Your Honor." Shaking his head, he returned to his seat.

"Your Honor, the defense rests," Eddie said.

"Are you prepared for your summation, Mr. Bender?"

"I am, Your Honor."

"Very well, you may proceed."

Eddie walked over to the front of the jury box. He looked at the twelve men and women for a long time before he spoke.

"As I look at you," he began, "I see people I have known all my life. I have asked you for your votes. I have attended picnics and county fairs and high school ball games with you. I know your wives and your husbands and your children." He pointed at Stump. "I know that most of you have known Stump Pollard for as long as you have known me. He served as chief of police for the Delta Police Department, honorably and well, for many years. And many of you also know that Stump and I are not exactly the warmest of friends. We have had our differences over the years, and once, on the front lawn of this very courthouse, we took our disagreement to a somewhat more than verbal stage. Fortunately for Stump, someone pulled me off him before I got hurt."

The spectators and jurors laughed.

Eddie pointed to the prosecutor's table. "Now, I want you to consider Jim Conway. You've known him, Stump has known him, and I've known him since the three of us were boys playin' marbles together on the school grounds. Well, that's the way it's always been around here. We're all one big family here in Panola County, Mississippi, and when someone comes in here to be tried, why, it's a little like settlin' a family dispute. Even our coloreds were like family.

"But now suddenly everything has changed. Our squabbles aren't family squabbles any longer; now we're attemptin' to settle our differences under the bright glare of the national spotlight. The coloreds we see aren't the coloreds we've known and grown up with; they're from places like Ohio and Michigan and New York. As I look out over this courtroom, to the lawn outside, I see unfamiliar faces and I hear voices talkin' in unfamiliar accents. Cameras and microphones and clackin' typewriters are carryin' a blow-by-blow account of everything we say and do here to the rest of the nation—to the rest of the world, even.

"Our task, then, is to ignore all that if we can. We should not be intimidated by these outside influences, nor should we attempt to send them a message. What we should do is close our eyes and ears to all but the fundamental truth. So let us get to that truth.

"You have heard Stump Pollard's version of what happened that mornin'. Accordin' to his testimony, he did not initiate the action. He returned fire, meanin' he was shootin' in self-defense. Although Alicia Canfield, Jerry Wiggins, and Violet Simmons are honest enough to admit they did not actually see Harley Mack fire first, they have all stated that it is their belief that Harley Mack did indeed fire first.

"The two principal witnesses for the prosecution have no such compunctions in their testimony. They have both sworn that not only did Stump Pollard shoot first, he was the only one who did shoot. They would have you believe that a marksman so skilled as to be able to hit his target between the eyes from a distance of a hundred and fifty feet could have also accidentally shot one of his own companions in the back. When you consider this testimony, however, you should also consider the source of the testimony.

"It's hardly a secret around here that both Charley Good and Peter Field have long histories of difficulty with the law. You know as well as I that they've been arrested for such things as assault, burglary, car theft, and bootleggin'. In addition, Peter Field now stands accused of raping Miss Simmons, and though we are not tryin' that case, it certainly casts a shadow on the impartiality of his testimony. Charley Good and Peter Field are not honorable men.

"Stump Pollard *is* an honorable man. Durin' his long and distinguished career as a law enforcement officer, he received decorations and letters of commendation from three Mississippi governors as well as numerous citations from the Mississippi State Law Enforcement Association and from the National Law Enforcement Association. He has established a reputation of honesty and integrity that even his political enemies—people like me—recognize. Stump Pollard does not have a history of lyin'. Even if there were no physical evidence to support his story, a reasonable person would have to take the word of a man of honor and integrity over that of a legion of thieves and brigands."

Eddie paused for a moment to let the words sink in, then held his index finger aloft.

"Ah, but we *don't* have to depend on that. For now there is physical evidence supporting Stump Pollard's testimony. The spent bullet has been found, and a ballistics expert—the same ballistics expert the prosecution used—has matched it to a bullet fired from Harley Mack Teasdale's pistol. Now, I ask you not to be confused by the smoke screen of the missin' empty shell casin'. If some good ol' boy friend of Teasdale, Good, and Field wanted to support Field's story, he could have quite easily gone back out there, found the shell casin', and disposed of it. Anyway, it doesn't matter because in his own argument with regard to the two empty chambers in Stump's pistol, Mr. Conway was ready to conveniently discard the fact that only one empty casin' was found. So I submit to you, ladies and gentlemen of the jury, that what is sauce for the goose is sauce for the gander. And regardless of how you feel about integration, regardless of how you feel about registerin' the coloreds to vote, regardless of how you feel about civil rights workers or outside agitators comin' down from the North to cause trouble for us, I do not believe you could sit there, in good conscience, and find any verdict for Stump Pollard but not guilty."

As Eddie Bender came back to take his seat at the defense table, Alicia watched him with pride. While a student in law school at Jefferson University, she had read the closing summations of Clarence Darrow and had studied the brilliantly reasoned speeches of such figures as Adlai Stevenson, Winston Churchill, and William Jennings Bryan. But today, watching this unknown, small-town country lawyer, she felt as if she had just taken a postgraduate course from a man who, within his own element, was every bit their equal.

Prosecution did not give up without a fight. Conway asked the jury to consider the profit motive of Brad Mitchell's convenient finding of the spent bullet, and he would not let go of the matter of the empty shell casing not being found. In fact, his closing argument was so good that it left a knot of apprehension in Alicia's stomach—a knot that seemed to grow the longer they sat waiting in Eddie Bender's office for the jury to return.

"Eddie," Stump said quietly as they waited, "regardless of how this thing turns out, I want you to know that I have absolutely no quarrel with the way you handled the case. You were brilliant."

"Brilliant? He was magnificent!" Alicia insisted.

Eddie grinned. "Hell, Stump, I've always been brilliant. Only you've been too pigheaded to notice."

The telephone rang shrilly, making everyone jump. Alicia picked it up.

"Hello? Okay, thanks." She hung up the phone and looked at the others. "The verdict is in."

By the time the defense team returned, the courtroom was so jammed, with spectators spilling out of the seats and into the aisles, that the bailiff had to clear a path for Stump, Eddie, and Alicia to walk through. Jerry, pushing Deon's wheelchair, and Violet, following close behind, took advantage of this parting of the sea to move down to the front where they, too, would be able to hear the verdict.

The clerk announced the entry of the judge, and everyone stood as Judge Dowling came in through the side door.

"Be seated," he said. "Bailiff, bring in the jury."

Alicia studied the jury members as they came in, trying to determine by their expressions what the verdict might be. But their faces were frustratingly impassive.

"Who will speak for the jury?" Judge Dowling asked.

"I will, Your Honor," a large, gray-haired man said, rising to respond. "I am the foreman."

"Has the jury reached a verdict?"

"We have, Your Honor."

"How say you?"

"We find the defendant . . . not guilty."

There was an outbreak of cheers from the gallery as Alicia embraced first Stump and then Eddie. Jerry and Violet wheeled Deon through the gate that separated the gallery from the defense table so they, too, could join in the celebration.

"Mr. Bender, I want you to know that I learned more from you during this trial than I learned during my two years of law school," Alicia told Eddie.

He laughed. "Hell, girl, that's no big thing. Everybody learns more from their first real case than they do from law school. That is, if they're worth their salt. But you did all right. In fact, if you get tired of livin' around all those Yankees up there in St. Louis, I'd be proud to take you on as a partner in my firm."

Alicia smiled. "I'm afraid I've already accepted a position in St. Louis. But I want you to know that I consider it a great honor to be asked."

"What about you, Deon?" Stump asked. "Where do you go from here?"

"Me?" Deon grinned. "Well, now that we have this taken care of, I'm going back into the fight."

CHAPTER
THIRTEEN

JUNE 29, 1963, FROM "TRAILMARKERS" IN
EVENTS MAGAZINE:

THE OCTOBER MISSILE CRISIS IN
RETROSPECT

An extraordinary tension gripped the world for
seven days last October as the United States and
the Soviet Union stood on the brink of nuclear war.

The crisis began when a U-2 spy flight brought
back unmistakable evidence that the Soviet Union
was building intermediate-range missile sites in
Cuba. In a televised address to the nation, President John F. Kennedy asserted that the missiles
were in position to strike "most of the major cities
of the Western hemisphere."

At first the Soviets and the Cubans denied the
existence of the missile bases, but photographic evidence given to the world in the arena of the United
Nations proved President Kennedy's allegations.

It can now be told that fateful discussions were

254

held long into the night at the White House to determine how the U.S. should react to the challenge. Some favored invasion, most favored air strikes, while a few preferred the more cautious approach of a naval blockade. The cautious approach won out, though the military was placed on full alert, and troops and equipment were moved to Homestead Air Force Base in Florida, poised for an invasion of Cuba if need be.

Tensions sharpened as Nikita Khrushchev threatened military retaliation against the American blockade. No one knew what would happen if one of the Soviet ships was actually sunk, but the U.S. was prepared to do just that if it became necessary.

During the crisis the U.S. continued to monitor the situation with spy planes, and the crucial conflict escalated when a U-2 was shot down over Cuba and its pilot killed. Other planes were fired upon, and the U.S. warned it would launch air strikes if fired upon again.

The world held its breath as the crisis deepened. Then came a respite as Soviet ships pulled back. During this friction-filled lull, negotiations between Kennedy and Khrushchev continued. Finally an agreement was made whereby the Soviet agreed to remove all its offensive missiles from Cuba in return for a U.S. pledge not to invade.

Though the crisis continued until November 20, the most critical moments were over.

"ICH BIN EIN BERLINER," KENNEDY TELLS BERLIN CROWD

One hundred fifty thousand citizens of Berlin gave President Kennedy a tumultuous welcome when he visited the divided city. Referring to the wall the Communists erected to keep those in the Eastern Bloc captive, Kennedy said, "There are many people in the world who really don't understand, or say they don't, what is the great issue between the free world and the Communist world. Let them come to Berlin! There are some who say in Europe and elsewhere we can work with the

Communists. Let them come to Berlin! And there are even a few who say that it is true that Communism is an evil system, but it permits us to make economic progress. *Lass sie nach Berlin kommen!* Let them come to Berlin!"

The crowd rose and roared, but the applause rose to near-hysterical pitch when Kennedy declared, "All free men, wherever they may live, are citizens of Berlin, and, therefore, as a free man I take pride in the words *'Ich bin ein Berliner'* ('I am a Berliner')."

FIRST WOMAN IN SPACE

Last month when Major Gordon Cooper's Mercury capsule circled the earth 22 times before landing in the Pacific, America celebrated its longest manned space flight—34 hours and 20 minutes. But the Soviets' record four-day flight leaves that feat in the dust, and now they have chalked up another first, the first female aastronaut, with the space flight of Lieutenant Valentina Tereshkova. The Soviet spacewoman's voyage lasted three days, more than twice the duration of America's longest orbital mission.

SHERI WARREN WINS COTY AWARD

Sheri Warren, founder and president of Contempo Clothes, has been awarded the prestigious Coty Award for brilliance of design for her latest line of fashions.

Official recognition was virtually inevitable since Miss Warren first established a major foothold in the fashion field through her SheriWear designs, the highly successful clothing line produced by E. J. Buckner and Company that still maintains the name, even though Sheri Warren is no longer creating them.

"When you consider that she had to start over again, without being able to build upon the reputation she had developed, her accomplishment in winning the Coty and achieving such economic

success is truly phenomenal!" a spokesman for the
award committee said.

NEW YORK

Someone was handing out leaflets to male passersby on
the corner of Forty-second Street. He didn't offer one to
Sheri Warren, but she glanced down at one lying on the
sidewalk and read the copy as she walked by:

> SULTAN'S PLEASURE
> TEN BEAUTIFUL GIRLS
> ENJOY A CHAMPAGNE MASSAGE

She smiled, wondering just what a champagne massage
was.

Walking over to the theater district, she entered Rosie
O'Grady's, where she was supposed to meet Ian Dunnigan,
the theater producer. The previous week he had called her,
asking to meet to discuss the costumes for his newest production. Costume design wasn't anything Sheri had ever done
before, but the thought of being connected with the theater,
in any capacity, was intriguing—so much so that she had
arrived a good thirty minutes before she was supposed to.
She had been too antsy to wait any longer.

It was dark inside the barroom, a warm, mahogany dark.
A group of people stood around a piano singing, laughing,
and waving their glasses in time to the music.

Sheri started toward the bar. One of the people singing,
a large, jolly-looking bearded man, motioned to her and patted the empty stool beside him. Sheri smiled and on impulse
joined them.

Without interrupting the song, the bearded man signaled for a fresh glass and poured Sheri a beer from a large
pitcher. She raised her glass and began waving it in time to
the music, joining with the others until the song was finished.
Then they all laughed and applauded the piano player and
each other. The bearded man spoke to her.

"Well, my pretty colleen, and what would be bringing
the likes o' you into this place?" he asked in an accent either
genuinely Irish or marvelously put on.

"Good drink, pleasant company, and beautiful music," Sheri replied, laughing.

Her answer met with cheers, and the questioner smiled broadly and stuck out his hand. "Sure'n I couldn't have said it better meself. You would be Sheri Warren, I'm thinkin'."

"You're Ian Dunnigan?" Sheri replied, taken aback.

"Aye, lass, 'tis Dunnigan himself at your service." He stood up. "Come to the booth in the back. We can talk there without the evil pryin' eyes and ears of the heathen."

With good-natured good-byes to his fellow singers, Dunnigan led Sheri to a booth in the corner. He ordered drinks for both of them: whiskey for himself, another beer for Sheri.

"I've never been involved with the theater," Sheri remarked after their drinks had been served. "It strikes me as very exciting."

"'Tis an ancient and wondrous profession, sure enough," Dunnigan said. "One that I have followed since I was a lad in Dublin."

"Why did you come to New York?"

He laughed. "For the same reason everyone comes to New York. Here is where all the opportunity lies, whether it be in the theater or the world of fashion—or the world of the gangster."

"Gangster?" Sheri replied with a nervous little laugh.

"Now don't be tellin' me you aren't aware of a certain underworld character who tries to hide his Mafia connections by stealin' a name from the old sod."

Sheri looked up at him, surprised. "Are you talking about Kerry O'Braugh?"

"An' who else would I be talkin' about, lass?" His eyes bored into hers. "I've been told he's your silent partner. Is that true?"

"Evidently the partnership isn't all that silent," Sheri said dryly. "You seem to know about it."

"I know about it, and so do many others. And therein is the rub, you see."

She cocked her head at him. "No, I don't see."

Dunnigan took a drink of his whiskey, then put the glass down and studied her for a long moment.

"Sheri, me pretty, a Broadway show is no little thing," he finally said. "It takes a prodigious amount of money to launch. Not my money, you understand, but the money of investors, big and small."

"I can understand that. But I don't know where you're heading with this conversation."

" 'Tis those self-same investors I've got to be keepin' happy," Dunnigan said. "When I asked you about designin' costumes for the show, I had no idea you were mixed up with the likes of Kerry O'Braugh. Surely you can understand now when I tell you that I can't be usin' you."

Sheri leaned back in her seat. Her hair fell over one eye, and she impatiently swept it back from her face. "No," she said quietly, "I can't understand."

"Then let me explain it to you. Organized crime pollutes, fouls everything it ever touches. It started with the unions, stealin' from the workers their hard-earned legacy. And look what it has done to the manly sport of boxin' and the kingly sport of horse racin'. It has wormed its way into night-club entertainment, the record industry . . . some say it's even tryin' to gain some influence in Hollywood. Well, so far the legitimate theater has resisted it, and I certainly don't intend to let the Mob use my show to get a foot into the business."

"Surely, Mr. Dunnigan, you can't think my costume designs would be the ruin of the legitimate theater."

He smiled sadly. "Not directly, lass, not intentionally. The devil has desecrated you. He has done that, hasn't he, lass? He has stolen your soul."

"I . . . I must be going now," Sheri said, standing quickly, her eyes filling with tears. She bumped her hip painfully on the corner of the booth in her haste to get away.

"I'm sorry, lass," Dunnigan called after her. " 'Twould have been a lovelier production with your costumes. I'm sure of it."

Stepping outside into the humid night air, feeling angry and hurt, Sheri impatiently wiped her wet cheeks with her fingers. She could not stem the flow of tears. She hurried away from the bar.

Lights were just beginning to come on as she strode purposefully down the street between great, sky-high slabs of steel and glass, and their irregularly lighted windows made surrealistic designs. As the sights, smells, and sounds of the city washed over her, the tears finally subsided.

She walked on. She passed a man playing a violin for coins from passersby and a vendor selling hot pretzels. A young woman stood in a doorway, looking up and down the street. She wore an imitation leather jacket, very shiny and red, and pants so tight they seemed painted on her every curve and crevice. The pants were tucked into boots the same shade of red as her jacket, which was halfway unzipped, and as Sheri drew closer she could see that the woman was wearing nothing under it. Her hair was colored somewhere between strawberry and orange, and she wore glittery eye makeup. The woman smiled and stepped out toward a man walking by, but he swerved to avoid her.

Without realizing where she was going, Sheri suddenly found herself outside Plaza Towers, a luxury apartment building of fifty-five floors. It was where Kerry O'Braugh lived.

"Good evening, Miss Warren," the doorman said, recognizing her and opening the door for her.

"Is Mr. O'Braugh in tonight?" she asked as she stepped into the lobby.

"Yes, he is. But I don't believe he is expecting you, is he?"

"No, he isn't. Please announce me."

The doorman cleared his throat. "Uh, maybe now is not such a good time to visit him."

"It'll be all right," Sheri said, sweeping past the doorman and crossing to the waiting elevator. She pressed the button for Kerry's floor, and as the doors closed, she saw the doorman frantically dialing a number on his house phone.

The high-speed elevator ride was brief, and she stepped out into the small carpeted alcove with its two facing doors. The door to Kerry's apartment opened even before Sheri could ring the bell. He was wearing a robe and slippers.

"Uh, Miss Warren," he said. "I wasn't expecting you tonight." He looked ill-at-ease.

"I'm sorry I didn't call ahead," she apologized. "But something has just come up, and it's very important that I talk with you."

"Yes, well, uh—"

"Aren't you going to invite me in?"

Kerry sighed. "Sure," he said, stepping back and opening the door wider. "Sure, come on in."

"Thanks."

He closed the door behind her. "I'll be back in just a moment," he said and headed down a long hallway.

"Oh, you don't have to get dressed on my account," she called after him.

Kerry looked back at her and smiled. "It's not exactly that." He pointed to the bar. "Fix yourself a drink. Actually, fix both of us a drink, if you don't mind."

For herself, Sheri took a beer from the under-the-counter refrigerator; she made a martini for Kerry. She was just finishing when a young, extremely attractive woman came out of a back room, pouting and buttoning her blouse. Kerry, still in his robe, was right behind her.

"Honey, if you have to have more than one woman a day," the woman muttered, "it seems to me like the least you could do is wait until you're finished with one before you bring another one in."

"I'm sorry," Kerry said sincerely. He handed her a large bill. "Here. This is for cab fare."

The woman looked at the bill, smiled broadly, then stuck it down into her bosom. She looked at Sheri. "He's all yours, honey," she said. "And take it from me—if you treat him nice, he can be very generous."

She left the apartment, and Kerry stood there for a moment, looking at the door, his back to Sheri.

"I, uh, seem to have come at an inopportune time," Sheri said softly, highly embarrassed at being a witness to the scene.

Kerry turned toward her, shaking his head slowly. "You don't know *how* inopportune. If you had just been fifteen minutes later—hell, *five* minutes later . . ."

Despite herself, Sheri laughed. "I'm sorry." She walked around from behind the bar carrying the beer and the martini, which she handed to him. "Here. Maybe this will help."

Instead of going over to the sofa as she expected him to, Kerry settled onto the rug and set his drink on the coffee table. He stroked the place alongside him, wordlessly inviting her to join him. She slipped down onto the soft rug beside him, holding the beer in one hand, the other hand on the floor beside her thigh for balance. Her long hair fell sensuously over her cheek.

"You said you had some pressing reason to see me?" Kerry asked.

Sheri looked at him. What should she say to him? He had not been in the least dishonest with her about his background. If the theater didn't want to use her because of her association with him, there was nothing she could do about it —and there was nothing *he* could do about it. Bringing it up to him now would serve absolutely no purpose whatever.

"It's . . . not important," she said.

Kerry chuckled. "Not important, she says." He raised his drink to his lips, and as he did so, the top of his robe gaped open, showing a mat of gray chest hair.

Maybe it was the sexually charged atmosphere of having come in on him when she did, but suddenly, and totally unexpectedly, Sheri felt drawn to him. It seemed impossible that she would think of him in a sexual way, for he was more than thirty years older than she. Nevertheless, she felt the stirring of desire, and she knew that she wanted him to kiss her—had, in fact, been wanting it for several minutes and wanted it now as much as she had ever wanted anything.

Her beer and his martini were somehow placed on the coffee table as she and Kerry moved to each other, pulled by some magnetic force. Sheri lost her sense of self-possession as she felt his arms closing firmly around her. She went eagerly to his embrace, despite there being something dark, cold, and dangerous about him.

Easily, leisurely, he seemed to lift her clothes away; then she felt the woolly texture of the rug against the smooth skin of her naked back. His mouth left her lips, and, involuntarily it seemed, her back rose up to allow him access to her breasts. Dunnigan's words came rushing back to her: *"The devil has desecrated you. He has done that, hasn't he, lass? He has stolen your soul."*

Instead of pulling away, the words made her feel completely controlled by him, like the spider before the fly. It was a position she rarely, if ever, found herself in—and, to her surprise, the most erotically exciting sensation she had ever experienced.

As Sheri rode the elevator up to her apartment, she thought about the men she had been with. There was Scooter's father, of course. And there had been the fashion photographer in Chicago. He had been married, though she didn't find out about it until afterward. She had never gone to bed with Frank Corso, though he had tried many times. She hadn't gone to bed with Morgan Canfield, either—though over the last couple of years she had found herself fantasizing that she had. Until this evening with Kerry O'Braugh, she had not been with a man since she arrived in New York. There were plenty of opportunities—even in a profession as rife with homosexuals as fashion design—but she had chosen abstinence.

Tonight, however, her carefully constructed armor had been penetrated, and she could still feel the effects of being with Kerry. It had not been an expression of love or even romance. What they had done tonight was purely physical, for both of them. Yet she had to admit it had been a very satisfying experience. She just hoped that Mrs. Spranger, who was an extremely perceptive woman, would not read in her face what had happened.

Walking down the hallway to her door, Sheri touched her hair and her clothes as if such a last-minute laying-on of hands would create a screen beyond which not even Mrs. Spranger's probing eye could see; then she opened the door to her apartment.

"Mrs. Warren, you have a visitor," Mrs. Spranger said, coming into the foyer from the living room the moment Sheri stepped inside.

"A visitor? Who?"

Her answer, grinning broadly, stepped into the foyer behind Mrs. Spranger.

"Hello, Sheri," Morgan Canfield said. "I'm back from South America."

CONN KASERNE, SCHWEINFURT, GERMANY

As Bob Parker walked up the smooth steps of the headquarters building, he happened to glance up at the concrete bas-relief just over the door. It portrayed an eagle clutching a wreath. The symbol that had once been inside the wreath had been chipped away, but Bob could clearly see it had been a swastika—visible evidence of what he had been told when he received his orders for this place: Conn Kaserne and Ledward Barracks, the two military installations at Schweinfurt, had been army bases for the German Wermacht during World War II.

Additionally, the city of Schweinfurt had been the target of intense aerial bombardment during the war because of its large ball bearing factory. To come here now, Bob thought, was to see history close up. He was very much looking forward to his new duty.

His orders assigned him to the 7th Cavalry squadron, part of the 3rd Infantry Division. The shoulder patch worn by members of the 3rd Infantry Division was a square of alternating blue and white diagonal stripes. Bob couldn't help but notice this was exactly the same logo that decorated every box of Corn Toasties and all other Canfield-Puritex products. He wondered about the similarity.

A sergeant came out of the building, and as he passed Bob on the steps he saluted and said what sounded like, "Garry Owen, sir."

Confused, Bob nonetheless returned the salute, saying, "Good morning."

A moment later, when Bob stepped up to the administrative sergeant's desk, he was greeted the same way.

"Garry Owen, sir. Welcome to the Seventh Cav."

"Wait a minute. You are the second person to say that to me," Bob said. "What the heck does 'Garry Owen' mean?"

"Haven't you ever seen a movie about the Seventh Cavalry?" the sergeant asked. "You know, about Custer?"

"Yes, of course."

"Well, you know that catchy little tune they're always playing in the background as the troop rides by?" The sergeant whistled a few bars.

"Yes, I've heard that."

"That song is called 'Garry Owen.' It's the official song of the Seventh Cavalry. And it's the way we greet each other. Instead of 'good morning,' 'good afternoon,' or 'good evening,' it is always 'Garry Owen.'"

Bob snickered. "Are you serious?"

"Does a fifty-dollar fine sound serious, sir?"

"A fifty-dollar fine?"

"That's SOP from Colonel Rockford. Any officer who fails to use the words 'Garry Owen' in greeting will be fined fifty dollars."

"Oh. Well, Garry Owen, Sergeant. Catchy little phrase, isn't it?"

The sergeant laughed. "Garry Owen, sir. I thought you might come around to the colonel's way of thinking. I'll tell him you are reporting in."

A moment later Bob was ushered into his CO's office. Colonel Rockford was tall and thin, with brown eyes and dark hair. "Garry Owen, sir. Chief Warrant Officer Robert R. Parker reporting as per orders," Bob said, saluting.

"Garry Owen, Chief," Rockford said, returning the salute. He then stood and reached across the desk to shake Bob's hand. "I see you've signed on to our tradition."

"Yes, sir." Bob grinned. "I understand there is a fairly good incentive for doing so."

"Ah, yes, the fifty dollars. Well, you understand that I don't actually have the authority to fine you fifty dollars. But I can strongly suggest that you make a voluntary contribution of that amount to the officers' flower-and-cup fund. By the way, there is another tradition we follow here." Rockford pulled open the bottom desk drawer and pulled out a black, knobby stick about one inch in diameter and thirty inches long. He handed it to Bob. "All my officers carry this at all times," he said.

"What is it, sir?"

"It's what the British call a swagger stick." He chuckled. "It's just another of our traditions, along with using the greeting 'Garry Owen' and, of course, the kilts."

"Kilts? You mean I'm going to have to wear a kilt?"

Colonel Rockford laughed. "No. Fortunately for many of us, the only ones who wear kilts are the members of our drum and bagpipe corps. They perform at all official Seventh Cavalry functions."

"That's good. I can handle the swagger stick and the Garry Owen, but I think I'd have a lot of trouble with a kilt."

"Yes, well, I daresay I can appreciate your sensibility. By the way, is this your first time in Germany?"

"Yes, sir."

"I think you're going to enjoy it. Germany is the best assignment the Army has to offer."

Bob pointed to Rockford's blue-and-white shoulder patch. "Colonel, are you familiar with the Canfield-Puritex Company back in the States?"

"Sure. I eat their cereals and my dog eats their chow."

"Have you ever noticed how much the Third Division patch looks like their logo?"

"That isn't coincidence. Don't you know where the logo came from?"

Bob shook his head. "No, sir, I guess not."

"There was a young artist over here during the First World War. He didn't serve in the Third Division, but he was so impressed with the performance of the Third that later, when he was asked to come up with a distinctive logo for Canfield-Puritex, he adapted our shoulder patch."

"Well, I'll be . . . That's interesting."

"You'll find we are a unit steeped in history and tradition," Rockford said. "As you probably know, Custer once occupied the very position I now hold." He chuckled. "However, I don't intend to follow in that august gentleman's footsteps. Now, Mr. Parker, I have you assigned to Delta troop. You will be in charge of the maintenance platoon. Delta troop has eight Hueys and eight H-Thirteens to look after. I'm sure that will be enough to keep you busy. So, as our Navy friends say, welcome aboard."

Bob smiled. "Thank you, sir. I'm glad to be aboard."

Over the next three weeks he got into the swing of things. When one of the officers in the troop went home to the States, Bob moved from his bachelor officers' quarters room into the apartment the officer had vacated. The apartment was "on the economy," meaning it was off the base in an average German neighborhood. Though it cost a bit more to live on the economy than it did to remain in the BOQ, it was much more pleasant, and it afforded him more privacy for his writing.

The officer complement of D Troop consisted of four other warrants, six lieutenants, one captain, and one major. A most pleasant surprise for Bob was learning that Mike Rindell was one of the other warrant officers. Bob had gone to flight school with Mike, and the two quickly renewed an old friendship.

Bob was also somewhat of a celebrity in the troop, not because he was a published author but because he had been to Vietnam. Vietnam was being discussed more and more now, and Bob's ninety-day stint of temporary duty there had given him an insight into the situation. Because of that assignment, Colonel Rockford arranged for Bob to give a talk about his experiences in Vietnam during one of the TI & E— Troop Information and Education—sessions.

There were, Bob learned soon after arriving, two very important days in the lives of bachelor officers assigned to Germany. One was "Wheel Day," the day on which a newly assigned officer's personal car, shipped by surface transportation from the States, would arrive at the port in Hanover. Until then an officer was totally dependant upon friends or taxis for transportation. The second great day was "T Day," the day on which the "dependent schoolteachers," as they were known, arrived. The teachers, mostly women and mostly single, were in Germany under contract to the Department of Defense to teach in the school system the Army maintained for the children of servicemen.

As it so happened, both days occurred in the same week for Bob. On the day he returned from Hanover with the black '63 Chevrolet Impala he had purchased shortly before leaving the States, he learned that the new teachers had arrived that very morning. The excitement of their coming made the officers' club very crowded at lunch, but Bob managed to find a table near the partition separating the main dining room from the kitchen.

He ordered chili and a grilled-cheese sandwich and was waiting for it when a young woman approached his table. She was slender, with a Jackie Kennedy-type hairdo. In fact, with her brown hair, wide-set blue eyes, and high cheekbones, she rather reminded Bob of the First Lady.

"Hi," she said. "Uh, there's no other place to sit. Do you mind if I join you?"

"No, be my guest," Bob offered, standing quickly.

"I'm Jill King," the woman said as she sat down.

"You must be one of the new teachers," Bob said.

Jill laughed. "Which is the most obvious? That I'm a teacher or that I'm new?"

"Both, I guess," Bob said, laughing with her. When the waiter came for Jill's order, Bob told him to hold his in the kitchen until Jill was served.

After their lunch Bob volunteered to drive Jill to the PX so she could pick up a few things for her living quarters. Jill would be billeted in the dependent teachers' BOQ, and Bob offered to give her a few hints on what she might need.

"Make sure you buy toilet paper," he said when they reached the PX. "The billeting office is supposed to furnish it, but they're always late. Same thing with lightbulbs. And if you have anything electric you'll need a converter. German current is fifty-cycle, American current is sixty-cycle."

Going inside the post exchange, they walked by the book section and as luck would have it, Bob spotted his latest effort. It must have just arrived because he had not seen it before. In fact, this was the first time he had seen any of his books overseas, though it wasn't as if the book had been published in a foreign market, since the PX was a part of the Armed Forces Exchange Services. Nevertheless, seeing his book here did give him a little thrill. It was also nice that he happened to be with Jill when he saw it.

The book, *A Score to Settle*, was a Western, and Bob was particularly proud of it, being as it was a definite step up from the erotic novels he had been writing. As he had told his editor in New York, this one he could show to his grandmother.

The cover was typical Western fare, depicting a cowboy standing in the middle of the street of a false-fronted Western town, the pistol in his gun hand spitting out a streak of fire.

"Do you like to read Westerns?" Jill asked when she saw him examining the book.

"Yes," Bob answered with a smile. "And I particularly like this one. This is a *wonderful* book."

"I don't read Westerns," Jill admitted. "I guess there are too many on TV for me to get too interested in them," Jill said. "*Gunsmoke, Rawhide, Bonanza,* and all the rest."

"Yes, but this one is better than *Gunsmoke, Rawhide,* and all the rest put together. I mean, it is a *wonderful* book," he gushed.

"You are really singing its praises," Jill said with a little laugh. "What makes this one so wonderful?"

"I suppose the guy who wrote it," Bob said, holding it up for her to read the author's name.

"Robert Parker," Jill read aloud. She shook her head. "I don't think I've ever heard of him."

"Sure you have."

"No, I don't think I have."

"Sure you have," Bob insisted. "You just ate lunch with him."

"I ate lunch with him? When? I . . . Wait a minute! Bob Parker! You mean . . . this is *you*?"

"Yeah, little lady, it is," Bob said, affecting a Western drawl.

Jill looked at the book with renewed interest. "Oh, my. I don't think I've ever met a real author before. You wrote this?"

"Yep."

"Have you written any others?"

"This is my tenth book."

"Ten? You've written ten books? Are they all Westerns?"

"No." Bob smiled sheepishly. "To be honest, I wish they had been. But for the last few years I've been turning out pornography for the masses."

"*Pornography?*"

"Well, nearly so. I've been writing what the publishing world euphemistically calls 'contemporary explicit.' You know, the kind young boys and dirty old men read?"

Jill laughed. "So what? A book is a book."

Bob grinned. "Yeah. Yeah, that's pretty much what I think, too. And I make no apologies for the stuff I've done in the past; I feel it's helped me develop my craft. But I have to confess, I haven't been using my real name on them."

"What name have you been using?"

"Roger Pringle. So the initials would be the same."

"I see you used your own name for this one."

"Yes, well, this one's different. This is a traditional Western. And I'm happy to say that the raciest thing in this book is when the cowboy kisses his horse. No more sex for me."

Jill held the book up. "If I buy it, will you autograph it for me?"

"I'll do better than that. I'll buy it *for* you and autograph it besides."

Jill smiled. "Well, how sweet. I don't believe I've ever read a Western, but I'm looking forward to reading this one."

After driving Jill and her purchases back to the BOQ, Bob asked her if she would like to go for a drive. "We can see some of the countryside, then have dinner at Volkach."

"Where or what is Volkach?"

"It's a monastery on top of a mountain, overlooking a bend in the river," Bob said. "It's also a restaurant and a winery. The food is fantastic, and they serve the great wine that they make on the premises."

Jill didn't hesitate. "Sure, why not? That sounds like fun."

They hopped back in the car and left Conn Barracks, first driving through the city of Schweinfurt. The first thing Bob showed her was the ball-bearing factory.

"It's nice," Jill said noncommittally as they drove by it.

Bob chuckled. "You probably think you're about to get the industrial tour, don't you? Well, don't worry. I just pointed this place out because if you know anything about World War Two, you've heard of the great Schweinfurt raids. This very plant is what they were after, and in one mission we lost more than a hundred bombers. That's over a thousand men."

"Good God, how dreadful."

"Yes, it was. And the irony is, we thought the losses were justified by the success of the mission, but we learned later that the Germans scarcely missed a beat. They were back in full production within two days."

"And a thousand lives were lost?"

"Yes. Well, many more than that if you count the Germans on the ground. When we go through the center of town you'll see a beautifully landscaped park, complete with hills. The only thing is, there weren't any hills in Schweinfurt. The hills are the remains of the old city. The Germans just covered the rubble with dirt and planted a park."

Jill shivered. "Isn't it wonderful to know all that is over?"

"Fortunately it was only the cities that were bombed. The villages were for the most part undamaged by the war, so as we drive through them, you'll see buildings that have stood unchanged for hundreds of years."

"And this place we're going to is like that?"

"Yes."

When they reached Volkach a short while later, Jill remarked that it looked like a picture on a calendar. The monastery was a beautiful example of old German architecture, with huge carved blocks of stone, turrets, towers, and walls. They parked down below, and then Bob led her up the carved-stone steps to the flagstone patio and out onto the far corner, from where they had an excellent view of the valley. He took her hand to help her up the steps, and since it seemed so natural, he didn't let go.

"I use this place as my five-minute checkpoint," Bob said.

"Five-minute checkpoint? What does that mean?"

"When I'm flying back to Schweinfurt from this direction, I'm exactly five minutes out when I pass over this point."

"Do you enjoy flying?"

"I love it."

"I should think it would be terribly exciting."

"It is." He gestured to the tables behind them. "Well, what do you say? Shall we order now?"

"Do we have to go inside to do that?"

"No, we can order from out here," he said, signaling one of the buxom blond waitresses.

Bob ordered roast deer with peas and noodles for both of them, plus a bottle of wine. "Be careful of the wine," he cautioned when it arrived and he poured a glass for her. "It's so good and mellow you may drink more than you intended, and you'll pay for it tomorrow."

"You speak as if with the voice of experience," Jill replied, smiling at him over the rim of her glass.

Bob grinned ruefully. "I suppose I am. One of the officers got married the first week after I arrived, and there's a tradition that the bride is kidnapped and the groom must find her by looking in every *Gasthaus* in town. At each inn he searches, the groom must buy the entire wedding party a drink."

"And you drank at every stop?"

"I really don't know," Bob admitted. "They tell me that by the fourth *Gasthaus* they were pouring me in and out of the car."

Jill laughed.

"It's not a condition I enjoyed, and I assure you it has never happened again."

"Thanks for the warning," she said, taking a sip of the wine. "I promise I'll be careful."

They dined slowly and stayed out on the patio after they had finished, watching the sun set over the valley below, exchanging personal histories. Bob told Jill about his divorce from Marilou and about his twin sons who lived with their mother. He also talked about what he called his two careers: the military and writing.

"Of course, I depend upon the Army to make a living," he explained. "So far the writing hasn't really paid much, but I do have hopes of it developing into something concrete in the future."

"How did you get into writing?"

"I can't remember when I didn't want to write," Bob said, shrugging. "It's a part of me, like my soul." He laughed sheepishly. "Oh, I know that's a bit pretentious sounding—I mean, coming from someone whose best-selling novel to date has been *Co-ed Sex Club*. But one of these days I'm going to write something people will take seriously. Or at least that's my ambition."

"You will," Jill said, reaching across the table to hold his hand. "I know you will."

"So, tell me about you," Bob requested.

"There's not much to tell. I was a schoolteacher in Long Beach, California, since I graduated from Compton College."

"Any siblings?"

"I have a younger sister who's a senior in high school. We're not at all alike. Dar is much prettier. She's bouncy and outgoing. Just to give you a comparison, she's the head cheerleader; I was secretary of the math club."

"You're being unfair to yourself," Bob countered. "I think you're very pretty. If your sister really is prettier than you, then all I can say is she must be a knockout."

"You're being kind," Jill said, looking embarrassed.

"No, I'm serious. Anyway, go on with your story. I want to know more about you."

"I've never been married," Jill continued, "but I was engaged to a man named Wolfgang Schultz."

"Wolfgang? You mean there really is someone named Wolfgang? Other than Mozart?"

Jill laughed. "Isn't it a terrible name?"

"He's German, I assume?"

"Yes, he was born here, but his parents emigrated to America right after he was born. That was just before the war, and Wolfgang's father was against Hitler."

"You said you were engaged. What happened?"

"Nothing."

"What do you mean, nothing? You aren't still engaged, are you?"

"I don't think so. I mean, there was never a formal breaking off of the engagement. But our relationship didn't seem to be going anywhere. We had never set a date for the wedding. And sometimes Wolfgang would go for two or three weeks at a time without even calling. I wasn't quite sure what to do or how to handle it. Then one afternoon when I was in the teachers' lounge, a man from the Department of Defense came to recruit teachers for the dependent school system in Germany. I signed up for it, and here I am."

"What did Wolfgang think of that?"

Jill grimaced. "I don't know. I didn't tell him. I just left."

"Good for you," Bob said, squeezing her hand.

"But I kind of like the irony of it: me leaving him by ending up in the place he's from."

It was full dark by the time they left Volkach. Riding back, they listened to Armed Forces Network on the car radio, and Bob sang along with The Animals' version of "House of the Rising Sun." At the BOQ, Bob walked Jill back to her room and kissed her good-night, suddenly realizing that this was the first time he had kissed a woman since he and Marilou divorced.

It felt good.

SAIGON

When Colonel Nguyen Van Tran was summoned to the Presidential Palace to meet with South Vietnamese President Ngo Dinh Diem, he invited Jarred Hawkins to go with him. As they waited in the reception room for their appointment, Jarred's gaze wandered around the once-elegant room. He looked up at the ceiling. It was no less down-at-its-heels than the rest. At the point where the chandelier was anchored a crack had started, working its way across the entire width of the ceiling. The crystal and brass fittings were dirty, and the wires leading to the candle-shaped lightbulbs were frayed.

Tiring of the tattered scenery inside, Jarred looked out the window at the lush, manicured lawn and well-tended flower garden. At least *it* still looked august. In the middle of the garden was a flagpole, at the top of which, floating in the hot breeze, was the national flag of the Republic of Vietnam, a bright yellow banner whose top was divided from the bottom by three narrow red bands.

A group of uniformed girls between the ages of sixteen and twenty came marching up the drive, swinging their arms stiffly and singing loudly. These, Jarred knew, were members of Madame Nhu's Young Women's Military Auxiliary. Reaction to the YWMA was varied throughout the country. Some thought it a good idea in that it fostered discipline and self-confidence among its members. Some were opposed because they considered it unladylike. And a few feared it as one more arm of the total control Diem, his brother Nhu, and Nhu's wife had over the country. Most, however, thought the entire thing was rather foolish.

At that moment a skinny man with a prominent Adam's apple and dark, piercing eyes came out of President Diem's office. "Nguyen, Colonel Hawkins, my brother will see you now," Ngo Dinh Nhu said.

Though Nhu held no elected office, he was clearly the second most powerful man in Vietnam. He derived his power not only from the fact that he was his brother Diem's most trusted adviser but also because he was chief of the Can Lao, which was loyal only to Nhu and answerable only to him.

Many insisted that Nhu, by virtue of his cunning and his personal control over the Can Lao, was even more powerful than Diem. There were even a few who said that President Diem actually ranked only third, with Nhu's wife, Madame Nhu, occupying the second-most powerful position. And, indeed, Madame Nhu—who held neither elected nor appointed position but who was generally considered the "first lady" since Diem was a bachelor—was an extremely powerful figure. She was both beautiful and outspoken, a combination that made her the darling of the international press. As a result, many of South Vietnam's national policies were first articulated by Madame Nhu.

"Ah, Colonel Hawkins, you are enjoying my wife's girls, I see," Nhu said, coming out of his brother's office and seeing Jarred staring out the window.

"They seem well disciplined," Jarred remarked, not knowing what else to say.

"Yes. Well, your press calls them the Dragon Lady's Gun Girls, I believe."

"I'm sorry for the disrespect. The American press is not known for subtlety or good taste."

Nhu chuckled. "Don't apologize. I like the name. I think it fits my wife quite well. Like the Dragon Lady in the American comics, *Terry and the Pirates,* Madam Nhu is a beautiful woman. And she is a powerful woman, of strong will."

"Yes, I agree," Jarred murmured, still not knowing quite what to say.

Jarred and Nguyen followed Nhu into the president's office to find Diem standing by a window, looking outside—though at what, Jarred couldn't tell. Diem was shorter and much more rotund than Nhu. He also had a more pleasant visage, and, like an older brother who was a Roman Catholic cardinal, Diem had once studied for the priesthood.

"Colonel Hawkins," Diem said, turning from the window and coming toward Jarred with his hand extended. "How are you? It is most kind of you to visit with me."

"I am honored that you have invited me, Mr. President," Jarred replied. He couldn't help but notice that though Diem was impeccably dressed in his trademark white suit, he was barefoot. Diem seemed oblivious to the fact, but it struck Jarred as awfully odd to be received by a head of state wearing no shoes.

"Yes, well, I did want to speak with you," Diem said. "It is my hope that you, being one of the few Americans who truly understands our language and our people, might be able to mediate with your government for me."

"Mr. President, I am only a lieutenant colonel," Jarred replied. "My influence with General Stillwell or General Harkins is quite limited."

"I am looking for your knowledge and your heart," Diem countered. "Not your rank or position."

"What my brother is trying to say," Nhu interrupted, "is that we want you to carry our words to the Americans in the same spirit and meaning that we give them. We are certain that much of the current difficulty between us lies in a lack of understanding."

"Your government has forced several concessions from us," Diem said. "They have told me that if we are to continue to receive your aid, we must make major modifications in how we treat our Buddhists."

"We want the American government to understand that how we treat the Buddhists is nobody's business but our own," Nhu added.

"I'm afraid it isn't just the American government, Mr. President, Your Excellency," Jarred said to the two brothers. "The Buddhist situation over here has aroused the ire of the entire American public."

"Why should the American public be concerned with how we deal with the Buddhist question? The U.S. is a Christian country, isn't it?" Nhu asked.

"Although Christianity is the dominant religion, the U.S. is a country of all religions. And the American public is concerned with fairness, especially when it comes to the matter of freedom of religion. If you continue to persecute the Buddhists, I'm afraid you are going to lose a lot of support."

Diem frowned. "The American public wouldn't even be aware of the problem if the news media didn't make such a big issue of it. I don't understand why the press won't just leave us alone and let us settle the difficulties ourselves. After all, what is going on here? Just some minor demonstrations in a few universities and some Buddhist temples. Is that any different from the Negro demonstrations that are now taking place in America?"

"Yes, there is a difference," Jarred defended. "In America the federal government is supporting the rights of the Negroes to demonstrate. Here your government is suppressing demonstrations. To Americans it looks as if you are concentrating your efforts on eliminating your domestic enemies, not fighting the VC."

"That is because the Americans are too naive to understand that the battle against the militant Buddhists *is* the battle against the Communists. By crushing the Buddhists we are crushing the seat of power of the Communists. And I want you to explain that to your people."

"Mr. President, I will convey your words," Jarred promised, "but I don't think I can make them believe them because I'm not sure I believe them myself."

"I told you you were wasting time by trying to make the Americans understand," Nhu spat. Until then, the conversation had been carried on in English, but now Nhu was speaking in Vietnamese. "You should never have made the concessions in the first place."

"My brother, have you forgotten our guest's linguistic ability?" Diem asked innocently.

"Excuse me for resorting to my own language, Colonel Hawkins," Nhu said, still speaking in Vietnamese. "But I find that words of anger are best when expressed in one's own language. I meant no offense."

"No offense taken," Jarred replied.

"Colonel Hawkins, if anyone can understand the psyche of the Vietnamese, it should be you," Diem said placatingly. "We are not a people used to democratic government. Change in this country, when it has occurred, has generally come about by the violent overthrow of the government in power. I fear there is a small but powerful band of people around who would like to see that happen to me. I am closed in on all sides by dissidents who would, given half the chance, mount a coup against my government."

"Do you know who these people are?"

Diem nodded. "In most cases I know who my enemies are. Some are in the military. Some are hiding in positions of authority and responsibility within my own government. Many others are in the schools and universities. All of those people, however, are but tentacles of the octopus. To cripple those tentacles we must kill the head. At the head of this octopus you will find the Buddhists. It is they who constitute the biggest threat."

Jarred shook his head slowly. "Mr. President, you have an army equipped with the latest in guns, tanks, and planes. It's going to be difficult for the average American to conceive of a Buddhist monk carrying a rice bowl as a legitimate threat to a government that U.S. tax money has bolstered for so long."

"If they knew that the Buddhists were being manipulated by the Communists, perhaps the Americans would understand," Nhu suggested.

"Without proof of that, it's going to be a tough sell."

"If proof is what the Americans need, then proof is what I shall give them," Nhu declared. He looked at his brother. "And now, Mr. President, don't forget you are meeting with a delegation from the provinces."

"Yes, yes, we must be going." Diem stuck his hand out to Jarred. "Well, Colonel Hawkins, thank you very much for coming in to talk with us. I do hope you are able to explain our position to your government."

Jarred nodded. "I will do what I can, Mr. President."

As promised, Jarred reported his conversation to Brigadier General Breckenridge, conveying as best he could the depth of Diem's anti-Buddhist feelings. In military parlance, General Breckenridge was Jarred's "next higher," and protocol required that he be the recipient of the report. Breckenridge was as far as Jarred could go with the information without violating strict military protocol, so when Breckenridge thanked him and said he would handle it from there on, it was out of Jarred's hands.

When he returned to Can Lao headquarters that afternoon, he felt a degree of frustration for not being able to do more to satisfy Diem's request. If Breckenridge had authorized him to speak directly to General Harkins, he might have been able to establish a dialogue between the two governments. Instead, he had done absolutely nothing to improve the situation. There was still a deep current of mistrust running between the American "country team" and the Diem government.

Jarred had hoped to report on his lack of success to Colonel Nguyen, but Nguyen wasn't there. Not only that, something was going on. He didn't know what it was, but twice he had gone from his office to the large room where the information-processing department was, and both times all conversation came to a halt. The first time it didn't really register, but the second time, when he walked over to the percolator for a cup of coffee, the cessation of conversation was so abrupt that it was immediately noticeable.

Jarred stirred sugar into his coffee, looking around the room at the Vietnamese workers. They all seemed extremely busy, filing documents or filling out reports, but it was obvious that the flurry of activity was to cover something up. He wondered what was going on but thought it would be improper to ask.

When he got off work that afternoon, he passed up dinner in the officers' club, opting instead to spend a quiet evening in his apartment, reading and listening to music. He put on a Joan Baez tape, then toasted a couple of cheese sandwiches and settled into his most comfortable chair to read. The book was *The Ugly American*, a novel that was strikingly close to the truth.

The telephone rang.

"Colonel Hawkins's quarters," he answered.

"Jarred?" It was Ly, and there was an edge to her voice he had never heard before. It frightened him.

"Ly, what is it, sweetheart? What's wrong?" he asked, putting his book down.

"They are burning the orphanage in Di Hoa," she said in a choked voice. "Please, you must do something!"

"The VC are burning the orphanage? The bastards! All right, where is Nguyen? I'll get hold of him, and we'll take some men up there."

"No, Jarred, you don't understand. It is Nguyen who is doing it!"

The headlamps of Jarred's jeep threw two spears of light into the enveloping darkness as he drove hard and fast up Highway 13. He was, he knew, a perfect target for a VC ambush. There was very little traffic on the road at night, so anyone who might be lying in wait would be able to see him coming for a long way.

If an ambush didn't get him, there was an equal chance he could get killed in an accident. Even in the daytime the road was a difficult one, full of twists, turns, and potholes, some so deep they had to be driven around. At night the road became even more treacherous, and Jarred wasn't improving his odds any by his breakneck driving speed.

As he approached Di Hoa, he saw an orange glow underlighting the overcast sky. Until that moment he had harbored the hope that Ly's information had been wrong. But a few minutes later when he pulled to a stop just outside the grounds of the burning orphanage, he could see that she was, tragically, correct.

A line of soldiers formed a perimeter around the grounds. They stood at parade-rest, as motionless as statues, faces painted orange in the flickering flames, gleaming eyes reflecting the hellfire.

The villagers of Di Hoa, who were being kept away from the burning buildings by the line of troops, were gathered in small groups, the terror of the evening mirrored in their faces. A number of the village men, women, and children had bloodied faces. Some were having their wounds attended to, but most were just looking at the fire in shocked silence, apparently so numbed by what they were seeing that they were totally oblivious to their injuries.

Nguyen Van Tran was standing halfway between the line of soldiers and the burning building, feet spread apart, hands on his hips. He, too, was looking at the fire, and his eyes followed a piece of fire-blackened paper that pirouetted crazily as it rode a column of heat and smoke high into the night sky. At first Jarred wondered what Nguyen was doing commanding an army unit; then, as he looked more closely at the uniformed troops, he saw they weren't part of the regular army at all but were Can Lao men dressed as soldiers.

"Nguyen, my God! What are you doing?" Jarred shouted, stepping unmolested through the Can Lao line to approach the Vietnamese colonel. He pointed to the burning building. "That's an orphanage, for God's sake!"

Nguyen took out a silk handkerchief and wiped his hands before he replied. "To you this may be an orphanage. But our intelligence sources confirmed it was harboring a nest of militant Buddhists."

"Militant Buddhists? Are you crazy? Nguyen, the name of this orphanage is St. Mary's. *St. Mary's!* Since when did Buddhists start recognizing the Mother of God?"

"Lieutenant Mot," Nguyen called to one of his men. "Bring Than Cao Duong." Nguyen finally turned and looked at Jarred. "Even though you speak our language, you are as easily deceived as any other westerner. Perhaps this will convince you."

A moment later a group of Nguyen's men came out of the darkness and into the circle of orange light, laughing and shouting obscenities at the elderly man they were leading by a rope tied around his neck. The man was very old, hollow-cheeked and extraordinarily frail. His skin had the texture of parchment, and the hair of his beard was as fine as threads of silk. His eyes were downcast, but he did not wear a look of fear as he stood before Nguyen.

"This is Than Cao Duong," Nguyen said, smiling maliciously. "I am sure you have heard of him."

"Yes, I have heard of him," Jarred said.

Than Cao Duong was one of the principal leaders of the Buddhist movement. He had been interviewed by an American reporter several weeks earlier. The reporter's story ran in several American newspapers, then in newspapers around the world, and finally in some of the bolder Vietnamese newspapers. According to the syndicated story, Than Cao Duong stated that Diem and Nhu had lost all popular support among the people of Vietnam. Diem was still in power only because he was being propped up by United States aid and protected by a brutal police force and an army that were more intent on terrorizing their own people than carrying on the war against the Communists. Shortly after the story came out, Than Cao Duong's name was moved to the head of the target list maintained by the Can Lao. In their eyes, he was now a bigger threat than all the known VC commanders in all the districts and provinces.

"The orphanage was providing this criminal sanctuary," Nguyen said. "Not only for him, but four other Buddhist priests as well."

"And you took it upon yourself to burn the orphanage out for that?"

"Like you, Colonel Hawkins, I am a soldier. I do not act without specific authority." He looked back at the Buddhist priest. "President Diem gave me a mission, and I followed through."

"Diem gave the orders? Or Nhu?"

"But, of course, Nhu speaks for his brother. And if I have orders, I must obey. What else is a soldier to do?" He had been speaking in English, but now he turned to Lieutenant Mot and barked an order in Vietnamese. "Throw this dog in the back of the truck with the others."

Complying, the old man's captors dragged him toward one of the trucks. Nguyen looked back at Jarred; at that moment, with the fiendish expression on his face and backlit by the fire, he could have just stepped out of hell.

"Go back to Saigon, Jarred," Nguyen said coldly. "Go to the American Officers' Club. Have a beer and—what is it you Americans do? Oh, yes, you 'shoot the shit.' Go and shoot the shit with the other Americans. Like them, Jarred, you do not belong here."

CHAPTER

FOURTEEN

AUGUST 3, 1963, FROM "TRAILMARKERS" IN
EVENTS MAGAZINE:

BUDDHIST MONK COMMITS FIERY
SUICIDE IN SAIGON

While a crowd watched in mesmerized horror, a Buddhist monk, protesting the Diem regime's treatment of the Buddhist population, poured gasoline on himself, sat down, then calmly lit a match and set fire to himself. While the crowd looked on and cameras clicked away, the monk remained silent and motionless as the fire leaped up around him. Minutes later his charred body fell over, dead.

The dramatic action of this solitary monk has had greater impact than the protest march last week of more than 60,000 Buddhists. The U.S. State Department, which has already expressed some concern over the Diem government's conduct, has now sent word that Diem had better move promptly to redress the grievances of the Buddhists. "Victory against the Communists will be impossible unless the Vietnamese leadership enjoys the full confidence of all its people," the message from the State Department said.

Inside information has indicated that Diem's brother, Ngo Dinh Nhu, is more stridently anti-Buddhist than Diem. Nhu's wife, Madame Nhu, is said to have referred jokingly to the self-immolation as a "monk barbeque."

SOVIETS CONTINUE HELICOPTER FLIGHTS OVER WEST BERLIN

Despite warnings from the three western powers to discontinue the provocative action, the Soviet Air Force penetrated western air space above West Berlin four times last week.

The Soviet helicopter, referred to by NATO as a "hound dog," has been taking off from a field in East Berlin and, flying low, crossing the infamous wall into western territory. Although every flight has included at least one "buzzing" of the West Berlin Congress Hall, there seems to be no other plan to its somewhat erratic flight path.

Apparently the Soviet pilot knows just how long he can stay over West Berlin before fighter aircraft are scrambled toward him, for he has managed every time to depart western air space before Allied aircraft arrive.

The Federal Republic of Germany, in a show of solidarity with West Berlin, had declared that for one week its Bundestag will meet in Berlin. That, according to the Soviets, is a violation of the Four Powers agreement—and it is believed the helicopter flights are a direct expression of the Soviet's displeasure with the Bundestag meeting.

ST. LOUIS

> *YOU ARE CORDIALLY INVITED TO A GALA BALL*
> *ON AUGUST 9, 1963, AT SEVEN P.M.*
> *IN THE HOME OF MR. AND MRS. JOHN CANFIELD*
> *TO RAISE MONEY FOR THE ST. LOUIS BALLET*
> *LEAGUE*
> *AND TO WELCOME THEIR SON, MORGAN,*
> *BACK FROM HIS SERVICE WITH THE PEACE CORPS*

"Actually, the *primary* reason for having the party is to welcome Morgan home from Ecuador," Faith told the young reporter from *The St. Louis Chronicle*. "But it also seemed like an ideal fund-raiser for the St. Louis Ballet League."

"Everyone is saying it's going to be the ball of the year," the reporter gushed. "And in a city known for its balls, that's saying quite a bit."

"Yes, isn't it?" Faith replied delightedly. "Well, of course, *I* wouldn't go so far as to say that. There have been some truly lovely balls in St. Louis this year, and no doubt there will be many more. But I do believe our guests will particularly enjoy this one."

Morgan was listening to the exchange from the hallway. He had been about to step into the living room but stopped when he heard his mother giving the interview. He didn't want to intrude; more than that, he didn't want to be asked any more questions about what the last couple of years had been like, or what his plans were now. And he especially didn't want to be asked if there was any woman in his future. In fact, he didn't even want to attend this ball, even though it was in his honor. But he knew he couldn't get out of it.

He took the back stairs up to the second floor, then walked down the long corridor to his old room. He still considered it his room when he was here, though he had taken an apartment in a high-rise complex overlooking the Missouri River.

The room still contained a few artifacts from his youth, and he walked over to a shelf to pick up a baseball autographed by Stan Musial. He was tossing it casually from hand to hand when his sister poked her head in the door.

"You remember what Dad used to say about that, Morgan? 'If you keep playing with that baseball, you're going to wipe off the ink, and it won't be autographed anymore.'"

Morgan chuckled, then put the baseball back on the little silver mount. "The name is half rubbed off now," he said. "It says Stan Mu-blob."

Alicia shook her head. "I never could understand why you kept playing with it. You could have tossed any ball back and forth."

"It wouldn't have been the same. Musial held this ball."

"Yeah, I know." She came into the room and sat on the edge of the bed. "It's good to have you back—though I'm sure you had a wonderful adventure down there."

"I didn't have nearly the adventure *you* had."

"Yes, well, I had a little more adventure than I really wanted," Alicia chuckled.

"I guess so, but you have to admit, you did get your law career off to a rousing start. You were in all the news magazines in all the airports."

"I would trade that rousing start in a heartbeat if I could change what happened," Alicia said quietly. "One person was killed, and Deon is crippled for life."

Morgan squeezed his sister's shoulder. "Just be glad it wasn't worse."

"I know."

Morgan reached for the ball again and, smiling, Alicia took it from him. "Don't *do* that," she scolded.

"I'm sorry. I'm just not thinking."

"Yes, you are thinking. And that's the whole problem. You're thinking about Sheri Warren, aren't you?"

"No," Morgan said quickly. Then he sighed. "Yes," he admitted. "I am. Did you know I asked her to marry me? I asked her to marry me, and she turned me down."

"Be glad she turned you down. She's not right for you, Morgan."

"You sound like someone else I know. I know Sheri doesn't come from what Mother calls good stock, but—"

"I'm not talking about her breeding," Alicia interrupted. "Sheri Warren is beautiful, intelligent, talented, ambitious, and well on her way to being extremely rich, and 'good stock' has nothing to do with it. She just isn't for you."

"Why not? Wouldn't you call those qualities assets?"

"Yes, they are assets—if one is building a fashion empire. But they're liabilities if one is planning to become the wife of a Canfield."

"The wife of a Canfield?" Morgan snorted. "You make it sound as if it were a position one would apply for, complete with references and vitae."

"It is," Alicia said simply. "And it's a position with a very precise job description."

"Is that so? Gee, I'm interested in just what you think that job description might be, Alicia."

She smiled. "Scoff all you like, but I could write the recruitment ad for you. 'Wanted, young woman between twenty-three and twenty-seven, educated at Lindenwood, Stevens, Bryn Mawr, Vassar, Sarah Lawrence, or similar school. Applicant should be attractive, but exceptional beauty is to be eschewed. She must have some knowledge of the arts though not be an artist, possess the skills of a gracious hostess and the diplomacy of a statesman. While an interest in socially accepted charities is to be desired, a commitment to causes is not. Intelligence should be implied rather than demonstrated, and all personal talent and ambition must be subverted to that of her husband-to-be.'"

Morgan laughed. "Is that what you think it takes to make a Canfield wife?"

"It's not what I think, it's what I *know* it takes to make a Canfield wife. That's why Sheri Warren was never really in the picture."

"Never in the picture? I told you, I proposed to her."

"Of course you did. But you didn't truly want her to accept."

"What makes you think I didn't?"

"Because if you had, you wouldn't have taken no for an answer."

"I think you're being unduly harsh."

"Do you? I don't think so. But if it's any consolation to you, I've also written the job description for anyone who might be foolish enough to apply for *my* hand."

"Good. Don't be one-sided in this thing. Let's hear it."

"'Wanted, young man between twenty-eight and thirty-five. Must have MBA from Jefferson U., Washington U., University of Chicago, or a school of similar or greater prestige. Applicant must be athletic but not be an athlete. Military obligation must be already fulfilled and must have been served as an Army officer. Anyone who was an officer in one of the other branches of service need not apply.'"

"Why is that?" Morgan asked. "What's wrong with the Marines, Air Force, or Navy?"

"Marine officers are too rigid, Air Force officers are too technical, and Navy officers are too clannish."

"And Army officers aren't any of those things?"

"No. When you get right down to it, they're generally just civilians getting their service obligation over with as quickly and painlessly as possible."

"I see. And what about ambition, intelligence, talent— that sort of thing. Can your suitor have any of that?"

"'Applicant's ambition should be limited to whatever goals are established for him by a generous father-in-law,'" she continued in an arch tone. "'Intelligence should take the form of recognizing one's true position and talent limited to the ability to display through creative groveling the gratitude he would feel for being accepted into the family business.'"

Morgan laughed again. "Ouch! My God, Alicia, what a cynic you have become."

She grinned. "I know. It's outrageous, isn't it? Maybe it will pass. Maybe it's just a stage I'm going through."

That evening the Canfield home was filled with splendid yet unobtrusive classical music, provided by a chamber ensemble from the St. Louis Symphony. Morgan drifted through the party, greeting with effusiveness his old friends and meeting with wit and charm new ones. Elegantly gowned and bejeweled women and dinner-jacketed or tuxedo-clad men mingled and mixed, constantly changing the dynamics of the several conversational groups.

After one circuit of the ballroom floor, Morgan found himself standing in front of a splashing champagne fountain. On the other side of the fountain, staring at it and holding a crystal goblet, was an attractive young woman. He moved around to speak to her.

"Hello. I'm Morgan Canfield."

The woman smiled. "Yes, I know. The reason for the party."

"Well, not really. I am the *excuse* for the party. I think

raising money for the Clarinet Marching Society or some such thing is the reason."

The woman laughed. "I believe it is the St. Louis Ballet League."

"Whatever. So, you know who I am. How about giving me the same advantage? Who are you?"

"My name is Jan Bower."

"Bower? As in Edward J. Bower and Company, the stockbrokers?"

"One and the same. Edward was my grandfather. My father is Deermont Bower." She pointed to the champagne fountain. "I was wondering. Does one actually drink from such a thing? Or is this entirely for show?"

"I really don't know the answer to that. Do you want some champagne?"

"Yes, I thought I might."

"Well, then, come with me. We'll get some at the bar outside."

"All right," Jan agreed easily.

"Lindenwood?" Morgan asked as he led her out onto the patio where one of the bars had been set up.

"I beg your pardon?"

"Did you go to school at Lindenwood?"

"I matriculated at Stevens School for Women in Columbia."

"Is that so? Well, I've known quite a few women from Stevens."

Jan laughed, low and throaty. "I daresay you have. Your legend lives on. You established quite a reputation among the Stevens girls."

"Really? What kind of reputation?"

"From all the stories, I gather you were quite the bon vivant."

"Lies, all lies," Morgan said, gesturing airily. At the bar he pointed to a bottle of Dom Perignon, and the bartender filled two champagne glasses. Morgan took them both, then motioned for Jan to follow him over to the low rock wall that separated the flagstone patio from the beautifully manicured lawn beyond, which sparkled with moisture from a recent watering. Morgan sat on the wall, then handed Jan her drink, inviting her to sit beside him.

Picking up on their conversation, Jan remarked, "Really

now, Morgan, you don't expect a girl to just accept your word that such a reputation is undeserved, do you?"

"No," Morgan replied lightly. "I expect you to let me prove it to you."

"And just how do you propose to do that?"

"We could start with dinner tomorrow evening," he suggested. "That is, if you aren't otherwise occupied . . . or involved."

Jan took a sip of her champagne, eyeing him over the rim of the goblet. Then she lowered the glass and answered, "I am neither occupied nor involved. And I would be delighted to have dinner with you."

SCHWEINFURT, GERMANY

When Bob Parker reported to the D Troop orderly room at 0200 hours on the morning of August 15, he was surprised to find all the enlisted barracks dark and no trucks out on the airfield being loaded with field equipment. Where was everyone? When his phone had rung thirty minutes before, he was told by the duty officer that this was an alert. By all rights, the entire troop should be loaded and ready to go by now.

Alerts were routine exercises during which the entire division would be summoned, generally in the middle of the night, to report immediately to predetermined positions in the field. They were an important part of overall unit readiness, designed to test how quickly the division could respond in case the Soviets decided to move across the border.

But this morning there were no trucks being loaded, no aircraft being readied, and no men responding to the call. Not only that, but the parking lot was quiet and dark, exactly the opposite of what it should be if this really was an alert.

Bob concluded that the alert had been canceled, so he reported to the orderly room to get the official word. There he found Colonel Rockford, Captain Greenly, Lieutenant Fillion, and Chief Warrant Officer Mike Rindell. Like Bob, the other officers were in flight suits.

"What's going on?" he asked. "Has the alert been canceled?"

"Not exactly," Rockford answered.

"Then I don't understand. Where is everyone?"

"This is a very special alert," Captain Greenly explained. He was holding his "Garry Owen" stick, slapping it against the palm of his hand. "We are the only ones involved."

"Oh?"

"Have you been reading in *Stars and Stripes* about that Soviet helicopter that's been coming across the border in West Berlin to buzz Congress Hall?" Rockford asked.

"Yes, sir, I've read a little about it. Frankly, I haven't paid much attention to it."

"You should have," Greenly said. "Because if he comes across this morning, we're going to be there."

"And do what?"

"Shoot his ass down," Mike answered with a grin. "We are about to make history. We're going to be the first helicopter ever to shoot down another helicopter in air-to-air combat."

"Not if Captain Greenly and I see him first," Lieutenant Fillion insisted smugly.

"Are you serious? We're going to West Berlin to shoot down a Russian helicopter?" Bob asked.

"If he violates western airspace again, yes," Rockford answered. He looked up at the clock. "Gentlemen, you'd better get going. We've already filed a corridor penetration for you. You'll fly through to Berlin while it's still dark, so you can be on the ground at Templehof by first light. Good luck." He smiled. "And what is it they used to say in all the movies? Good hunting?"

The four officers walked through the darkness toward the two helicopters that gleamed softly under the floodlight mounted on the front of the hangar. The crew chiefs for each ship had already untied the blades and removed all the covers.

"You two take seven-seven-one. We'll take two-five-oh," Greenly instructed Bob.

"Yes, sir," he replied, peeling off to the right with Mike.

"Since you outshot me on the gunnery range, how about I fly and you shoot," Mike suggested to Bob.

"All right." Bob looked at the four 7.2-millimeter machine guns attached to the helicopter, two per side. The guns were on swivels controlled by a sight-and-trigger mechanism hanging down in front of the cockpit. The gunner flew from the left seat, the pilot from the right.

"Hey, Chief," Specialist Hanvey said as Bob and Mike approached 771. "We were told to load up with live ammo. Is that right?"

"That's right," Bob said.

"Jeez, what's happening?"

"A Russian helicopter has been violating western airspace over Berlin. We're going there to shoot him down."

Hanvey grinned. "Awright! Let's get us some commie ass!"

"I do wish he could show a little more enthusiasm for the job, don't you?" Mike deadpanned.

The sun was bright and warm at ten in the morning and, after having flown without incident through the corridor, both helicopters were now waiting on the ground at Templehof. Hanvey was asleep, stretched out on the canvas bench in the back. Bob and Mike remained strapped into their seats, talking. Their orders were not to leave the aircraft for any reason until specifically released. They were allowed to remove their helmets as long as someone maintained contact with mission control, and Lieutenant Fillion in the other ship was fulfilling that requirement.

Mission control was not a part of the tower or flight operations. It was a special Army unit set up in a remote radar trailer. All communication would be handled through what was normally one of the ground frequencies and thereby be hidden from the Soviets and East Germans who routinely monitored all air traffic control. The call sign for mission control was "Vexation"; the call sign for the two helicopters was "Saber"—"Saber One" for Captain Greenly, "Saber Two" for Mike and Bob.

As it so happened, just the night before, Bob and Jill had been over to Mike's house for an outdoor barbeque. Mike's wife, Maria, and Jill had taken immediately to each other, becoming instant friends.

"You know what Maria told Jill last night, don't you?" Mike asked, when the subject of Jill came up.

"No, what?"

"She told her not to let you get away."

Bob chuckled. "Sounds like Maria is trying to do a little matchmaking."

Mike snorted. "A *little* matchmaking? We're talking major league wife-and-baby stuff here. Don't forget, Maria was born in Italy, so she still has a lot of the Old World attitudes. If she had her way, she would be a professional matchmaker. She really eats that stuff up."

"Well, it doesn't hurt anything, I don't guess," Bob said.

"Okay, but don't blame me. I'm giving you fair warning. If you don't want to get stuck with this girl, you'd better not bring her around anymore."

"Come on, Mike, you're exaggerating a bit, aren't you?"

"Hell, no, I'm deadly serious. I'm telling you, once Maria gets her mind made up about something, she never lets go. She'll have you hog-tied and dropped in a trick back, then dragged kicking and screaming all the way to the altar. You mark my words."

"Maybe I won't," Bob mused.

"Maybe you won't what?"

"Maybe I won't kick and scream all the way to the altar."

Bob thought about last night. After leaving Mike and Maria's, he had gone back to Jill's room over at the teachers' BOQ. He had taken his portable typewriter and was going to write while she graded papers. Instead of working, though, they wound up making love while a tape of Henry Mancini's *Charades* played softly in the background. Afterward, he had to dress to go back home. It would have been nice to have left her in bed this morning.

"*Start 'em up!*" Greenly abruptly yelled through the open window of the other helicopter. "We just got the word! The son of a bitch has come over again!"

The warm, erotic thoughts of the night before flew out of Bob's head as the flight teams were galvanized into action.

"Hanvey! Stand fire guard!" Mike shouted as he began flipping switches.

It took less than one minute from start-up to liftoff, and, faster than Bob would have thought possible, the two helicopters were beating their way across the city toward Congress Hall. By prior arrangement they flew low—so low that Mike was having to dodge chimneys and antennae.

"*Vexation, this is Saber One,*" Greenly said over the air, which Bob was picking up in his headset. "*We're scrambled with two.*"

"*Saber One, your target is three miles north, bearing*

three-five-zero from your point of departure," mission control instructed from the ground.

"Roger," Greenly replied. *"Three miles, bearing three-five-zero."*

"Tally Ho!" Bob suddenly called. "I've got him in sight."

"Where?" Mike asked.

"About one o'clock. He looks a little like one of our old H-Nineteens. Do you see him?"

"I've got him," Mike said.

Bob pulled the sight-and-trigger unit down from its overhead holder, then freed the guns so they would track with him.

"Saber One, do you have him?" Mike called.

"Roger, we've got him," Greenly replied. *"I'm going to break right. You continue straight ahead. If he tries to run we'll have the angle on him."*

"Roger that," Mike replied.

The two turbine-powered Hueys were considerably faster than the reciprocating-engine-powered Russian Hound Dog. As a result they closed on him quickly. The Russian pilot was on the lookout for the Air Force fighter jets that had been scrambled earlier and apparently had no idea that two American helicopters were coming up on him. The Hueys were approaching from the Russian's blind spot, below and behind him.

As they drew closer, Bob put the target ring on the Russian and watched as the helicopter grew bigger and bigger. They would be within range within seconds.

"Guns are hot," Bob said, arming the system.

"Saber, are you close enough to engage?" Vexation asked.

"Roger," Greenly replied. *"We are within range, and guns are hot. Request permission to fire."*

"Negative. Do not engage," Vexation said. *"I say again, do not engage."*

"What?" Mike said angrily. He was talking over the intercom only, so his words did not go out. "What the shit is this? Why don't we just shoot the asshole down and be done with it?"

"Roger, understand we will not engage," Greenly said. *"Saber Two, secure your weapons."*

"Shit!" Bob said over the intercom. He flipped the arming switch off. "Weapons secured," he reported over the air.

Bob didn't realize until that moment that his palms were sweating—and had been sweating since they took off. He wiped them on his pants leg.

"What do we do now?" Mike asked. "Just wait until the son of a bitch sees us?"

As if answering Mike's untransmitted question, Vexation came back. *"Saber, this is Vexation. Has the Russian pilot spotted you?"*

"Negative," Greenly answered.

"It is imperative that he knows you are there. He must know you could have shot him down if you had wanted to."

"So that's it," Mike grumbled over the intercom. "They never planned on us shooting him down. We were just running a bluff on the son of a bitch."

"Saber Two, this is Saber One. Give him a close pass. Let him know he has company."

"Will do," Mike replied. He moved to the left to uncover, then climbed up to the Russian's altitude and eased up alongside. It wasn't until they were almost even with him that the Russian pilot even suspected anyone else was around. His eyes widened with surprise and fright.

"Up yours, asshole!" Mike shouted, sticking his hand out the window and extending his middle finger to the Russian.

The Russian bottomed his collective, then threw his cyclic hard to the right so that his helicopter dropped down sharply and started to the east.

"Saber One, he's coming your way," Mike said.

"Roger," Greenly replied. *"I can make one more pass."*

Bob watched as the Russian beat his way back toward the Eastern sector. Suddenly Greenly's helicopter flashed by on the other side of the Russian, and the Russian had to turn hard to the north to avoid him. That gave Mike the angle he needed to close in a second time. This time when they drew even with the Russian, Mike, Bob and Hanvey all gave him the finger. They stayed alongside until the Russian reached the dividing line between the sectors.

"Saber Two, do not penetrate!" Greenly called.

"Roger," Mike said, putting the Huey into a very tight turn to the right. "We're breaking off pursuit now."

*   *   *

Two days after the adventure in Berlin, Sergeant Malloy, Bob's maintenance sergeant, came into his office. "Chief, I think maybe you'd better come out here and take a look at seven-seven-one," he suggested.

"Why?" Bob asked. "What's wrong with it?"

"I just think you should have a look at it," Sergeant Malloy insisted.

"Okay." Bob picked up his "Garry Owen" stick and followed the maintenance sergeant out to the flight line. As he approached 771, he was surprised to see his entire maintenance platoon standing around looking at it. Specialist Hanvey and Mike Rindell were also there.

" 'Tenshut!" Sergeant Mallow called as they approached, and all the men came to attention. Bob noticed that everyone but Mike was smiling. Mike was beyond smiling. He was barely able to control his laughter.

"Mike, what the hell is going on?" Bob asked suspiciously.

"You know how fighter pilots paint little flags on their airplane to keep count of their victories?" Mike replied.

"Yes."

"Well, partner, they don't have one damn thing on us." He pointed to right front door, just below the window. There, stenciled on very neatly, were three hands, each making a fist and giving the finger. Bob laughed out loud, and when he did all the others, who had been fighting to restrain themselves, joined him.

"What do you think of it, sir?" Hanvey asked. "Can we keep it?"

"Hell, yes, we can keep it. The only question I have is, why are there three? There was only one Russian helicopter."

"Yes, sir, that's true," Hanvey agreed. "But you have to admit, that one Ruskie got rammed up his ass three times."

AUGUST 28, 1963, WASHINGTON, D.C.

The crowd was not yet a cohesive unit, even though thousands upon thousands of people had come together for the same purpose. A group from Georgia, holding up signs that proclaimed their place of origin, was singing "We Shall Overcome." Another group from Mississippi was singing "We

Shall Not Be Moved." Still others were singing, "Woke up this morning with my mind set on freedom. Hallelu, hallelu, hallelujah!" There were signs, banners, sashes, buttons, balloons, and shirts all bearing ringing phrases of freedom.

Artemus Booker, whose Cadillac displayed a special pass in the window that allowed it access to restricted areas, was waved through by members of the Capitol Police. He parked the car within sight of the great stage where the day's events would be taking place, then removed the collapsible wheelchair from the backseat and opened it. After that he lifted Deon out and sat him gingerly in the chair.

"How's that?" Artemus asked his brother. "Are you okay?"

"Yeah, I'm fine, thanks," Deon said. He looked around at the crowd and grinned. "So, what do you think? Was it worth coming?"

"Are you kidding?" Artemus gazed around at the teeming mass of people. "Look at this crowd, will you? I thought you said you were expecting one hundred thousand. There's three times that many people here."

"Incredible, isn't it? I understand that so far this morning twenty-one charter trains have arrived at Union Station. And I heard that buses have been coming through the Baltimore tunnel all night at the rate of a hundred per hour. That's not even counting the cars and planes full of demonstrators."

The demonstration was set to take place on the Mall, which stretched from the Lincoln Memorial to the Washington Monument. Television and newsreel cameras were set up at strategic points throughout the crowd to capture for posterity the events that would occur. The Freedom March on Washington was the largest demonstration of its kind ever held, and organizers had been working on the logistics for the previous two months.

All sorts of things had to be dealt with in planning an event of this magnitude. Many nervous whites in the city feared having so many Negroes gathered together. What if riots erupted? What if the Negroes started looting? Dreading what might happen, store owners moved out ninety percent of their inventories into warehouses in Maryland and Virginia. The federal government had four thousand soldiers standing by in the wings and another fifteen thousand waiting to come in if necessary.

The organizers were well aware of these fears—and aware, also, of how much damage could be done to their movement if the March on Washington got out of hand. They did not plan to let that happen. To make sure it didn't, they arranged everything down to the last detail. All the speakers were told they were limited to seven minutes and seven minutes only. People would be standing by with long shepherd poles, with instructions to jerk a long-winded speaker off the platform if need be. The idea was to get the rally started on time, have each event take place on time, and get it over early enough to allow most of the city to be evacuated before dark.

Deon had been one of the organizers of the demonstration, and to him had fallen the responsibility of designating where on the Mall the facilities should be situated to accommodate the crowd.

"I've got twenty toilets in place out here," Deon said to his brother, "and twenty drinking fountains. But from the looks of things, that's not going to be nearly enough."

Artemus chuckled. "Too late to worry about that now."

"Hey! Hey, my man, you Artemus Booker?" a young Negro man called.

"Yes," Artemus answered.

"The basketball player? That Artemus Booker?"

"Yes."

"How 'bout that? Hey, this is Artemus Booker," the young man said to his friends, and for a moment there was a flurry of handshakes as Artemus greeted his fans.

Finally he managed to break away from them and continue pushing his brother's wheelchair toward the VIP stand that had been constructed at the foot of the Lincoln Memorial. Entry onto the VIP stand was very carefully controlled, and both Capitol police and event security men were turning away anyone who didn't have the proper credentials.

Deon and Artemus had the proper credentials—Deon because he was one of the principal organizers of the event and Artemus because Deon had secured the pass for him. They would have no trouble getting on the stage, but they were having a lot of trouble getting *to* it. The closer they came to the stage, the more solidly packed was the crowd and the more difficult the passage.

"Let us through!" Artemus started calling. "Let us through, please!"

"Hey! Hey, look who that is!" someone shouted.

"Looks like some more of your fans," Deon said. "Maybe your being famous is going to be a help after all, and they'll let us through."

Artemus smiled to greet the approaching young Negro man, but to his surprise the young man stopped in front of Deon's wheelchair.

"You're Deon Booker, aren't you?" the young man asked. He was wearing a suit and tie and tortoiseshell glasses.

"Yes," Deon answered.

"Mr. Booker, you don't know what a thrill it is to meet you."

"To meet *me*?" Deon asked.

"Yes, sir, you. I've read all about you. You've been part of the movement from the very beginning—in Montgomery during the bus boycott, in Mississippi last year. . . ."

"Yeah," Deon said, subconsciously rubbing his useless legs. "I was in Mississippi, all right."

The young man winced. "I'm sorry. I've reminded you of how you suffered for it."

Deon smiled kindly. "I'm reminded of it every moment of every day."

"I guess you are. You know, the rest of the country owes you a lot, Mr. Booker. For all you've been through and for what you've endured, you are one of the true heros of our time." He glanced at the VIP pass on Deon's lapel. "I'm sorry. I'm holding you up, aren't I? You're trying to get up on the stage."

"Yeah, well, we aren't having much luck with it. There are so many people we can't get through."

"You let me take care of that," the young man offered. "Hey!" he shouted to his companions. "Help me get these two men through here. You know who this is? This is Deon Booker. Help me get him up to the stage!"

The young man's enthusiastic energy paid off. The crowd parted for them as the sea had parted before Moses. And as they traversed the path made for them, scores of young men and women, drawn by the flurry, cheered and applauded Deon. Many reached out to touch him.

"We're with you, Deon!" someone called. "We're all in the fight together!"

As Deon and Artemus approached the VIP stand they

saw such celebrities as Harry Belafonte, James Garner, and Marlon Brando. Like the ordinary people in the crowd, the Hollywood luminaries were applauding Deon's arrival.

"Deon," Artemus said, his voice breaking, "I have never been prouder of anything in my life than I am right now of you."

He looked down at Deon, then looked away quickly, not wanting to infringe upon his brother's private moment. Tears were streaming down Deon's face.

Just after they took their places on the VIP platform, the public address system came alive. Folk singer Joan Baez sang "Oh Freedom," which was followed by Odetta singing "I'm On My Way" and Peter, Paul, and Mary performing "Blowin' in the Wind." But it was Mahalia Jackson who really brought the crowd to life with her a cappella rendition of "I Been 'Buked and I Been Scorned," which stirred the deepest emotions in tens of thousands of people, and tears flowed like rain.

There were dozens of speeches throughout the day, some reasoned and articulate, some impassioned and rambling. The sun grew hotter, the day grew longer, and the meeting droned on. From his position on the stage Deon could look out over the solid mass of humanity that filled the Mall to overflowing, lining both sides of the reflecting pool, which stretched to the front of the Washington Monument, and spilling into the trees. Black faces predominated by far, but enough white faces were scattered throughout the great crowd to prove the movement had definitely crossed racial lines.

Finally, A. Phillip Randolph was called upon to introduce the man whom everyone had come to hear. "It is my great privilege to introduce the moral leader of our nation," Randolph said. "I give you Dr. Martin Luther King, J-R." He pronounced the letters *J* and *R* rather than the word "Junior."

Martin Luther King stepped up to the microphones. He paused for a long moment, looking out over the vast crowd, and as he stood there, the three hundred thousand demonstrators fell silent, waiting expectantly.

"I am pleased to be here with you today, on a day that will go down as the greatest demonstration for freedom in our nation's history," King finally said. Although his opening line elicited applause, he delivered it almost as an aside. Then, in his clearest diction and stateliest baritone, he began his speech.

"Fivescore years ago, a great American, in whose symbolic shadow we stand today, issued the Emancipation Proclamation, ending the Negroes' long ordeal of slavery.

"But one hundred years later the Negro is not free. One hundred years later the Negro is an exile in his own country. One hundred years later the Negro languishes on an isle of poverty in the midst of a great sea of material wealth."

As King spoke, ovations began to pour forth from the crowd, starting in the distant rear and rolling to the front like a mighty surf. Here and there people shouted out their encouragement with "Yes," and "Right on!"—words that might have interrupted an ordinary speaker. But King wasn't ordinary. He skillfully wove those shouted words into the measured pace of his speech.

Continuing with his speech, he didn't stray from his text until near the end. Then, as if he, too, were caught up in the great emotion of the moment, he abandoned his text and began to deliver his words not from the page but from the heart.

"And so I say to you today, my friends, that even though we face the difficulties of today and tomorrow, I still have a dream. It is a dream deeply rooted in the American dream.

"I have a dream today. I have a dream that one day this nation shall rise up and live out the true meaning of its creed: 'We hold these truths to be self-evident, that all men are created equal.'"

Deon had heard Martin Luther King give speeches before, and he had seen him move people, but never had he witnessed anything like the response King was generating today. The feeling he had had earlier that the crowd was merely a collection of several different groups was no longer valid. Now the crowd had but one focus, one life, and one soul. It was the embodiment of Dr. Martin Luther King Jr.'s soaring words.

"I have a dream today. I have a dream that one day on the red hills of Georgia sons of former slaves and the sons of former slaveholders will be able to sit down together at the table of brotherhood.

"I have a dream that even the state of Mississippi, a state sweltering with the heat of injustice, will be transformed into an oasis of freedom. I have a dream that even down in Alabama, with its vicious racism and with its governor whose lips drip with words of vileness and hate, that one day in that place little black boys and little black girls will be able to join hands with little white boys and little white girls as sisters and brothers. I have a dream today."

Now the pounding surf of cheers and applause from the crowd had swelled to a constant roar, not drowning out King's words but, somehow, underscoring them and giving them even more power. He continued on with his dream, and then he moved to the conclusion of his speech, bringing everyone with him in a burst of energy and metered oratory.

"So let freedom ring from the prodigious hilltops of New Hampshire. Let freedom ring from the mighty mountains of New York. Let freedom ring!

"Let freedom ring from the heightening Alleghanies of Pennsylvania! Let freedom ring from the snowcapped Rockies of Colorado! Let freedom ring from the curvaceous slopes of California, let freedom ring!"

King was soaring now, his words rising and falling, lifting the hearts and spirits and igniting in the minds of everyone present the certainty that they were witnessing one of the defining moments of American history.

"Let freedom ring from Stone Mountain of Georgia! Let freedom ring from Lookout Mountain of Tennessee! Let freedom ring from every hill and molehill in Mississippi! From every mountainside, let freedom ring!

"And when this happens, when we let it ring from every state and every city, we will be able to speed up that day when all God's children, black men and white men, Jews and Gentiles, Protestants and Catholics, will be able to join hands and sing in the words of the old Negro spiritual, 'Free at last! Free at last! Thank God Almighty, we are free at last!' "

Then, as the cheers of three hundred thousand rolled across the Mall like crashing thunder, King abruptly turned and walked away. In some mystical way his sudden absence from the podium allowed the words he had just spoken to take on a life of their own.

Hearing the words reverberating inside his head, Deon knew that this was a moment he would remember and cherish for the rest of his life.

*   *   *

In St. Louis, Eric Twainbough watched King's speech on television. When it was over he turned to look at Tanner and saw that she was wiping tears from her eyes.

"Oh, my," she said. "That was really something, wasn't it?"

"Something? It will go down in the books as one of the greatest speeches ever given," Eric replied somberly. "Like Lincoln's Gettysburg Address, it will be studied for generations to come."

"Do you think it will do any good? Do you think the Civil Rights Bill will be passed?"

"No doubt about it. The Negro movement has reached what physicists call critical mass. It can't go back. It has turned the corner. There will undoubtedly be racial prejudice for a long time to come, but those who would keep segregation and other forms of racial discrimination as a part of public policy, even local public policy, have just heard the bell tolled on their bigotry. I am certain that what has happened in Washington today was the defining moment in the Negroes' battle for equal treatment under the law." He sighed. "I just wish . . ."

"What is it you wish?" Tanner asked.

"I just wish that Loomis could have lived long enough to see this day."

Tanner walked over to her husband and put her arms around him. "You lived to see it for him," she said, kissing his cheek gently. "And I think somehow he knows."

CHAPTER

FIFTEEN

OCTOBER 26, 1963, FROM "TRAILMARKERS" IN *EVENTS MAGAZINE*:

CANFIELD-PURITEX NEGOTIATES WHEAT SALE TO RUSSIA

John Canfield, president and CEO of Canfield-Puritex, is not an ambassador, but President Kennedy probably wishes he were. At a time when relations between the U.S. and the U.S.S.R. are more strained than they have been for some time, there is, to quote the President, ". . . a hopeful sign that a more peaceful world is both possible and beneficial to us all."

President Kennedy made the remarks in regard to the $250 million wheat sale negotiated by Mr. Canfield. Kennedy went on to say that besides engendering good relations between our two countries, the grain sale would also ". . . help American farmers as well as shippers and the entire agricultural complex. Furthermore, it will reduce the American balance-of-payment deficit."

Canfield-Puritex is one of the largest agri-business industries in the United States.

GATEWAY ARCH TO BE BUILT IN ST. LOUIS

Final plans have been approved for the construction of a towering 600-foot arch to be built on the banks of the Mississippi River. The arch, to be officially called the Jefferson Expansion Memorial, will commemorate the purchase from France by Thomas Jefferson of the land west of the Mississippi River known as the Louisiana Purchase.

"Missouri was a part of that purchase," a spokesman for the memorial committee said. "And St. Louis played a vital role as the gateway city in opening up those new lands. This arch will represent that gateway."

It is hoped by planners and the people of St. Louis that the memorial will become as identified with their city as the Eiffel Tower is with Paris.

U.S. STATE DEPARTMENT SAYS DIEM BECOMING MORE DIFFICULT TO WORK WITH

The U.S. State Department has expressed concerns over recent events in South Vietnam. "There has been much more emphasis placed on the persecution of the Buddhists than in the prosecution of the war," a spokesman for the State Department said.

The Kennedy administration has made no secret of its belief that President Ngo Dinh Diem's brother Ngo Dinh Nhu and Nhu's outspoken wife, Madame Nhu, are the main stumbling blocks impeding improvement in the situation.

"If Diem is to continue enjoying the support of the American government and people, he must show a willingness to move away from the hard line he is taking toward his country's Buddhists," the spokesman continued.

Although only 28 percent of Vietnam is Chris-

tian (Roman Catholic), Diem and most of his power
structure are a part of that religious minority.

SAIGON

Jarred Hawkins had known Colonel Khanh Cao Tri for a
very long time. He had met Tri when both men were junior
officers during Vietnam's war with the French. Because of
this long-standing relationship, the two always exchanged
pleasantries whenever they happened to encounter each
other, though they had never become close friends. Therefore, when Tri invited Jarred to meet him for a beer and "a
discussion of subjects of mutual concern," Jarred suspected
he had more on his mind than an afternoon of nostalgia. He
went to General Breckenridge with his suspicions.

"What makes you think there's more to it?" Breckenridge asked.

"You remember the execution of Captain Sanh?" Jarred
asked.

"Yes, how could I forget? It was a very nasty business.
But what does your meeting with Tri have to do with that?"

"Captain Sanh was Colonel Tri's nephew. Captain
Sanh's father was killed during the war with the Viet Minh, so
Tri raised Sanh. They were like father and son."

"Go on," Breckenridge urged.

"If Captain Sanh really was involved in some sort of anti-
Diem plot, it seems highly unlikely that Colonel Tri wasn't
aware of it—or, indeed, didn't support it."

Breckenridge took another puff of his cigarette, but he
said nothing, just squinted at Jarred through the smoke.

"I am convinced that Tri is a part of the same group his
nephew was associated with," Jarred concluded.

"An interesting surmise," Breckenridge said. "But
where do you come in? Why do you think he wants to meet
with you?"

"General, if you want my opinion, I believe a coup is
imminent. And I think that, through Tri, they are sending out
feelers to see how the U.S. will react to such a thing. Tri is
going to ask me for our support. So what do I do now? What
will the U.S. do?"

General Breckenridge stubbed out his cigarette in an

ashtray made from a 105 howitzer shell casing, then drummed his fingers on his desk for a long moment as he stared at Jarred. The stare was so intense and lasted for so long that Jarred grew uncomfortable. Finally Breckenridge sighed, then took off his dog tags. There was a small key on the dog-tag chain, and with it he opened a locked drawer, from which he removed a folder. He slid it across the desk to Jarred.

"I think it's time I showed you something," the general said.

The front of the folder bore a red diagonal line; printed in large bold red letters across the top and the bottom were the words TOP SECRET.

Jarred opened the folder. There was a cover page, also marked "Top Secret," then the document itself, a cablegram, again with the top-secret designation. Jarred looked up at Breckenridge questioningly.

"This cable was sent by President Kennedy to Ambassador Lodge," Breckenridge explained.

Jarred began to read.

TOP SECRET

It is now clear that whether the military proposed martial law or Nhu took advantage of its imposition to smash pagodas with special police loyal to him, it has placed onus on the military in eyes of world and Vietnamese people. It is also clear Nhu has maneuvered himself into commanding position.

U.S. government cannot tolerate a situation in which power lies in Nhu's hands. Diem must be given chance to rid himself of Nhu and his coterie and replace them with best military and political personalities available.

If, in spite of your efforts, Diem remains obdurate and refuses, we must face possibility that Diem himself cannot be preserved.

We now believe immediate action must be taken to prevent Nhu from consolidating his position further. Therefore, unless you, in consultation with General Harkins, perceive overriding objections, you are authorized to proceed along following lines:

(1) Impress on appropriate levels of Government of Vietnam (GVN) the following:

(a) USG cannot accept actions against Buddhists taken by Nhu and his collaborators under cover of martial law.

(b) Prompt dramatic actions to redress situation must be taken, including repeal of Decree 10, release of arrested monks, nuns, etc.

(2) We must at same time inform military leader that U.S. would find it impossible to continue supporting GVN militarily and economically unless above steps are taken immediately, which we recognize requires removal of Nhu from the scene. We wish to give Diem reasonable opportunity to remove Nhu, but if he remains unrelenting, we are prepared to accept obvious implication that we can no longer support Diem. You may also tell appropriate military commanders we will give them direct support in any interim period of breakdown of central government mechanism.

(3) We recognize necessity of removing taint on military for pagoda raids and placing blame squarely on Nhu. You are authorized to have such statements made in Saigon as you consider desirable to achieve this objective. We are prepared to take same line here and to have Voice of America make statement along lines contained in next numbered telegram whenever you give the word, preferably as soon as possible.

Concurrent with above, ambassador and country team should urgently examine all possible alternative leadership and make detailed plans how to bring about Diem's replacement, should it become necessary.

Assume you will consult with General Harkins re any precautions necessary protect American personnel during crisis period.

You understand we cannot from Washington give you detailed instruction how operation should proceed, but also know we will back to hilt actions you take to achieve objectives.

We have held knowledge of this telegram to minimum essential people and assume you will take similar precautions to prevent premature leaks.

Jarred closed the document and put it back in the folder, then handed it to General Breckenridge. For several moments he mulled over the information he had just been made privy to.

"General," he finally said, "just so there's no question about my misunderstanding what I've just read, this cablegram is giving the go-ahead to a coup, is that right?"

"Your understanding of the cable concurs with that of everyone who has read it," Breckenridge replied.

"It stated that knowledge of the document was to be kept to the 'minimum essential people.' How many know of it?"

"Ambassador Lodge, of course. General Harkins, General Stillwell, and I. One or two of their key people may also be aware, but I doubt that more than ten know. I've taken it upon myself to include you. If, as you suspect, Colonel Tri does represent a coup element, then it would behoove you to be armed with the information that our government would look with favor upon a successful overthrow of Diem."

"Yes, sir," Jarred said.

"Of course, at this point it would not be wise to let Tri, or anyone else for that matter, know of our position. At least not until we have assessed the probability of success."

"And you want my appraisal of the people with Tri?"

"Precisely. Go to the meeting with him. Listen to what he has to say, find out who he represents. Then we'll go from there."

"Very well, sir." Jarred stood to leave, but when he reached the door he stopped and turned back to Breckenridge. "General?"

"Yes?"

"Has it occurred to anyone that if we assist in the overthrow of the Diem government, we will be doing the very thing we are supposed to be over here to prevent?"

"What do you mean?"

"Correct me if I'm wrong, sir, but our mission is to support the legally elected government of South Vietnam.

And yet we're about to embark upon an adventure that is the absolute opposite of that mission."

"What's your point, Hawkins?" General Breckenridge asked sharply.

Jarred sighed. "Nothing, sir. I'll meet with Colonel Tri."

The great overhead fans of the Majestic Hotel turned noisily but did little to dispel the heat that hung over the lobby like an oppressive blanket. Colonel Tri had advised Jarred to be in the Majestic's lobby at noon, where, he was told, he would be met by Tri's adjutant, Captain Cheu, for transportation to the place where the American colonel and the Vietnamese colonel would meet.

Jarred was sitting in a wicker chair, a cold gin and tonic on the table beside him, reading a newspaper and waiting for Tri's man. It was just after noon, and he had the hotel lobby to himself because everyone else was in the midst of the midday *ngu traua*, or siesta. Even the desk clerk dozed, stretched out unconcernedly across the top of the counter.

"Colonel Hawkins? I am Captain Cheu."

Jarred looked up to see a Vietnamese officer. He was a bit startled because even though he had been looking for Cheu, he had not seen him come in.

He drained the rest of his drink quickly, then stood up, indicating that he would follow. Outside the hotel, a battered old Renault was parked against the curb, and at a signal from Captain Cheu, Jarred climbed in. They rode without conversation, the normally traffic-clogged streets now nearly empty because of the siesta.

Jarred looked through the car windows at the festering boil that was Saigon's inner city. Saigon had seen its population increase almost tenfold in twenty-three years. Those newly arrived from the country moved into one-room hovels with relatives already living in the city, or they built small shanties onto existing structures, which bulged out into the already crowded lanes and alleyways. Streets once broad enough to allow a double stream of cars had been turned into narrow, twisting labyrinths, barely wide enough to allow passage of a man on foot. Among these structures and behind them, in dark, damp corners in the intricate maze of paths, were cubicles used for prostitution and opium smoking. They were also, Jarred knew, the spawning grounds for rebellion—whether the rebels be Viet Minh or Viet Cong . . . or non-Communists plotting a coup.

The alleys stayed dark even at high noon because the overhangs blotted out the sun. Through holes and passageways leading from one alley to another people scurried like moles through tunnels, sometimes going for months at a time without ever seeing the light of day.

The Renault left Saigon and entered Cholon, the Chinese district. Although Saigon and Cholon had grown into one large megalopolis, united under a common administration, they maintained distinct and separate personalities, and Jarred could determine quite easily the exact point where Saigon ended and Cholon began.

Cholon was like Chinese districts everywhere in that it maintained its Chinese identity. Whereas France had left its colonial mark on Saigon, Jarred could see little evidence in Cholon that the French, the Americans, or *any* foreigners were ever there at all. The overcrowded hovels that pocked Saigon were absent in Cholon. Instead, as Jarred gazed silently at the passing scene, he was looking at row upon row of spick-and-span shops stacked high with a variety of products. Indoor and outdoor restaurants, he noticed, were many and permanent, as opposed to the portable sidewalk soup stalls in Saigon. He even saw playgrounds for the children, nonexistent in Saigon. All the signs were in Chinese characters, as were the newspapers, books, and magazines he saw on the stands. A theater was on every block, the marquees depicting some thrilling scene such as a glaring swordsman holding a bloodstained sword in one hand and the severed head of his enemy in the other.

When Captain Cheu reached his destination, he stopped and pointed.

"In there," he said tersely. They were the first words spoken since leaving the Majestic.

Jarred thanked him, then got out of the car.

The place Colonel Tri had chosen for the rendezvous was a store that sold wicker baskets and earthenware pots. An old man clacking an abacus looked up as Jarred entered. He didn't speak but pointed with a bony finger to the back of the shop. Jarred went through a beaded curtain, across a yard with an open cistern, then up a flight of rickety stairs to a small room. Inside, an old woman motioned for Jarred to sit at a crude table, and she set a bottle of warm beer in front of him.

A few moments later General Tri, dressed in nondescript civilian clothes, came into the room. The butt of a cigarette burned close to his lips. The very strong smell of the cheap Asian tobacco was oppressive in the close room. Tri lit a new cigarette from his old one before speaking.

"Tell me, Colonel Hawkins, what is the American position vis-à-vis the Buddhist problem?"

Jarred appreciated his directness. "I think you are aware, Colonel, that my government is very displeased with the way this whole business is being handled," he replied.

"Do you agree with me that we should exert more zeal in fighting the Communists than in persecuting the Buddhists?" Tri asked, squinting through the smoke of the cigarette clamped in his lips.

"I think that would be an appropriate statement."

For a moment Tri said nothing as he stared at Jarred through the smoke. Then he spoke again.

"Jarred, we have known each other a long time now," he said, switching from the more formal address. "You were here when the French were here. We have fought together, we have seen our comrades die together. Because of that we can trust each other. Do you agree?"

"Yes, I agree wholeheartedly."

"Suppose I told you that there were some people—some officers in our military—who hold a position similar to that of the American government? What would the U.S. government's reaction be to that?"

"I think my government would encourage those officers to petition Diem to change his policy," Jarred answered carefully.

"It is already too late for that. Besides, as I am sure you know, Diem is no longer the real power. He is a puppet being controlled by his brother and his brother's wife."

"That is unfortunate."

"There is another way to change the policy of our government so that it is in compliance with what the U.S. wishes," Tri suggested cautiously.

"What way is that?"

"We are prepared to remove Nhu from any position of authority."

"How do you propose to do that while Diem remains in power?"

"By removing Diem."

"I see."

"We are also prepared to replace the present government with a new government, one that will work in close harmony with the Americans as well as serve the best interests of the Vietnamese people."

"You are talking about a military overthrow of the government," Jarred said. It was a statement of fact, not a question.

"Will the Americans help?" Tri asked, thus acknowledging Jarred's statement.

"What would you need?" Jarred asked in turn, being careful not to make any concrete commitments.

"How far will the Americans go? Would you help us fight against the troops that will remain loyal?"

Jarred had not discussed this aspect with General Breckenridge, but he was certain that what Tri was asking was further than the U.S. would be willing to go.

"You won't be able to count on us for armed support during the coup," Jarred replied. "But after the coup, if it is successful, we will aid in maintaining order."

"Will you give us logistical support? Will you provide us with transportation and communication facilities?"

"We will not withhold matériel that is already committed to the Army. Nor will we place any restrictions on how it is to be used. But to coordinate the support we can give, we must know with whom we will be working. Who are the principal officers involved?"

Tri took several puffs of his cigarette, studying Jarred carefully through the cloud of noxious smoke he produced, before saying, "I think the time has come for trust between us. General Duong Van Minh, the one the Americans call 'Big' Minh, will be in charge. General Tran Van Don will be second-in-command."

Jarred nodded. "I know both of them. They are good officers. You may tell them they will have the support of the U.S."

Tri stood up. "Wait here for one minute," he instructed.

"Then return to the place where Cheu let you off. He will be there to take you back to your home." With that he was gone.

Jarred sat there, pondering what had just happened. Although the cable he had read in General Breckenridge's office indicated clearly that the highest authority in the United States government would welcome a coup, it had just fallen to him to be the instrument of its implementation. The U.S. role of passive support had, with this commitment, taken its first step toward active intervention.

HYANNIS PORT

A touch-football game was under way out on the lawn, and there was a sudden outbreak of cheering and laughter when a Secret Service agent caught a pass and ran for a touchdown.

"Uncle Jack! Uncle Jack, come on out here! The Secret Service is beating the clan! We need you!" one of Bobby's younger children called.

"I can't come now," President Kennedy called through the screen of the front porch.

"Why not?"

"Because I've been traded to the Chicago Bears," the President quipped.

"You're going to play for the Chicago Bears? Wow!" The youngster ran back to the others. "Did you hear that? Uncle Jack is going to play for the Chicago Bears!"

"No, he isn't. He's just teasing," one of the older children said.

"He's the President of the United States. I'll bet he could play for the Bears if he wanted to."

Jack Kennedy laughed, then turned toward John Canfield. John and Faith were in Hyannisport as weekend guests of the Kennedys, and John was sitting in the porch swing, drinking beer from a can.

"John, you did one hell of a job for us on that wheat sale deal with the Russians," Kennedy said. He used his finger to stir the ice around in his Scotch and soda, then licked the finger. "And I want you to know that I'm grateful for your patriotic service."

John chuckled. "Hell, it's not all that hard to be patriotic when it's good business. My company stands to make a great deal of money from the Soviets over the next several years."

"You mean, provided the Russians will need our wheat again."

"Out of bounds! Out of bounds!" a player outside shouted.

"I was not!"

"You were, too!"

"Oh, they'll need our wheat, all right," John said, raising his voice slightly to be heard over the tumult. "You'd be hard-pressed to design a more inept farming policy than the one the Soviets follow. And their transportation system is worse. They can't move the crops they do produce from where they're grown to where they're needed. Half of their entire farm production spoils in transit. I tell you the truth, Mr. President: If their military is as fouled up as their civilian infrastructure, we have nothing to worry about."

"Unfortunately, their military *isn't* fouled up," Kennedy replied. "In fact, the reason everything else in their country is so fouled up is because they've put everything into their military at the expense of their society."

"Maybe so," John mused.

"I got you!" a childish voice yelped.

"You didn't touch me!"

"Yes, I did. I got you way back there!"

Kennedy looked over his shoulder at the game, smiled, then turned back to his guest. "I'm glad you and Faith could come visit us for the weekend. I think Faith's being here has been good for Jackie."

"How is Mrs. Kennedy doing?"

"Physically, she's doing fine. But emotionally she still hasn't gotten over losing the baby."

"That's a tragedy the whole country shares with you," John said.

"I know. The letters to the White House have been wonderful. Still, the baby is gone. Sometimes I think it would have been better had he been stillborn than to live for just a day and a half. That made it worse somehow."

"Mrs. Kennedy will bounce back," John offered. "She's young and strong."

Kennedy smiled. "I know she will. I plan to get her out

on the campaign trail again. That'll be good for her. She's always liked that."

"You aren't starting your campaign for reelection yet, are you?"

"John, for a politician the natural order of things is to *always* campaign. Besides, if I don't get out there soon, Barry Goldwater is going to have me for lunch. He's working hard and has been for the last three years."

John made a wry face. "I'll admit, Goldwater does seem to find a lot of ways to get his name in the papers and his face on TV."

Kennedy shook his head. "It's pretty easy from where he sits right now. All he has to do is watch what I do, then issue a statement as to how *he* would have done it better. He has the answer for everything—the Berlin Wall, the Negro unrest, this nasty business with Diem and the Buddhists in Vietnam. . . ." He chuckled. "But, of course, if I were where Barry is right now, I'd be doing the same thing."

"You won't have any trouble getting reelected," John insisted.

"I wish I could be as certain of that as you are. Unfortunately, I've lost a lot of ground in the South."

"Because you sided with the civil rights demonstrators."

"Yes. And for several federal actions we've had to take to ensure their protection. Did you know Alabama has actually issued a warrant for Bobby's arrest? Can you imagine that?"

"I know that passions have been running high down there. I got a close-up glimpse of it when Alicia was involved in that trial in Mississippi."

"Yes, I followed that with a great deal of interest. You should be proud of your daughter. She came across very well in all of her interviews. And Morgan. The reports on him from his time with the Peace Corps are outstanding. They are both fine young people."

"I am proud of them," John said, beaming. "And I'm proud of the way you have stood up for what is right. I know that by doing so you've made a lot of enemies in the South— but I believe you've made just as many friends."

"I know what I'm doing is right," Kennedy replied. "But I do wish this all had waited until my second term. I could do a lot more for the movement if I didn't have to watch my political fences. And then there's that business with King."

"What business with King?"

"This is just between us, you understand," Kennedy said in a confidential tone, "but the FBI has had Martin Luther King under surveillance for quite a while."

"Really? Why? Surely the FBI doesn't buy into all those bigoted charges that King is a Communist."

Kennedy sighed. "Unfortunately, King doesn't always choose his company wisely. Bayard Rustin, for example."

"Rustin is a brilliant man."

"He is also a man with a Communist past."

"But you don't believe—"

Kennedy held up his hand. "Actually, I don't believe any of it. But there is a perception out there. The perception is fanned by the flames of bigotry, I'll admit, but it is there nonetheless. And in politics, perception is nine tenths of reality."

"What has the FBI learned?"

"Other than that King is quite a cocksman, not a damned thing." Kennedy finished his drink, then put the glass down. "And I'd be the last one to ever say anything about him on *that* score."

Uncomfortable with the oblique reference to the President's own promiscuous behavior and anxious to get away from that subject, John said quickly, "I'll say this for him: Martin Luther King gave one hell of a speech at that Freedom March."

"Didn't he, though," Kennedy agreed. "That was the first time I ever heard him all the way through. I was very impressed."

"Getting back to the campaign, what are you going to do to shore up your strength in the South?"

"Well, for one thing, I've accepted an invitation to go to Texas next month. And when I go, I'm going to have Lyndon and Governor Connally squire me around so I can shake every hand and kiss every ass in the entire state if that's what it takes to beat Goldwater there. If I can win in Texas, I can lose the rest of the deep South and it won't make a damn bit of difference."

"Mathematically, I guess that's right," John agreed.

"I think you could help me in Texas, John. I would like you to go with me."

"I'd be glad to go if you really think I'd be of any help.

But how would I be? I don't have much influence with Texas politicians."

"You let me worry about the politicians," Kennedy replied. "I have another reason for wanting you there. Goldwater is beginning to make some inroads with his tactic of portraying me as antibusiness and himself as the great savior of capitalism. Well, as far as I'm concerned, there is no more astute or highly visible businessman in this entire country than you. So if you are riding in a motorcade with me when I go down there, it's going to send a message to the entire business community."

"All right, Mr. President, if you think it'll help, I'll be there," John promised.

OCTOBER 31, 1963, SAIGON

It wasn't yet dark, but Jarred Hawkins's apartment was in shadows. He sat there peering through the gloom, preoccupied. He had spoken to Colonel Tri a short while earlier and learned that the coup was set for sometime during the night. Already soldiers were massing outside Saigon, ready to move in the moment they received orders to do so.

Jarred thought of Ly. He had not told her about the coup and could not tell her without compromising the entire operation. After all, she was married to a member of Nhu's innermost circle of officers. Even if Ly had sworn to keep the secret—and Jarred believed she would have—the secret wouldn't be safe. Her husband had ways of finding out such things. Yet despite the compelling reason for not telling her, he couldn't help but feel as if he were somehow betraying her by keeping her in the dark.

He got up and poured himself a drink at his bar, then walked out onto the balcony to look down at the city below. A cacophony of street noises floated up to him—though, remarkably, he could discern a soft melody being sung by a woman sitting on the sidewalk, rocking a baby on her shoulder. Motorbikes and cyclos sputtered and popped and trailed blue streams of exhaust as they zipped up and down the street. The evening bread woman was making her rounds through the narrow alleys, and her lilting *"Bun Mae"* blended harmoniously with the lullaby the woman was singing to her child. Barefoot urchins ran through the paths, clacking sticks together to announce the soup vendors, and already customers were coming out of their homes carrying bowls.

Life was going on here, just as it always had and always would. What did the soup vendor or the bread woman care who was in power? Would their lives be improved by the overthrow of Diem? Would their lot be worsened if the coup failed?

Vietnamese did not tend to think in terms of one lifetime but rather a flow of lives, with one life but a drop in the generational river. They had patiently weathered the occupation of the Chinese, the French, the Japanese, and then the French again. Against such patience and fortitude, could any outside people make any impact? Could America, even with the best of motives, turn this centuries-old stream toward a new path? Jarred thought not.

The door rattled and then opened behind him, and Jarred turned to see Ly come in. When she saw him, she smiled an uncertain but pleased smile.

"Ly," he said. "What a wonderful surprise." He put his glass down and crossed to her quickly, taking her in his arms. Finally, after a long, slow kiss, they separated. Ly put her head on Jarred's shoulder, and he held her tightly. "I wasn't expecting you tonight."

"I wasn't sure you would be here," Ly said. "I was afraid I would be too late."

"Too late? Too late for what? Where did you think I would be?"

"It doesn't matter now. Jarred, Nguyen knows of us."

Jarred stiffened. "He knows?"

"Yes."

He released her and walked to the bar to fix her a drink. "How did he find out?"

"I don't know. He has spies everywhere. Who can say?"

"How long has he known?"

"From the very beginning."

Jarred brought the drink to her and questioned her with his eyes.

"I must confess, Jarred, that I have known for a very long time that he knew about us," Ly admitted.

"Why didn't you say something?"

"I was afraid. I was afraid that you wouldn't want to see me anymore."

"But weren't you running a terrible risk?" Jarred asked, confused. "Weren't you afraid of what he would do if he caught you?"

Ly choked out a scornful laugh. "He didn't care. It just gave him more opportunity to be with his little boys."

Jarred looked at her in sharp surprise. "Little boys? My God, you mean Nguyen is homosexual?"

"You didn't know?"

"I had no idea."

"I'm surprised. Though he used to be very secretive about it—the only reason he married me was to hide it from everyone, in fact—lately he has gotten careless, almost as if he doesn't care who knows."

"I'll be damned."

"Jarred, there is going to be a coup, isn't there?" Ly asked abruptly.

He frowned at her. "Where did you hear that?"

"From Nguyen. He says there is to be a coup. He says the Americans are making the coup, and you are in charge of it."

Jarred sighed. "America isn't making the coup, and I'm certainly not in charge of it. But I did act as the liaison between my country and those who *are* making the coup."

"When will it be?"

"Ly, I can't tell you that."

"Is it to be tonight?"

"Stay with me, Ly. Stay the night with me."

She slipped into his arms again, and he could feel her shivering. "I'm frightened," she whispered.

He didn't know if she was frightened by the coup or by the prospect of staying the night with him.

"Don't be frightened. It will be all right. Don't be frightened."

They kissed again. The kiss when she arrived had been a kiss of joy, of love, and of welcome. But this one was a kiss of sex, an open invitation to share physically what they were feeling emotionally.

Jarred carried her to his bed and laid her down gently. She didn't say a word, but her eyes burned into him as she removed her clothes and watched him remove his. Ly's soft skin, though lightly scented with perfume, had a distinctly womanly smell about her that tantalized Jarred's senses. They made love then, with hunger and desperation.

The last vestige of light had gone, and with the darkness came a cool breeze that carried with it the promise of rain. Jarred could smell it before he heard it, and he heard it before he could feel it. And then finally the rain was there, drumming on the balcony and blowing in sheets of fine spray, settling like a mist on Jarred's skin, giving him a pleasant chill. Ly rested her head on his arm, and he pulled her close, spoonlike, listening to the drenching rain and rumbling thunder. He felt the softness of the woman with him, the woman he loved, and he drifted off to a pleasant sleep.

Much later, after the storm had passed, Jarred awoke to find that he was still holding Ly as he had been when he fell asleep. He knew intuitively that she was not sleeping, and when he touched her gently, she turned over and snuggled against his chest. He wondered what had kept her awake.

They made love again, this time more slowly, more tenderly, and when they were finished, it was she who drifted off to sleep and he who was silent in the quiet bed with only her measured breathing for company. Finally he, too, drifted off.

Jarred heard no sound, but in the midst of sleep, mind at peace, body at rest, a sudden awareness told him to wake up. He sat up in the still-dark room and saw a figure standing quietly just inside the door. Slowly he reached for the holstered pistol hanging from the bedpost.

"Who's there?" he demanded in a harsh whisper.

"Captain Cheu, adjutant to Colonel Tri," the figure answered quietly.

"Jesus, Cheu, what is it? What do you want?"

"Colonel Tri wants you to come to the Defense Ministry building."

Jarred got out of bed and began pulling on his pants. "Has it started?" he asked.

"Yes."

"Jarred? Jarred, what is it?" Ly asked, coming awake and sitting up. Seeing Cheu, she gasped and pulled the sheet up to cover her naked body.

"I must go," Jarred said. "You stay here."

"When will you come back?"

"I don't know."

Now, despite her nakedness, seemingly oblivious to Cheu, Ly got out of bed, went to Jarred, and put her arms around him. "I love you, Jarred," she whispered. "I love you."

Jarred smiled. "I love you, too, but I'm afraid if you don't get back under the sheet, our friend will go blind."

Cheu had closed his eyes in embarrassment and was pushing his fingers hard against the eyelids as if afraid they would pop open of their own volition.

Ly giggled, sounding grateful that something had eased the tension. Then she got back into bed and pulled the sheet over her again.

"After we leave, go back to your house," Jarred instructed her. "Go home and stay there. Do not go out onto the streets until all this is over. Promise me."

"I promise."

"I will come to you as soon as I can."

"Jarred, I love you," Ly called once more as Jarred and Captain Cheu headed out the door.

"Go home," Jarred called back to her. "Go home and stay there!"

As they clumped down the stairs, Cheu assured him, "She will not be harmed."

"I would certainly think not. She is no danger to anyone." They reached the street, and Jarred asked, "Did you drive over?"

"I walked."

"Then you can ride back with me."

Jarred's jeep was damp from the rain of the night before, and the steering wheel was wet and slippery in his hand. The engine started sluggishly, and his foot slipped off the clutch pedal so that it sprang back painfully against his shin, causing him to yelp. Angrily, he threw the jeep into gear and sped away from the curb.

It was a short drive to the Defense Ministry building, only a few blocks from Jarred's apartment. When they reached the building, which was just behind the Continental Hotel, there was nothing to indicate a coup was in progress or even imminent. The guard at the front gate was eating a bowl of rice and didn't even look up as Jarred and Cheu drove by.

It was only after they were inside that anything looked different. There, in one of the conference rooms, several high-ranking officers were standing around nervously while others were on telephones talking with field commanders. Jarred saw Colonel Tri and went over to him.

"Has anything happened yet?" Jarred asked.

"Only the execution of a traitor," Tri replied, lighting a new cigarette from the old one, as was his habit.

"An execution? Who was killed?"

"Ho Tuu-Quang, chief of the Navy."

"Chief of the *Navy*? For God's sakes, Tri, the Navy has no power. Why did you kill him?"

"He refused to join us. Those who aren't with us are against us, and they must be eliminated," a brutish-looking captain answered for Tri.

"And just who are you?" Jarred asked.

"This is Major Nhung," Tri said. "He is General Don's personal aide."

Suddenly two shots sounded from a room nearby. Jarred jumped, then looked toward the door. He started for it, but Tri caught his arm.

"No, my friend," he warned. "It is much better if you don't interfere."

"Tri, what the hell is going on in there?" Jarred demanded.

The Vietnamese colonel let out a long puff of smoke before answering. "In addition to Tuu-Quang, two more senior commanders refused to join us. The junta sentenced them to death as well. Their sentences were just carried out."

"My God, Tri, have we opened Pandora's box? How many more must be killed?"

"As many as are required to ensure the success of the coup," Major Nhung said. "Why are you here, if you have no stomach for this? We have no need for Americans on this night."

"His presence here is important to our operation," Tri said sharply. "And you will treat him with respect."

Nodding curtly, Nhung went to stand near General Don. A telephone rang, and Don answered, spoke a few words, then hung up.

"The orders have been given," he announced. "Our

troops are moving into Saigon. The liberation of our people has begun."

Nguyen heard the sound of gunfire and knew the military revolution had been launched. He had come to the palace that morning to warn Diem and Nhu of the impending coup, but they had dismissed the warning out of hand. But now, as the day was getting on toward three o'clock and the sound of gunfire was growing ever more frequent and ever closer to the palace, they would have no choice but to believe him. Nguyen hurried back to Diem's office to try to talk sense into them one last time.

When he went in, he found Diem sitting at a long mahogany table, drumming his fingers nervously. Nhu was pacing back and forth in front of the windows.

"What is it now, Nguyen?" Nhu asked.

"Do you hear the gunfire?"

"Yes, of course. We would have to be deaf not to hear it. I have already made a telephone call. There is some minor disturbance in one of the Army units, that's all. I assure you, the situation will soon be under control."

Nhu's words of assurance were followed by a long chatter of machine-gun fire, several rifle shots, and finally a heavy explosion. The shock wave caused the chandelier to swing back and forth, and the glass tinkled musically. Almost immediately another huge stomach-jarring explosion followed; it shattered the windows.

The three men ducked away from the flying glass. After a few moments Diem sat up and looked toward his brother, who had scurried away from the windows. "That is no minor disturbance, my brother. That is an uprising."

"No, that is impossible," Nhu insisted. "I have spies everywhere. If this were a mutiny, they would have warned us."

"But I *did* warn you, Excellency," Nguyen reminded him.

A messenger hurried into the room then. His uniform was torn and smoke-stained, and his head was bandaged. He handed a note to Diem, who read it without comment, then closed his eyes and pinched the bridge of his nose. He remained that way for several seconds.

"Well?" Nhu asked anxiously. "What does it say?"

Diem slid it across to him. "Naval headquarters has fallen. And Admiral Tuu-Quang was executed."

Nhu paled. "Do something!" he demanded of his brother. "You are the commander-in-chief of all the armed forces! Give an order that will override those given by their officers!"

Outside the palace, in the inner core of the city, the fighting came closer. A few tanks and the troops still loyal to Diem moved into position around the palace and began returning the fire. The booming explosions of tank guns shook the palace to its foundation.

Diem grabbed the phone, got through to the Defense Ministry, and spoke with General Don.

"What are you doing, General?" Diem demanded. "I did not believe you would commit treason against me—against your own country!"

"I am fighting *for* my country, not against it," Don replied. "Sir, we have proposed to you many times that you reform your policy to conform with the wishes of the people. You ignored us. Therefore, the time has come for the *Army* to respond to the wishes of the people. Please understand us."

"I'm ready to reform my policy," Diem said quickly.

"Why didn't you agree to do so before now?"

"I needed time to think about it. Why don't we sit down together? We could talk about the strengths and weaknesses of this regime and seek ways to improve it."

"I am sorry. It is too late now. There is nothing to be done," Don said.

"It's never too late," Diem insisted. "I hereby invite you all to the palace to discuss the matter together and find a solution acceptable to both sides. I promise no reprisals against the officers."

"I'm sorry, sir, I cannot stop it. It is not my decision. It is the decision of the junta. Perhaps if you spoke with General Minh—"

"I will not speak with that traitor!" Diem barked.

"You must speak with Minh if you are to speak with the others," Don said.

"*No!*" Diem shouted. "That traitor stabbed me in the back!"

"Then it is no good," Don said.

Diem slammed the phone down in anger.

"What did they say?" Nhu asked anxiously. "What did they say? Can you force them to call it off?"

Nguyen watched Nhu in surprise. The man normally had ice water for blood; now he was displaying intense agitation.

Diem shook his head. "They said it was too late for negotiations. But our men seem to be holding their positions fairly well. As time goes on and the traitors see that a quick victory is impossible, I think they will negotiate with us."

Nhu's panic increased. "Time? There is no time!" He grabbed the telephone and dialed the Defense Ministry. "I'll talk to them. They'll listen to me. I'll *make* them listen!"

He got Don on the phone. In a more controlled voice he said, "General Don, let us now call a truce, and you bring your fellow conspirators to the palace. Here we can discuss all your grievances and make concessions."

"As I told your brother, it is too late for that," Don replied. "However, we can offer you safe conduct out of the country, but only if you capitulate now."

"I will convey your offer," Nhu said. He covered the mouthpiece and told Diem, "They have offered us safe passage if we surrender now."

"You don't believe them, do you?" Diem asked.

"This may be our only chance!"

Diem took the receiver from his brother and hung up the phone, his intransigence deepening. "That is *not* our only chance. I refuse to capitulate. We will make our own escape somehow. We will prevail."

"How?"

Diem's mind was racing. Reaching for the phone again, he said, "I'll call the American ambassador. Perhaps he can help us."

When Henry Cabot Lodge answered, Diem spoke with the voice of one still in authority and unconcerned about his fate. "Some units have made a rebellion, and I want to know what is the attitude of the United States."

"I do not feel well enough informed to be able to tell you," Lodge answered. "I have heard the shooting, but I'm not acquainted with all the facts. Also, it is four-thirty A.M. in Washington, and the United States government cannot possibly have a view."

"But you must have some general ideas," Diem said in a tone now less confident. "After all, I am a chief of state. I have tried to do my duty. I want to do now what duty and good sense require. I believe in duty above all."

"You certainly have done your duty," Lodge acknowledged. "As I told you only this morning, I admire your courage and your great contributions to your country. No one can take away from you the credit for all you have done. Now I am worried about your physical safety. I have a report that those in charge of the current activity offer you and your brother safe conduct out of the country if you will resign. Have you heard this?"

"No," Diem lied. He paused, then added quietly, "You have my telephone number."

"Yes. If I can do anything for your physical safety, please call me."

"I am trying to reestablish order," Diem said. "Will you help me achieve this?"

Lodge remained silent.

Diem hung up and looked at Nhu. "The Americans won't help."

"The bastards!" Nhu bellowed. "This is all their doing!"

Nguyen walked over to one of the shattered windows and looked out at the lawn. He could see the palace guards darting about, scurrying across the courtyard like crabs, squatting low, holding their helmets on with one hand as they ran, the other hand gripping their rifles. He could hear the shooting and explosions from just a few blocks away. Behind him, using his private transmitter, Nhu was radioing his handpicked province chiefs to come to his assistance, but none of them responded. He even tried to reach his youth and women's organizations for help, but he failed there, too. Either his messages were being jammed by the insurgents or his supporters had gone over to the rebels to save themselves.

"We are trapped!" Nhu said. "Trapped here like rats!"

Nguyen spoke up. "I can help you."

Diem turned and looked sharply at him. "How?"

"Frankly, sir, I feared this very thing might happen, and so I have kept a car out back, a battered Land Rover. Very nondescript. No one would think to look for the president in such a car."

Diem grinned. "Excellent! We could go to Cholon, to

Ma Tuyen's. I have had my agents equip his villa for an emergency—though, of course, I never expected one would actually occur."

"Cholon?" Nhu asked. "We'll never make it. All the roads will surely be blocked by now."

"Call Father DeJager. He will know the best way."

A call was placed to the Catholic priest who had been Diem's roommate in seminary. It was nearing dark when they hurried down the back stairs to the Land Rover. Slipping out of the palace grounds, they followed Father DeJager's directions and managed to avoid rebel troop patrols. As Nguyen had predicted, the old car was not challenged. At a place near the Saigon River they switched cars again, from the Land Rover to a black Citroën, a further precaution Nguyen had taken. Finally they reached the villa of Ma Tuyen, a rich Chinese merchant who had financed the Ngo brothers' covert political network for years.

With the coming of dark, a gray drizzle fell over the city, depositing the ash and soot from the day's fighting. The ring of troops around the palace moved closer, firing flares that burst over the grounds and painted the low-hanging clouds, the trees, and the buildings with a devilish red glow. At around nine o'clock the order was issued to stage a full-scale assault on the Presidential Palace—the attackers not knowing they would be waging a siege on an empty building, the defenders unaware that the leader they were fighting for had left. Artillery and mortars were moved into position and shot off, raining high explosives into the confined area. The bombardment was kept up for several hours; then a force of tanks and armored cars closed on the last outpost. The tanks poured point-blank fire at the protective walls.

A high explosive round slammed into a loyalist tank, which literally flew apart with flaming pieces arcing away from the point of impact as if launched by rockets. A second tank joined the first, and then a defensive bunker was wiped out as the loyalists fell back before the murderous rebel fire.

At 6:15 in the morning, after a night-long siege, the rebels called for a five-minute grace period to allow the President to emerge and surrender. It was now November 2, the Day of the Dead.

When Diem didn't come out, the angry rebel commander ordered the attack resumed, and at close range cannons, machine guns, and rifles fired into the palace, pulverizing what little glass was left, splintering doors, and smashing great chunks of stone and cement from the walls. Finally a white flag fluttered pitifully from a window, and the rebels, realizing they had won, whooped and hollered and fired their guns into the air as they dashed into the palace to tear down draperies, grab silver and china and Madame Nhu's negligees and Nhu's whiskey, and celebrate their great victory over Ngo Dinh Diem and Ngo Dinh Nhu, whom they combed the palace in search of.

Their quarry, however, was well out of reach. Just before dawn they, along with Nguyen Van Tran, had left the Tuyen villa, deciding to take refuge instead at St. Francis Xavier, a French church in Cholon.

"Father Guimet," Diem told the French priest who greeted them, "we need sanctuary. May we stay here?"

"Of course," Father Guimet replied. He let them in, then looked back toward the street nervously before shutting the door.

"There has been a rebellion," Diem explained. "Many of my faithful troops have been killed. I have loyal soldiers but traitorous generals."

Nguyen saw Nhu's eyes dart around the room, flashing with fright. He seemed unable to stop shaking, and Father Guimet put his hands on his shoulders to comfort him.

"How may I be of assistance?" the priest asked Diem.

"Would you let my brother and me say confession and let us take Communion?"

"Yes, of course."

"Thank you, Father."

"And you, my son?" Father Guimet asked Nguyen.

"I am Buddhist," Nguyen replied.

Nhu looked at his henchman in surprise. "You are Buddhist? But how can this be? You willingly took part in sacking Buddhist temples."

"I placed my loyalty before my religion," Nguyen replied simply.

He walked over to one of the pews and sat, waiting as

the two brothers went one at a time into the confessional. Afterward they took Communion, and then Diem came over to Nguyen.

"Colonel Nguyen, call the generals," he ordered. "Tell them where we are."

Nhu grabbed his brother's arm. "Why?" he asked.

"It is over. I will run no more. I will not become a hunted animal in my own country."

"But they'll kill us!" Nhu protested.

"Yes, there is a good chance of that," Diem agreed. "But I have made my confession, and I am at peace with God. I am ready now to die, if need be."

Nhu rubbed his hands together repeatedly, as if washing them. "Why do they want to kill us?" He licked his lips nervously. "Everything we've done, we've done for the good of the country. Diem, plead with them as president. Beg them to spare our lives!"

"They mean to kill me."

"Well, you, yes. But why kill me? I have no authority. You are the president. You are the one they are making the rebellion against. I have merely been an adviser to you!"

Diem looked at his brother—a look filled, surprisingly, not with disgust but with compassion. "I am sorry," he said quietly. "I really am sorry."

The phone call was made.

Diem ate a sweet cake while they waited, but Nhu nervously paced back and forth in the rectory, and every few minutes he walked to the window and peeked through the blinds.

Finally they heard squealing brakes and strident shouts. Nhu jumped to the window and peered outside. He saw an armored personnel carrier and two jeeps.

"They are here," he said, his voice a guttural whisper.

"Are there any generals with them?" Diem asked. "I won't surrender to anyone less than a general."

Nhu looked out again. "Yes, I see General Mai Huu Xuan in one of the jeeps. And there are a number of other officers."

"The arrogant young Turks," Diem said scornfully. "But

the presence of a general means at least we will be accorded a military execution and be spared a lynching."

"Diem, no one is watching the back door. It isn't too late," Nhu said. "We can still escape."

"Nhu, pull yourself together!" Diem said sharply. "Now, come. We will surrender like men—and as befits a chief of state."

Diem, Nhu, and Nguyen walked out into the light drizzle. Soldiers were standing in a semicircle around the door, their guns pointed at the three men.

"My, are we as dangerous as all this?" Diem chided, taking in the armed troops with a small wave of his hand.

The door through which they had come slammed shut from the breeze, startling one of the privates. The young man dropped his gun and let out a fearful yelp.

"Don't be nervous, son," Diem told him. "We are, after all, only three."

He and Nhu approached Xuan's jeep. The general looked at them dispassionately, then ordered one of his men, "Bind them."

"How dare you!" Nhu snapped. "Show respect for your president!"

One of the soldiers struck Nhu, who fell to his knees. Another grabbed him and tied his hands behind his back.

"General, I protest the improper manner in which you are handling this," Diem said sharply as his hands were bound. "I will give a full accounting to your superiors when we reach headquarters."

General Xuan smiled coolly but said nothing.

Diem eyed one of the officers. "I know you. You are General Don's aide."

"That is correct. I am Major Nhung," the officer replied. "I am glad you recognize me. I want you to know who brought you to justice."

"Major Nhung, what about this one?" one of the soldiers asked, pointing to Nguyen.

"Him, too," Nhung said.

"No!" Nguyen shouted. He looked at General Xuan. "General Xuan, I support the rebellion! I am the one who called to tell you where to find Diem and Nhu!"

Nhu turned and glared at his former comrade. "You despicable—" But his outburst was cut off by a vicious stroke from a rifle butt.

"He believes I betrayed him," Nguyen said. "He doesn't understand that my loyalty is to my country, not to him."

Diem, too, turned and stared at Nguyen. His penetrating yet pitying gaze made Nguyen look away, unable to meet his eyes. It would have been easier had Diem cursed him as Nhu had.

"Put Diem and Nhu in the personnel carrier," General Xuan said.

"What about Nguyen?" Nhung asked.

"He is one of us. He can ride with the troops. No need to bind him."

"Thank you, General Xuan," Nguyen said.

"Major, the ropes are uncomfortably tight," Diem complained.

"You won't be uncomfortable for long," Nhung said, smirking, and then he shoved Diem and Nhu into the bottom of the armored carrier. Major Nghia, the tank officer, climbed into the gun turret overlooking them, while Nhung sat with the prisoners below. Xuan and the other officers got back into their jeeps, and the convoy left the church.

Crammed together on the floor of the vehicle, lying on their backs, Diem and Nhu were jostled painfully as the armored car got under way. Blood clotted on Nhu's mouth where he had been struck. He was biting his lip and blinking his eyes.

"It is not a long trip, my brother," Diem consoled.

They had been moving only a short while when Major Nhung whipped out his pistol and straddled the prostrate Nhu, then jammed the gun against his nose. Nhu tried to turn his head away, but Nhung maintained the pressure, shoving so hard that Nhu's nose began to bleed. Nhung laughed.

"When General Don hears of this, you'll be severely punished!" Diem warned, glaring up at his enemy.

The vehicle abruptly stopped moving.

"What is it? Why have we stopped?" Captain Nhung shouted up.

"It's a railroad crossing," Nguyen called down. "We won't be stopped long."

"It will be long enough," Nhung said half to himself. He glanced up at Nghia. Suddenly Nghia opened fire from the gun turret, shooting the brothers point-blank with an automatic, while below, Nhung sprayed them with bullets. The sound inside the closed vehicle was deafening. Satisfied at last, Nhung holstered his pistol, then removed the bayonet from his rifle and stabbed the brothers repeatedly, hacking at their bodies.

Now swimming with blood, the armored car continued on. Up ahead in the jeeps, the passengers did not look back. Nguyen sat stiffly on top of the carrier. He did not say a word.

Jarred Hawkins was waiting at the Defense Ministry headquarters with Colonel Tri, General Don, and General Minh when the convoy arrived. There was a general movement toward the armored personnel carrier, then shouts of shock and disbelief when Nhung stepped down, hauling out the two corpses and dropping them to the ground. His hands and clothes were stained with blood, and he grinned triumphantly and unconsciously wiped his hand across his face, leaving a crimson smear on his cheek.

Some of the soldiers dipped their handkerchiefs into the blood; others shouted out cheers over the death of the two men who had, until hours before, been the leaders they were sworn to serve.

"My God," Jarred muttered, turning away in revulsion.

"Believe me, Colonel Hawkins, it wasn't supposed to be like this," Tri said. "They were supposed to be given a military execution, not butchered."

In the tumult at the Defense Ministry, Nguyen Van Tran managed to slip away, and he reached his house a short time later.

Hearing him come in, Ly rushed to meet him. "Nguyen! What has happened? For two days now I have been listening to gunfire and explosions. I didn't dare leave the house. The radio says that the coup has succeeded. Is that right?"

"Yes. General Minh is now in charge."

"In charge of what?"

"Of everything, my dear," Nguyen said dryly. "He has been appointed, or shall I say he has appointed himself, chief of state, president, king, emperor, God. . . ."

"Were there many killed?"

"It was not a bloodless coup," he replied cryptically.

"Was anyone we know killed?"

"Are you asking about your lover?" Nguyen laughed. "My friend and military adviser? He was there, you know. He was right in the thick of things."

"Nguyen, you must tell me! Is Jarred all right?"

"Do not fear. Your Jarred is perfectly safe. He did exactly what the Americans have been doing ever since they arrived in our country: He stood by and watched others die."

"Thank God he is all right," Ly breathed.

"You did not ask about your president and his brother."

"Diem? Nhu?" Ly chuckled derisively. "I'm not worried about them. No doubt the Americans will evacuate them to some place like Hawaii, where they will live in a big house with a large staff to see to their every need."

Nguyen shook his head. "I am afraid not, my dear. Diem and Nhu are both dead."

Ly blanched. "Dead? How do you know?"

"Because I watched as they were butchered. I watched, and I didn't do a thing to stop it."

"Don't be foolish. What could you have done?"

"I could have been less the coward and died with them."

"And what would that have accomplished?"

"It would have preserved my pride."

"Your pride?" Ly scoffed. "What reason have you for pride? You abandoned your pride and your humanity long ago when you sold your soul to serve Nhu."

"I fear you may be right," Nguyen said. He pulled his pistol and jacked a cartridge into the chamber. "So there is only one thing left for me now."

"Nguyen! What are you doing?"

He lifted the gun.

"Please, no! Put that gun down!" she screamed.

He pointed the pistol at Ly.

"Nguyen! No!"

"Oh, but I must. Don't you see? I am the loyal officer, and you are my loyal wife. This is how it must be for us."

Nguyen pulled the trigger. The gun bucked in his hand, and the bullet slammed into Ly's chest. The impact of the heavy .45-caliber slug drove her back against the wall, and as she slid down, a smear of blood marked her passage. The front of her *ao dai* turned dark red. Her eyes were still open, but the fear they had evinced the moment before Nguyen pulled the trigger had already faded, glazed over with the opaque film of death.

When Nguyen was certain that his wife was dead, he put the gun to his temple and fired.

THREE WEEKS LATER

Colonel Jarred Hawkins stared through the window as, far, far below, the coast of Vietnam slid beneath the wing of Pan Am Flight 393. There was a soft *ding*, followed by a rush of air in the speakers. Then the stewardess began speaking.

"Ladies and gentlemen, the captain has just turned off the no-smoking and the seat belt signs. You may smoke and walk around the cabin if you like. However, for your comfort and safety, we ask that you do keep your seat belts fastened when you are in your seat."

The man in civilian clothes in the seat next to Jarred took out a pack of cigarettes. He was thin and bald, with thick horn-rimmed glasses. He held his pack out toward Jarred.

"Smoke, Colonel?" he asked.

"No, thank you."

"Mind if I do?"

"No, go ahead."

The man lit his cigarette, then blew out a long column of smoke. "Are you rotating back to the States or just going back on leave?" he asked.

"I'm rotating back."

"How long have you been over here?"

"Five years."

"Five years?" The civilian stared at Jarred incredulously. "You stayed in that hellhole for five years?"

"Yes."

"You must've liked it."

"I did."

"Well, to each his own, I guess. But if you liked it, what happened? Did you get tired of it?"

"Let's just say it became time for me to move on to something else."

"I know what you mean. Take me, for instance. I wasn't there very long, but I was ready to get out."

"What were you doing there?"

"The name is Chapel, Henry Chapel," the man replied, holding out his hand. "Like you, I work for the government, only I'm not in the military. I did my bit during the Korean War. Well, not really. I mean, I didn't go overseas or anything. I was a private at Fort Dix. Now I'm a trend analyst."

"I beg your pardon?"

Chapel laughed. "Don't try to understand it. Half the people I work for don't understand it. Basically it has to do with taking society's pulse, then recommending what action be taken as a result of what I find out."

Jarred shook his head, indicating that he still didn't understand.

Chapel laughed again. "Well, let's put it this way. When I came over here ten months ago, the State Department was really beginning to get miffed with Diem—you know, the way he was treating the Buddhists and all? But they thought there was nothing they could do about it because he had been elected by a large majority and everyone figured he still had the support of the people."

"I believe Diem did have the support of the people ten months ago," Jarred said.

"And what makes you think that?"

Jarred shrugged. "Just a general feeling. Things I heard and observed."

"Unfortunately, you weren't the only 'old hand' over here who thought that. But our government cannot formulate policy on such general feelings or things you hear and observe. It must have scientific data, and it was my job to provide that data."

"How did you do that?"

"Oh, come now, Colonel, you don't think I could break something like that down into a few easy sentences, do you? It has taken me years to develop the system. There are all sorts of things involved in such an analysis. Trends in newspaper articles, attendance at state-sponsored events, tobacco consumption . . ."

Now it was Jarred's turn to be incredulous. "Tobacco consumption?"

Chapel grinned. "Yep, believe it or not. When people

begin losing confidence in their government they get anxious. When they get anxious, they smoke more. There are many other things one must consider as well, such as movie attendance, trends in music, how much rice a family has on hand at any given time, a correlation of moon stages with incidents of civil unrest."

"Did you wave any dead cats around?" Jarred deadpanned.

Chapel laughed. "I told you you wouldn't understand. But suffice it to say that my reports did bring about a change. The U.S. went from unwavering support of Diem and everything he did to questioning and then openly challenging him. And it's a good thing, too. If we hadn't changed our policy, we would have been caught flatfooted when the generals overthrew the government. As it is now, we are in position to work with the new people. Our new attitude may, in some small way, even be responsible for them. Yes, sir, I believe things are going to be better now. Much better. And I don't mind telling you, I have a little pride in the way things have turned out. You could almost say a proprietary pride."

CHAPTER SIXTEEN

NOVEMBER 22, 1963

Faith Canfield looked through the window of the company Lear Jet, but there was nothing to see except a layer of clouds. They lay beneath her like a great ocean of cream, fluffy and whipped into swirls and peaks. In the window's reflection she could see her own face and that of her husband, sitting across from her. John was reading a copy of *The St. Louis Chronicle* that he had picked up at Lambert Field just before they left St. Louis.

"Unbelievable," he said quietly.

"What's that, dear?" Faith asked, turning away from the window.

"This article about what's going on over in Vietnam." John folded the paper and laid it on the plush leather seat beside him. "The members of the junta are already beginning to quarrel among themselves. I'm afraid we may have jumped out of the frying pan and into the fire by getting rid of Diem."

"You talk as if *we* got rid of him," Faith said. "We didn't do it. The Vietnamese people did it. Or at least, their army."

"I don't know. Maybe it was spontaneous. But if we didn't have any overt role in it, we certainly sent signals to the generals who launched the coup. We've been denouncing Diem for the past year."

"John, you aren't taking up for him, are you?" Faith asked. "The man was a monster. The way he burned all those pagodas and brutalized the Buddhists. Instituting martial law and rounding up hundreds and hundreds of monks, nuns, student activists, and plain ordinary citizens—for no reason other than that they protested. Anyone who opposed him was his enemy."

"It was more Nhu than Diem, but since Diem gave Nhu free rein, he was just as guilty." John stroked his chin. "But are these new clowns any better? I think not," he said, answering his own question. "I'm afraid our troubles over there are just starting. I wonder what Kennedy thinks of the situation now. If I get the chance during this visit, I'm going to talk to him about it."

"Good heavens, dear, you aren't going to have any time for that. Did you see the schedule the White House sent us? Every moment we'll be in Dallas is accounted for."

"That's the way it is when you're campaigning," John said. "You have to take advantage of every opportunity."

"Can you imagine how exhausting that must be?"

John laughed. "Not to someone like Jack Kennedy. He thrives on this. Campaigning is to a professional politician what whiskey is to an alcoholic. He has to have it."

"But poor Jacqueline. She certainly isn't campaigning for any office."

"No, but she likes it almost as much as he does. You've seen the way she lights up when the spotlight is on her."

"She projects very well, that's true. But I get the feeling she would prefer to be a much more private person."

"If Jackie wanted—"

"Jacqueline," Faith corrected. "You know she doesn't like to be called Jackie."

"But that's what everyone calls her."

"Everyone doesn't know her. We do. And those of us who do know her should call her what she prefers to be called."

"Mr. Canfield, we've just been given immediate clearance

into Fort Worth," the pilot announced over the speaker. He looked back into the cabin, and John waved at him.

"Well, that didn't take long," John said, glancing at his watch. "I told you we'd get here in time to fly over to Dallas with them."

"It seems foolish to fly in that big airplane from Fort Worth to Dallas," Faith said.

John patted his wife's hand. "It's all politics, honey. Nothing projects presidential power and prestige like an arrival in Air Force One. With Fort Worth and Dallas you get two for one."

"Oh, no," Faith groaned as the Lear Jet started down, leaving the white fluffy clouds for dismal-looking gray ones. "Are those rain clouds?"

John picked up the telephone and asked what the weather was like on the ground. Told it was light rain, he passed the word on to Faith.

"That's too bad," she said. "I was hoping for a pretty day."

"Maybe it'll clear up."

"I hope so."

The jet touched down smoothly; then the engines roared as the pilot activated the thrust deflectors. John could see little puddles of water shining gold in the sun that was already beginning to peek through the clouds. He also saw a light-blue Boeing 707 with the words UNITED STATES OF AMERICA printed above the windows and the presidential seal just forward of the front door. For security reasons, Air Force One was sitting majestically apart from everything else. Sitting in almost equal isolation was another 707, almost identical to Air Force One, which John knew was the Vice President's plane.

A Cadillac was waiting for John and Faith at the flight apron. They stepped out of the Lear Jet, skirting a puddle of water to get to the car. By the time the jet's engines were shut down the car's engine was starting, and they were whisked off to the Hotel Texas.

The ride was a swift one, and as they stepped into the hotel lobby, a young man approached. "Mr. Canfield?"

"Yes."

"Sir, the President asks you to join him in his suite."

"Faith?" John said, looking at his wife.

She laughed. "Don't worry about me. I'll wait here."

John gave her a quick kiss. "Thanks."

The bellhop escorted him into the elevator and up to the Presidential Suite. Three or four people were with the President when John stepped into the large sitting room, but the only one John recognized was Dave Powers.

"Hi, John, glad you could make it," Jack Kennedy said. "Listen, have you had breakfast?"

"I had coffee and a roll in St. Louis, so I'm fine."

"Well, have another cup," the President offered. "Mike, pour him a cup, will ya?"

"Thank you. Black," John said to the man Kennedy had called Mike.

"The crowds were great in San Antonio and Houston," Kennedy said. "Weren't they great, Dave?"

"Yes, sir, they certainly were."

"And they loved Jackie." Kennedy grinned. "And don't kid yourself. Jackie loved every minute of it. I told you this would be good for her."

Another man came into the suite, carrying a briefcase. He placed it on a table by a chair.

"Ah," Kennedy said. "My morning reading." He put his glasses on and reached for the first folder. "Others get to read the backs of Cheerios or Wheaties boxes." He looked up at John and smiled. "Or Corn Toasties," he added in deference to one of the cereals manufactured by Canfield-Puritex. "*My* breakfast reading is situation estimates on Vietnam, Cyprus, and Korea or the latest statements made by De Gaulle and Khrushchev."

John started to say something about the military junta in Vietnam, then decided this was neither the time nor the place. He sipped his coffee as the President read without comment the prepared reports.

When Kennedy finished reading, he reached for the first in a stack of newspapers, asking, "How did they treat our visit to Houston and San Antonio yesterday?"

"The *Chicago Sun Times* had good things to say about Mrs. Kennedy," Mike replied. "They say she might even win Texas for you."

Kennedy chuckled. "Look, don't knock it. I'll take votes

any way I can get them. Oh, damn. Will you look at this? 'Storm of Political Controversy Swirls Around Kennedy on Visit,'" he read aloud. "And this: 'Yarborough Snubs LBJ.' And this: 'President's Visit Seen Widening State Democratic Split.'" He angrily shoved the papers aside. "What the hell is going on here?"

"They don't know what they're talking about," Dave Powers said.

"Listen, Mike, get Kenny on the phone," Kennedy ordered, referring to Kenneth O'Donnell. Mike picked up the phone and dialed. "We've got to get this business between Yarborough and Lyndon straightened out."

"I've got O'Donnell, Mr. President," Mike said, handing the phone to his boss.

"Kenny, you see to it that Senator Yarborough rides in the car with Lyndon today." There was a pause while O'Donnell responded. "I don't care what he says," Kennedy growled. "Listen, you tell Yarborough I will not take no for an answer. He'll either ride in the car with Lyndon, or by God he'll walk." He slammed the phone down, then raked his hair with his hand. "I don't have time to wipe every runny nose in the Democratic party. I wonder if Goldwater has to put up with this?"

The others laughed.

"Listen, where is Faith? Didn't she come with you?" Kennedy asked, suddenly turning his attention to John.

"Yes, Mr. President. She's waiting downstairs in the lobby."

"Down in the lobby? What the hell is she doing down there? Get her up here. She can visit with Jackie while Jackie's getting ready."

John picked up the phone and had Faith paged. When she answered the phone he said, "Come on up."

Faith's laughter tinkled through the receiver. "Where do you think I am?" she replied. "I'm just on the other side of the door from you, my love, in the bedroom. Jacqueline called down for me several minutes ago, suggesting I come in through the bedroom entrance so as not to disturb all you strategists. I'm helping her decide what to wear today."

"And what is she going to wear?"

"A pink suit. Wait until you see it. It's gorgeous."

"Knowing her, I'm sure it is."

*   *   *

Faith hung up the phone and turned back to Jacqueline Kennedy, who was sitting at the dressing table. At the moment Mrs. Kennedy was wearing only her pink skirt over a full slip. Mary, her maid, had the still-hangered top half of the suit—a pink jacket with a dark-blue collar and dark-blue trim on the pockets—hanging from a hook on the closet door. A matching pink pillbox hat was on a nearby table. Jacqueline, who had just finished putting on her makeup, leaned forward and put a long, lacquered nail to her cheek.

"Is that a wrinkle?" she asked. "I believe that's a wrinkle."

Mary laughed. "Mrs. Kennedy, you don't have a wrinkle on your entire body."

She sighed. "Perhaps not. But I do look tired, don't I? I swear, one day on the campaign trail can age a person thirty years."

"You could age thirty years and still outshine most of the people I know," Faith said.

Jacqueline laughed. "Faith, you are an outrageous flatterer." She touched her hair. "Is it still raining? I hope it is. I would much rather ride in the bubble top than the open car. I hate getting windblown."

Next door, Ken O'Donnell answered a ringing phone. "I told you what the President wants," O'Donnell said to the caller after listening for a few moments. "He wants Yarborough to ride with Johnson. No, I don't care what kind of fuss he makes. The President wants him in the car with the Vice President even if you have to pick him up and bodily throw him into the backseat."

"Who is that?" Kennedy asked, interrupting his own conversation when he overheard O'Donnell's.

"It's Larry O'Brien. Yarborough is still balking at riding with Johnson."

Kennedy took the phone from O'Donnell. "Listen to me, Larry," he said forcefully into the mouthpiece. "*Get . . . him . . . in . . . the . . . car!*"

While his boss was on the phone, O'Donnell walked over to pick up the newspaper Kennedy had been looking at earlier. He leafed through it casually until he reached page fourteen, then was stopped by a full-page ad bordered in black.

Watching him, John noticed the expression shift on his face. "What is it?" he asked.

O'Donnell showed John the paper.

The ad was placed by a group calling itself "The American Fact-Finding Committee." The headline stated: WELCOME, MR. KENNEDY, TO DALLAS. It then went on to accuse the President of the imprisonment, starvation, and persecution of "thousands of Cubans." The ad also claimed Kennedy was selling food to Communist soldiers who were killing Americans in Vietnam and suggested bluntly that he had "reached a secret agreement with the U.S. Communist party." It asked, "Why have you ordered or permitted your brother Bobby, the Attorney General, to go soft on Communists, fellow travelers, and ultra-leftists in America, while permitting him to persecute loyal Americans who criticize you, your administration, and your leadership?" The ad concluded with, "Mr. Kennedy, we demand answers to these questions, and we want them now."

"Oh, shit," John muttered.

By now Kennedy had hung up the phone and, seeing the two men perusing the paper and guessing correctly that they weren't pleased by what they were reading, held out his hand and said, "Let me see it, John."

Wordlessly, John handed it to him.

Kennedy had just finished reading the ad when Faith and Jacqueline came into the room. It was as if they had come in on a funeral.

"What is wrong?" Jacqueline asked.

"There's an ad in one of the papers," John told her. "A very unfavorable ad."

Kennedy handed her the folded-over newspaper. "Can you imagine printing a thing like that?" he asked testily.

Faith watched Jacqueline's face as she read the ad; her vivaciousness perceptibly faded.

"This is awful," Jacqueline said quietly.

"Oh, don't worry about it, Jackie," Kennedy said, flashing a grin. "You know we're heading into nut country today."

Faith took the paper from Jacqueline and began reading, getting angrier by the minute. "How could a respectable paper print something like this?" she asked. "This is absolutely libelous."

Her question was met by silence.

"Look," Kennedy suddenly said, turning to the window, "I think the rain has stopped. *There's* a bright spot, anyway."

Faith smiled to herself as she thought of how Jacqueline had hoped the rain would continue so the bubble top would be used.

Kennedy grew animated and cheerful again. "You know, last night, with the rain and the fog, it was a perfect night for intrigue, don't you think? I mean, suppose someone was sneaking through the crowd, carrying a small pistol concealed in his coat pocket." Kennedy assumed a slight crouch and walked on the balls of his feet, looking about furtively. "He could reach in his pocket, pull out the pistol like so, shove it into the President's side, and *pop, pop, pop,* then drop the gun, whirl"—Kennedy demonstrated—"then vanish into the crowd and the night."

"Oh, Mr. President," Faith shuddered. "Don't say things like that. It makes me nervous."

Jacqueline smiled. "Don't worry. This is Jack's fantasy. He would love nothing better than to write some cheap, trashy novel full of night and fog and intrigue."

"And sex," Kennedy added, holding up his finger. "Don't forget the sex."

Everyone laughed, and Faith realized this was Kennedy's way of buoying Jacqueline's mood, which had been nearly scuttled by the newspaper ad.

Outside the hotel, three rows of cars were waiting to take the presidential party to the airport. The automobiles were arranged according to rank and position: The farthest cars were the congressional convertibles, the cars in the middle were closed Mercurys for midlevel staff people, and the cars nearest the curb were open-top Lincolns reserved for the more powerful. As the Canfields stood at the curb, waiting to be told which car they would be riding in, John saw—and eavesdroppped on—Larry O'Brien talking with Senator Yarborough.

"We wish you would reconsider, Senator," O'Brien was saying.

"I'd be glad to issue some sort of conciliatory statement," Yarborough replied.

"Senator, you could say ten thousand words and it wouldn't be as effective as getting in that car."

"Mr. Canfield, Mrs. Canfield, here is your car," someone announced. Reluctantly turning away from the political imbroglio being played out in front of him, John took Faith's arm and helped her into the backseat of one of the curbside Lincolns, then slipped in beside her. Almost immediately the driver started the car, and they pulled away to join the others.

Though impressive looking, the motorcade was nothing like the one planned for Dallas. There the carefully calculated route would wind through the heart of the city in a way as to afford the maximum number of people an opportunity to see the President. This motorcade, by contrast, was strictly logistical: getting them from point A to point B. There were, however, sizeable crowds on both sides of the street, waving and shouting enthusiastically as the motorcade passed by.

When they finally arrived at the airport, John saw Senator Yarborough getting out of the Vice President's car. He chuckled.

"I notice O'Brien got Yarborough in the car with Johnson after all," John commented to his wife.

"Why are you grinning? Is that significant?" Faith asked.

He made a wry face. "I guess you had to be there."

Faith and John were invited to fly on Air Force One. The flight from Fort Worth to Dallas took only thirteen minutes, and the fact that the airplane got no higher than five thousand feet in the hot, muggy air made it a rough, bouncy, uncomfortable flight. Faith was relieved when, looking out the window, she saw a ribbon of concrete approaching closer and closer beneath the wings until, finally, they were on the ground.

The airplane shuddered with the power of reverse thrust; then it turned off the runway and headed toward the green and red terminal building. Before reaching there, though, it veered away and taxied toward a building marked "International Arrivals." A spot had been designated for the plane near a high chain-link fence. Here the Dallas Police Department and Secret Service agents were very much in evidence, standing guard on the low roofs of nearby buildings and walking around on the concrete apron.

On the other side of the cyclone fence hundreds, perhaps thousands, of people were cheering, waving, jumping up and down. Faith's own father had been a United States senator, and she had personally known every president since Herbert Hoover. Nonetheless, she had never gotten used to the wild adulation the public showed its presidents. She commented about it to John.

"I'm afraid it isn't all adulation," he remarked. "Look around."

Faith did so and saw what he was talking about. Scattered throughout the cheering spectators were an alarming number of people expressing hostility to the President. Two men were holding aloft a giant Confederate flag. Another held up a sign reading: HELP KENNEDY STAMP OUT DEMOCRACY. Another, crudely lettered and misspelled sign said: YOUR A TRAITER. One long sign editorialized: MR. PRESIDENT, BECAUSE OF YOUR SOCIALIST TENDENCIES AND BECAUSE OF YOUR SURRENDER TO COMMUNISM, I HOLD YOU IN COMPLETE CONTEMPT. There were more. IN 1964, GOLDWATER AND FREEDOM. And: KENNEDY, LEADERS OF COMMUNIST PARTY WANT YOU RE-ELECTED. Finally there was: YANKEE GO HOME AND TAKE YOUR EQUALS WITH YOU.

Seemingly oblivious to the hostile proclamations, the Kennedys walked down the steps from the plane, smiling and waving as they ascended. As a native of Texas, Vice President Johnson was symbolically welcoming the Kennedys to Dallas, so he stood at the foot of the ramp and shook their hands as enthusiastically as if he hadn't been with them all morning.

The Kennedys walked over to the chain-link fence to greet some of the people on the other side. Accompanied by the Secret Service agents, they walked for about fifty yards along the fence, and Kennedy energetically reached up and down, left and right, touching fingers that were thrust through the fence grid.

"Good morning," he would say, grinning warmly. "Hello! It's good to see you! I'm glad you could come down!" Occasionally he would answer a shouted question.

"How do you like Texas, Mr. President?"

"I love it, I love it. Who wouldn't like it here?"

The more hostile comments, and there were a few, were ignored.

Someone had given Jacqueline a large bouquet of roses when she stepped off the plane, and she was carrying them now as she accompanied her husband along the fence, smiling at the crowd, saying a few well-modulated hellos, and occasionally pushing a lone strand of dark hair away from her eyes.

Kennedy finally finished working the crowd and turned to get into the big open Lincoln that had been driven out to him. Governor and Mrs. Connally were already in the car, riding backward in the jump seats.

"Remember, Mrs. Kennedy," Dave Powers said to Jacqueline as she got into the car with her husband, "be sure to wave at the people on your side of the car, away from the President. It's wasted effort for both of you to wave at the same person. He can vote only once."

"You don't have to tell me how to campaign, Mr. Powers," Jacqueline replied, smiling sweetly. "I've been doing it for quite some time now."

"I'm sorry; I know. I'm just touching all the bases, that's all."

"You're doing a good job," Jacqueline said sincerely.

John and Faith were shown to their car. It, too, was a convertible, though not one with additional jump seats. As a result, they rode alone except for the driver and a front passenger who identified himself as someone from Governor Connally's staff.

"Do you mind?" he asked. "I have no official function. I just wanted to be a part of it."

"Be our guest," John said.

Though three other cars would be behind the presidential car, Faith thought that they were still close enough to see the President quite clearly. And even if the cars pulled farther apart, she could readily identify the occupants by the two hats prominent in the President's car: Jacqueline's pink pillbox and the governor's cowboy hat.

At exactly 11:45, two motorcycle policemen started the procession, followed by the lead car, an unmarked white Ford filled with law officers and security agents. Three more motorcycles were behind this car, leading the rest of the motorcade by some distance.

The presidential car was next, a long, dark-blue, open Lincoln limousine. Behind it was another open limousine, this one filled with Secret Service agents. Dave Powers and Ken O'Donnell were also in this car.

The Vice President's car was third in line. Senator Yarborough, who had agreed to ride in Lyndon Johnson's car, was on the left side of the rear seat, the Vice President on the right. Like the President's car, this one was followed by a carload of Secret Service agents.

The convertible in which John and Faith were riding was next, followed by the press pool car, then the photographers' convertibles. The motorcade was rounded out by assorted cars containing congressmen and other city and state officials whose political positions had earned them the honor, and, finally, by a bus carrying the logistics people. Police motorcycles were scattered throughout the procession.

At first the motorcade drove through streets that were nearly barren. John and Faith sat back in their seat, frequently holding their hands over their eyes to shield them from the sun.

"My, that sun is bright," Faith observed.

"What happened to our nice clouds?" John asked.

"I know. Contrary to what I said earlier, I certainly wouldn't mind them back. And look at poor Jacqueline. She looks hot, doesn't she?"

"No hotter than anybody else."

"Well, her suit is wool. They should have put the bubble on. Then they could have used the air conditioner."

"Yes, but the humidity would fog up the inside. Besides, it would cheat the people."

"What people?" Faith asked dryly. "There's no one here." With a wave of her hand she took in the bare streets and stark billboards.

"There will be when we get downtown," John assured her.

He was right. As the caravan moved farther downtown, the crowds got larger and larger. Many of the waving, cheering people held up signs, most of which, unlike those at the airport, were friendly.

Suddenly the motorcade stopped.

"What is it?" John asked. "What's going on?"

"Look," Faith said, pointing to a sign held up by a group

of children that read: MR. PRESIDENT, PLEASE STOP AND SHAKE OUR HANDS. Kennedy readily complied, going so far as to get out of the car.

John laughed. "Well, you've got to hand it to the kids. I'll bet when they came up with that idea, everyone laughed at them."

After a few moments with the children, President Kennedy got back into the limo, and the motorcade started again.

By the time they reached Live Oak Street, the cheering had become a constant roar. People were standing as many as twelve deep on the sidewalks, and office workers were leaning out of windows, waving and cheering. Though everyone in sight seemed to be a Kennedy supporter, John noticed that the security men were checking all the windows very carefully.

By now the crush on the sidewalks was so thick that the people in the front were being pushed forward by those in the rear, to the point where they were shoved off the curb and into the street. Some of the flanking motorcycle policemen had to slow almost to a stop, creeping along and keeping their bikes upright by dragging a foot on the ground.

"Jackieee! Jackieee! Jackieee!" the crowd roared. One of the Secret Service agents in the follow-up car, seeing that Jacqueline was getting a little frightened by the crowd closing in on her, jumped out of his vehicle and ran up to put himself between her and the crowd.

The motorcade reached Main Street and started down a nearly mile-long furrow of screaming, waving humanity. The noise and heat pounded down on those in the open cars, and Faith suddenly felt dizzy. She put her hand to her forehead.

"What is it?" John asked, concerned. "What's wrong?"

"I'm not sure." Faith closed her eyes for a moment and shivered. "I'll be glad when this motorcade ends."

"It's probably just the sun, the heat, and the noise," her husband reassured her. "Oh, look. There's an underpass just ahead. We'll get a break from the sun."

Faith craned her neck and looked at the underpass, just beyond a large building that had a sign identifying it as the Texas Schoolbook Depository. They couldn't reach it too soon, as far as she was concerned.

"It's twelve-thirty," John said, pointing to a large digital clock on a nearby Hertz sign. "I think we're supposed to be at the Trade Mart in five minutes, so it won't be much longer. Wave at the crowd, honey."

"They aren't here to see us; they're here to see the President."

"We're all part of the same package," John said, waving and smiling at the people jammed along the street. He just happened to look toward the President at that moment, and he saw Kennedy suddenly jerk his hand to his throat. At about the same time, he heard a flat, popping sound. A second later an odd pink spray misted around the President's head, like a halo, followed by Kennedy jerking violently backward and then to the left, toward Jacqueline. A second pop sounded.

John got a dizzy, sickening feeling, very much what he might experience in an airplane that took a sudden, startling dip.

"John, what's happening? My God, look at Jackie!" Faith cried, too distressed to remember her own rule of always referring to the First Lady as Jacqueline.

Inexplicably, Mrs. Kennedy had climbed out onto the trunk of the car. A Secret Service agent was running hard to catch up to the presidential vehicle. Reaching it, he jumped up onto the back bumper, physically pushed the First Lady back into the seat, then threw his body over the top of the couple.

"Oh, my God, Faith! The President's been shot!" John shouted.

The driver of John and Faith's car now accelerated in concert with the other cars in the motorcade, racing through the streets behind the speeding President's car, sometimes going over seventy miles per hour. The crowd lining the street looked on in wide-eyed, openmouthed shock. Most people did not yet understand why the motorcade was going so fast, but a few comprehended even without being told that the unimaginable had happened.

The motorcade wound up at Parkland Hospital, and the harried policemen directed the incoming cars, miraculously preventing any collisions.

The cars' occupants spilled out into the driveway of the emergency entrance, then through the doors and into the lobby. They were all dignitaries in their own right, so no one assumed the authority to try to stop them. Others came as well, drawn by an overwhelming compulsion to get as close to the stricken President as they could.

John and Faith looked at Jacqueline, standing just beyond, her face stricken, her pink suit splattered with the President's blood, a gruesome testimony to what had just happened. Faith started to go to her, but just then someone came and led Jacqueline deeper into the hospital. Faith assumed the First Lady was being taken to her husband—or at least to a place as close as she could get.

There was a constant chatter of conversation in the hospital lobby:

"Not Dallas. Oh please, God, don't let this terrible thing happen in Dallas."

"Who was it? Who shot him?"

"I didn't see who it was, but it came from a hillock right alongside the road."

"No it didn't. It came from that big building we were going by. What was that place?"

"The Texas Schoolbook Depository?"

"Yes. It came from there."

"Really? I thought it came from that knoll, too."

"How bad is it, do you think?"

"I don't know. We can pray that it's not too bad."

"No, it's bad. It's very bad. The whole top of his head was blown away."

"Jesus Christ. Well, still, I wouldn't give up hope yet. The doctors can do amazing things nowadays."

"Where's Jackie?"

"She's in there with him."

"Well, there must be some hope then, don't you think? I mean, they wouldn't even let her in there if there was no hope, would they?"

"Did you see Jackie's suit? She's covered with so much blood that when I first saw her, I thought she was hit, too."

"That all came from the President. He was hit in the head."

"Don't be so negative."

"I'm just being realistic."

"Oh, God. There goes a priest. They must be giving him final unction."

"What?"

"Last rites."

"Oh, my God."

The Canfields were pushed along by the crowd in the lobby. When they found themselves by an unmanned triage desk, they walked up another corridor that went to the right, away from the press of people. It led them to an area designated "Minor Medicine." Here were several small rooms, and though a few other people had already found their way into this area, it was much less crowded and much quieter than the main corridor had been.

John and Faith tottered like sleepwalkers into one of the rooms, where they found a metal-framed couch. They sank down onto the green plastic cushions.

"John, what do you think? Will the doctors be able to save him?" Faith asked in a small voice.

John sighed and took her hand in his. "I saw the bullets hit him, Faith. I don't think he's going to make it. In fact, I think he's already gone."

Faith started to cry. "Dear God, how awful!" she burbled. She took a handkerchief from her purse and dabbed her eyes.

A Secret Service man stuck his head into the room. "I'm going to have to ask you folks to leave," he said. "We're bringing the Vice President in here."

"Of course," John murmured, standing, then offering his hand to Faith.

"No, no, let them stay, Roy," Vice President Johnson said, coming into the room. Lady Bird was with him. "I know Mr. Canfield. He's all right."

"Very well, Mr. Vice President," the agent said.

John nodded solemnly at Johnson. "Thank you, Mr. Vice President."

"Take your seat, John," the Vice President suggested with a wave of his hand. "God, this is awful. To think that something like this would happen in Texas." He put his hand to his forehead and shook his head slowly.

Someone else came in. "Mrs. Johnson, you asked me to find out if Mrs. Kennedy would receive you. She said she would like that."

Lady Bird looked at her husband.

"Yes, go," he said. "I think that would be nice."

She left, and the Vice-President walked over to the window and stopped in front of it. The fact that the blinds were shut and the curtains were pulled didn't seem to matter. He looked out anyway.

The next several minutes passed quietly. Johnson said nothing, and John and Faith spoke only in occasional whispers to each other. However, a constant babble of noise came from outside.

At 1:15, exactly forty-five minutes after the rifle shots had been fired, Malcolm Kilduff and Kenneth O'Donnell stepped into the room. Lyndon Johnson was still standing at the window with his back to the room. Kilduff cleared his throat.

"Mr. President?" he said.

John immediately noticed the change of title. So did Faith, who squeezed his hand hard, and Johnson, for he turned around and looked quizzically at Kilduff.

"Mr. President, I have the sad duty to report that John F. Kennedy is dead. I would like your permission to make the announcement to the public."

Still not saying a word, Johnson nodded, and Kilduff started out of the room.

"No, you had better wait," Johnson suddenly called. "We don't know whether this is a Communist conspiracy or not. I'd better get out of here and back to the plane. Are they prepared to get me out of here?"

"I'll check, Mr. President." Kilduff left the room, and for the next five minutes no one said a thing. Johnson turned back to the shuttered window, continuing to blindly stare at it. John studied him, trying to imagine what thoughts would be going through his mind at that precise moment.

Kilduff returned at 1:20. "Everything is ready, Mr. President. I'll make the official announcement as soon as you leave."

"Yes," Johnson replied, starting out of the room then. "As soon as I leave, you announce the death."

John and Faith were left alone.

"The President is dead," John said quietly, tears streaming down his face. "Long live the President."

SCHWEINFURT, GERMANY

It was Friday, the twenty-second of November, at nine o'clock in the evening. Except for the adjutant's office, which was the duty station for the Officer of the Day, it was dark and silent in the 7th Cavalry headquarters building.

Chief Warrant Officer Bob Parker had the duty. As he had told Jill when explaining why he couldn't go to Nuremberg for the weekend as they had planned, this was not a very pleasant way for him to spend his birthday.

Officer of the Day was not a difficult duty. He had only to hold guard mount, which he did at 1500 hours, then answer the telephone and act as the commander's representative until relieved the next morning. At 1645 hours the Duty NCO had played "To the Colors" over the camp loudspeaker. This alerted everyone that the Retreat ceremony was imminent. At 1700 hours he played "Retreat." At that time the flag was lowered and folded respectfully into the tricorn so that no red would show. "Tattoo" and "Taps" were lined up for the last two official bugle calls of the day. "Tattoo" would play at 2145 hours, "Taps" at 2200 hours.

Bob was acutely aware of military tradition and ceremonies this evening because he was reading *Troopers with Custer*, a factual account of Custer's last days. In the quiet darkness of the empty headquarters building, Bob could almost feel the presence of the long line of 7th Cavalry officers who had pulled this same duty before him—an unbroken line stretching back one hundred years, all the way back to those days when the 7th was fighting the Indians.

The feeling had been so strong, in fact, that Bob had opened the glass display case that was the repository for several Custer artifacts. The Custer memorabilia were here as a part of the 7th Cavalry's legacy.

Custer's actual saber was, at that moment, lying on the desk in front of Bob, and Custer's hat, though too small, was on his head. He also had an original duty officer's log. An entry dated 6 June, 1876 read:

> *Under way at 4:30 A.M. Weather cool, clear and breezy. Pvt. McWilliams from Troop H accidentally shot himself with his revolver, bullet entering calf of*

leg. He rides in an ambulance. Distance covered today, 16 miles.

The phone rang, and Bob reached for it.

"Garry Owen, Seventh Cavalry, officer of the day Mr. Parker."

"Mr. Parker, this is Captain Fontaine, duty officer for the Third Infantry Division. I have an immediate action message. Are you ready to copy?"

"Ready to copy, sir," Bob replied, picking up a pencil.

"Action required, notify commanding officer soonest possible. Message follows: 'President John F. Kennedy died in Dallas this day, twenty-second November '63, at thirteen hundred hours, Central Standard Time, as the result of a gunshot wound to the head inflicted by person or persons unknown.' End of message. Do you copy?"

Bob was silent.

"Mr. Parker, do you copy?" the captain asked again.

"Yes, sir," Bob said quietly. He felt a sinking sensation. "I copy."

He hung up the phone, then made the entry in the duty log.

2030 hours. Received immediate action message from duty officer of Third Infantry Division, informing this command that President Kennedy had been shot in Dallas by person or persons unknown. President died at 1300 hours.

Bob couldn't help but think of the historical significance of this log entry. Years from now a 7th Cavalry duty officer as yet unborn might well read this entry with the same awe Bob felt for the log entries he had just been reading.

He called Colonel Rockford.

"My God," Rockford breathed upon hearing the news. "I haven't been listening to AFN. I haven't heard anything about it."

"Is there anything I need to do, sir?" Bob asked.

Rockford thought a moment. "Call all the troop commanders. Tell them to report to squadron headquarters as soon as possible. I'll meet them there."

"Do you want an alert?"

"No, I don't think so. Not unless one is called by Division. But I think we had better be prepared for any contingency."

"Yes, sir." Bob hung up, then lifted the receiver again and called all the commanders as ordered. When his task was completed, he gathered up the Custer artifacts and walked down to the far end of the long, dark, hallway to return them to the display cabinet.

Then, alone in the dark, he wept.

ABOUT THE
AUTHOR

Writing under his own name and twenty-five pen names, ROBERT VAUGHAN has authored over 200 books in every genre but science fiction. He won the 1977 Porgie Award (Best Paperback Original) for *The Power and the Pride*. In 1973 *The Valkyrie Mandate* was nominated by its publisher, Simon & Schuster, for the Pulitzer Prize. Mr. Vaughan lives with his wife in Sikeston, Missouri.

THE AMERICAN CHRONICLES

by Robert Vaughan

In this magnificent saga, award-winning author Robert Vaughan tells the riveting story of America's golden age, a century of achievement and adventure in which a young nation ascends to world power.

"The American Chronicles . . . [are] not only historical fiction, but also romance, thriller, travelogue, and fantasy." —*Entertainment Weekly*

___29661-2 OVER THERE $4.99/$5.99 Canada

___56510-9 THE IRON CURTAIN $5.50/$7.99

___56077-8 COLD WAR $5.50/$7.50

___56082-4 THE NEW FRONTIER $5.50/$6.99

Ask for these books at your local bookstore or use this page to order.

Please send me the books I have checked above. I am enclosing $_____ (add $2.50 to cover postage and handling). Send check or money order, no cash or C.O.D.'s, please.

Name _____

Address _____

City/State/Zip _____

Send order to: Bantam Books, Dept. DO 11, 2451 S. Wolf Rd., Des Plaines, IL 60018
Allow four to six weeks for delivery.
Prices and availability subject to change without notice.   DO 11 11/95